TREELIGHT

TREELIGHT

A Star Brothers Adventure

Colleen Drippé

PRESS

Cover design and map by Joseph Drippé
Studio Sæculorum
jdrippe@gmail.com

Interior design by Lisa Nicholas
Mitey Editing
miteyediting.com

ISBN: 1548854018
ISBN-13: 978-1548854010

DEDICATION

To my husband, Paul.
We've been putting up with each other's
artistic temperament for a mighty long time.

ACKNOWLEDGMENTS

Thanks to Dr. Seddon, Lisa Nicholas, Joseph Drippé and many other appreciators and encouragers including Karina Fabian, Tom Johnson, and Anna Rögnvaldsdottir.

TREELIGHT COLONY

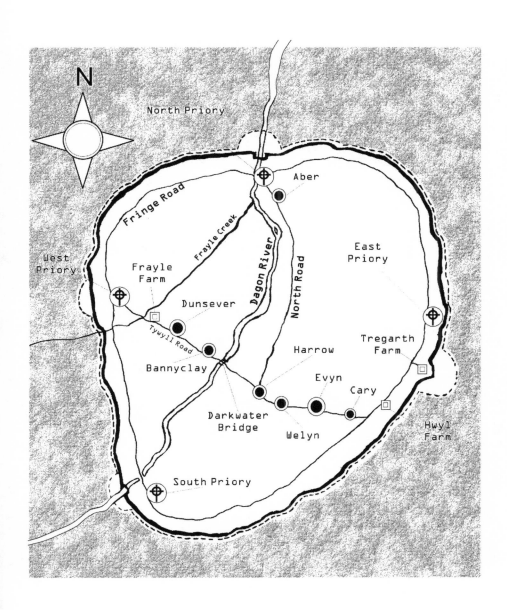

PRELUDE

THE SHIP DRIFTED SLOWLY WHILE the planet turned beneath it, chasing the sunset. In the blackness, stars gleamed like jewels, freed in their glory from the concealing curtains of the atmosphere. There was a certain grandeur about the shining craft with its retractable solar sails spread wide to catch the energy gift of the triple suns of Sachsen.

Yes, it *was* beautiful, but only if you did not look too closely at the scarred hull and the many repairs on its protruding sensors. Beneath that exterior lay the warren of its inner workings which were even less prepossessing. The *St. Balthasar* was nearly as old as the company of its owners, a netship that predated almost everything else in common use.

In the daily crises of *St. Balthasar's* decrepitude, crew and passengers were often indistinguishable since both must work to keep the vessel in operation. As Father-Captain N'Gombo put it ruefully, "Entropy dwells among us."

Night had been declared for the time, as the *St. Balthasar* matched its clocks to those of the capital city below, and most of the crew not on watch were sleeping. There were of course, the usual exceptions but, once more to quote the captain, "Those two are always on watch."

The chamber in use by the wakeful pair was small, crammed with machinery and screens, along with two very utilitarian chairs which took up most of the remaining space. Their occupants completed the job of filling the cabin until it would literally hold no more. One of these, who had been forced to duck in order to get through the doorway, had to extend his long legs beneath one of the consoles in order to fit in front of a screen.

Through habit, Chief Gaed Alfred Snowtyger almost never sat properly in a chair. The *St. Balthasar* had been designed for smaller men – the chief was just a hair less than seven feet tall – and he accepted this limitation as he accepted everything else: that the facilities were overcrowded, the hatchways somewhat small and the general comfort level even lower than the ceilings.

As he leaned forward to read a screen, even the reduced gravity of the ship allowed his silver hair to fall forward into his eyes. Once or twice, shoving it back, or when he banged into some part of the equipment, Chief Snow-tyger thought wistfully of his home colony, longing for the mountains of Lost Rythar. In memory, he hunted wolves on the snowy slopes, spear in hand, seeking their lairs among the coils of the serpent spruce while two suns made doubled shadows –

"I'm accessing Networld 326," his companion said, as he reached over to tap a key. "We've got a problem."

The speaker was as small and neat as Gaed Alfred was large and sprawling. Long association had erased even the awareness of their physical disparity from both minds as it had also negated the great gap between their cultural origins. Now, heads together more or less above the console, one must hunch down while the other strained upward to see what was in front of them.

"326," Gaed Alfred repeated. "A buyout, isn't it?"

"Right. We've had visiting rights all along, though. It's a Christian colony."

"Is that likely to change?"

The other man frowned, giving his oriental features a look of rather more sternness than he realized. That frown when it came, combined with his wispy beard and tufted eyebrows – as much grey as black – had been known to strike fear into his underlings. The chief, however, did not notice.

"When dealing with the corporations," Father Moto said precisely, "change for the worse can only be expected."

The Faring Guard continued to stare at the screen. "Pesc," he rumbled. "That corporation's got a bad name."

"They have."

"Colony first settled by Dagon Ltd – hmm. That would be some time ago. A century and a half by my reckoning."

"The Star Brothers have sent a visitor every ten years. We'll call up the journals on those visits when we're through here but I think we've got most of the information in this entry."

Gaed Alfred's face did not change as he concentrated. He was, like most of his people a simple man. Exiled from his homeworld as the result of a blood feud, the chief had spent over half his life in the Faring Guard. Those wistful memories of the wolf hunt dated back nearly thirty standard years.

"What does Pesc intend to do with their purchase?" he asked.

"Well," Father Moto said slowly, "as you can see from the readout, the place was settled on spec. Dagon had to do some terraforming before they could plant the colony."

"And the colonists, who had no better option, signed away their souls, I suppose."

"Not quite," the Star Brother said with a small smile. "As you can see here they were recruited from a world named Cymri something or other – translates as New Wales. There had been a civil war but it doesn't say what they were fighting over."

The Lost Rythan grunted. "It doesn't take much to get up a fight," he said, thinking of his own past.

"Of course the contract these people's ancestors signed placed them in the corporation's debt. How this is understood by the present colonists is anyone's guess."

"But they were guaranteed freedom of religion?"

"Oh, yes. The Star Brothers saw to that. Our order had more influence back then and we were called in at the request of the would-be colonists to approve the contract."

"So what happens now?"

"That depends on Pesc. There is no reason they should object to our continued visits to the colony but –"

The Faring Guard grunted. "It all depends on what they have in mind, I suppose," he muttered.

"Well naturally the normal *modus operandi* is to industrialise – quickly and drastically – set up a repayment schedule and then open the colony to interstellar trade."

"Which means," the other man said thoughtfully, "they will have to manufacture something that pays well enough to warrant export via the net."

"Of course. Or they might do some mining. Was there a survey done on natural resources?"

Gaed Alfred scrolled down. "Yes. Nothing out of the ordinary. The colony mines a few metals and does some simple refining." He shoved another strand of hair away from his eyes. "I suppose there are other things they might do. Set up a med center or a university. Or make a resort out of it."

The Star Brother's mouth twisted in distaste. "That's *all* we'd need," he said, thinking of some of the pleasure centers already extant.

"Probably the colony's religion wouldn't survive something along those lines," the other man agreed. "But there doesn't seem to be anything special as far as natural beauty. A star cluster and a nebula nearby –" He went on reading. "The colony itself is surrounded by native forest and everything beyond the borders marked as a hazard zone."

"Then no resort." The smaller man crowded closer to the screen. "It's almost certain to be some finished product they can produce. We'll just have to see what they come up with and how much it's going to disturb the status quo."

"And whether it's dangerous." There had been a few colonies depopulated by massive pollution and other industrial accidents. There were laws, of course, but in the case of the major corporations, these were seldom enforced.

Father Moto nodded. "I've already thought of that," he admitted.

"Someone will have to go down and check things out."

"Of course," the Star Brother agreed. "One of ours and perhaps two of yours."

This was pretty much standard. Star Brothers were almost always accompanied by Faring Guards when they traveled. The Lost Rythans acted as aides to the priests and brothers who served the stellar colonies, though admittedly their presence sometimes caused more trouble than it saved. The Faring Guard had originally been formed as a kind of foreign legion for the many Lost Rythan colonists who, through no special malice, got into trouble in their home colony. Frequently that trouble involved manslaughter.

The truth was that Lost Rythar had not long been civilized – a little over two centuries ago they had still been making blood sacrifices to the sungods – and they owed both their "taming" and their Christian Faith to the efforts of the Star Brothers. In repayment for this and for the fifty or so missionaries who had not survived the process, they held themselves ready – and embarrassingly eager – to serve their benefactors.

Father Moto was frowning again as he pondered the matter. "I have someone I think will do," he said at last. "Not a priest, because the colony already has its own priests. A brother newly out of the noviciate – Brendan Stillman. We'll stay in touch with him and he can report from the ground, so to speak."

"Mingle with the colonists?"

"Our visitors usually do. The colony language is Basic, so that won't be a problem. Changing over from whatever they spoke originally is standard procedure when someone sets up a colony like this." He turned away from the screen. "And we have contacts on the planet, places our people usually go."

"I expect that means your delegate can tell you things you wouldn't learn officially?"

Father Moto cocked one bright eye in the other man's direction. "Those are usually the most useful things to know, aren't they?"

The giant chuckled. "I've got a pair of helpers for him, then – a little more settled than most. Two of my better men, in fact."

"Fine," the priest said. "That should do very well. We don't know what they may run into down there once the people learn they've been sold."

"My men are here on the ship," Gaed Alfred told him. "They were both wounded on their last assignments and they've been on light duty. Probably eager to get back in the thick of things." The chief did not exaggerate, for he knew his people pretty well. "I suppose you'll need to have this youngster sent up?" he added.

"I'll call for a shuttle," the priest said. "He's down in Bloomhadn right now at our house there." He still looked a little worried. "If we weren't spread so thin," he admitted, "I'd send a more experienced agent. But with all these other stations to keep track of – and Brother Brendan has some good qualities. He's adaptable and eager to serve."

"Are there any more buyouts on your list?" Gaed Alfred asked, diverting his friend's anxieties.

"Not yet. But don't forget there are over two hundred and eighty corporate colonies and we try to maintain at least a visiting presence on every one of them. Though," he added ruefully, "some of that *is* underground work."

The other man nodded. He knew of several martyrs and, beyond that, a number of his and Father Moto's operatives had simply gone missing.

"You do what you can," the Faring Guard reminded his friend, "and God takes care of the rest."

Without answering, the Star Brother cleared the screen and punched in his next problem. The two worked for most of the night watch, only emerging in time for Matins.

CHAPTER 1

"YOU ARE ANGRY," THE VOICE said, and Marja Sienko did not bother to deny it. She listened to the insistent murmur of the river – but what river? Where? – and she felt the soft wind on her face. It was a green sort of wind, supposing a wind could have color, and it smelled like flowers. For some reason, this annoyed her even more.

"Someday," the voice murmured – or maybe it was the wind itself – "there will be a reckoning. You will pay them out."

At this, she roused slightly. "No," she protested. "It's all too late for that."

"But you did –"

Marja shrugged. "I didn't mean it that way."

"Lie back," the voice said soothingly. "Remember now. Tell me –"

She told it about her home in the land of stiff-necked peasants. "The stars," she said bitterly, "were nothing but lights in the sky. I thought they must be cities, far away."

"You wanted to see those cities?"

"They were not for the likes of us. We were born to work."

"So you worked?"

"Yes," she said, raising one arm as though to ward off the searching wind. "I worked. But," she added, "there was a school. I went to school."

"Not a very good school," the voice said.

"It was not. But I studied hard. I learned about the people in the north. They lived in apartments high above the city and they could look out on the lights. Their clothes were always clean and they had vids and gravity wells and they could fly through the air."

"Did you hate them?"

"Yes!" Marja said. "But I loved them, too."

There was a moment's silence as though something – the air and the river – digested her words. Then the voice came again. "Now you have an apartment of your own above the city. How did this come about?"

"On testing day at the school."

"You were chosen for the academy at Bloomhadn?"

"Not the first time." She turned over, feeling softness beneath her, curling herself into a ball. "Not – then."

"What happened that first time? You were twelve years old, weren't you?"

"Yes," she answered unwillingly and someone made an adjustment to the wind. The smell of flowers intensified.

Breathing the gas, she began to relax. It was as though another person were speaking and that made it alright. "It was the day of the examinations," she said dreamily. "They knew about it at home. The night before, I mended my best skirt and I borrowed real shoes from my cousin. I didn't want to go before the city people wearing boots."

"And you had studied?"

"Oh, yes." Once more she started to draw her body into a knot and the questioner increased the calming dose.

"What happened?"

"My mother was not feeling well the next morning. I think she had one of her headaches. She said I would have to stay home and help in the house. It was washday and there was churning and the younger children to care for. My father said I would soon be leaving school in any case."

"So you did not appear for the examination?"

"No."

"You worked at home all day?"

She shook her head. "I did as little as I could. I was angry and I hated everything about the farm. My mother grew angry too – and then I spilled a basket of clothes when I went out to hang them up."

"So you were beaten?"

"When my father came in for his noon meal, yes."

"But they let you remain in school for another year."

"Yes." For the first time, she wondered why. Perhaps they had not thought her strong enough to work in the fields. Certainly she had no aptitude for housework.

"And when testing time came again?"

"I said nothing to my parents. They didn't know the day. I went in my work clothes *and* my boots." She listened to the river for a moment. "I made one of the highest scores in the district."

"Ah. Then you were accepted at the academy in Bloomhadn and later the Sachsen Colony University."

"That too."

"You never went back home?"

The flowery wind blew through her mind. "No," she murmured drowsily. "I never went back."

After that she was left alone with the river and the moss and the green scent of growing things until it all turned into sleep.

"ACCEPT," THE PSYCH EXAMINER SAID. "With reservations."

The personnel officer looked down at the screen. "Will she need treatment?"

"Only if this is a long term placement. Then there might be problems." The examiner waited, curious as to what he would say.

The personnel man did not comment on this. "Feed in the specs on her assignment," he said, "before you get her up. And then make an appointment for her briefing. This is a rush job."

With a shrug, the examiner turned back to the bank of controls. It wasn't any of her business if Pesc wanted to take a risk on Dr. Sienko. There might be problems and there might not. The subject seemed to manifest a very strong personality. But whether she could overcome such deeply held feelings of resentment and inferiority remained to be seen.

It was not usual to hire someone before the psych scan but Marja Sienko was already classed as an employee. She had been offered a contract almost as soon as she completed the physical.

When Marja roused, she had no memory of the scan. She was, however, unpleasantly conscious of the mass of undigested material that had been fed into her memory. For some minutes, she sat on the edge of the couch, trying to find places in her mind for it all. Once she looked up at the examiner but the other woman kept her own eyes on her terminal.

Finally, she rose and began to gather up her things. At this, the examiner handed her the appointment disk. "It's for tomorrow," she said. "They're not wasting any time, are they?"

"No," Marja said, glancing down at the display. Only the time and date were visible but once she activated it, it would give her directions to the place she was to go.

She left the examiner's curiosity unsatisfied. She had much to do, if she were to be ready. All that afternoon and night, she continued to digest facts and images. In the morning, she reported for the final briefing, still feeling rather unbalanced by the overload of data.

Networld 326 would be her destination. The world was unnamed unless its inhabitants called it something else. Settled by its original owner, Dagon Ltd., some century and a half previously, checked on regularly every five years. Otherwise it was a closed world and remained unvisited except by the Star Brothers who had an agreement with the corporation.

The colony had been deliberately left low tech for fear non-directed development might interfere with its future usefulness. Because of this, the Brothers had not been permitted to establish any of their schools.

For a moment she paused in the corridor picturing to herself the lives these colonists must live, comparing them to her own early prospects. Low tech, enforced ignorance – well at least she had had an opportunity to read books brought in from outside her community. It wasn't hard to imagine the drudgery and misery in which such people lived. Pesc would be doing them a favor!

Their world had been classified as habitable with reservations. Now what did *that* mean? She sought further among her new memories. Continents and oceans fairly evenly distributed, but the settled area confined to only one landmass and only the center of that. Almost every available bit of land had originally been covered with native forest and most of it still was. However, a large area had been sterilized and inoculated with offworld flora ...

This happened sometimes. The native life on a world might be utterly unusable, but why had they been obliged to *sterilize* the colony's land? Perhaps her briefing would clear this up.

Then there were seasons, but not reliable ones. Six stars in the cluster, four of them not very bright. Well, Sachsen orbited a three star cluster and managed to have reliable seasons.

After this, she drew a blank. Networld 326 had probably been such a small part of Dagon Ltd's investments that no one had bothered to gather more information. Most likely the corporate visitors had only taken time to note down a few token statistics before they left to check on Dagon's other colonies.

At any rate, the population had grown sufficiently that there should be no shortage of potential employees for whatever Pesc intended, though these would have to be trained to manage robot workers. It would be part of her job to lay the groundwork for that training and, considering Dagon's negligence, it looked like she had her work cut out for her.

She strode briskly into the anteroom and gave her name to the robosecretary. With an obviously manufactured smile, the thing told her to take a seat and wait. Marja still found it hard to deal with machines masquerading as people, mainly because she had grown up in a place where the only machines she saw were farm implements. Now the android's bland and distant affability struck her as condescending.

There were two other people already waiting in the room – Henri something or other whom she remembered as an anthropology student and, on a chair near the inner door, a somewhat older man who regarded her curiously as she came in. No doubt Henri – was it Merlot? – and she had been hired for the same sort of jobs. But regarding the other one, she could not even make a guess.

Then she spotted something gleaming on his left wrist. A slave band! At this, she looked away hastily, hoping he had not noticed her staring.

But as she waited for her turn in the inner office, her eyes kept wandering back to that banded arm and the man to whom it belonged. The slave had a weathered looking face and wore his straight brown hair tied back. His eyes were also brown with the kind of lines at the corners that might mean a lot of time spent in the dry air of starships and space stations.

Before she could turn away from this scrutiny, he smiled at her, his teeth even and white. "Dr. Sienko?" he asked politely.

Dumbly she nodded, failing to conceal a mixture of embarrassment and chagrin. Then, "How do you – I mean –"

"Networld 326," he said simply.

"Oh God!" She stared at him in consternation, her own face alternately reddening and paling.

"I've been assigned as your bodyguard," he added.

"But –"

"Claiming a colony can be dangerous work."

She looked away, biting her lip. She had expected there would be difficulties ahead, but not the sort that required a bodyguard! After all, she was a social engineer, not a revolutionary.

She felt the man's eyes still on her, measuring what he saw. She was young – very recently graduated – and, she was forced to admit, not bad looking. Her shoulder length hair was the pale shade found among Sachsen's plains farmers, her face wide at the cheekbones with a generous mouth and the characteristic green eyes of her race.

She did not, however, believe he was admiring her looks. As she tried not to stare openly at him, she began to feel as though he might be weighing her in some other way, his look detached and unembarrassed. Calculating.

"I did not expect a bodyguard," she said stiffly breaking in on his observation. "I hope you won't be needed."

"We always hope that," he agreed.

She bit her lip. "So, who are you? I mean what shall I call you?"

"Franz Wells." He did not offer her his hand, though he quirked another tentative and somewhat ironic smile in her direction.

She stared at him blankly.

"We do have names, you know. We're not robots."

"All right. You've made your point."

He studied her for another moment. "No point, Doctor Sienko. I shouldn't have said that. You've never worked with a corporate slave before, have you?"

She shook her head. "I've never worked for a corporation before," she admitted, wondering why, despite everything, she felt she could trust this man. "This is my first job."

"Just think of me as something that comes with the job."

Before she could further entangle herself in social difficulties, Marja was called in for her briefing.

Once inside the over-decorated office, she reached two conclusions at once. The first was that she disliked the director on sight and the second was that she *would* not show him that she was impressed either by him or by the power he represented.

From the crown of his carefully arranged hair to the tips of his over-polished boots, this man was everything she had ever hated about the fabulous city in the north. She was quite sure that *he* had never worked the muddy fields south of Bloomhadn. He would have ridden the skyways of the city, placed himself at the window of an apartment tower to survey the domain spread out beneath him and, if he had ever thought about the farm country at all, would have curled his lip in disdain.

Had she been able to analyse her feelings at that moment, Marja Sienko would have been appalled at both their complexity and their intensity, quite justifying the psych examiner's caveat. She aspired to equality with this man at the same time that she held him in contempt – and also despised herself for envying him. It was these two conflicting emotions that guided her behaviour now. Without waiting to be asked, she walked over to a chair and sat down, crossing her legs defiantly.

"Dr. Sienko. " This he accompanied by the calculated raising of one eyebrow. "I am Director Quintus. Do please take a seat." He waited to see if this would embarrass her.

"Thank you," she said and her voice was clear.

With a shrug, Quintus pulled up another chair. "You have been given the preliminary material on your assignment?"

She nodded.

"Questions?"

"A few." She chewed on her lip for a moment. Then, "Why sterilize the land?"

"Ah, you go for the jugular." He reached over and took a folder from his desk. "I'm told it's because of the forest, Doctor. It supplies oxygen, but it's pure hell on anyone who goes in there. According to Dagon's recon, the trees aren't really trees at all. Neither are the vines real vines. Despite their color – purple, I believe – they live mostly by photosynthesis, but that is their only resemblance to plant life as we know it."

He gave her a ghoulish smile. "The first team lost three members in there, trapped, if you can believe the testimony of the survivors, and eaten."

"By predatory animals, you mean?"

He shook his head. "There are *no* predatory animals, Dr. Sienko."

"Then by the – the foliage itself?"

"So it would seem. We have no further details; the survivors were too busy getting out of there to make observations. The place was only an investment after all, not a scientific study, and Dagon really didn't care. They left most of the forest intact because of the atmosphere, burned away enough to plant the colony, made an artificial ecosystem and let it go. The colonists could deal with the trees later if they needed more space and, apparently, they have done so."

She frowned. "How?" she asked. "They didn't have the technology, surely."

"That we don't know, but there is slightly more land under cultivation now than there was before."

So – one more question left for her to answer when she go down there.

"Now as to your immediate assignment," Quintus went on, "you already know what you are to do. We need a report on the current state of culture and a working plan to turn this into a paying proposition. Of course that last part isn't your job, but you must help us get the population ready. We'll provide anything you require – within reason, of course."

Suddenly she thought of a way to unsettle him. "Director," she said abruptly, "I think Mr. Wells had better hear this too. Please call him in."

He stared at her blankly. Then, "Oh – of course." He activated a sensor on one wrist. "Send in Dr. Sienko's guard," he said and a moment later, the slave was ushered into the office. Quintus did not offer him a seat.

"Now," the director went on, "we're assigning you a robosecretary who will accompany you everywhere you go. Also Dagon's usual contacts on Networld 326 will be told to receive you. You must inform them about the sale and gain their cooperation. They were always paid well in the past and we will continue the payments as long as we need their services."

Quintus looked up from the screen, his gaze passing over the bodyguard as though the man were invisible. "The robosecretary should be the equivalent of an entire research team," he said. "It can store information and access anything further you need to know from the ship's databank. It will also be your means of communicating with your supervisor. We'll keep one of our smaller vessels in orbit until we have a station built, so you won't have any trouble staying in touch."

He saw Marja looking at the bodyguard and interpreted that look as a question.

"This sort of robot can't kill to protect you," he said. "It might intercept an attacker but –" Here he gave a little shrug. "Anyway, they're too valuable to waste."

The implication was plain. Wells was expendable but corporate robots were not.

Marja's lips made a thin line.

"So, Dr. Sienko," the director went on, pretending not to notice, "you know what we expect of you. Once you have made your observations you will work out a plan to get the colonists ready for modern life. Enlist the help of their natural leaders, of course –"

"That is standard procedure."

"Right. Any more questions?"

There were, but she doubted that Director Quintus could answer them. Across the room, Wells waited impassively, his hands linked behind him. What thoughts did he hide, she wondered? How must it be to live in a world where men like Quintus had the power to dispose of him as though he were less than a machine?

The director rose, his face showing no more than that of the slave as he dismissed her. He must rank all underlings together, she thought – slaves, robots and employees. She resisted an impulse to reassure herself that she was wearing shoes – for a moment it had seemed to her as though she might still have on her old muddy boots.

Her bodyguard held the door for her. She was touched by his simple act of courtesy which made her feel as though being Marja Sienko was good enough after all.

She even gave Wells a conspiratorial smile as he closed the door on Quintus, but there was no answering smile on the guard's face. Had he after all classed Marja with the directors and the masters he must endure? Somehow, she hoped not.

❧

BRENDAN STILLMAN WAS A SMALL, wiry man. Rapier like in his black habit, he moved restlessly about the central chamber of the starship, enjoying the low gravity and the prospect of – finally – an assignment of his own.

A closer look would modify the first impression, for he had a ruddy, friendly face, topped with uncompromisingly orange hair. His generously freckled nose turned up ever so slightly and there was an odd mix of mischief, innocence and dedication in his keen blue eyes. He was a product of Gaelway Colony, a place not known for the reliability of its citizens, but he had proven the exception to the rule.

Young Stillman had served much of his Star Brothers' novitiate in the train of a series of overworked interstellar missionaries, visiting world after semi-abandoned world until everything spun together in his head as a vast amalgam of humanity as diverse as it was needy. He had spent the last half year on Sachsen, however, to finish up his spiritual formation before taking vows.

The sudden announcement of his posting had come as a surprise. Despite his eagerness to serve, he could honestly have named a dozen or more men better qualified than he was. His obligatory session with the sleep tapes had briefed him quickly if not painlessly – he was prone to headaches when he used the things – so at least he knew where he was going and what he was expected to do when he got there.

A few crewmen passed through the open space and one or two off-duty brothers were working out with equipment as antiquated as the ship. Everyone who spent much time on the *St. Balthasar* had to exercise strenuously in order not to lose bone mass in the low gravity.

"Brother Brendan!" a voice said behind him and he whirled about to see Father Moto's face suddenly appear from a hatch midway up the wall. "Welcome aboard."

The younger man grabbed the edge of a walkway and swung himself up. A moment later he entered a room not much larger than the superior's workroom. Luckily, since it already held two Lost Rythans as well as Father Moto, there didn't seem to be any breakable items.

"Let me introduce your assistants," the priest said without preamble. "This is Ard Matthew Third-Blade –" He indicated a tall, straight-nosed man with shoulder length auburn hair and a short, trimmed beard. Ard Matthew's features proclaimed his membership in the Third-Blade clan, the nose longer and the cheekbones higher than was the norm for his colony.

"And Gris Wolfgang Bloodbear." Another tall, straight-nosed man whose shoulder length hair was only a shade or so lighter than that of the first leaned forward and extended a hand. Gris Wolfgang had a streak of syntho-flesh on one cheek that interfered slightly with the growth of his beard but otherwise the two looked very much alike to the newcomer's eye.

"Pleased to meet you," Brother Brendan said. They would be Faring Guards, he concluded, recruited after committing some sort of mayhem on their homeworld. It was the usual way troublemakers were disposed of – and reformed – in that colony.

Father Moto indicated chairs and, as usual, the Lost Rythans had to fold themselves carefully into seating meant for smaller folk.

"You've all been briefed, I believe?" the Star Brother glanced around at the group, bright-eyed and obviously not missing a thing.

There were nods as Brother Brendan winced a little, remembering his sleep tape headache. Not everyone was affected as he was by the process of memory infusion, but he made up for it by not suffering from the net-travel sickness which affected so many of his confreres.

"Good. I will now tell you what is probably in store for the colony you will be visiting and what we hope to do about it." The priest paused for a moment, ordering his thoughts before he began. Then, "As you know, Net-world 326 is one of nearly three hundred planets originally colonized on spec by corporations like Dagon Ltd. The original colonists came, knowing that their planet belonged to the corporation and that they or their descendants would eventually have to pay for the privilege of settling there."

The Lost Rythans, whose own world had never been touched by corporate investment, looked at one another uneasily.

Father Moto continued. "Since then – about 160 years standard – they have been on their own, building a little, farming much and reproducing themselves into a healthy population. We are normally permitted to visit them every ten standard years.

"There isn't much we can do for them, of course. The corporation wouldn't allow us to build anything, least of all a seminary, so the local clergy are not very well educated. We try to root out heresies and to encourage anything worthwhile – for example there's a native religious order, the Brothers of St. Hubert – but that is the limit of our influence."

Mention of the Brothers of St. Hubert earned an approving nod from the Lost Rythans whose own colony was much given to founding religious houses. It was a characteristic of these people that they measured almost everything by their own culture, which might have been one of the reasons they could be challenging to work with.

"Now," Father Moto went on, "we know what the new owners seem to be planning. Chief Snowtyger has set some inquiries on foot using an operative he has employed in the past. This man, Dust, tells us that Pesc's official plan is both expensive and not very likely to accomplish what they *claim* they want to do."

Uh oh, Brother Brendan thought. Wheels within wheels. And then he reproached himself for running ahead of his superior's explanations.

"Gaed Alfred's man is trying to learn more, and we expect to have ongoing updates from him, but so far we have only these hints that all is not what it seems. Because of this uncertainty, we have decided that you three will remain on Networld 326 for the duration of whatever transition there may be and report back to us as you can. In the mean time we will continue our own investigations and decide what to do about the results."

Brother Brendan could not repress a grin which he covered up immediately. When Chief Snowtyger and Father Moto put their heads together almost anything could happen, and a quick vision of the pair, so oddly matched, plotting away, always appealed to his sense of humor.

Father Moto gave him a reproving look. "What is it, Brother Brendan?" he asked.

"A – a question, Father," the young man said quickly. "What we are doing – this is not within the agreement with Dagon Ltd., is it? I mean coming when it isn't the right time and all and then just staying down there. Won't someone object to having us?"

"They might," the priest agreed, not at all taken in by his quick thinking reply, "if they knew. But the operative word here is 'transition'. We expect things to be in disorder for a while. And we do not yet have an agreement with the new owners."

"So we are to tour the colony?"

"Yes. But naturally you will proceed as quietly as you can. Even though Pesc has not done anything to alter our arrangement with their predecessor, that could change at any time. So far they've had other things to worry about, but there's no sense drawing attention to yourselves."

Once more Brother Brendan had to cover some confusion as he wondered how he was going to avoid attention in his Star Brothers' habit while traveling with a pair of six and a half foot warriors who had never been called upon to exchange their colorful and barbaric native costumes for something less noticeable. But that was just one of the problems he would have to solve on his own, he supposed.

"In light of this new information, I wish we had a priest we could spare, but at the moment, we do not." He sighed. "You may, of course, reveal your presence to anyone you trust and give out information as needed. It is only against *public* revelations that I caution you and that only until we have come to some kind of understanding with Pesc.

"You will shuttle down to our regular landing place on a farm near the edge of the wildwood – that is what they call the native forest. You may hide the craft there. The family knows us and we have left a landing beacon on their farm. Gris Wolfgang is a pilot, so we needn't involve any more personnel."

At the mention of his name, the man with the synthoskin nodded respectfully.

"We cannot keep a ship constantly in orbit without attracting too much attention, and anyway, there isn't one to spare until we know whether the situation is serious enough to require it. But we'll leave a transmitter satellite where you and we can leave messages for one another. Chief Snowtyger and I will be traveling the Net – we have other business to see to, of course – but we will check in with you as often as we can."

He did not add that both he and the Faring Guard chief had pegged Networld 326 as potential trouble and that they anticipated Dust's further reports with some concern. There was no need to alarm their operatives unnecessarily, Father Moto thought. Young Brendan should have enough sense not to reveal himself to the Pesc representative.

The priest rose briskly and the others did likewise, somehow finding room in the cramped cabin to kneel for his blessing before they departed.

On their knees, the two Faring Guards were almost as tall as Father Moto standing up.

IT SEEMED ODD, MARJA THOUGHT, that even though he was corporate property and undoubtedly conditioned to serve Pesc first, she went on feeling that she could rely on Wells – or perhaps it was only that she wanted to. There was no real reason she could give for this conviction, though the psych tester would have been quick to point out that here, at last, was someone even lower on the social scale than she had imagined herself to be.

It did occur to Marja – but she rejected the thought before it took hold – that her confidence in Wells might have been implanted by the corporation along with the information on Networld 326. But even if they *had* done so, they had certainly neglected to prepare her for the inconvenience of having a bodyguard in constant attendance.

She had given up her apartment as soon as she was hired and had taken quarters in the Pesc complex while she awaited her posting. Wells was given the room next to hers with a connecting door keyed to his hand. He knew when she rose in the morning and was waiting for her in the corridor when she came out, and this – as well as the key – did much to try her patience.

Worse, he accompanied her everywhere, remaining unobtrusively in the background while she communed with the robosecretary, or stationed himself against a wall in the cafeteria while she ate – until she finally ordered him to sit and eat with her. Probably he would have gone shopping with her if she had had time for such things. She didn't. There was too much to do before she left for her assignment.

While she familiarized herself with the resources and workings of her robosecretary, Wells sat nearby, an implant engaged. He, too, must be absorbing information – or perhaps he was only listening to music. Who could say?

One evening, three days after the interview, when they were eating together he looked up suddenly. "Have you ever been to the park?" he asked.

"You mean here in Bloomhadn? No. It isn't safe."

"So I've heard."

She frowned and set down her glass. "What are trying to say?"

"You would be safe enough if we went together."

"I still don't understand you!" Her voice was sharper than she had meant it to be.

Wells shook his head, smiling faintly. "Training," he explained, "for when we reach Networld 326. There are some things you need to learn about safety and you need to learn them before we get there."

"But my safety is *your* job! You're supposed to protect me, aren't you? Even here – I suppose you dog my footsteps in order to get me used to it."

"I'm not an army, Dr. Sienko. A time may come when you need to look out for yourself."

That was why, reluctantly to be sure, Marja agreed to visit Bloomhadn Park in the company of Franz Wells. Worse, they were to make their visit late at night.

"It's beautiful after dark down near the ocean," he told her. "Of course you can't see the sky very well because it's generally cloudy, but sometimes there's a sort of glow on the water. It does that itself."

And so, with only three days remaining before she set off on her first major assignment, she made a date with her bodyguard to drink wine in Bloomhadn Park.

WHEN BROTHER BRENDAN CAME OUT of cold sleep, the first thing he saw was Ard Matthew standing over his berth. The Lost Rythan didn't look too steady on his feet, but that was probably a combination of low gravity and low ceiling as well as his obvious case of net sickness.

"Here," the Lost Rythan said, holding out a flask. "Drink this before you get up."

Brother Brendan propped himself up on his elbows. "Thank God, I don't need the stuff," he said. "But it was good of you to think of it." He unhooked the straps and slid to the floor. With no more than a slight weakness in his legs, he preceded the other man out into a lounge. Though the word hardly applied to the spartan area with its utilitarian seating and very prominent basins for those travelers who could not make it to the restroom in time.

He found two crew members waiting along with Gris Wolfgang Bloodbear. Bloodbear, looking somewhat better than his friend, indicated a wall screen. "There it is," he said.

The image showed what might have been any other habitable planet – one of the dozen or so Brother Brendan had already visited. The landmasses were a purplish color and the oceans were blue, while white cloud masses alternately obscured and revealed the places where these came together.

And then he did a double take. It was the light he noticed first. Each of several suns shed a different radiance on the world so that only the smallest rim of the planet lay in darkness. There were no polar caps – not, he recalled from the sleep tape, because it was an exceptionally hot world, but because the poles were seldom turned away from all of the suns at once.

He remarked on these things to Gris Wolfgang.

"Look some more," the Lost Rythan said. "No bare mountain ranges, no deserts. Hardly any beaches."

Brother Brendan looked. "Yes – and everywhere that color," he marveled. "Solid purple."

"The wildwood," Father Moto said, suddenly appearing beside him.

The young man's eyes were drawn back to the screen. "Solid trees. A forest that covers the entire world!"

"No," the priest told him. "That is exactly what it is not. Don't even think of the wildwood in those terms. There are real trees in the settlement lands – we'll see them soon as we orbit the planet. But not these –"

"And they are dangerous," Brother Brendan murmured, remembering. "Yes. A killer forest."

"To most." Father Moto frowned. "However I've been reviewing the reports on past visits and it seems that Father bor Stein, our most recent visitor, heard a few stories about people living in the wildwood. *Druids*, they were called, which is ridiculous, of course. Anyway, he wasn't quite sure whether those were folk tales or rumours."

The young brother peered more closely at the screen. "That wasn't on the tape," he said uncertainly. "And I don't see how anyone could survive in there."

"Every colony has stories like that." The new voice came from a huge man, moving nimbly in the low gravity as he crammed himself into the chamber along with the others.

The two Faring Guards did not quite come to attention – there wasn't room – but the feeling that they did so was strong. Chief Snowtyger allowed himself to be introduced to the Star Brother, whom he looked over as though evaluating one of his own men. It made Brother Brendan nervous.

"Things do unravel on some of these colonies after a while," Father Moto was saying, "especially when we have our hands tied by the corporations. We often run into superstition, even a drift into paganism. There's no reason it couldn't happen here."

Brother Brendan listened with one ear, meanwhile keeping his eyes glued to the screen. The St. Balthasar was passing over water now, dotted with a string of islands. Ahead of them he could just make out a rim of lavender – another forested continent. "When do we go down?" he asked without looking away.

"I will say mass for you first and then you may take the shuttle."

The young brother nodded. "It's beautiful," he said, "even if the forest isn't safe."

"Look over there. That's the colony coming up."

They watched the forest shredding away as, far below them, shades of green took its place. Mottled tones succeeded these and lines that were probably roadways, but the whole break passed away beneath them even as they watched. Once more the wildwood dominated the landscape. The colony certainly didn't look very large from space.

Some hours later, as Gris Wolfgang guided the shuttle down on the Star Brother's beam, the three visitors had a better view of the wildwood. The purple mounds might well be taken for treetops and they *did*, Brother Brendan remembered, have trunks, though these were not woody. Slowly the alien forest gave way beneath them. It was early evening on the continent, the reddish light of two setting suns spilling across the land.

This time the cleared area seemed huge – a small country, which is what it was. As the shuttle swept lower, its passengers could make out both creeks and roads as well as pastures and planted fields, farmsteads and, far to their left, what might have been a village with a church tower, everything lost to sight again as they neared their destination.

The beam directed them along the fringe of the wildwood, the craft dropping until one side – the east, Brother Brendan thought – consisted of nothing but the purple landscape while the western plain might have been that of almost any other settled world.

At length, they entered a sort of inlet in the purple, where a large area of planted land looked as though it had been literally wrested from the native flora. As they dropped nearer the ground, a band of dead earth became visible, separating the green from the violet.

The shuttle landed in a pasture near a barn. Immediately a small crowd of people erupted from a nearby house, converging on the craft almost before Gris Wolfgang cut the power.

"These must be our friends," Brother Brendan murmured, running one hand through his unruly hair.

"Looks like they're expecting us, anyway," Ard Matthew agreed.

The Star Brother gave him a sharp look. "They're not supposed to have any means of communication beyond their world," he said. "No radio, no com –"

"Of course not," the Lost Rythan said. "You Star Brothers are restricted by treaty from giving them anything like that."

"But not your own people, I take it?"

"Faring Guards always try to operate within the law," Gris Wolfgang told him virtuously. "We would never deliberately compromise anything the Star Brothers do."

"The letter of the law, anyway," his even more honest companion added.

"I'm glad of that," Brother Brendan said in what he hoped was a businesslike tone, though a slight twisting of the lips gave him away. "We'll try to keep it that way. Though with this buyout," he admitted, "the law is bound to slip around a bit."

The two Faring Guards, sensing that their superior was an understanding man, relaxed. "We have never brought in anything that was *expressly* forbidden by the treaty," Ard Matthew told him. "But over the years, our people have made our own contacts while the Star Brothers conducted other business. There are many things a man can explain quietly to those interested, without violating the ban on technology."

"So these colonists may be more sophisticated than we were led to expect?"

The other man shook his head. "Not at all. Everything we have done has to be kept secret for the safety of those involved – and for the colony's good as well. The things you have been told about their general lack of knowledge are true."

"But," Gris Wolfgang added, "we may have tampered with the beacon a little."

The Star Brother stared at his assistants. "Have either of you ever been here before?"

Both shook their heads.

"Then you had your own briefing, separate from mine?"

Ard Matthew looked a little embarrassed but his companion nodded. "Gaed Alfred wanted to make sure we knew our jobs."

"Naturally."

There was no time for further discussion as Gris Wolfgang reached down to release the hatch. Almost at once, Brother Brendan found himself face to face with the man who was, he hoped, to be their host.

The colonist was tall and somewhat on the lanky side. He had longish dark hair beginning to grey at the temples, and eyes as blue as the brother's own. His face was bearded and here the grey had made even greater inroads, though he moved lithely enough as he hauled himself up to the hatch.

"Welcome to Treelight," he said in very passable Basic. "Dinner's waiting!"

CHAPTER 2

IT WAS A TYPICALLY OVERCAST evening when Marja and Wells took a robo-cab to the edge of the city nearest the park. All around them soared metal-plast towers, aerial byways connecting level after level above the canyon-like street. Only a few people were visible on the ground and most of these were of a furtive sort, watchful and skulking. True citizens, those with memberships in the various living co-ops, would be riding the skyways that connected the upper levels.

Marja was wearing a shield harness and when Wells told her to activate it, she did so willingly.

"You will wear this whenever you go out among the colonists on Networld 326," he told her. "Of course you needn't keep it activated all the time, but you must be able to turn it on instantly if you have to." He instructed her to slap one shoulder with her other hand. There came an odd tingling in her flesh as though the air around her had changed somehow into something electrical, something precarious.

"It's proof against most energy weapons, slows projectiles and can partially stop a knife."

"And how many energy weapons do you think I'll encounter on Networld 326?" she asked him, squirming about within her half felt cocoon. Of course there wasn't *really* anything there, she kept telling herself, but it stifled her nonetheless.

"Probably none at all," Wells replied to her question, unperturbed. "The colony's supposed to be pretech. But Pesc is always thorough."

She wondered if she heard something ironic in his tone, but it was gone when he spoke again.

"A shield won't save you from kidnapping. Someone could easily turn it off if they got a good grip on you. Nor would it protect you long from repeated blows, from a bludgeon, say. You'll have to be alert, quick on your feet."

"And where will *you* be," she inquired, "while I am being bludgeoned?"

He paused to adjust something beneath his jacket. "I could be otherwise occupied. Or dead."

She looked at him quickly. "You really think –"

"It's my job to think about all the possibilities, especially the really bad ones. And now, if you want to enjoy that view, we must pass through the park and down to the terraces by the sea. The water should be very beautiful this time of night."

"You've been here before." she said. Guarding someone else, she wanted to add, but did not.

"Of course." He gestured toward the path at the end of their street. "That's the park. Mostly it's a giant campground for squatters. They are left alone as long as they don't cause too much trouble in the city itself."

"I know about the squatters. This city is my home, you know, even if I've never – never gone *slumming*."

He gave her a quick grin at this, but didn't say anything.

There were lights ahead and what had once been thick plantings of trees and shrubbery, now sadly depleted – probably for firewood, she thought. As they moved into the area, she could hear voices, arguments and song, shouts and screams and laughter that had nothing in it of joy.

"The loud ones are no trouble."

The path bent a little to the right until Marja could no longer see the city street, though Bloomhdan's towers still loomed above the ragged treetops. Not far from the verge, a tent wall glowed with the flickering light within. There were shadows passing against the fabric.

The path curved again and the terraces ahead came into sight far ahead of them, glittering with lights. Wells took her arm, forcing her to slow down. There was a steady glow now from the direction of the sea. That was a safe zone, guarded. There would be tables, autoservice.

Abruptly Marja felt her companion stiffen, but he did not release her arm. Gravel crunched ever so faintly behind them, out of sight beyond the curve.

She inhaled more quickly and tried to speed up.

"Not that way," he breathed. "Never run in panic. You must plan ahead –"

"I haven't p-planned anything," she gasped. "I just w-want to g-get away!"

She had barely finished speaking when someone lunged against her and there was a short, snapping sound. She was thrown to the ground beneath a long, tattered form which moved spasmodically and then was still. The weapon snapped again and another figure staggered, dropping something that clattered against the stone curb. A third leaped on Wells from behind, one arm hooked around his throat.

She pushed the body off her legs and tried to stand up. She was shaking so that she could barely keep her balance. Somehow her protective field had become deactivated, maybe when she fell. She reached over and slapped her upper arm once more while, a short distance away, the wounded attacker was moving in to help his friend.

Wells had not raised his arms to his throat as the other man's grip grew tighter. Instead, he shifted his stance, keeping a grip on his gun. Then with a sudden heave, he freed himself, wriggling snakelike from the grasp of what had suddenly become two assailants, somehow eluding the downward slash of a long-bladed knife in the process. Or had he? His own shield was probably up, but Marja thought she saw the blade slam home in his side before it was withdrawn for another blow.

In sudden fury, she ran toward the fight, not in the least knowing what she would do. Before she reached the bodyguard however, the gun came up, making that strange snapping sound again and the wounded man fell. The other threw down his knife and fled.

"Come on," Wells said, taking her arm once more. "The scavengers are on their way."

This time they did run, not stopping until they had gained the terrace. A few people glanced over at them as they snapped off their shields and straightened their clothing. Wells held out an arm to her once more. The gun had disappeared beneath his coat and he seemed fully recovered from the struggle

Still, she had seen what she had seen.

"Are you hurt?" she whispered loudly.

"Bruised a little. Now, let us pretend that nothing has happened. Walk with me over to one of the tables. Don't attract attention –"

"But – but don't we have to report this!"

"If we do, we will. The company can cover for us. But probably we won't."

He led her to a seat at a small autoserve and took one opposite.

"But you shot those men!"

"Those were trank darts. They have to hit near the heart to put someone out right away, which is why that one didn't go down the first time I hit him. Still, I don't think the scavengers will be gentle when they strip those two – so it might come to the same thing."

She stared at him, caught between anger and laughter. Maybe he saw the rising hysteria in her face, because he leaned closer. "What would you like to drink?" he asked her as his eyes bored into hers. "Sweet? Dry?"

"Damn you," she got out.

"Something in between, then," he said and punched in an order. "You did fairly well, by the way. But you should have picked up the knife if you really meant to help me."

"Help you! I thought you'd been killed!"

He shrugged. "I warned you that might happen. At least you remembered to reactivate your shield. That was quick thinking."

She was still shaking when the wine appeared in the slot and he poured into the two glasses that came with it. "I'm sorry this had to happen," he added belatedly as he handed her a glass.

"You're sorry! I should think you'd get into trouble for things like this! Do your superiors know how – how irresponsible –"

He sipped his wine without looking at her. "I get into trouble now and then," he admitted in a different tone from the one he usually used. "But not for this."

"Surely you don't mean you were following orders!"

"In a way I was. The park is a good training ground for my clients and I use it when I can. Civilised people sometimes try not to believe in raw violence. Survivors must lose that innocence –"

She choked on her wine. "Well you've done a thorough job of it, you bastard," she said. "I'm surprised you didn't rough me up yourself!"

He waited until she stopped coughing. "Dr. Sienko," he said then, "I am assigned to protect you. My owners set the policy and I follow it. Did you think this was a date? We both have jobs to do and we must make sure we do them."

It was a brutal speech – another part of her toughening? She caught him watching her in the dimness – they hadn't turned on the table light – and a series of emotions washed over her. Anger, certainly, and mortification, because she had begun to see him as a man who deserved her consideration. She shook her head.

"Better?" he asked. "Would you like more wine?"

She held out her glass. "I must get back to work. Will we have to –?"

"No, we won't walk through the park again. I'll call a robocab to the terrace."

They drank in silence. Then, "I saw that man stab you –"

"The shield took most of it. I doubt the skin is even broken."

"You expect violence," she stated. "You've been conditioned to it."

"I'm still alive because of that conditioning. A lot of guards don't last as long as I have."

She tried to see his face, a smudge in the dimness. "How old are you?" she asked abruptly. "If you don't mind a personal question, that is."

"Forty-seven standard years. The corporation keeps us as long as we remain useful."

"And what happens then? You retire to a desk job?"

He didn't answer this.

"But have you always – always belonged to them?" she persisted, her face reddening, though he could not see it.

He poured himself some more of the wine. "We come from training centers," he told her. "They take us on when we graduate."

She was glad they could not see one another very well. "Like me," she said shakily. "This is my first job."

"Yes."

"I would like to ask you something," she said then. "Not – not about yourself. About my – *our* job."

"I'll answer if I can."

"Have you been interfacing with the robosecretary? As I have, I mean?"

"Some. But I don't have the education you've got. I've set my input to dumb it down a little."

She nodded. "But this isn't something technical. It's about the forest." She drained her glass and set it down. "As soon as we have the population in hand, there's going to be a lot of construction. Factories going up, robot workers, and the natives trained to supervise them. Mining everywhere."

"I got that much." There was something hesitant in his voice.

"The corporation plans to poison the trees. They'll design a disease and kill them all except for a few islands and places they don't need."

"That seems to be the quickest solution," he agreed.

"But what about oxygen? Isn't that why Dagon Ltd. left them there in the first place?"

"They must have found some way around the problem," he said vaguely.

"Not in the data I've been given."

He set down his own glass. "Then I guess they'll leave enough trees to take care of things."

She shook her head. "No," she said slowly. "There won't be enough – not in the long run."

"Then they'll think of something else. Find some other way to keep the atmosphere going." He sounded as though the conversation was finished.

She rose. He could be right, but she wanted to know. She would access the databanks when they got back.

Later in the night, after she had set the robosecretary to transmit her question, there was a delay in getting the answer. She ordered sandwiches for herself and Wells and was just unwrapping hers when the reply finally arrived. They would plant the oceans with oxygen producing algae, the robot said.

But then, she wondered, why hadn't such algae grown there already? She spoke the question aloud. The machine must have still been linked because the answer came immediately.

"This is not your concern," the thing told her in its emotionless voice. "You exceed your job description by asking questions like these."

She gaped at it. 'What –?"

"This is your first warning. Unwarranted research is logged with corporate center. You will cease at once."

She looked over at Wells who laid one finger across his lips.

Nodding that she understood, she got up and followed him out of the room.

"What did you think of that?" she whispered when they were well out in the corridor.

"I think it was good advice and I hope you take it."

This time she thought she sensed a businesslike good will in him. Now that she had come out on the other side of innocence, any kindness was welcome.

"Thank you," she told him. "I'm very tired now and I know you must be. There won't be any more work tonight."

The next few days were too busy for further speculation. She had barely finished interfacing with her robot secretary when it was time to depart.

IT HADN'T BEEN ALL THAT hard to get the first stuff for Gaed Alfred. There wasn't anything very secret about this part of Pesc's files and for Dust the hack was routine. He filed the report away for when the chief contacted him again.

Sometimes after a job, he gave himself a virtual body, and he did so now. He couldn't be working all the time, nor could he be always studying – though his enhanced memory made things a lot easier than they would have been before. He'd been picking up on the education he'd missed, starting pretty much at the bottom and then taking off on anything that caught his fancy.

Right now that was a field called physics, only it branched off a lot and he was always having to make choices to follow this or that. It was sort of like exploring tunnels, he supposed – you couldn't go everywhere at once, but you could back out and start over if one of them didn't seem to be going anywhere.

He thought about that now, letting his virtual body sit back in his virtual chair. Net Theory was great, but then there was also some stuff about particles he liked a lot. Each subject had its own guy who came in – not a real guy, but just someone who looked like Dust's idea of a teacher. A lot of them resembled the bigger kids at the orphanage, the ones who'd been decent, that is. Or maybe some social worker he'd met when he was in jail. Anyway, they explained things and answered questions and Dust got smarter. He even did virtual experiments and built stuff – only the things he built were no more real than his tools.

One of his teachers said he should see what would happen if he did an experiment wrong but he'd only fallen for that idea once. It was too much like the *accident*. The accident was why he was in here and he didn't like to be reminded of it. So maybe he wasn't learning as much as he might have but that was okay.

Which reminded him of the other thing he had to do. Dream.

"You'll go mad," the psych program told him, "if you don't dream. You don't need to sleep but you can't just stay conscious all the time."

"So make me some nice dreams."

But it didn't work that way. That was the hell of it – the literal hell.

And it was almost time again. He could tell by the way his thoughts were getting twisted around. Dust could take a certain amount of weirdness, but if he let things go on that way too long, his mind could just check out. He'd been warned about the danger. If that happened, he would become a *real* vegetable and they might just as well turn off the machinery that housed what was left of him.

So he closed his virtual eyes and let them come. For one moment, before he went under, he thought about his friends. There were two of them, one new and one, his old partner who still came to see him. It was good to have friends who were real and not something programmed in –

And then the nightmares began.

ℜ

BROTHER BRENDAN RETURNED THE COLONIST'S greeting and quickly introduced himself and his companions. He was a little dizzy with the sudden shifting sunlight as it came from at least three different angles. Besides the problem of the sunlight, the rank smell of greenery was a shock after the dry antiseptic air of the shuttle.

"We weren't expecting such a timely welcome," he said. "I believe your name is Tregarth? It was in the briefing, though I'm still digesting everything."

Their host indicated the land around them. "Tregarth Farm. And yes I am Master Tregarth, while these," he added, jumping back down, "are my family. He indicated a smiling, dark-haired woman and a crowd of children and young people. It must be an extended family, the Star Brother thought. In the light of the suns – the largest westering and turning red – their faces seemed to glow with cheery good health.

"It looks like you knew we were coming," Brother Brendan said, one eyebrow raised in the question he wasn't going to ask. "But this isn't the regular time for a visit."

"Sure we knew. The beacon showed when your ship came out of the net and we guessed you would bring the shuttle down while it was still daylight." Master Tregarth raised an eyebrow of his own. "But you *are* nearly three years early, you know."

"Oh – yes." Of course these people would be familiar with the Star Brothers' visiting schedule.

"And Faring Guards," Tregarth added, turning as the other two climbed down. "I remember the last visit. There were two of you then, but they came with a priest."

"As you have guessed," Brother Brendan told him, "this is not a routine visit."

"Then we will speak of your business after dinner. Unless it is an emergency?"

"We don't know yet," the Star Brother admitted. "It might be eventually, but there is no immediate danger."

Tregarth led them toward the house, wading through children. He seemed to be digesting these words.

"Did you clear this land yourself?" Brother Brendan asked, staring around at the well-ordered farm. On three sides, the alien forest was a distant smudge, lavender above and dark plum below. The contrast between the oddly hued crowns and the more normal greens of offworld foliage was as glaring here on the ground as it had been from orbit.

The Master shook his head. "No. We have the Order of St. Hubert to thank for that," he said. "They established my grandfather here before I was born."

"So they own the land?'

"No one owns land on Treelight. It's all held in fief – from the company. I am their vassal and this farm is in my care."

Brother Brendan had to admit the arrangement made sense. While no one was allowed to forget that the corporation owned the colony, there were not the bad feelings that might have sprung up if the people had been treated as mere tenants. He wondered how the news he brought would affect this arrangement.

Tregarth House was built of stone and wood, so hemmed in by outbuildings that the party had to pass through what amounted to a courtyard before coming to the dwelling proper. They followed their host into a fine, big house, walking straight into a dining room where a table stood weighted down with food and dishes.

To his secret amusement, Brother Brendan caught the two Lost Rythans peering anxiously at the jugs on the table. They had no sooner come in, however, before great tankards of beer were poured and given into their hands. Obviously Tregarth had entertained Lost Rythans before.

When grace had been said, well over twenty people sat down to devour an enormous tureen of vegetable soup, bread and cheese and an assortment of cooked vegetables. There was fruit as well, stewed together until the visitors could not say what sort it was.

Surreptitiously Brother Brendan studied the wainscoted room in which they sat. There was a crucifix above the door and a tapestry on one wall, embroidered – or was the design woven in? – with stylized images of foliage and animals, many of them familiar. All wildlife, he remembered from the tapes, had been brought from offworld. There were no native fauna.

"How large is your farm?" he asked, looking away from the tapestry while his host passed around bowls of cracked nuts.

"As you see," Tregarth answered. "We are a notch in the wildwood. Not the first and not the only one."

"It's a big notch."

"Oh," the man said, understanding. "There are more people here than you see. The rest live in cottages scattered about."

"But it's all one farm?"

Tregarth nodded. A farm-master was a sort of overlord, he explained. A working overlord. "I remember well the last visit," he added. "It was Father Taran. He stayed here for a day or so and then made a tour of the colony."

"Oh," Brother Brendan said. He did not go on. Such things as he had to tell the master had better be said in private.

Later, while the women were clearing up and the sons had gone out to do their chores, Tregarth led his visitors down a wide hallway and out onto a veranda at the back of the house. It was still daylight – maybe it always was, the Star Brother thought – though the largest sun had gone down with a lingering display of red and gold. Another one almost as large still lit up the landscape, but the ruddy light was gentler now. What might have been a third sun was so dim and far away that he could look directly at it.

The farm master settled himself on a bench, indicating seats to the others. He reached for a pouch at his belt – he was dressed in a long homespun jerkin over breeches, the whole belted with leather – and cut himself a chew of something. He offered some of this to the others, but they declined. Once he had the plug settled firmly in his cheek and had replaced the pouch, he sat back and waited.

Without preamble Brother Brendan plunged in, telling him first about the sellout. "We don't know exactly when Pesc Corp's representative will arrive, but it will be soon," he finished. "And so far, we have only a partial idea of what they plan for you."

"You'll be staying in the colony, then?"

The Star Brother nodded. "My assignment is pretty open at the moment."

He ran one hand through his hair – at least they had sent him to a place where its color would not attract attention. About a third of Tregarth's family had red hair.

"There will be changes," he said. "We can't do anything about that. But I can and will file a report on any irregularities. It's one of the reasons I'm here." He did not add that should something go wrong, whatever aid these people received would almost certainly *not* be coming from Net Central. The government had an arrangement with the corporations that seldom worked to the advantage of the colonists.

He wondered just how far the Star Brothers' treaty would hold the Lost Rythans if problems arose. As Faring Guards, they were bound to obey *him* – at least to the letter. But he must be very careful about what orders he gave.

"I don't see much this Pesc can change," Tregarth said presently, pausing to spit. "But I expect they'll bring more technology down from the stars. They'll want their payment – and it's right they should have it. We knew this would come."

"The corporation means to turn a profit," Brother Brendan agreed. "But with all that forest, there isn't much room."

"No, there isn't. They'll clear more land. And maybe move in more people. *That* makes me nervous, I'll admit."

The Star Brother shook his head. "They *can't* bring more colonists," he said flatly. "The settlement contract was with your ancestors and even if they wanted to make new contracts with someone else, it would be far too expensive and complicated to scoop up another group of settlers. There aren't so many useful people at loose ends these days."

"So you think they will increase manufacture," the other man said thoughtfully.

"It's the only thing that makes sense. Agriculture won't pay them back."

Master Tregarth considered. "We don't have much they're likely to want – out among the stars," he agreed. "Our colony was terraformed which means there's nothing unique about it – no delicacies and things you can't get anywhere else."

The first sunset faded into a pale and shadowy glow while the next sun began tinting the west with its own evening shades.

"What can you tell us about the Brothers of St. Hubert, sir?" Ard Matthew asked during a hiatus in the conversation. "You said they cleared this land."

Tregarth turned toward him. "Our own order," he said. "Founded less than thirty years after the colony. They fight the trees."

Brother Brendan had been staring at the sky, wondering if a bright spark above the horizon was a star, a planet or another of the six suns of Networld 326. He swiveled about to stare instead at their host.

"They keep back the wildwood," the master was saying. "And extend the lands of men."

"Are there many of them?" Gris Wolfgang asked.

"Yes," the master said slowly. "And no." He worked the plug in his cheek and spat again. "They join and make their vows – and when they are ready, they go into battle."

Gris Wolfgang sat forward. "*Battle*?" he repeated. "With whom?"

"I told you. With the wildwood."

His visitors were silent, thinking about this. To the Lost Rythans there was something rather fine in an idea which seemed to combine the things that most appealed to them – fighting and piety.

"This forest," Brother Brendan said remembering what his superior had told him, "is supposed to be very dangerous, isn't it? The trees are not real trees."

Tregarth nodded. "No, they are not. And yes it is a very dangerous place. It costs lives for every bit of land they reclaim."

Gris Wolfgang looked up. "They fall in battle," he said, understanding at once. "You meant that there are many, but most of them are now with God."

The master nodded. "You put it just about right," he agreed.

"I would like to see where they live," Brother Brendan said, having decided that his tour must start somewhere and the Brothers of St. Hubert was as good a place as any.

Tregarth considered. "I don't see why that can't be the first leg of your journey. Especially –" But he did not finish what he started to say.

The Star Brother waited. He could see that his companions were quite willing – even eager – to see the place. "That will be fine," he said quickly. "But we will need a map."

"A map you shall have, but I can also send you a guide. We all know the way, we of Tregarth Farm. Some of ours have gone to them in the past." He rubbed his chin thoughtfully. "There's a man I've got working here who can take you. He's already visited them once or twice."

The evening passed slowly, the master telling them a few legends about the wildwood and asking questions in his turn. All the suns were down – everything apparently set except for one that was too small to matter – and a great nebula had risen to light the midnight sky by the time they went to their rest. It was huge, resembling nothing so much as the mythical kraken etched in shades of violet.

"No moons?" the Star Brother asked when he parted from his host.

But the other man did not know what a moon was and it had to be explained. No, there were no moons.

Mornings on Networld 326, or Treelight as its inhabitants had named it, were a long drawn out affair. Less than three hours after they went to sleep, the first of the dim suns rose, chasing the nebula westward but not giving much more light than a full moon on some other world. The timing was not exact, of course, since Treelight made a rotation about every 28 hours standard. Nor were the suns entirely reliable.

As far as Brother Brendan could understand from his briefing, sunrise times were contingent on the planet's position as it wobbled about in a highly eccentric orbit. That was why the seasons could not always be predicted. Anyway, there were two dim suns in the sky when he woke and the world beyond the open shutters was a misty, pearl-colored dreamscape.

No one seemed abroad when the Star Brother rose and said his morning prayers, but the persistent bellowing of cattle was punctuated by the crowing of what had to be a rooster, familiar from his boyhood home in Gaelway Colony. He had not finished praying when he heard a door slam and a boy appeared outside the window, striding purposefully toward one of the sheds with a bucket in his hand.

At last he rose from his knees, only to find Ard Matthew waiting for him outside the door. "Gris Wolfgang has gone to help with the milking," he said in answer to the other man's query.

Brother Brendan looked at him in surprise. He had never heard of a Faring Guard milking a cow. Did they even *have* cows on Lost Rythar, he wondered? He put the question to Ard Matthew.

"Goats," the Lost Rythan told him briefly. "It can't be too different, can it?"

Brother Brendan, who had milked both in his time, did not bother to answer. Gris Wolfgang could find out for himself.

"I've got the map," Ard Matthew went on. "Master Tregarth gave it to me before he went out." He handed over a sheet of very coarse paper, apparently homemade, and carefully inked.

"Shouldn't we go and help with the chores?" the Star Brother asked.

"He said they didn't need us."

"Then come in and we'll see how far we are from the monastery – or whatever they call it."

They hunched over a low table, spreading out the drawing. Tregarth Farm had been clearly marked and on the side of the notch away from the forest, there was a road. This seemed to run north and south with several turnoffs which led to other holdings, each of them, if he could judge the scale, as large as Tregarth Farm.

"Look there," Ard Matthew said, running one calloused finger along a line drawn directly into the forest.

"Pennderen Krik," the brother spelled out. He didn't think the written language would have changed too much – it was more likely the word was supposed to be "creek" and that Tregarth had not learned to spell.

Further on, a road branched east toward the forest verge. It seemed to end directly beneath the trees. "St. Hubert Pryeree," Brother Brendan read aloud. "Now I wonder how far that is from here."

"Are we walking?"

"I don't know. Don't they have horses?"

Ard Matthew looked at him for a moment. "Yes," he said, "And Gris Wolfgang and I were taught to ride as part of our training for this assignment." He did not look too eager to put his new skills to use.

"They didn't have any horses on my home colony," the Star Brother admitted. "We used something else – not in the same family, I think. But we had saddles." Riding a horse would be like milking a cow, he suspected, when all you had milked before was a goat.

They were interrupted by one of the younger boys who called them to breakfast. Brother Brendan carefully rolled up the map and set it aside. He hadn't decided whether they should make their visit to the priory the beginning of a tour of the colony or whether they should first return to Tregarth Farm. He had better consult Master Tregarth.

Word would spread when the corporation made its first move and that too would become a factor in their decision. Still, the colony was a large place – or so it seemed from the ground. In the absence of radio, a lot could go on elsewhere before news of it reached the eastern fringe.

The dining room was crowded with farm workers who ate breakfast with the family and there were already platters of whole grain pancakes on the table along with basins of porridge. The master said grace and everyone fell to. More than one pair of eyes were directed toward the visitors while their owners chewed, but custom – or command – kept the eaters silent.

Tregarth motioned his guests to a bench near the head of the table. Another man sat there already, a hulking, scruffy fellow, who did not look as though he were related to the family.

"This is Gwern," the master said. "He'll go with you to the brothers."

The stranger gave each of the newcomers a measuring glance, his gaze lingering longest on the Lost Rythans. His own shoulder length hair was of the same ruddy shade as the Star Brother's, his eyes a brilliant blue, and he wore a drooping moustache. "You come from the stars," he observed in a deep, growling voice. He sounded as though he didn't quite believe it.

Brother Brendan assured him that they had. The Lost Rythans did not say anything.

Tregarth introduced them.

"How far is it to the priory?" the Star Brother asked as he picked up his cup, still eyeing Gwern. They were having beer for breakfast, he noted, something the Lost Rythans relished more than he did.

"Take a wagon," Master Tregarth said. "Leave in the morning, get there by evening."

Brother Brendan nodded, more relieved than he had expected. He *had* been nervous about the horses. "When will you be going?" he asked Gwern.

"Couple days. Got to finish some jobs here first."

"Gwern is a blacksmith," Master Tregarth explained. "He's working for his board while some business of his gets settled."

The blacksmith gave him a wry look and went on eating.

"When you get back, you'll be wanting to see the colony, of course," the master went on. "And your best way to do that is to join up with the travelers."

"Those are traders, aren't they?" the Star Brother said, fishing the information out of his overloaded memory.

"Yes. I've sent word out to Boss Sergay and he should be here when you get back."

"Then you may as well put us to work," Brother Brendan told him cheer-fully now that all was decided. "We'll earn our keep while we wait."

Master Tregarth grunted. "There's always work," he allowed, "and I'm grateful for extra hands." While he spoke, he was assessing the strength of the Lost Rythans. "Yes, I think we'll find something for your assistants to do."

The Star Brother gave him a crooked smile. "I'm stronger than I look," he said.

At this Gwern spoke up. "Come help me," he suggested in his hoarse voice. "I had a boy but he's laid up with fever right now."

The Star Brother turned to him. "Fine," he said.

"Soon as you're ready," the blacksmith told him, shoving his moustaches out of the way as he finished his beer.

The three visitors ate quickly and rose with the others. There was one surprise when their guide stood up, for he was nearly as tall as a Lost Rythan and looked a bit like one, though the color of his eyes showed a different heritage from theirs.

The next two days were strenuous, but none of the offworlders minded. While they worked, they learned what they could about the colony's affairs. By the third morning, as they prepared to leave for the priory, Brother Brendan had begun to feel at home on Treelight. The multiple suns no longer bewildered him and the scents of barnyard and spring growth were not so very different from the smells of other barnyards and other springs out among the stars.

They left the farm soon after breakfast on a cloudy morning. Since Master Tregarth expected the travellers within the next day or two, it was plain their holiday would be at an end when they got back. They would have to get down to business.

Brother Brendan mentioned this to Ard Matthew and the other nodded.

"This is a fine place, though," he said. "And these are good people." That was high praise from a Lost Rythan.

"All the more reason to learn what Pesc intends to do to them, don't you think?"

Because Tregarth was a large farm, it was a longish drive to the main road. Once they reached the highway – broader than the lane they had been traveling, though still unpaved – the wildwood lingered only as a sinister smudge on the eastern edges of the cleared land.

There were two board seats. Gris Wolfgang sat next to their guide while, behind them, Brother Brendan and Ard Matthew studied the map. Once or twice Gwern glanced over at the Lost Rythan beside him and more than once Gris Wolfgang gave him a curious but not unfriendly look.

"You tall ones come from – where?" the guide asked finally.

"Lost Rythar. I am of the Bloodbear clan and Ard Matthew is a Third-Blade."

"Lost Rythar is a colony?"

The other nodded.

"We might be kin."

"You sure look like it," Brother Brendan said, glancing up. "But Lost Rythar was settled long before we had star travel. It was one of those accidents when the starnet touched down somewhere on earth and –" He stopped. This man had no idea what the starnet was and he was not about to launch into an explanation.

How could he make a primitive understand that the net was an artifact found and used but not understood? That all the openings came out near habitable worlds and, due to leakage, one often found familiar things mixed with alien? Once in a while there would be a world where that leakage had included human beings, but never so far had anyone discovered an intelligent race that had not originated on earth.

"They say our ancestors came from two different places on the motherworld," Ard Matthew explained to the bemused colonist. "We seem to be a mixture of Polynesians and some Baltic tribe. But of course there have been a lot of changes over the years."

Gwern grunted. "I don't know much about the motherworld," he admitted. "But I guess we all come from there if you go back far enough."

"Where is your home?" Brother Brendan asked.

"West of here."

"Maybe we'll visit your farm when we return," he began but the other man shook his head.

"I'm not coming back."

For a moment the Star Brother did not understand – and then he did. "You're going to join the Order of St. Hubert?"

"That's right. Best place for someone like me."

Gwern and Gris Wolfgang exchanged a glance while some sort of understanding seemed to pass between them.

After that, the colonist turned his eyes to the road. "Killed a man," he said after a silence of some minutes. "Took sanctuary in a church and Father Olwyn got me safe conduct to the fringe. Helped out Tregarth, but now it's time to do what I promised I'd do."

"To save your honor," Gris Wolfgang suggested.

"More than that, I reckon."

"Of course." Brother Brendan tried not to look at either of the Lost Rythans, knowing as he did, that they, too, were paying for crimes of their own.

"It's not so different offworld, maybe?" Gwern said at last.

"Not on Lost Rythar," Ard Matthew told him promptly.

"You have a wildwood?"

The Lost Rythan shook his head. "The stars are our wildwood."

Gwern thought this over. "Star Brothers?"

"No. That's something different."

"So what are *you*?"

"Faring Guards."

After that they went on in silence. Gwern apparently needed no further explanation.

Treelight, for all its confusion of suns – there were four in the sky now, five if you didn't count smallest one which gave no more light than a star – was a beautiful place. Slowly Brother Brendan relaxed and began to watch for turnings in the road.

THE CORPORATE VISIT WAS ALMOST due and because of this, an early announcement was less of a surprise to Master Madoc of Harrow than the Star Brother's visit had been to Master Tregarth. Despite company policy, he had been allowed to keep a net receiver – safe enough in his hands, for he treated the thing with an almost superstitious respect. He responded only when the lights came on and a voice – the voice of his overlord – told him to.

It was not usual for the corporation to send a woman, though it had happened a few times before. These great ladies were not like the females of the colony. Bryn Madoc's father had once told him that if it happened, he was to treat the representative as a man, which seemed like good enough advice until he actually heard a woman's voice on the receiver.

Assuming the visitors came for news, he expected to pass on everything he had gathered in the five years since their last visit. On the last three occasions, his caller had been the same man – a cold and perfunctory lord who seemed to age very slowly and listened impatiently to what the master had to say, delivered the overlords' largesse and always departed on the same day that he came.

This time it would be different. Her name was Doctor Sienko and she brought news of her own. She had recoiled from his respectful address, hinted that what she had to tell him was good, and had a few questions for him before she cut off.

"You are head of a village," she began. "Isn't that right?"

"I am Master of Harrow, Great One," he told her. "But I live at Madoc Farm."

"Don't call me Great One," she said, her friendly manner slipping a little. "Can you arrange quarters for me and – and my staff – in the village itself?"

"Certainly, Gr—I mean, ah, Lady."

This title didn't suit her either. "Call me Dr. Sienko," she said.

He did not dare to ask what *that* meant.

"I have much to tell you," she went on. "I will need to speak to your leaders, to prepare them for changes that are coming. I believe you are a member of the ruling council of the colony?"

"In – a way," he said cautiously. "We seldom meet, but I have a vote when we do." Already, even though she was nothing more than a voice from space he was finding it hard to deal with her. Mustering his courage, he asked when the shuttle might be expected.

"This evening. I gather Madoc Farm is the usual landing place?"

"Yes, Great One – I mean, pardon me, Dr. Sienko. That is where your illustrious predecessors have set the beacon."

"This evening, then," she said and cut off.

Master Madoc was sweating a little as he left the room. Because he had company in the house, he could not take time to collect himself. Instead, he hurried back into the sitting room. Master Frayle of Frayle Farm was there on business – they were working out a marriage between one of Madoc's daughters and Frayle's oldest son. Father Caron, pastor of St. Dyved's, had come to help plan the wedding.

Both guests knew that Madoc Farm was the corporate visiting site. It was not a secret exactly, though Madoc normally didn't discuss the matter with outsiders. But this was different and he decided after all to take counsel with the other two before the agent arrived.

Calling for more drink, he reseated himself on the bench. His guests had seen, on the amulet he wore at all times, the blinking light that accompanied the summoning vibration. And Father Caron, at least, already knew what that meant.

Quickly Master Madoc told them about the call, but not mentioning the prospect of news. Whether it was really good still remained to be seen. He also told them about the corporate representative's request for accommodation in the village.

If Frayle was impressed, he didn't show it. He was master of a prosperous estate, larger than Madoc Farm, though he did not, like his host, have the mastership of a village. He was, to his inferiors, a rather formidable personage with a lean, saturnine face and piercing blue eyes. His dark hair was but lightly touched with grey and he kept his beard well trimmed. Now he poised like a hunter stalking prey, obviously waiting to learn something he could use.

The priest, on the other hand, looked like a peasant. Only the unmistakable intelligence in his expression gave warning that he was not. Humility was not current among the masters and they seldom recognized that quality for what it was. At any rate, neither of his companions took him very seriously.

Father Caron was well aware of this and it did not bother him. There were times he preferred to remain invisible for quite practical reasons. This, he suspected, was going to be one of those times.

CHAPTER 3

THOUGH **D**UST DID NOT KNOW it, Chief Snowtyger was praying for him. It wasn't just one of those all inclusive "lead all souls to heaven" prayers, either. Gaed Alfred kept a mental list of people he dealt with in the course of his affairs, especially those who, in his opinion, really needed prayers.

His list included a variety of souls from government officials to beggars he had met in the alleys of a dozen colony cities. He was acquainted with corporation types, merchants and even outright gangsters. Dust himself might once have fallen into the latter category, but Gaed Alfred didn't know for sure. Now the man was a specialist in breaching corporate security.

"In season and out of season", the apostle had said and Gaed Alfred took him at his word. He supplied Dust with some of the programs he was using to further his education, mixing in anything he could find that might lead him in the right direction. He also talked with him whenever he had a chance, fueling his imagination with Christian imagery. Dust considered him a friend.

At the moment, Snowtyger was exercising in the *St. Balthasar*'s central chamber. The prayer was part of the exercise. Long ago he had come up with a formula to which he stuck, even though he knew very well that God would know what he meant even if he just gave Him a list of names – or didn't, for that matter. The chief, however, tried to be thorough.

Up went his arms, thrusting what would have been an impossible load on Earth, but which came to somewhat less in the lower gravity of the starship. "For the man who tried to pick my pocket on Networld 46. I didn't get his name, Lord, but I ask Your mercy for him, and I'm sorry I broke his arm. Please do not let him be lost."

Down came the weights. "For the so-called Duke of Rahman Colony, I ask Your mercy. A kick in the pants might also help, but I leave that up to You. Please do not let him be lost–"

As usual, he was interrupted.

The *St. Balthasar* was dropping off a Star Brother and his aides on one of the worlds in the same sector as Networld 15 – should they stop there? Father Moto had business with the local bishop, but it could wait if there was something more pressing elsewhere. However, Father-Captain said he needed parts for the water recycling system if they didn't mind, and several other parts for ongoing breakdowns on the starship.

Networld 15 was Dust's current home. It would be an opportunity to check in with him personally on that Pesc business and Snowtyger said so.

"Right, Chief!" The messenger, Heth Justin, spun about, moving more gracefully than a Lost Rythan had any right to in the low gravity. He was, however, a lot younger than his superior and not quite as large.

Up went Snowtyger's arms as he flexed his muscles, feeling the stress meant to preserve his bones. "For Dust, I ask Your mercy. He's had a lot to bear. Please don't let him be lost.

"For the Pesc representative on Networld 326, I ask your mercy. Please don't let him – or her – be lost."

He tried to squeeze in as many prayers as he could before his duties called him away.

THERE WOULD CERTAINLY BE A space station. Already the materials were arriving as unmanned cargo ships emerged one after another into realspace above Networld 326. If the sunsets had not been so prolonged and the nebula so bright, any colonist might have seen the accumulating supplies and equipment as freighters crossed the night sky like moving stars. But so far, no one did.

In the confusion, *Pesc 7*, the company ship now orbiting Networld 326, failed to note the departure of the somewhat smaller Star Brothers' vessel. Because it was company policy not to leave unnecessary technology within the reach of the colonists, the *Pesc 7* shuttle would not remain on the world's surface during Marja's mission. She had her robosecretary and her bodyguard, besides which there would be – already were – Master Madoc and his associates.

"You'll set up in Harrow," Coordinator Hu had told her and she had told Master Madoc. "You might be able to see the place when we pass above the colony."

So far she had seen nothing except great masses of purple alternating with the rich blue of the sea and an occasional lake or river. The colony, when it came in sight some hours later, was a disappointment. So much of the planet remained unclaimed that this small patch looked like nothing more than a scar among the purple.

Beside her, Franz Wells was also studying the screen. Harrow lay near the center of the green expanse of colony land. From space it was one pale blotch among many, surrounded by what looked like farmland.

"How large is the town?" Marja asked.

"It's a good-sized village," the coordinator told her. "But of course that will change. That's where we'll put our headquarters once we get started. The only larger city is Bannyclay which grew up after Dagon chose Harrow for its center of operations."

Marja shrugged. She hadn't liked the sound of Madoc's oily voice and would have been happy to choose a different liaison person. Perhaps that would be allowed if he proved difficult. It was also possible he might be no more than a typical example of the colonists, ignorant and fawning and if that were true she had her work cut out for her.

To manage the establishment Pesc was planning to build – factories and mines, which would eventually cover the world from pole to pole – these people would need not only education but a much more modern outlook than they had now. Their cooperation would have to be based on enlightened self interest rather than an exaggerated respect for their "betters."

If all went well, of course, the colonists would eventually become redundant. Robot labor could be supervised by a cadre of company inspectors. In a generation or so, the descendants of the present inhabitants could be given token jobs and a life of comparative ease in some reservation specially set aside for them. At that point, they would be encouraged to either use birth control or to emigrate until their numbers dwindled to a token occupation – the minimum number of permanent residents required for colony status.

While Marja was pondering the future of people she had yet to meet, Wells had kept his eyes on the screen. She would have liked to hear what he thought but with Hu standing there, she hesitated to bring him into the conversation.

Eventually they boarded the shuttle. The skies through which they descended were a chaotic mixture of light and shade, as different suns shone each at its own intensity and its own angle while clouds sailed above the purplish land. For a time, they passed over a sea as blue as any she had seen on Sachsen, fringed with golden beaches. But always there was the forest filling in the center of every continent and every island.

Their pilot was another slave – Marja had spotted the band when the cuff of his jacket slipped upward momentarily – and he was also armed as her own bodyguard was. A dark, hawk-faced man, no older than Marja herself, he hid himself beneath a coldly professional exterior. Expertly, he took them down over the twilit colony, roads and river gleaming faintly below in the rather confused, crepuscular light. Here and there the roofs of a village showed briefly and were gone.

"Sit back, fasten belts," the pilot said tonelessly. His passengers complied, even the robot, which had been designed in human form, though it looked no more human than it was.

They moved more slowly over rooftops, peaked, thatched, even tiled, heading beyond the village to the farmland beyond. Marja kept her eyes on the screen while the crowns of real trees planted by Dagon Ltd. went by beneath them, breaking off at a crossroads where stood an odd construction of timbers from which something depended, swinging gently in the evening breeze. The last of the sunset showed what looked like drapery with a sagging irregularity on top.

"What was that?" she asked involuntarily as the thing passed out of sight.

Wells did not turn. "That was a gallows," he said.

In the front of the shuttle, the pilot made a small sound that might have been a chuckle. Immediately afterwards, he brought them down into a quadrangle formed by the houses and outbuildings of a farm. A man was already running toward them, or at least trying to run. He was rather fat and this slowed him down. Behind him, two other figures waited in the shadows of a porch.

Marja pulled herself together, trying not to think of what her bodyguard had just told her. If he spoke truth, then what she had seen was a body hanging there and it meant that she would have to revise her opinion of the colonists even further downwards.

Almost before the fat man came puffing up to the opened hatch he gaspingly introduced himself as Master Madoc. In the light of the shuttle he proved to be middle aged with faded auburn hair and a jowly face with a trimmed beard. He fixed his eyes on her in a way she didn't like and made a low bow.

"Lady Doctor Sienko!" he cried with false heartiness when he had got his breath. "Welcome to Networld 326!"

"That is what you call it?" she asked. "I should think you would have a name for your colony by now."

He looked confused. "Oh, yes, of course," he said. "The, ah, common people call it Treelight. That is – if it pleases you." Behind him, the other two approached more slowly, their eyes fixed on the shuttle hatch. Marja caught sight of a distinguished looking man about the same age as the master and another, nondescript fellow, who appeared to be a priest.

Naturally religion would be a potent force in a place like this, she thought, though the presence of a cleric made her nervous. She had long since abandoned the faith of her parents, along with their ignorance and poverty.

She allowed the master to help her down from the shuttle, his soft hands fumbling on her arm. Wells was right behind her, eyeing the colonists as though he expected an attack at any moment. As for Marja, she kept seeing in memory that swinging bit of drapery hanging from the gallows outside the village. She found it impossible to match the execution with this genial toady, busily trying to lay the entire colony at her feet.

"May I present Father Caron and Master Frayle of Frayle Farm," he said when it became apparent that his companions were not going to fade back into the shadows. They had stuck to him like burrs ever since the call.

Marja greeted the pair politely, aware of Frayle's keen eyes on her. Presently, the robot descended from the shuttle, carrying her luggage and that of her bodyguard. The hatch closed immediately and, without any further delay, the craft begin to lift. Their pilot had fulfilled his duty, and saw no reason to remain.

Her host continued plying her with compliments as he guided her toward the house, remarking on her youth and wondering how it was that such a beautiful young woman should be entrusted with such an exalted job. He apologized for the dampness, for the chill of the evening and for the smallness of his house – which was actually of a very good size – and for the accommodations she would find within.

"I asked for quarters in the village," she said, cutting him off.

Somewhat taken aback, he was nevertheless quick to assure her that everything had been arranged.

Wells came in for a share of attention. Apparently the colonists did not realize he was a slave and the other two walked with him. The robot however made everyone nervous. It was an attractive model, androgynous and by no means grotesque. It had been decently clothed and though it did not have hair, its face was set in an expression of plastic friendliness.

Master Frayle kept glancing at the thing curiously while Father Caron only looked disapproving.

"You are Dr. Sienko's assistant?" the priest asked Wells.

"Her bodyguard," the other replied. "I am a corporate slave."

Frayle seemed to divine his meaning at once. "Then you are bound to our new masters," he said, his tone altering slightly. "A serf?"

Wells nodded. "If I understand your use of the word, that should be about right, sir."

"This woman is your mistress?"

Wells shook his head. "I belong to the corporation," he said. "My duty is to keep her safe."

"You are very welcome here," the priest told him. "You and Dr. Sienko. We already know that this is not a routine visit."

"No, Father, it is not."

"You are not allowed to tell us anything, I presume," Frayle suggested.

"Not until Dr. Sienko gives me leave. I'm sorry."

Master Frayle gave him a quick look. Perhaps he was not used to being addressed by a slave in quite this manner.

"Only once before was I here when a representative of Dagon Ltd. arrived," Father Caron was saying. "It is not everyday we meet a man from the stars."

At this Wells unbent a little. "No," he agreed, "I suppose not."

They entered a vestibule and then came into a room obviously intended to awe them with its richness, and indeed it did, a little. There were tapestries on the walls – all filched from other rooms and hung that day – and a carpet on the floor. Their host gestured toward a settee covered in hide where Marja sat down gingerly, feeling as though she had been enthroned.

Candles burned on every table, great masses of them, and now a timid woman came in bearing jugs and carved cups. She offered them beer.

Marja took a cup from politeness, though Wells rather spoiled the moment by leaning over to dip a tester in the liquid. He nodded briefly when it came up negative and she dared take a sip. She really didn't like beer anyway.

Not quite understanding, but inclined to resent whatever had occurred, the master gestured Wells and the robot to another bench where the serving woman came over hesitantly to hand the bodyguard a cup of his own. She would have given some to the robot had not Wells prevented her. "It cannot drink," he explained gently, causing her to withdraw in some confusion.

The others found seats, everyone gazing expectantly at Marja. After a moment, she launched into the first phase of her planned explanation. She dwelt on the benefits of industrialization, the modern wonders soon to pour into the colony, and the generosity and kindness of her employer.

All the time she spoke, she kept remembering that not far away at the crossroads a body dangled, moving ever so slightly in the evening breeze. Fortunately, she had not seen the way its bird-picked face reflected the ghastly light of the rising nebula.

Nor did she know that above the planet in the corporate ship, the shuttle pilot was getting quietly stoned. As long as he took a detox pill the next morning, no one cared.

~

THEY HAD LONG SINCE MADE a brief halt to eat the dinner Tregarth's wife had provided and Brother Brendan had taken the opportunity to call in an account of his observations so far. The message was duly transmitted to Father Moto, but its sender did not expect an immediate reply. He didn't even know where the *St. Balthasar* was headed when the ship re-entered the net. His report might be held for some time before it could be sent on.

The afternoon was waning when the road finally forked, one branch turning due east. The wildwood had been a constant presence on their right side as they moved north, sometimes near enough that they could make out individual crowns and then receding once more to a vague purplish haze. Now they were headed directly toward it.

There were still trees and bushes on both sides of the lane, offworld foliage with green leaves and flowers, birds and insects. Beneath their wheels the way was half grown over with grass. A cool, spicy breeze blew from the wildwood ahead. It almost smelled like cloves, though there was an undertone less pleasant.

"Like cleaning a deer," Gris Wolfgang said when Brother Brendan remarked on this. "Not blood but something like it."

Yes, that was it – something like the insides of things.

"Been close to it before," their guide said. "The farm had a big cleared space so you wouldn't have seen much. But out here it's different." He gazed ahead as though weighing the strength of this foe while his hands tightened on the reins.

"How much further is it to the priory?" Brother Brendan asked him.

"Not far. It's close to the edge."

The road did not run straight. Sometimes they almost lost sight of their goal but after a while, the wildwood began to tower over the greenery until the jagged canopy started to resemble treetops less and less. The offworld foliage grew more sparsely, finally tapering off to grasses and low-growing weeds. The birdsong ceased.

Presently they came to a broad meadow where cattle grazed on the thin grass. A man was herding the beasts toward a barn some distance away, but he stopped and waited as the wagon came in sight.

"Is the priory ahead?" Brother Brendan called and the herder nodded.

He was wearing some sort of religious habit.

"God's blessing on you. Keep on and you will see it."

Silently, Gwern flicked the reins and started them on their way. Soon enough they came to a crude, sprawling structure built almost entirely of laid stone. The roof was thatched and there were small windows along each wall – very small windows. A sturdy wooden door stood half ajar and two men came out of this as they pulled up.

Both were clad in grey homespun robes with a plain cross of lighter fabric sewn on the breast. Their hair was tied back and they wore short, trimmed beards. Their racial resemblance to Gwern and the Tregarths was plain both in their coloring and in the cast of their faces. One of them limped slightly and there was an odd sort of irregular tattoo on one side of his face.

"Welcome guests, in the name of God," the marked one called.

Their guide tied the reins to the front of the seat and climbed down. Slowly he walked toward the pair. "I have come," he said woodenly. His fear was a palpable thing, though he tried to hold it in check.

The tattooed man inclined his head. "Welcome, Gwern," he said, recognizing him. "We have been expecting you. And these others? I see that one of them is a Star Brother."

At this, Brother Brendan jumped down and introduced himself and the Lost Rythans. "We've come to visit the priory," he said. "And also I have news for your – prior?"

"We call him the marshal," the other man replied. "As he cannot come to you, I will take you to him."

Leaving the others to put up the horses, the Star Brother accompanied the tattooed man into the house.

Inside the building, the stonework continued. There was no wood to be seen except for the ceiling beams, while the floor was of packed earth. They passed from the entryway into a short, narrow corridor, where the visitor recognised on one side what had to be a barracks, its stone walls lined with small windows. Simple pallets lay in rows on the floor.

A smaller room – almost a cell – opened off the far end, the doorway hung with a leather curtain.

"Will you come in?" his guide asked.

Not knowing what to expect, Brother Brendan followed him into the room. On a blanket spread beneath the window, a man half lay propped up against a leather sack leaking hay. His gaunt face was flushed and marked with more of the same tattooing Brother Brendan had seen on the guide.

Now that the light was a little better, he saw that both men bore similar designs on hands and arms as well.

"This is Marshal Gwilym," the other man said. "Brother Brendan," he added for the marshal's benefit, "of the Star Brothers."

Marshal Gwilym fixed sunken eyes on his visitor's face. "You are welcome in the name of God," he whispered. "I know of your order, though I have not seen one of you before."

Brother Brendan gestured with one hand. "May I?" At a nod, he hunkered down beside the other man. "I am sorry you have not," he said frankly. "But there are scarcely enough of us to serve the colony worlds as we would like. Normally we visit Treelight only once in a decade, but this is not an ordinary visit. I was sent on a special mission to you."

The sick man fixed him with feverish eyes, waiting.

"There are changes coming and I am here to help you if I can." His voice trailed off as he wondered what exactly he could do to protect these people. By himself, nothing. As representative of the Star Brothers – not much more.

"I am here," he resumed more firmly, "because it matters to us – to the Star Brothers – what becomes of you."

"There is – some threat to our world?" the marshal inquired.

"I should think that has always been the case," his visitor told him. "You must know that your colony has been left in peace all these years since its founding only because Dagon Ltd. was waiting for an opportunity to sell it at a profit."

"These things are in the hands of God," the marshal said with a faint smile, rallying a little. "Now, I gather, it is God's will that we be sold."

Brother Brendan met his eyes. "I wish I could bring you better news," he said frankly, "but I can only say that God's will is sometimes hard to bear." He kept glancing from one man to the other, realizing that both of them were ill, though what was wrong with them, he did not know. "You may say that I spoke out of turn," he added. "And I have. I think you already know better than I what it is to suffer –"

"What is the instrument of this coming trial?" the marshal asked.

"Your new owner is the Pesc Corporation. Like Dagon Ltd. they plan to make a profit."

The man on the pallet gazed up at a crucifix on the opposite wall. "What exactly do you think will happen?"

"Your way of life will change. We think they are planning to set up industries, a manufacturing economy. A new culture –"

"They will expand the colony?"

Brother Brendan nodded. "I don't see how they can avoid it. The corporation cannot legally bring down more settlers – or at least we don't think they can – but there is no ban on machinery. Robots for instance."

"What is a robot?"

His visitor explained about artificial intelligence. "They have no will," he added. "They are really nothing but tools. True men will have to tell them what to do."

The other brother snorted. "Abominations," he growled, his weathered features wrinkling with distaste.

The Star Brother shook his head. "Not necessarily." He had lived among the things for most of his life and had never thought of them as anything except walking computers – appliances of a sort. "But," he had to admit, "I doubt your people will be comfortable with them."

"Then they are simulacra – mindless as the dead save that they walk – and obey." The marshal seemed to have a fairly good grasp of things despite living in a pre-tech colony, but his choice of images shed a light that had never occurred to Brother Brendan before. Country-bred himself, he suddenly remembered the first time he had actually met a roboclerk. He had taken it for a banshee and run crying to his mother.

"I will be traveling throughout your colony," he said, shaking off the unpleasant memory. "And soon – if not already – a corporate representative will also be arriving. When he reaches the colony, we will all learn more about the situation."

"This corporation might not like having a Star Brother at large," the marshal observed.

"I hope they won't know I'm here," his visitor replied. Then, "I am sorry," he said, changing the subject, "to find you ill, Marshal."

"Ah. You have seen our beauty marks?" The sick man held up one arm, smiling grimly. "It is the wildwood. We all come to this in the end, for we take such wounds in the fighting that, after a time, must kill us. But at least we die as free men."

The Star Brother looked at him blankly. What did the marshal mean by *that*, he wondered. He did not ask, though his perplexity showed on his face.

The marshal saw this. "I grow weak," he whispered, "and I shall have to rest now. Brother Alwyn can show you about and answer your questions." He indicated the other man. "I will see you – later – in the chapel for Compline." He closed his eyes and Brother Brendan saw both weariness and pain etched on his face.

"Of course," he said, rising hastily. He turned to Brother Alwyn, indicating his readiness to leave the marshal in peace.

In silence, the other man led the way back down the corridor until they came to a turning which led into a larger room filled with stone tables and benches.

They found the Lost Rythans seated at a table drinking beer with another – unmarked – brother. Ard Matthew looked up as he came in.

"Where is Gwern?" the Star Brother demanded.

"They took him somewhere else. Since he's come to join them, he isn't really a guest." The Lost Rythan set down his beer, waiting expectantly.

"I saw the marshal," Brother Brendan told him. "He is ill." He eyed Brother Alwyn. "Something to do with the wildwood."

The brother nodded. "It is the mark," he said. "The trees – only they are not real trees – send out their vines to attack us. Sometimes our brothers are engulfed and – and devoured." He saw the look of incredulity the others gave him. "Things in there can move fast enough at times. But," he added, "we are not helpless against them. We strike and we kill. When we sever their connection to their roots, or what passes for roots, they are mortally wounded."

He held up his arms, letting the sleeve fall back to show the strange designs beneath his skin. "It is the vines that sting us. Though we wear protection, we cannot avoid them entirely when we go against the forest. They die when their hosts die but not so quickly. We have tried setting fires, but they go out. And so we suffer what we cannot avoid."

"And what, exactly, do you suffer?" the Star Brother asked, eyes narrowed as he regarded the branching lines on the other man's cheek.

"The toxins build up. Our bodies fight against them for a time – sometimes a year or two – but in the end even one sting can be too much. Especially if it is in the face or torso. When that happens, the signs come on more quickly."

"You have no cure?"

"Not one that we would use. There are others who do – at least we have heard."

"Why can't you take the remedy?"

An expression of distaste came over the other man's face. "The poison attacks more than the body," he explained. "It also lays siege to our will, pulling us to serve the wildwood, to eat of its produce, to live in its shadow. In short, it would make us *its* creatures. This pull even we must suffer before the end, but we fight it as we fight the other evils of our flesh. None falls to this, by God's mercy, because we die before completely losing our free will."

"But if someone did survive?"

"What life would they have as minions of a mindless creature – yes, the wildwood is all one – cut off from their fellow men, working ever to promote the destruction of their own kind?" Brother Alwyn looked away. "It does not bear thinking of."

At this Gris Wolfgang spoke up. "But it is thought of," he said. "That is what you are telling us."

The other man did not answer.

"You describe what amounts to possession," Brother Brendan said thoughtfully.

Brother Alwyn shook his head. "It might seem so, but no. To possess another there must be an intelligence. There is no such thing here. Say rather it compels its victim to serve its interests but leaves him free to go about this as he sees fit. And they are not very clever, these slaves of the wildwood. Not as they were before. Or so we are told," he added hastily.

"A form of brainwashing," the Star Brother murmured. "And this is what you fear most?"

"More than death."

Obviously, the visitors thought, seeing death in the man's marked face.

"Yet you still clear the land," Brother Brendan said wonderingly. "And this is the price you pay."

"We rarely clear new land these days. Mostly we reclaim what the wildwood takes."

The others looked up in surprise. "Surely you don't mean that the forest is moving in on the colony?"

"Only in a few places. And there we have our priories. Mostly," Brother Alwyn added, "things are quiet along the fringe. But it has been many years since we took any *new* land from the wildwood."

"Master Tregarth said the Brothers of St. Hubert had made a notch in the wildwood. In his grandfather's day."

"Yes, Tregarth and a few other places. But not recently." He shrugged. "It is as though they – *it* is beginning to recover from the poison the corporation used when our ancestors came here. Or perhaps it is growing stronger for some other reason."

Brother Brendan set both hands on the stone table, not feeling the chill of it in the deeper chill of this new revelation. "But the corporation," he said finally. "Surely they will deal with the wildwood – I mean they have the technology to destroy it. They must or there would be no point in coming here."

"Do they promise *that*?" Brother Alwyn said with a grim smile. He turned away. "Will you come with me to the chapel? We eat no evening meal and soon it will be time for prayers."

The visitors followed him into another stone-walled chamber. To his surprise, Brother Brendan saw that Marshal Gwilym had left his bed, propping himself up with a staff, as the community gathered to sing the office. There were about fifty of them, most marked by the jagged purple signs of poisoning. Gwern, too, knelt with the brothers, still wearing the shirt and breeches he had come in, his face bearing a look both exalted and resigned as he prepared to offer himself to the life – and death – of the Brothers of St. Hubert.

IT HAD BEEN A TAXING evening with much to explain and much to gloss over. Marja was exhausted, the Nebula had sagged far to the west, and even Wells was looking pinched about the mouth when she and her party were finally taken by wagon to the village.

To her relief, they did not pass by the gallows but turned off into another lane, which presently became a street leading into the market square. A wooden house had been set aside for her use near the corner and she could only hope the original inhabitants had not been evicted. To her dismay, she and Wells were received by a small staff of servants.

It was on the tip of her tongue to demand that these people be moved out of the house for she had no doubt they would report everything she did to Master Madoc. Then she saw Wells looking at her. He gave a slight shake of the head to remind her that security was *his* problem.

After their hosts had gone, she was soon installed in a surprisingly comfortable bedchamber by a kindly farm girl who had already laid a small fire on the hearth. She must, Marja thought, ask for a portable heating unit when she contacted the ship in orbit. And there would be other things to send down as well – gifts for the company's supporters and for the many influential people she must persuade to help her in the first stages of her work. She resolved to make up a list of those who should be presented with tokens of the corporation's good will.

They had provided Wells a room at the other end of the hall, but this he refused to accept, politely explaining that he must be within call of his client. At his insistence, the room next to Marja's was hastily cleared of some stored goods and a mattress was thrown down for him on the floor.

Fortunately, Marja did not see the knowing looks exchanged between the maid and manservant. She would have been humiliated if she had, though Wells, who *had* seen, remained unruffled as he set the robot to patrol the house. Not needing sleep, this was a logical job for it and, since security fell within his provenance, it was obliged to obey. The relations between slave and machine were sometimes hard to decipher – as Marja was to learn before too long – and might sometimes go in the opposite direction with Wells subject to the robot.

After setting the machine its task, her bodyguard took it on himself to examine every door and window, to look into every room – even those occupied by the staff – and to carry a candle down into the cellar, making sure there were no other ways into or out of the house. Only then did he tap on Marja's door and ask if she had any further tasks for him.

She wanted to talk to him, to ask him a few things, some trivial, some less so, but she was too tired. Instead she wished him a cordial good night – as though, she thought ruefully, this were some sort of house party – and heard him enter his own room.

He'll put a listening device against the wall, she told herself and waited. But if he did, it was done silently. The next thing *she* heard was the young maid coming in to mend the fire and open the curtains. Already there were three suns in the sky and another, brighter one on the rise.

Marja sat up abruptly, startling the girl. "Have – What time is it?" Immediately she realized the stupidity of the question. What meaningful answer could the colonist give?

The maid turned on her a nervous smile. "Will you have your breakfast in bed, Lady?" she asked timidly. From outside the window came sounds of horses, the creak of wagons, shouts and calls.

Marja set her feet on the floor. "Certainly not! Is Wells – my bodyguard – awake?"

"Yes ma'am. He is entertaining visitors."

Then she had certainly overslept! And to leave such things in the hands of a man with no training! She threw on more of the clothing her employers had supplied – fine-spun blouse, a long pleated skirt and real leather shoes – and hurried into the corridor. She heard voices below.

At the bottom of the stairs she met the robosecretary.

"Who is Wells talking to?" she demanded in a low voice.

"Father Caron and Constable Wynn," it said in it's artificially inflected voice. "They are paying a call."

Her lips quirked into a mirthless smile. A call. They hadn't wasted any time! She wondered what her bodyguard was telling them.

She found the group in what must be the sitting room, each holding a cup of some hot beverage. Everyone rose when she came in, the constable trying not to stare, the priest regarding her with a neutral expression, and Wells merely watching her.

Her first impulse was to demand an explanation as to why she had not been woken, but this she stifled as it would give the colonists the wrong impression. "Good morning, gentlemen," she said and waited to hear what they would say.

"Sorry, ma'am, to intrude on you so early," the constable told her, reseating himself when she took a chair. "It's my duty, see, to make sure you're settled in comfortably and, besides, it's market day."

She looked at him blankly.

"Saturday," he explained. "There'll be a lot of people in town. Not all of them honest."

"Oh, of course." She considered for a moment. "Perhaps I might see this market?"

"Yes, ma'am. Master Madoc sent word you might. Be some more of the Farm Masters in town and he was sure they'd want to meet you."

She nodded. So things *were* falling into place, she thought, and Madoc might be more perceptive than he had seemed the day before. "Of course," she told Wynn. "I will want to meet as many people as possible. You may tell them that for me." She gave him her best and friendliest smile.

The constable rose and bowed. "I will do that, Lady," he said, taking this as dismissal. "I've got a couple of men posted outside the house. Whenever you choose to go out, they'll go with you."

It was only after Wells closed the door behind him that she remembered the body hanging at the crossroads. There was no tactful way to inquire about that, she supposed; but she would have to make it clear that there could be no more hangings. Pesc did not permit capital punishment in its holdings.

And then she realized that the priest was still seated. He gave her an apologetic smile. "There was no opportunity to speak to you last night," he explained. "Naturally the Church will be concerned about the news you bring. I hope your corporation's policies won't interfere with the free practice of religion."

She called up another smile, not a very convincing one, as she reentered the room. "Of course not, ah, Father," she said. "I look forward to working with you in the days to come. There are many problems to solve, and your help will be invaluable."

Father Caron gave her a long look. "I don't suppose you are a Christian yourself?" he said, looking as though he already guessed the answer.

"I – I'm afraid not. But we should have no trouble working together."

The priest rose, turning his gaze on her bodyguard. "That remains to be seen," he said. He, at least, showed none of Master Madoc's fawning deference. "Perhaps you will do us the honor of attending Mass tomorrow? That will be Sunday according to our calendar."

She thought she detected a shade of irony in his speech but, covering her irritation, she answered him as graciously as she could. "Of course," she said. "I am here to see everything you have to show me. Believe me, Pesc has your best interests at heart."

Wells was looking down at the cup he held. She could not read his expression. "Perhaps my bodyguard may be excused," she added. "And of course the robot."

"I would be happy to welcome Mr. Wells," the priest said precisely. "But you had better not bring the machine."

When he had gone, she turned on her guard. "Why didn't you wake me?" she demanded. "It's not your job to deal with the natives!"

His face remained expressionless. "I will remember that in future."

She glared at him. "We've got to get this straight *now*, Wells. You are not to meddle! And," she added, "as long as the constable has provided me with protection, it won't be necessary for you to accompany me everywhere I go."

"I'm sorry I won't be able to obey you there."

"What do you mean?" she snapped. "You were provided by the corporation to serve me!"

"Not quite. I must obey my conditioning first," he explained. "My owners have set certain imperatives. I am *their* property, you see, just as you are their employee. I promote their interests best by watching over you."

"Then you expect to follow me about, mixing with the people here –"
He nodded. "I must."

"And you'll be attending the – the Mass tomorrow?" Already memories of her childhood were crowding unpleasantly into her mind.

Once more that nod.

"This is ridiculous! Do you think they'll murder me in the church?"

"No, I don't think that. But such things have happened on other colonies."

"But not here. *I* need the good will and cooperation of the clergy. Why must you push yourself in?" She could not understand why she was so angry, but she was.

For a moment, she thought he wasn't going to answer. Then, "You are right, Dr. Sienko, that I am not bound to go inside the building with you to worship." For some reason, his choice of words made her even more angry.

"But as I would have to accompany you to the door and wait for you outside anyway, I would like your permission to hear Mass."

At first, she did not understand him and when she finally did, she was so taken aback that she almost forgot her anger. "*You* are a Christian?" she said, appalled.

"That surprises you."

She got control of herself. "Yes, it does," she said coldly. "I thought that a man conditioned to violence, to obedience no matter what is asked, would – would hardly –" She felt her annoyance growing even though there was no real reason for it. It wasn't as though *she* held any faith that might be affronted, but bringing Wells seemed almost as bizarre to her as taking along the robot.

Wells watched these different passions move across her face while his own expression remained unchanged. "Once more you have spoken the truth," he told her when he thought she had control of herself. "My conditioning runs deep. But there is still some small part of myself that is mine to dispose of as I wish. My *leisure*, you might say. *That* is left to each one of us for the sake of balance. We each use it differently, of course, but it is supposed to keep us sane."

Her anger dissolved as quickly as it had come. "Then I won't interfere," she said. "Just be discreet about it."

He made a half bow and turned away. "More visitors," he observed, glancing out the window. "Looks like Master Madoc and Master Frayle."

With a groan, she seated herself and tried to draw back her hair. She was hungry but she would have to make do with a cup of tea – or whatever the stuff was. "Let them in," she said.

As it happened, Marja was not to see the Saturday market after all. At least not that day …

CHAPTER 4

CHIEF SNOWTYGER HAD BEEN PLANETSIDE for some days, meeting with several of his connections on Networld 15. Copper, as the place was called, had an idyllic climate, if you liked sunshine and almost uninterrupted summer weather, but not much land. Every inch of it was built up, under and over, while the colony's food supply was grown on farms in the sea.

The chief had not come for the cuisine, however. He was a busy man and had several commissions to perform before he went to see Dust. Whenever he could, he paid a personal visit to his agent since Dust was, of course, unable to do any travelling himself. On coming in to the office, one saw nothing except a bank of machinery. Dust did not keep a secretary.

Gaed Alfred's friend, whose second career was proving to be even more lucrative than his first – Dust was a mercenary who had gotten too closely involved with a grenade – specialized in the sort of things people like Chief Snowtyger often needed. That was how they had met. The chief had never even seen a likeness of Dust in the flesh, having known him only as a mind encased in metalplast.

"We were right about Pesc," the hacker said after the two had exchanged greetings. "They've got a programme laid out, but there doesn't seem to be anything to back it up."

"What do you mean?"

A set of symbols came up on a screen. "This is a copy of the development schema for Networld 326," he said. "It's very complete – and expensive. The payoff time is estimated at three centuries."

"Three *centuries*?"

Dust would have nodded, but lacking a body, he was confined to a plain affirmative.

"And you say there's no backup for this? Nothing allocated?"

"Oh, there are allocations. I haven't dug all that out yet. But I can already tell they are not for the right things."

The Faring Guard grunted.

"There's a chance I won't be able to get everything you want. An alarm went off as I went in, though I don't think they can trace the source of the break-in. Still, there will be new codes and I might have to start over."

Chief Snowtyger combed his beard with one hand. "I guess you'd better keep trying," he said. "Father Moto has a bad feeling about this business, and so do I.

"Yes," the chief continued, wondering whether Father Moto had made a mistake sending someone as inexperienced as Brother Brendan to the colony. "You've done well so far, Dust. And if you have to put in some extra work, it's covered."

"Right. The Star Brothers always pay well." A pause, and then, "I guess you have another meeting somewhere after this?"

Gaed Alfred looked down at the complex of machinery that held the life of his friend. "No," he said. "I saved you for last. The *St. Balthasar* is waiting in orbit and I'll shuttle up in a few hours."

Immediately another screen came to life, set with chessmen. After a moment, a panel disgorged a large mug of cold beer.

Obviously he had been expected.

There was silence after Compline and in that silence, the visitors were escorted to a low, stone room not far from the chapel. Here straw mats had been provided along with wool blankets and a chamber pot which told them plainly that they were not to go outside during the night. Other than one candle and a crucifix on the wall, there was nothing more.

Brother Brendan drew off his outer clothing and settled himself on one of the crude pallets. The others did the same, though, before undressing, Gris Wolfgang stepped over to the small, shuttered window and tried to look outside. He could not get the covering open.

The Star Brother had a lot to think about. It was plain that his order's infrequent visits – no more than routine checkups – had sufficed only for the barest spiritual needs of the colony. He wondered if Pesc knew about the priory and the appalling things these brothers took for granted. He wondered why *he* hadn't been told. Didn't the Star Brothers know?

In the end, everything came back to what the corporation planned to do with their new acquisition. He could still think of no alternative to what he had told the marshal – that Pesc would want to industrialise the place, building robot-run factories and utilizing the resources available. But even *he* knew it would take something pretty profitable for them to recoup their investment.

One rather uncomfortable idea had occurred to him, which he could not entirely banish from his thoughts. There were some things whose manufacture was so dangerous that most colonies would not allow their production. Was it something like this that Pesc had in mind? If so, could anything be done to prevent their exploiting and endangering the colonists in this way? There might be legal means to stop them but, if so, his superiors would have to be the ones to make use of them. The colonists would be helpless in a contest with any of the interstellar corporations, let alone one as powerful as Pesc.

When these thoughts had tormented him for some hours, he finally fell asleep, only to be wakened by the bell for matins. Along with his companions, he emerged into the awful twilight of two pale suns already risen. Apparently the daytime hours were measured by the larger pair which had not yet begun to redden the sky.

When they had finished their prayers and stumbled back to their beds, the Star Brother fell into a dream-riddled sleep, wandering in a great purple wood where trees spoke to him in a language he couldn't understand, telling him terrible things he would forget when he woke. After a while, he struggled into wakefulness to see sunlight pouring in through the now unshuttered window. He held out his hands to that light and saw that both were covered with purple designs ...

Stifling a shout, he woke once more, shuddering and sweating in the candlelit room. The Lost Rythans were already pulling on their clothing. In silence, they made their way back to the chapel for Lauds. This was followed by Prime, and then a priest – one of the Order – prepared to say mass.

There were four suns in the sky by the time they went to breakfast. Actually there were five, but the fifth was so distant that only someone who knew where to look would know it for what it was.

Brother Brendan chewed his bread and strips of some flavorless dried vegetable slowly, as he looked around the room. The marshal wasn't there. As for the brothers, many of them had laid aside their habits and were dressed in leather – leggings, boots and jackets. Heavy gloves – almost gauntlets – waited beside their plates while they ate. Brother Alwyn, who sat with the guests, explained that they would be going out to patrol the perimeter, grubbing up smaller incursions of the wildwood and noting "restless" spots. Presently he invited Brother Brendan to come and take leave of the marshal. The Star Brother rose at once, leaving the Lost Rythans to finish their meal.

He found Marshal Gwilym propped up as before, his tattooed face drawn and even more deeply shadowed about the eyes, as though yesterday's exertion must be paid for. "You return to Tregarth?" the marshal whispered so that the other man had to bend down to hear him.

"Yes. From there we are going out with the travelers."

"That would be Sergay. I know him. He is a pagan, poor fellow."

The Star Brother nodded. "Thank you for telling me."

"You are – only one man. Your order little more." The marshal paused, gathering breath. "This – discourages you, doesn't it?"

Brother Brendan flushed slightly. The marshal was echoing his own thoughts.

"Yet you have come. You – throw in your lot – with ours."

This time embarrassment kept the Star Brother silent. Beside the gallant folly of the Order of St. Hubert, what did *his* trifling sacrifice matter?

"God sees. I tell you this," the other man said, his voice momentarily strengthening, "I who stand – at the gate of eternity. Do not be afraid!"

Exhausted, the marshal slumped down, panting. A tremor passed over his frame.

Brother Brendan knelt beside him and took one tattooed hand in his own. "Thank you," he murmured, seeing that the man could no longer speak. "We will pray for one another, I hope."

Leaving the marshal, he rose and followed Brother Alwyn out into the courtyard. There was no sign of the Lost Rythans.

Tregarth's horses were already hitched to the wagon. Within the stone walls of the barn, two of the brothers were inspecting the cows before letting them out one by one. They were dry this time of year, most of them big with calves.

He watched for a moment.

One of the pair, a young man with hair as red as Brother Brendan's own, grinned at him. He pointed to the purple markings on his own arms and hands and then to the cows.

The Star Brother understood. They were making sure the animals had not been infected. He shuddered a little.

"I have two friends with me," he said aloud. "Do you know where they are?"

The other brother, who was older, nodded politely. "They have gone to see the edge of the wildwood," he said. There were marks on his face as well as on his arms. Brother Brendan wondered how long it took before the brothers became disabled by the gradual poisoning. And why, he thought, in irritation, must Lost Rythans seek out every peril that came their way?

But when he had gone outside, avoiding the cows and their steaming droppings, he met his companions returning, Ard Matthew in the lead. Both wore the heavy swords Lost Rythans deemed appropriate for visiting low tech colonies, though the Star Brother would have been willing to bet they were also armed with smaller and only marginally permitted weapons.

Still, it was true that the Faring Guards had an affinity for more primitive gear and took it up whenever they had the chance. Gris Wolfgang held his drawn sword in one hand and was wiping it with the tail of his shirt.

"It's alright, Brother," Ard Matthew called, seeing the expression on his superior's face. "They said the sap isn't dangerous."

The Star Brother bit back what almost any other man would have said about common sense and attention to duty. Instead, he gestured toward the wagon. In silence, they left the fringe of the wildwood behind.

Their return trip took a little longer, since none of them had had much experience driving horses. Since Brother Brendan had at least driven the horse-like draft animals of Gaelway Colony, it wasn't long before he took over from his companions.

When they arrived at Tregarth farm, a line of wagons stood encamped in the pasture, complete with cook-fires and lean-tos. Bright skirted women moved about among these, while children were everywhere. The farm hand who met them near the barn seemed distracted as he took the reins. There was no sign of the master.

"He's over with the traders," he said in answer to the Star Brother's question.

With a nod of thanks, Brother Brendan hurried in that direction, followed by his two companions. They could all smell meat cooking and, knowing that Tregarth was keeping Treelight's strict version of the Lenten fast, took this as confirmation that these people weren't Christians. Still, the aroma was tormenting to men who had had little to eat that day save bread and whatever it was the Brothers of St. Hubert dried from their garden. Turnips, maybe? They had been given more of the same for their midday dinner, which they had eaten quite some time before.

They spotted the master almost immediately, sitting with another man on a wagon tongue. The two were drinking something from mugs and for the sake of the Lost Rythans, the Star Brother fervently hoped it was beer.

Tregarth spotted his guests almost at the same time they saw him. He stood up and waved them over. "Come and meet Boss Sergay," he called.

His companion also rose. The traveler proved to be a much smaller man, thin and wiry, his dark hair and beard gone mostly grey, his eyes darker than those of the people they had met so far on Treelight. He studied the offworlders almost without seeming to, giving Brother Brendan the feeling he was sizing them up according to some code of his own. Certainly he did not miss the weapons of the Lost Rythans nor the fact that the Star Brother, at least, might almost have been of the same race as the colonists.

"These are the men from the stars." Tregarth introduced them while a younger man fetched more mugs and poured for them from a foaming pitcher. He had to pour again for the Lost Rythans almost at once.

Sergay nodded approval. "These two tall ones," he said to Tregarth, "seem as human as we are and as for the other, he might have grown up on your own farm."

Brother Brendan came over and shook hands with him. "As a matter of fact I did spend part of my life on a farm," he said pleasantly, "though it was a smaller one than Tregarth."

Master Tregarth gave him a curious look. "You come from a world such as ours?" he asked.

The Star Brother shook his head. "I've never seen a world like yours." He turned to Sergay. "We've just come from the Priory of St. Hubert," he said. "I'm afraid I've never seen anything like *that* before either."

The traveler nodded. "Likely not," he agreed. "There are stranger things in this world than even Tregarth here has seen, though he's greedy enough for news."

Brother Brendan seated himself on the grass. "And *is* there any news?" he asked.

The Lost Rythans hunkered down beside him. Already a crowd of Sergay's people had gathered to stare at them. Not only were the Faring Guards much taller than the colonists, but their clothing, while it went well with the weapons they carried, was equally outlandish. Lost Rythar was a bleak world and its people were fond of bright colors, a taste they did not abandon in exile.

"The corporation has wasted no time," Tregarth said abruptly. "They've sent someone to Harrow." He emptied his own mug and then held it loosely in both hands. "We already knew Dagon Ltd. had contacts in that district but their visits were usually kept pretty quiet. Not this time."

Brother Brendan glanced up at Sergay. "How far is Harrow from here?" he asked.

The traveler shrugged. "It's a good way. And I've not seen these foreigners myself yet," he admitted. "Rumour travels faster than horses, though, and I had word of their coming not long after we turned off the Harrow Road onto the Fringe Highway."

"So you know nothing about their plans?"

"Oh, I will soon enough. People know we'll be coming back that way and that we're partial to news. That is, we'll head that way if it suits you, of course." He grinned crookedly. "I owe Ben Tregarth a favor or two –"

The master laughed heartily at this. "One or two," he agreed and then turned toward the visitors. "My men and I saved him from hanging once, back when we were all a bit younger than we are now."

"A lot younger," the traveler agreed. "I've got smarter since then."

Brother Brendan was beginning to like this man, pagan or not, and he could see that Sergay had made a favorable impression on the Lost Rythans as well. But he was curious nonetheless and decided to speak out. "I was told," he said tentatively, "that this colony was entirely Christian."

Sergay gave a shrug. "They always let a few bad lots through when they gather up settlers," he said cheerfully and the Star Brother knew this was the only explanation he was likely to get.

But Tregarth did not let it rest. "The travelers have their own ways," he told his guests, "but they are always welcome wherever they go. They carry news and goods. But –"

"We're not always welcome to *stay* wherever we go," Sergay finished for him with a laugh. He gave the Star Brother a direct look. "To each his own, and I hope you'll see it that way."

Brother Brendan took the warning. "We are grateful for your help," he told the other carefully. "As to my view of your religion – or lack of it – that's less important than God's opinion. Since I'm only His servant, I'll leave that up to Him."

"Well said!" Sergay laughed again and pointed toward the nearest cooking fire. "Have you eaten yet?" he asked wickedly.

This was too much for Gris Wolfgang who turned on their host a rather bleak look. "Your beer is very good," he said. "That should be enough for us."

At this, Tregarth cast a sidewise look at the traveler. "They've got bread," he told the Lost Rythan, "and dried fish from the ponds near Harrow. Don't you, Sergay?"

In answer, their host summoned the youngster and told him to bring food for their guests. Instead of the boy, however, a striking girl arrived bearing a platter of bread and fish along with some dried fruit – at least Brother Brendan hoped that's what it was – and offered this to the visitors.

They thanked her, said grace, and fell to.

As the girl showed no sign of going away, Sergay introduced her. "My daughter, Rhosya," he said briefly. "She's a midwife and one of the best herb women in the colony."

She looked about twenty years old, brown-eyed with classic raven hair. The Lost Rythans stared at her with frank admiration and even the Star Brother felt a stirring at the sight. Quickly he turned back to his meal.

"One of the best?" she said, smiling at her father. "Is that all?"

"Now don't you start putting yourself forward," Sergay told her. "A woman's got to know her place."

"This place will do," she said, motioning her father to move over so she could seat herself beside him on the wagon tongue.

"Likely it will," Sergay agreed amiably. "Now," he addressed the offworlders, "I'm told you've come to learn what you can about this new corporation we're saddled with and you're not the only one wants to know. But since you've just come from the Priory, maybe you have some other questions?"

Brother Brendan nodded. "They told us the wildwood is moving," he said abruptly. "That it's beginning to grow onto colony land."

"I've heard that too," Sergay agreed. "They don't talk a lot at the priory when we bring them supplies, but things get out."

"Tregarth Farm is as near the wildwood as any," the master said slowly, "and we've had no trouble."

"There are tales," Rhosya said. "From the north. The druids –"

Her father lowered his brows, shaking his head at her. "Those are only tales," he said warningly.

"It might be better," Tregarth said quickly, "to wait until you have seen more of the colony –"

But Brother Brendan was staring at the girl in surprise. "Did you say *druids?*" he asked. "Those people who used to worship oak trees?"

"Not oak trees," she said quietly. "The wildwood."

Marja's many visitors had kept her from seeing the market, though she vowed she would eventually. But on that first Saturday, callers followed one after another steadily for most of the day. There were masters of farms and of guilds, officials of the village, and all sorts of ladies along with other people she could not classify. Some, she suspected, were not even respectable, though the constable tried to weed out the worst of them.

As she received her guests, she was aware of Wells in the background watching everything. And yet it was impossible, as the day progressed, to stay angry with him. His extreme conscientiousness – and his faith – were rather pitiable than otherwise. In fact, she looked forward to discussing her visitors with him later.

Master Madoc and Master Frayle were to join her that evening for dinner. She left the menu to her staff and was surprised to find soup and vegetables on the table but no meat.

"It's the custom," Wells explained. "We're in Lent by their reckoning, which is a little ahead of the stellar calendar. The cook told me."

She nodded. Wells had the advantage of her in that the servants would confide in him.

"There are only three places set," she observed.

"That too is the custom. I cannot eat with you in the presence of men such as these."

She had forgotten. Now they discussed where he had better station himself during the meal and finally decided on the sitting room. He would take a place at the worktable with the robosecretary, from which post he and it could see everything that went on in the dining room and hear most of it as well. He stepped into the kitchen for a quick sandwich.

Meanwhile, Marja prepared herself carefully. These two were influential men, apparently among the most powerful in the colony. Madoc was master of the town besides being a wealthy man in his own right and Frayle, Wells had learned, owned extensive mining interests in the west as well as a very large estate.

Somehow she must convince them that their positions were not at risk – that no matter what happened, they and their families would still come out on top. Madoc, as the scion of a clan long used to collaborating with the colony's owners, should be little trouble. As for Frayle, she only wished Wells had been able to learn more about him.

She had already noted that he was more intelligent than his companion. Also there was something ruthless in his makeup, if the calculating way he watched everyone was any indication. She did not think he would be an easy man to manipulate. Frowning, she summoned Wells to see if he had learned anything more than he had already told her about the masters.

Her bodyguard hurried in, swallowing hastily. To her delight, he *had*.

"They bring servants when they come," he explained. "Their men stay in the kitchen where the cook and your maid – her name is Tara – entertain them. One of Madoc's men is Tara's cousin."

"I see." Indeed she did. "So, tell me more about Frayle."

"Well, he's still staying with Master Madoc. His own farm is pretty far away, on the other side of river, with two villages between. His oldest son is to marry Madoc's daughter."

"And his family is influential?"

"Very. He is rich and connected by marriage with other rich people. He has two respectable sons and another one they don't talk about – the youngest, who the servants think ran off with the travelers. They say he might even have become a bandit since then. His name is Evan and he left one of the local girls in trouble. Frayle had to make some sort of arrangements about that –"

"Oh my," she said. "You do dig out the dirt, don't you? Is there more?"

"The hanging," he went on. "It was an old woman accused of witchcraft. Madoc served as one of the judges and since Frayle was here, he was the other."

Marja stared at him in shock. "Witchcraft?" she said faintly.

"The colony's a backward place."

"B-but how did they – I mean, what *did* the woman do? Surely they're not having witch hunts!"

"Oh no. Nothing like that. She poisoned her husband, using something from the wildwood. But no one wants to talk about that much. I gather it's considered a particularly heinous crime."

"So she was actually hanged for murder?"

Wells shrugged. "No. The man didn't die – but he disappeared not long afterward."

"I'll have to think about this some more. You've done a good job, Wells. I really am impressed!"

She stepped in front of a mirror to check her hair and costume. The corporation had created a wardrobe for her that would not only impress the locals but, by it's resemblance to their own costumes, would not violate their sense of fitness. "These masters are not very savory, are they?" she said over her shoulder. "And yet I've got to convince them it's in their interest – and *make* it in their interest – to help me with this project."

Wells gave her a somber look. "It is better – if you don't mind a word of advice – it is *easier* if we try not to judge those we work with. I mean–"

He trailed off in what might have been embarrassment.

"That would be good advice," she told him crisply, "for someone in your position. But I will continue to think of this Frayle as a real stinker. A storybook villain who probably did away with that poor girl his son got in trouble."

"You only make your job harder."

She shook her head. "I was joking, Wells," she said and saw him relax slightly.

He gave her a rueful smile but before he could say anything more, they were interrupted by the arrival of Marja's guests. In the bustle, Wells disappeared quietly to his place while she and the two masters took seats in the dining room.

They were obviously trying to charm her, Madoc obsequious, his companion gallant. As she sipped her wine, she tried to imagine Frayle making "arrangements" about his son's paramour – and yet, despite herself, she enjoyed his company. Between courses, she outlined the first steps they must take to prepare for the transformation of their world.

"I'll need to coordinate things with your churches to reeducate the people, I suppose," she said. "They seem to run the schools. And I believe there is a bishop at Bannyclay?"

"Yes," Madoc told her, glancing at Frayle.

"I'll want to talk to him. And to your other leaders. The people must be guided toward salaried work – we must bring the corporation closer to them. They've got to think of Pesc not as some distant foundation but as the immediate source of their livelihood."

"Of course," Madoc said eagerly. "And those of us who have always served Da- I mean the corporation – that is, Pesc now – are ready to stand behind you!"

Frayle was watching her thoughtfully. "When you say salaried work," he said, "that means you have something other in mind than agriculture, doesn't it?"

She nodded. "Of course. I know you need food, but your present system could be made much more efficient. And profitable." She smiled graciously, watching his face as he pondered that word, profitable.

"Then," she went on, "we will bring in the equipment to make of this a manufacturing center. The native forest can be cleared away as you expand, mining operations started –" She paused. "But you have mines already, don't you?" she said, hoping she had not made a faux pas.

"We do," Frayle said slowly. "But probably nothing on the scale you have in mind."

Madoc nodded. "Out Master Frayle's way, there is a refinery run by a guild."

"I see," Marja said, watching Frayle. "I suppose that can be made more efficient for a start. The guild system – if I understand it –"

The other two looked at her.

"This lack of centralization is what's keeping you down," she said.

"I thought," Frayle said dryly, "the ban on technology was what kept us from producing more wealth. And of course the fact that we have been isolated from the rest of humankind ever since the founding of the colony."

"But that was Dagon Ltd's doing," she exclaimed hastily. "We're going to lift the ban on imports! Offworld goods will begin pouring in as soon as you're ready for them."

Madoc could not repress a small grunt of pleasure, though Frayle was regarding her quizzically. "This should be an ambitious undertaking," he said. "Even for a corporation."

"We owe it to you," she told him warmly, watching his face. "Believe me, Pesc has your interests at heart in this. You mustn't think of the corporation as an owner but rather as a patron. The patron of your colony."

For all its glibness, this should be no more than the truth. The proposed arrangement was to the mutual benefit of the populace and the company. These people would be educated, would live in comfort they had never known – and their world would finally turn a profit.

The evening went well. While Madoc proved as provincial as she had expected, his companion was a very well-informed man for a colonist. He impressed her as much by what he left unsaid as by what he said – and by the way he looked at her. Frayle, at least, was not blinded by her nearness to the corporation. He made it plain that he saw her as a woman, as well as Pesc's representative.

Eventually, her guests departed – with something to think about, she hoped, as she followed them out the door. The nebula cast its eerie glow across the empty square as she stepped outside to see them off. They had come in a carriage, which waited for them outside the gate. It was as Wells had said; each had brought a manservant.

She turned her face to the sky. What a strange place this was! It was springtime, but the seasons were not reliable because the planet's inclination was not the only determining factor. There was also the matter of its near approach to one or other of the stars in the cluster, sometimes even moving *between* them. It was incredible that such an arrangement had resulted in a habitable world, though apparently a balance of some sort had been struck.

At which point she remembered that Networld 326 *hadn't* been habitable – at least for humans – when Dagon first developed it. She had forgotten the great purple forest.

The attack came as she turned to go back inside. There were two of them and it was plain their object was to abduct her rather than to kill her. Reflexively she slapped her shoulder and felt the shield like an invisible suit of armor. There were arms gripping her – or rather they gripped the shield – and she was thrown to the ground with enough force to knock the wind out of her.

And then something hit one of her attackers and he fell. A trank dart? She rolled over and felt her shield deflate. She had bumped her shoulder on something – rolled in wetness – and there were two figures struggling in the doorway! One of them was Wells, forcing someone backward – a hoarse cry –

Suddenly he was helping her up. In the nebula's light her skirt was covered in darkness. He led her inside and closed the door.

"What – who –?"

"Not yet," he said, guiding her to a seat. He fetched a glass of wine from the dining room, snatching the decanter from the hands of a shocked maid. The woman followed him into the other room and screamed. "Blood! She's covered in blood!"

Wells set down the decanter and slapped her. "Send someone for the constable," he called as the maid ran into the kitchen.

Marja accepted the glass and drank. She was bruised on one side and her skirt was darkened with something –

"Wells! What did you –?"

"This isn't practice," he said. "Mr. Wynn is going to find dead bodies out there."

But he didn't. There was blood, but the bodies had disappeared.

While the constable's men searched the premises, Wells helped Marja up to her room. "Who were those people?" she asked as they mounted. "Why was I attacked? Do they know?"

"No one is talking," Wells said. "But I don't think Wynn was as surprised as he should have been – about the disappearance of the bodies, I mean. As to who they were, he may know something. But whether he'll tell us is another matter."

In the absence of the maid, he began stripping off her bloodstained clothing with the impersonality of a nurse. "Here," he said, handing out a blanket to wrap herself. "I'll tell them to bring up hot water."

"Wells – who do *you* think did this?"

He looked at her soberly. "There are far too many possibilities for me to make a guess," he said. "At least not yet."

He left her sitting on the bed, recalling Master Frayle's cruel and handsome face smiling at her over dinner. His teeth were not good, she remembered, and he had tried not to show them too much.

Only later did she remember Wells' hands on her – those hands fresh from killing – and his quiet efficiency as he undressed her. He had treated her as though she had been a child and not a woman at all.

Tomorrow they were going to Mass together, she and Wells. She wondered if the masters would be there, too.

SERGAY'S DAUGHTER HAD DISCOMFITED BOTH her father and Master Tregarth, but that was not, Brother Brendan suspected, because she repeated an idle tale. His briefing had included hardly anything about the colony's interaction with the wildwood but now he was determined to ferret out everything he could about the so-called druids. He began at once to look for an opportunity.

None presented itself the next day, which was Sunday. A traveling priest said mass at Hywel Farm on the Fringe Highway south of the Tregarth turn-off and the entire household, as well as most of the laborers and their families, made the trek. They left Tregarth Farm an hour or so before the rising of the two largest suns.

The master ruled a good-sized community. Just what their relation was to the Tregarth family, he was not sure until someone told him they were serfs. This seemed to be the order of things in the colony, at least outside the towns. He wondered whether Dagon Ltd had concocted the social order.

What with Hywel's inhabitants and a few random dwellers along the highway, there was a good sized congregation. After the Mass, the priest hurried away to serve two more communities further south.

The following day the travelers departed, returning once more to the Fringe Highway. This they followed southwest until it met the Harrow Road. This highway, their guests were told, descended, with some hilly parts, many miles to the west where it dipped into the valley of the River Dagon. Bannyclay, where the bishop had his seat, lay on the far side of the Darkwater Bridge.

"We always pass through Harrow, trading, and there you may get a look at this company agent," Sergay explained. "It isn't far from the river."

Sergay and the Star Brother were riding together on the seat of the first covered wagon in the line. Bloodbear and Third-Blade had been welcomed into one of the others, where they were busily making friends with the travelers. As Pesc had not yet made an agreement with the Star Brothers, he did not consider his order bound any longer to remain silent concerning matters outside the colony. Accordingly, he told the Lost Rythans to answer any questions the travelers put. It was high time these people learned what they were up against!

"I suppose we'll remain incognito as far as outsiders are concerned, though," he told Sergay now, thinking of the corporate presence at Harrow. "Can you trust your people not to talk?"

The traveler grinned at him. "We've had a lot of practice keeping quiet," he said, pausing to take a swig from a jug beneath the seat. "Now tell me something about your own world, Star Brother. You were not born in a cassock, I think."

Brother Brendan grinned in spite of himself. "There isn't much to tell," he said. "My full name is Brendan Patrick Stillman and I come from Networld 87 – Gaelway, it's called. It's a sort of watery place with long strings of islands and lots of open sea. We live on islands mostly since the continents are almost all bare rock."

"You have farms? Woods?" Sergay had never seen the ocean and probably did not know exactly what an island was.

"Nothing like the wildwood," his companion said thankfully. "But everyone has something to bear. For us it's storms that make it hard to get from place to place. We have a little more technology than you've got here, but we still have to use boats."

"Ah. And your family?"

He looked down, remembering. "Well that's another story," he admitted. "We had storms of our own, you see. My father is a – a musician."

A sudden, poignant image of his hard-drinking, fiddle-playing father came between him and the other man. The elder Stillman had made a good enough living for a poor colony, but an awful lot of it went for whiskey. And their lives – his and his mother's and his seven brothers' and sisters' – had never been orderly. But Pat Stillman could *play*. The songs he composed were still performed all over Gaelway.

"Live on a farm?" Sergay asked, offering him the jug.

"Once or twice. Mostly we moved around. Two of my brothers went off to the Dominican School – one of them's a priest now. The other one drowned in a storm."

The traveler nodded. "Live in a wagon, then?"

At this, Brother Brendan brought himself back to the present. "As a matter of fact, we did for a while," he said. "But my father's made a real name for himself now, and the council gave him a house."

"Got respectable, you mean?" Sergay suggested.

The Star Brother shook his head. "Not so bad as that," he admitted with a laugh. "And I've got another brother who still takes to the road. He plays a harp – not a big one – it's the kind you carry around. He sings at ports and places where they're always glad to have him. I might have done the same if it weren't for the Star Brothers."

"You play – and sing?"

Brother Brendan flushed slightly. "There hasn't been much call for that these past years," he admitted. "But I did, once."

"You won't have forgotten."

He had a sudden absurd vision of himself playing and singing at the village fairs as they traveled along – and then it did not seem so ridiculous after all. If duty required it, he might end up doing just that!

"Tell me," the other man asked curiously, "are there any like us among you? Travelers, I mean?"

Brother Brendan nodded. "Yes, there are. We call them gypsies. But they have boats instead of wagons."

Sergay chuckled. "That would be something new. Would we get along alright, do you think, if we met them?"

His companion smiled. "I think you would. My father always did. Sometimes they took us along in their boats."

It was late afternoon when they reached Cary Farm at the junction where Harrow Road turned west off the Fringe Highway. The highway went on, encircling the entire colony, but according to the map, most of the villages lay more toward the center of the cleared area.

Treelight Colony really was a large place – practically a small country. The farms were widely separated by woodlands and open fields inhabited by imported animals gone wild or stocked wild in the first place. There was room, he could see, for many more people than there were, should the colonists choose to make use of the fallow land. But Pesc, he reminded himself grimly, would soon be filling in the open spaces. It had happened before on other worlds.

They remained at Cary until noon the next day, trading cloth from Tregarth and dried fruit from Hywel, not to mention the herbal decoctions Sergay's daughter had mixed from plants gathered along the way. These sold very well, for Sergay's people were well known and Rhosya's reputation as an herbalist preceded her wherever they went.

Master Tregarth had given the Star Brother a supply of native coins, copper mostly, stamped with Dagon's logo. The coins were made, Rhosya told him while she counted her receipts, in Dunsever at the foundry. But what sort of currency, he wondered, would the colony be using this time next year? Or in the years to come? Some offworld scrip, he suspected, or cheap coinage made of metalplast.

They reached Evyn that evening and camped there. This was a larger village than Cary, which had been no more than a lane or two, and it was set at the joining of several farms. Here the visitors saw shops and craftsmen at their work. There was a smithy, which set Brother Brendan in mind of Gwern. He hoped the blacksmith would be given a very long noviciate before he must go out and fight the wildwood!

After Evyn, the road began another descent amid ever thickening trees, variform oaks mostly. There were no more farms between Evyn and Harrow. Aside from a few isolated cottagers, the countryside was empty of humankind. There were deer, however, and the descendants of imported bears along with many smaller animals.

Usually they paused here to hunt, Sergay told Brother Brendan. But in Evyn there had been rumours of bandits. Indeed, the townsmen had gone out only a week or two before and captured several men who could not account for themselves. They had been hanged not far from the road.

While this news did not particularly frighten the Star Brother, he regretted the casual way these people dispatched their undesirables. The two Faring Guards took things in stride however, Ard Matthew only asking whether they had been shriven, which they had. He and Gris Wolfgang then asked leave to go to confession themselves, but it could hardly be managed without giving away their offworld origins.

"Wait until we reach Harrow," Sergay told them. "Father Caron won't ask as many questions. Or even at Welyn – their priest is a good sort and nearly as canny as one of *us*."

Wednesday night they camped in a clearing beside the road. A creek ran nearby and Sergay's people took advantage of this to refill their water casks. They were more than halfway to Harrow, the boss told Brother Brendan.

The next day as they jogged along, several men on horseback charged suddenly out of the woods, blocking the way while others emerged from the brush, aiming bows at the company. In a place where firearms were neither manufactured nor supplied, bows and arrows were the distance weapon of choice.

"It's that damned Lewis gang," Sergay muttered, tugging a spear from behind the seat. "This could be bad –"

From the wagons, his own people emerged bearing swords and shields. A few arrows hit the wood and one of the horses was injured before the mounted bandits actually charged the caravan. The Star Brother had scarcely time to realise what had happened before he found himself armed with another spear, warding off two horsemen who were trying to climb from their mounts onto the wagon seat. Sergay had disappeared into the melee.

Suddenly, something made a low, coughing sound, and one of the bandits dropped with a neat hole in his forehead. Following up the shot, Ard Matthew leaped down among the fighters, dodged a sword cut, and fired again. With shouts of surprise, the robbers began backing away from him in fear. At the same time, from the side of the road, a tall red-haired man took aim with his bow –

Gris Wolfgang was fighting back to back with one of Sergay's men, his great, heavy blade swinging tirelessly. They weren't doing too badly, even though some of their foes were on horseback. One horse was down already and several men.

Only Brother Brendan saw Ard Matthew fall and, had he not trained himself to avoid the colorful expletives he had learned from his father, he would have cursed heartily. If that gun fell into the hands of this lot, there would be hell to pay!

With a savage thrust, he sent one of his attackers from the saddle and saw the other unhorsed by one of the travelers. Taking advantage of the distraction, he leaped down from his seat and ran to the aid of the Lost Rythan. But Ard Matthew was already on his feet, bleeding from one shoulder – the left, fortunately, where the arrow still protruded – as he aimed once more and shot.

Whether it was the gun or the enthusiastic swordplay, the gang began to pull back. When their leader received a bullet in the hip and nearly fell from his horse, they melted into the forest. Several people lay on the ground, but before the Star Brother could reach them, Sergay's people had given their surviving enemies the coup de grace.

Taking prisoners was not a custom of the travelers.

CHAPTER 5

"YOU SAY THEY'VE SEEN SOME action?" Chief Snowtyger said as he dumped a stack of printouts on the table.

"A purely local fracas," Father Moto told him. "Nothing to do with the corporation."

"Well, that's something. And I suppose my fellows held their own?"

"Brother Brendan says the Third-Blade boy took an arrow in one shoulder."

The chief grunted. "Hope it was the left."

The priest hid a small smile at this typical expression of Lost Rythan optimism; it took a great deal to put them out of a fight. "What have you got there?" he asked.

"Not enough," the other man told him. "It's mostly old stuff I looked up myself." He squeezed into the seat and turned toward his friend. "Dust tells me it's a girl," he said. "Pesc sent in some young lady fresh from the university."

"If she's a competent young lady –"

"I suppose she is – a social engineer, whatever that is. But they've given her a lot of scope." The Faring Guard took up a sheet. "This bit is from Dust," he added. "He's still working on it. I didn't know exactly what to ask for."

"Let me see," the Star Brother said, reaching over. He scanned the printout. "They hired her right out of training, as you say. Didn't even wait for the psych test – did he get results on that for us?"

"Nothing special," the other man said. "It wasn't tagged."

"You have it?"

Gaed Alfred shuffled his papers. "Here," he said, handing over another sheet.

Father Moto scanned it while the other man waited.

"Well? Do you see anything?"

"I don't know." Suddenly the priest reached over and turned on the screen. "Let's see," he murmured. "Yes –"

After some time, he looked up at his impatient companion. "She should have been tagged for treatment or else rejected," he said. "With an attitude like that, she could hardly be considered fit for a job like this one."

He pointed to something on the paper.

"Don't look at me," Snowtyger said. "I don't know what all that means."

"Neither did I, quite. That's what I was looking up. How can they expect her to deal with a privileged class, when she resents the very idea of inherited status? And she is expected to persuade them to do whatever Pesc wants? Why, she'll be gritting her teeth every moment."

"Yes, I see." The Faring Guard scrolled down the screen. "But maybe she's good at working and gritting at the same time. I know, *I* am. I have to be in a job like this."

Father Moto smiled a little. "You succeed because you are trying to do God's will, Alfred," he said. "I very much doubt this young lady has such a resource going for her."

"Then I pity her."

"I wouldn't have hired someone like that," the Star Brother said decidedly. "Even if it's all on the level, she isn't qualified."

Snowtyger shook his head. "Looks like trouble in the making," he admitted.

The priest considered. "You had better instruct your friend to dig further if he can. I'm not at all satisfied with this."

"Right," the chief said. "I agree with you." He cleared the screen and put on the scrambler. After that he typed in a series of numbers and symbols drawn not from conscious memory but from some other place. If anyone had tried to force the information from him – even with a probe – it would have come out as gibberish.

Light years away, in his cocoon of machinery, the consciousness that was Dust left another problem and turned to receive Snowtyger's request. At this point, his own curiosity was aroused and, had he possessed a mouth, he would have bared his teeth in the joy of the hunt.

MASTER MADOC CAME FOR HER in the morning. Since she was a personage, this was an *appearance*. The great lady from the stars would accompany her vassal to Mass. He made no objection as Wells followed at their heels, though the bodyguard was not offered a seat in the carriage where Madoc's family waited. He was to walk behind with the servants.

Marja was uncomfortably aware of him there, still watching over her. After the attack, which had left her bruised and sore, she had ceased to take anything for granted. She had been careful to fasten the shield harness beneath her clothing and barely resisted an impulse to finger her left shoulder just to make sure the activator was in place.

And what would the colonials think if they knew, she wondered. Madoc seemed to live in his own cocoon of comfort and good living, but there were others – Frayle, for instance – who were more perceptive.

The church lay at the other end of the village, surrounded by a graveyard as old as the colony. Tombs and monuments, smaller stones and little fenced plots all attested to the piety and wealth of the inhabitants. The church itself was in an ancient style consciously copied among the more conservative colonies, with two towers and a crude rose window between. It reminded her uncomfortably of her childhood.

To Master Madoc's chagrin, Frayle was waiting for her at the bottom of the steps. Madoc, occupied with his wife and daughters, could do nothing as the other master stepped forward and offered Marja his arm. If he had heard about the attack of the night before – and almost certainly he had – his face showed no sign. He gave her a gallant smile as he led her inside.

If this was anything like the churches of her home colony, men and women would sit on opposite sides. And apparently it was – in all respects save one. For there were hardly any seats, only a vast empty space with a few pews near the front. Frayle left her at one of these where she was joined by Madoc's womenfolk, shy and uncomfortable as they found themselves alone with the great lady. The carriage ride had been a short one and none of the ladies had been formally introduced.

Marja endured the covert stares of the daughters and the more refined glances of the mother, while trying not to show that she despised them. These ladies had always taken precedence here, Marja thought. *They* had never been obliged to stand with the common folk.

On the other side she saw Madoc and Frayle kneeling side by side as though they had come for no other purpose than to worship God in purity of conscience. Some others of the more distinguished citizens knelt or sat on benches while the commoners crowded in behind. She wondered if Wells could still see her from whatever humble place he had been allotted. Not daring to turn and check, she felt suddenly vulnerable.

Presently two altar boys came up the nave, followed by Father Caron. Everyone, common and master alike stood respectfully until he reached the altar.

It was the same Mass she remembered, for the Star Brothers saw to it that nothing changed, and it brought back painful memories of her desperate struggle to escape a life as narrow and primitive as that of these colonists. At least *she* had been offered an education and, when she proved apt, a chance to rise. *They* had been given nothing.

For the first time, she wondered how such people would react to the new life Pesc had planned for them. Would they appreciate the opportunities offered? They had schools already, of course, but nothing that would fit anyone for modern life. That must change as their world changed.

If they were willing, she amended, listening to the ancient phrases, the prayers and responses of the choir. Only if they were willing –

The sermon was mercifully short. Father Caron looked right at her as he spoke of the evils of greed, of worldliness and the folly of grasping after the goods of this life at the expense of eternal things. This sort of talk would do the corporation no good, she thought grimly. Here was something else she must change.

She endured the rest of the Mass, thrusting away a memory of her first Communion and the childish faith, so quickly eclipsed, that had attended it. When the business was finally over, both Frayle and Madoc converged on her. There was a crowd outside, and here she was at last introduced to Madoc's family while many of the people who had visited her the day before came up, claiming acquaintance. She saw Wells standing at the edge of the gathering, watching everyone.

Apparently she was expected to go home with one of the worthy citizens – or all of them at once, it seemed. But before she could accept any of the invitations, a young man wormed his way respectfully through the crowd to her side and told her in a low voice that Father Caron would be honored if she and her bodyguard would join him at his house for some refreshment.

She caught sight of Wells' nod of approval – the young man must have spoken to him first – and, using this as an excuse, began to extricate herself from her well wishers. Madoc made as though to follow, thought better of it, and watched with annoyance as she joined her bodyguard and went after the servant.

Actually Marja was pleased that things had worked out this way. This was as good a time as any to sound out the priest, she decided – now while the memory of his sermon was fresh in her mind.

They passed through the cemetery and came to a house on the far street. It was not large, but the architecture matched that of the church.

Their guide left them in a small, square reception room with a fireplace on one side. The remains of a fire burned there, for the morning had been chilly, and before it a table was drawn up. Once more there were three places set and she wondered who the other guest was to be.

She was not left to wonder long as the priest came in carrying a platter of pancakes in one hand and a jug of syrup in the other. "Welcome to you both," he said. "You may either take seats or help me carry in the food."

Flushing slightly, Marja followed him out to what proved to be a kitchen. He handed her a plate of sausages – the Lenten restrictions did not extend to Sundays – and the teapot. Wells was given a big bowl of stewed fruit while their host stopped behind to turn more pancakes on the griddle.

The meal was superb, after which the teapot was refilled and Marja leaned over to breathe in the fragrance of the brew. Each world had its own version of the perennial beverage and this one, while like no other she had tasted, was quite palatable.

But their pleasant meal was not, as she reminded herself, a purely social event. While she and Wells helped clear the table – there was no sign of the young man who had summoned them – she watched their host surreptitiously. Why had he invited her, she wondered, and how might she best lead him to the subject she had in mind?

Presently they all took places in another part of the room where a padded bench stood beneath a window opposite two carved, wooden chairs. When they were seated, the priest turned to Wells. "I gather that *you* at least are a Christian," he said pleasantly.

The bodyguard gave him a startled look.

"You may trust a priest to know, even though you did not go to communion."

At this the other looked up at him. "You must know that I am the agent of Pesc, Father," he said. "You could hardly expect me to receive the Sacrament."

"Perhaps not. We are none of us lax in these things here on Treelight." He frowned slightly. "The Star Brothers have encouraged our people to go more often, I know, but it is not our custom."

Marja began to have the oddest notion that they had been invited here not because Father Caron wanted to open negotiations with her but because he wanted to speak to her bodyguard. She was a little deflated at the idea.

Seeing this, Wells made an effort to turn the conversation in another direction. "This is your – second spring, I think it's called?" he said diffidently.

The colonist wasn't stupid. He, too, glanced at Marja. "Yes," he said. "We don't always get a second and then we must make do with the first – which isn't very reliable. After this it will be summer. Already the fields are planted."

"Your lives must be hard," Marja said, seeing her opening while she fought down the dismal thought of those fields and all the work they entailed. "I hope my employers will be able to make things easier for you."

No one said anything.

"I mean," she went on doggedly, "that we should be able to work together to raise the living standard in the colony."

"Ah." Father Caron held up the teapot. "More, anyone?" he asked.

Marja accepted another refill while Wells shook his head.

She tried again. "We will need to work together, you and I," she said brightly. "All the clergy. You have the most influence over how the locals think, and I'm sure you know there will be many changes in the near future. We must make it as easy as we can."

The priest glanced at her. "Changes?" he inquired politely. He sipped his tea while Wells gave him a bleak look.

"Surely you can see," Marja said, her voice growing a trifle sharp, "that their way of life will have to change! We'll be providing better schools, training, more wealth. A lifestyle more on a par with that of the other colonies."

"Will we be linked to them? Will there be traveling to and fro?"

She bit her lip. "Not – not at this time. Pesc does not envisage anything like that at this stage. First your colony must be transformed into – into something more productive. For your own good –"

"It would be a fine thing," the priest mused, setting down his cup, "to visit Earth. To see the cradle of our race."

Wells winced at this, but Marja gave their host a quick, hopeful look. "I'm sure," she said, "there will be exceptions – especially after you have helped us with the reeducation of the colonists."

Father Caron glanced from one to the other of his guests. "I believe there would be," he agreed rather dryly. "May I ask just what sort of things you want changed?"

She leaned forward. "To begin, you would have to alter your – your *emphasis* a little," she said. "Obviously there must be more incentive to work with us. To appreciate the things we offer."

"What are those?"

"Why the – the *comforts* of life. Vids, recreational drugs, better quality food, birth control, employment for everyone, better health care, more personal freedom –"

"Freedom?" the priest repeated. "From what? For whom?"

"Why from – from superstition to begin with. They hanged a witch here! Did you know?"

"Yes. It was regrettable."

"*Regrettable*? Is that what you call it when a woman is accused of witch-craft without trial?"

"Oh, she had a trial. Anyway, she was guilty."

Marja bit her lip. Obviously she would have to educate the clergy first, if she was to make use of them. She tried another tack. "I don't think the posi-tion of women is at all equitable in the colony," she said. "How many jobs are open to them here in Harrow?"

Her host folded his arms and sat back in his chair. "Marriage," he said. "Before that, those who are able sometimes teach. Most work on the farms they were born on. And we have a few convents, though not many. Our pop-ulation is small."

"And is that all? None learn a trade, apparently. That girl provided with the house, ah –" She looked questioningly at Wells.

"Tara," he told her. "She comes from Madoc Farm."

"Yes. A drudge and a servant. And then she'll be forced to marry some laborer and spend the rest of her life bearing children."

"No one forces them to marry." The priest gave her a thoughtful look. "I gather our ways are not those of your own colony," he said, though she knew very well they *were*. Had the man read her mind?

"We must, of course, pay our debt to the corporation which has bought out Dagon Ltd, and we expect to work in your factories until that debt is paid. But it is not likely that we will put our women and our children to work. You would not expect that, would you?"

"Of course not! Children won't be required to work! In fact, no one will. Don't think of this in terms of *debt*, please." He seemed to imagine the colony would pay off a sum owed after which it would be free to go its own way. Obviously he had no conception of how the charter worked.

"What we want is for you to help us show people that it is in their best interests to have us here," she said desperately. "These farms, for example, can be combined into more efficient operations requiring far less labor. And your individual craftsmen – you can have more and better things if we replace them with robot labor, with factories. In all ways, you can have a better life!"

"A better life." He glanced at Wells. "You, too, are an employee of Pesc?" he asked. "A colonist?"

The other man gave him a guarded look. "I am a slave," he said. "I believe you knew that already."

Marja glared at him. This reminder was not likely to make things easier.

"Ah. We don't have serfs at large here; they are members of their farms and seldom travel about. I had supposed you referred to a form of contractual employment."

Like hell you did, Marja thought furiously.

"And do you remember your homeworld?" the priest asked politely.

It was plain that Wells did not want to answer. But the silence stretched on and on until he was forced to reply.

"'Yes, Father," he said at last.

"And was it anything like this one? Though if they bought and sold each other, I would guess not."

He stared at the floor.

"You won't speak? Perhaps you are not allowed to?" Father Caron glanced at Marja.

"Of course he is free to speak!" she said against her will. "I hadn't thought about you coming from a colony, Wells," she added, trying for naturalness and failing.

He looked up. "I know. You thought we were bred somewhere like cattle."

A look of distaste passed over Father Caron's face.

"It was called New Bohemia," Wells said suddenly. "When the ecosystem began to fail, there were too many people to relocate. So the colony's owner came in and took the children."

"And enslaved them?"

"No one was forced to sell."

Marja sucked in her breath. This was news to her. She had never thought to ask where Pesc got its slaves.

Father Caron frowned, his eyes fixed on the other man's face. "Your parents gave you up to save your life," he said at last. "But how did your colony become uninhabitable?"

But at this the bodyguard shook his head. "I was a child," he said evasively. "And as you say, they saved my life." She saw that his hands were shaking.

The party broke up soon after. She extracted a promise from Father Caron to view the company vids she had brought with her and to allow her to explain in more detail what she wanted him to do. Once she had the bishop's sanction, she did not doubt he would come around. After all, there would still be freedom of religion.

She and Wells walked back to the house in silence. A few people passed them, staring at the strange Lady from the stars and her servant, who paced beside her like a guardian spirit. Her expression – and his – discouraged the familiarity of the previous day.

Once more in her sitting room, she turned on him. "This is my fault," she said bitterly. "I should never have let you enter the church!"

He did not try to defend himself. At the worktable, the robot sat in silence, its pleasant face turned toward the pair as though listening politely. Almost certainly it *was* – listening, that is.

"You knew this was my first posting," she went on. "You might have thought of that, even if I didn't. You've dealt with primitives – with *priests* – more than I have."

"Father Caron is going to be difficult," Wells replied. "It will be hard to secure his cooperation."

"I know that! And if you sabotage me it will be impossible!"

"I cannot sabotage you," he told her unhappily. "I have been conditioned to absolute loyalty to the corporation."

She gave him a sharp look. "But you would if you could," she accused him. "You're almost a primitive yourself!"

He shook his head. "I am not a primitive."

"*He* saw it in you!" she said angrily. "That priest recognized an ally and now he'll try to play you against me!"

"No."

At the table, the robot smiled its carefully engineered smile, reminding her that it would soon be time to contact the ship in orbit – the robosecretary served as her communicator, after all. But she planned to edit her report of *this* day!

Later, after a careful and not at all satisfying conversation with Coordinator Hu, during which she did not mention her visit with the priest, she shut herself in her room, ostensibly to go over her programme. But mostly she just sat and thought.

Tomorrow she would send for the bishop. He, as a member of the upper class, would be much more likely to understand the situation. Certainly he could put his subordinates in their places!

She blew out the candle. She had asked Hu to send down some solar powered equipment both for her own comfort and as gifts to Madoc and Frayle, but none of it had arrived yet. Still worrying, she climbed early into the bed, but there was no sleep for her – or only a light doze.

Marja was half awake when the sound of distant voices roused her. She sat up. Visitors? Had that wretched priest come to see Wells? She listened intently. Yes, that was the voice of her bodyguard alright.

Slipping a robe over her native nightdress, she eased the door open. The sounds were coming from below, but there were no lights to be seen. She moved partway down the stairs. A faint greenish glow spilled around the edge of the turning, coming from the sitting room door. Robot light.

She listened to words spoken in the artificially inflected tones of the machine.

"—careless. You admit –"

"I was careless."

"You caused our representative embarrassment. You should have remained silent."

"That is so. I regret –"

"Your arm –"

She slipped down another step and then another. Peering around the angle of the wall, she saw something they would never have let her see, if they had known she was there. The robot stood over her bodyguard who sat hunched in a chair. As she watched, he extended his wrist – the one with the slave band. The robot clamped one metalplast hand directly to the band and something happened

He did not cry out, but she heard him draw in his breath, barely repressing a groan. She was afraid to move as the torture – for it could not be anything else – went on and on. Probably no more than five minutes elapsed before the thing released him, but it seemed much longer. She saw him sag back in his seat, drawing great, gasping breaths.

"This violation has been added to your record," the robot said in its mellow voice. "You are still considered viable but if there is another, you may risk early retirement."

He did not answer, but only sat there cradling his arm, while the robot resumed its own place at the table.

Stifling a whimper, Marja darted silently back up the stairs. No – they never would have shown her *that*! It was as though the shiny covering of life had been peeled back to show horrors beneath – things she had never imagined!

Much later, she heard footsteps in the corridor and then the quiet opening of a door. After that there was only silence until dawn.

THEY DID NOT STAY LONG in Welyn. The battle had occurred less than an hour's ride from the outskirts of the village and long before they reached the place, Rhosya had cut the arrow from Ard Matthew's shoulder and cleaned and bound the wound. Though the Lost Rythan seemed perfectly

satisfied with her treatment, Brother Brendan insisted he take one of the antibiotics they all carried in their kits.

Sergay's daughter rode with her patient and was still sitting with him when the wagons pulled up into the small square. With the efficiency of long practise, the travelers set out their wares and Ard Matthew's nurse was reluctantly drawn away from her patient to sell her tonics. She left him resting quietly after a dose of some liquid that smelled like mushrooms mixed with earth.

"Is he really so ill?" Brother Brendan asked the other Faring Guard as they watched the business being conducted in the square. Sergay had given them both dun-colored cloaks to hide their foreign clothing so that, by keeping in the background, they managed not to attract attention.

"He is in no danger," Gris Wolfgang assured him seriously. "It is the overflow of the girl's kindness that has kept her by his side."

The Star Brother gave him a quizzical look. Lost Rythans were not known for irony; apparently he must take the words as literally as they were spoken. "Was the wound very deep?" he asked.

"I've seen worse."

"Well, that's good. Sergay tells me we won't be staying here many hours. Now that we are back in settled country, we can travel the road after dark – or what passes for dark beneath the nebula. We should reach Harrow before midnight."

The other nodded, watching the traders at their work. "Brother Brendan," he said abruptly, "May Ard Matthew and I go to confession while we are here?"

His superior gave a sigh. "I supposed you would. You have mentioned it before. But surely Ard Matthew should rest, at least until we get to Harrow."

Gris Wolfgang shook his head. "We will have to be much more careful when we reach that place," he said. "You know that. And *now* there is blood on our hands."

Brother Brendan nodded reluctantly. There might be blood on his own hands too, or at least on the spear he had used to ward off his attackers. He hoped he had not injured anyone too badly. He sighed again. Having worked with Lost Rythans for most of his noviciate, he had become accustomed to their exacting and rather bizarre consciences. They killed – and then they prayed for the souls of those they had killed. They repented, if not the killing itself, then the eagerness with which they fought. Maybe they were right.

"I believe Sergay said the local priest was someone we could trust," he admitted slowly. "If Ard Matthew is able, we will go see him while everyone is occupied here."

After getting directions from one of the travelers, he joined the two Lost Rythans beside the last wagon. Ard Matthew did not look much the worse for his wound, though his arm was in a sling. His companion had draped one of the disguising cloaks over him, but the Star Brother could see the gleam of steel where it didn't quite hide a sword.

Twitching the cloth together, he led them off down a lane to the church. This proved to be a smallish building, made mostly of wood, with a shed-like structure behind it. Here, he had been told, they would probably find the priest, if he hadn't been called away to a sickbed or some other duty. Certainly he would not be at the travelers' market.

They were in luck, meeting a man coming out of the church. The villager looked up at once, a broom in one hand and a dustpan in the other. His hair was dark, his features partially hidden by a short black beard. His nose was somewhat crooked.

"Father Bryn?" Brother Brendan asked, correctly identifying the priest by something in his steady gaze as he watched them.

"That I be, stranger," he said. "Did you come in with the travelers?"

The Star Brother told him they had. In such a small community, everyone would be known, of course.

Setting aside his cleaning tools, Father Bryn regarded his callers. He did not miss the fact that they wore identical cloaks – somewhat too short in the case of the Lost Rythans – and that these latter two bore no racial resemblance to anyone in the colony.

"Sergay speaks well of your discretion," Brother Brendan told him frankly. He let fall his own cloak enough to show his Star Brothers' habit.

"Ah. You are all members of the order?"

"Only I. These two are Faring Guards. We have business in your colony."

"Men from the stars," he said, frowning a little. "You've come because of the buyout, haven't you? People here are talking about nothing else."

Brother Brendan saw no reason to deny it. "But," he added, "I'm only gathering information for my superiors right now. We are on our way to Harrow."

The priest nodded. "And why have you come to me?"

"We would like to go to confession, Father," Gris Wolfgang spoke up. "We have been in a fight, you see, and it is hard not to offend God in a situation like that." Considering the death toll of the encounter, this was something of an understatement, but the Star Brother let it stand.

The priest indicated the doorway behind him. "Come inside, then, before you are seen. That is, I suppose you would rather not have word of your presence get out just now."

They followed him into the church.

"Are you expecting trouble?" Brother Brendan asked.

"Don't you? Why else are you here?" the priest said impatiently as he gestured them into the nave.

It was a poor place, dirt floored for the most part, though the sanctuary itself was much finer, paved with stone and decorated with magnificent wood carving. A beautifully done crucifix hung above the altar and as they all knelt, the Star Brother could tell that his companions were moved by it and so was he. The figure on the cross showed such rough strength, such determination in the midst of suffering, that he was heartened for the first time since he had emerged from the shuttle. The carving might have been done on Lost Rythar itself!

Presently, Father Bryn led them one by one to the confessional at the back. He seemed a different man when he had rolled down his sleeves and set the purple stole about his shoulders. When his turn came, the Star Brother found the words easy to say – that he had been afraid, that he had doubted God's providence, that even now he rather resented the fact that he had no idea what he was to accomplish. He spoke of the impatience he sometimes felt for the two Faring Guards – that they seemed like children to him, an added burden he must bear. But always he came back to his cowardice –

"At least you know what you're worth," the priest said briskly when he had let the other man run down. "It could be a sign you're beginning to grow up yourself. Just don't let your fears keep you from doing your duty, whatever it is, and doing it well."

He paused for a moment. "And don't think you've been sent to save us all from the corporation," he added. "They don't give assignments like that to young men fresh from the noviciate. Only God knows how He plans to make use of you. Your job is to be ready for whatever comes."

Then he gave him absolution and left the three of them to say their penance while he finished sweeping out the church.

Later, they walked around outside of the building, pausing within a small grove of fruit trees. Ard Matthew had gone a bit pale from the exertion – or it may have been the potion he had drunk earlier. At a gesture from Father Bryn, he sank down gratefully against a tree.

"Now you'll be wanting to know the news about this Pesc person," the priest said, when he had settled them. "She's fastened on Harrow like a putrid fever, and her bodyguard with her. They've got a sort of simulacra with them, I'm told. Mannikin or golem or something. She and it are lording it over the masters there."

"*She*?" Brother Brendan repeated in surprise. No one had told him yet that the corporation's delegate was a woman.

"If you can call her that. Something female from beyond the stars, anyway."

The Lost Rythans looked at him in distaste. They had strong ideas about the dignity and role of women and had, in the course of their duties, met all too many of the sort the priest described. Imitation men, they called them, using an untranslatable but not complimentary word from their own language.

"She's commanded the bishop to come to her," their host was saying. "Sent word to Bannyclay that he was to meet her at Harrow to discuss the future of the colony."

This was no surprise. Treelight was a small colony, powerless in the hands of its owners. Certainly, there would be no respect shown for local authorities.

"Did he come?" Brother Brendan asked.

"No. And he isn't likely to." The priest spat. "As I understand it, we owed Dagon a debt for settling this world. And now Pesc has bought the contract. But it's a money debt – they didn't buy our souls."

The Star Brother gave him a look in which pity mingled with helplessness. "That," he said, "is almost certainly what they think they *have* bought, Father."

For a long moment, he and the colonist looked at one another. At last the priest spoke, "You are right, of course," he agreed heavily. "I do not want to believe you, but I must." His hard features grew bleak. "God help us now," he said. "There are some here whose souls they *will* have. Some they must own already."

He glowered at the three offworlders. "If it were not for the great power of this corporation to strike back at us, I would say that we were justified in ridding ourselves of these envoys of theirs. But it would do no good –"

"No," Brother Brendan told him. "Don't even think that. We must find some other way to come to terms with them."

The priest turned away. "Of course, there is still our debt," he said. "We owe them *something* in justice."

There was nothing more to say; the visitors rose to go. Father Bryn slipped out of the orchard first to make sure there was no one in the lane and then, at his signal, they made their departure.

When the three reached the square, Sergay and his people were still busy haggling with the villagers. Brother Brendan and Gris Wolfgang helped their companion back to the wagon and laid him down. His wound might not be serious by the reckoning of Lost Rythans, but he had bled and was bleeding again. Eventually they got this stopped and remained with him until the travelers began to close up shop. They had miles to cover before they could rest. And then – what?

MARJA HAD SENT FOR THE constable as soon as she came downstairs in the morning. Her sleepless night had left ravages in both her peace of mind and her physical looks, as well she knew. After what she had witnessed, it was all she could do to face Wells.

She sat down to breakfast however, indicating that he should join her. He told her he had already eaten but she did not believe him. She kept trying to trace in his countenance the marks of his interview with the company robot. She could not help herself. Now that she knew the truth, it was easy enough to see the suffering that lay just beneath his smooth exterior – it had always been there. She was ashamed of her blindness.

When Constable Wynn arrived, still swallowing his own breakfast, he presented himself in the dining room where Marja still sat toying with her own uneaten meal. She could read in his countenance the memory of Saturday's violence and it was obvious he expected to hear of more.

He had already made his own inquiries, assuring her that she was in no further danger. The culprits, he said, had undoubtedly been from among her many callers that day, perhaps members of a gang wanting to hold her for ransom. Whoever they were, they were long gone, the constable assured her, and not likely to return.

Marja wanted to believe him and, had it not been for something she had seen in her bodyguard's face, she might have. But that there was more to this matter seemed plain to both Wells and herself. There were things she wasn't being told.

As she greeted the constable, she reassured him that nothing further had happened, and he seemed relieved. This was another matter.

"I sent word yesterday that you were to summon the bishop," she told him. "He must know already that I am here and that I must confer with him as soon as possible. I believe his seat is at Bannyclay, isn't it?"

"Yes, Lady," the constable replied, not looking at her. "But it might be better if – if one of the masters were to go for him."

Marja glared at him. "You did send for him, didn't you?"

The man nodded unhappily. She could not know with what trepidation he had sent off a messenger with a politely worded request.

"I don't want to deal with the masters," she said presently and then stopped.

In the sitting room, the robosecretary waited at its table for her commands, her requests for information, her *communications*. It had been listening in when she chided Wells for his speech with the priest. If I told it that it must not torment Wells, she wondered, would I be obeyed? All the time I was receiving my briefing and he was jacked in – was he being threatened then?

"I want you to send again," she said after a moment's pause, "and tell him that I expect him to come. That Pesc orders him to come!"

With a bow, the constable withdrew, trying not to show his dismay.

When he had gone, Marja sat back, sipping her tea. Behind her, Wells paced the room, pausing at each window as though seeking enemies behind the curtains. At last he spoke.

"Someone is coming up the walk. Master Frayle."

Marja set down her cup with a crash. She hoped Wells had not noticed her start. Suddenly she determined to get rid of the robot before she saw anyone else. She could no longer bear to have the thing in the room.

She rose and went into the sitting room. "I want you to make an office out of one of the upstairs rooms," she told it, keeping her voice steady with an effort. "I'll need a place to work where none of the colonists can intrude. Please go up there and find a suitable space."

The robosecretary rose at once, its bland faces assuming an expression of helpfulness. "Coordinator Hu has asked that I monitor your health while you are here," it chanted. "He would like me to check your vital signs and take a sample of your blood this morning."

"I've had full spectrum inoculations," she told it crossly.

"Coordinator Hu is responsible for your welfare," the machine said, its voice as pleasant – and as inhuman – as it had been the night before. She wondered if it would tell her she was at risk for early retirement if she did not cooperate.

What a fool she had been! Retirement for a slave? When Wells was no longer useful to the corporation, they would kill him. They would activate something in the slave band and he would die. No one should need to tell her *that*!

She saw the robot hand extended, the emerging needle. "Not now," she told it desperately. "Can't you see someone is coming! Go – go upstairs. I'll be along later."

For a moment it hesitated. Then, as Wells ushered Master Frayle into the room, it turned and began to mount the stairs.

"I hope I do not disturb you at your work," the master said, smiling as he came forward to take her hand. He looked so human after the robot that, even knowing what a scoundrel he probably was, she greeted him with more warmth than she had intended. When she took a seat on the bench, he joined her there at once.

He *was* a handsome man, she thought – just as she remembered him from their last meeting. His face was marked with the experience of years spent guiding the fortunes of his – serfs? Employees? Dependents? – his keen, blue eyes bracketed with the lines of care and responsibility.

"You are tired," he told her, with a curious glance at Wells, as though wondering why the servant lingered.

She looked up. "You may go into the kitchen," she said. "Have the maid make some more tea."

The bodyguard nodded and left them, though Marja knew he would still be listening, alert to any danger.

"You have been given a great responsibility," Master Frayle was saying. "I know you are not the sole director of this project, but –"

"I've been sent to do a survey," she told him. "The preliminaries. My job is to deal with what you might call the *human* aspect of things."

"You have no power to make decisions?"

The question set her on guard, taking her by surprise. "Oh, yes. I will make recommendations," she said after a moment. "I have already begun." She thought of the supplies and gifts she had ordered. The shuttle pilot should be bringing them down to Madoc farm today or tomorrow. She must arrange for their pickup.

Frayle looked as though he might have said something more personal, but delicacy held him back. "It is a beautiful day," he observed instead. "I wish you could walk over my lands as they are now – in springtime."

"You must be eager to get back to them."

He started slightly. Then, "You seem to understand everything," he told her smoothly. "But the truth is I have responsibilities here and I cannot return as soon as I would like."

She studied his face, wondering what sort of man he really was beneath his mask of courtesy. He had kept himself in shape, she noted, and his teeth could be – *would* be fixed. He had an excellent understanding and should certainly become a leader in the remaking of the colony.

He seemed to be waiting for her to say something so she asked him the first thing that came into her head, "Do you have a family? I mean – of course you do. I suppose you miss them."

Frayle looked down, his smile resolving itself into something else. "I am a widower," he told her. "But I have sons. One of them is to marry Master Madoc's daughter. Perhaps you've heard."

"Yes, I *had* heard." She listened for the sounds of tea, but the girl must still be boiling the water. "The eldest."

"That is so."

She remembered what else Wells had said about Master Frayle's sons. That the youngest had created a scandal – and that girl! But with the master seated so close that he was almost touching her, she could hardly believe now he had done away with her. No, he might have sent his son's paramour away, perhaps even arranged an abortion. But that would have been the extent of it.

"You may have been told," he said as though discerning at least some of her thoughts, "that my youngest son – Evan is his name – has been a trouble to me." He watched her closely as he spoke.

"There was some gossip," she admitted.

"Yes. Servants talk." He moved away from her and stood up. He held himself well – a contrast to the tubby Master Madoc – as he stepped over to the window and turned. "Evan has disappeared," he said. "He may be dead."

"I am sorry –"

He straightened himself. "But this is not fitting," he said abruptly, "that I should trouble you with such personal matters. You, who represent our patron beyond the stars, have greater concerns than our petty problems."

She heard footsteps in the dining room and suddenly Wells walked in, bearing the tea tray. She could read nothing in his face – he might have been one of Master Frayle's own servants as he poured and offered the other man a cup.

"Thank you," Marja said when he had set down the pot. "You may go."

She wasn't sure he would do this. It might be against his conditioning to leave her alone with an untrustworthy colonist. But to her relief, he swung about at once and walked out of the room.

She turned back to her guest. "Please don't think of me as a great lady," she said. "I am an employee of Pesc, that is all. I am here to help you to make the transition from a low tech colony to a more modern commonwealth. Naturally I would appreciate your cooperation in this undertaking."

"And you have it," he told her eagerly. "What would you like me to do?"

"Speak to your own people," she said. "Prepare them. One of the first things I'd like to do is set up a model farm with modern equipment. We could teach your workers to operate the machinery and when the other masters see how much more you can produce –"

He was plainly startled at this. "You would like to begin with Frayle Farm?" he asked.

"What better place? You seem to be a man of progressive ideas. Why shouldn't you be the first to enjoy the fruits of what Pesc has to offer? And your workers – after they are trained, you won't be needing all of them. They could go out into the rest of the colony and train others."

"Ah – I see." He stared thoughtfully down into his cup. "And what does your corporation plan to do when the farms have been made over?"

"Oh, we won't wait for that," she told him eagerly. "We'll bring in the engineers, begin new mines, build factories, and – and expand the colony."

"Expand the colony?"

"Take out the wildwood. Poison it – as our predecessors did here."

His face was study in confusion. Was she going too fast for him? She had felt a mounting excitement as she talked, and suddenly she was almost hysterically confident. She set down her teacup.

"You don't know," she said, "what good things Pesc can do for you! They can build a whole new world here."

He began to catch the infection. "Yes," he said brightening. "A new world."

She talked on, forgetting Wells in the kitchen, where he sat fingering the slave band perhaps, and remembering his pain. She forgot the robot waiting upstairs, its amiable face turned toward the corridor, its blameless metal-plast hands in its lap.

And then she fainted.

Frayle caught her as Wells hurried in from the dining room where he had posted himself. After some time spent chafing her wrists, she opened her eyes to see both men bending over her, Frayle looking genuinely shocked, Wells grimly efficient. Yet somehow it seemed to her that Wells was not surprised at all, as though he had expected something like this to happen.

With many expressions of concern and apology, her guest departed while her bodyguard carried her upstairs to the waiting robot.

CHAPTER 6

CHIEF SNOWTYGER HAD ACTUALLY BEEN asleep when the call came in. An aide, Heth Xavier Wolfbane, was obliged to rouse him. The younger man, somewhat scarred and still getting used to a regrown leg, knelt awkwardly beside the cot. "It's Dust, sir," he said.

The chief sat up at once and Heth Xavier handed him the comm. It said much for the high (and expensive) level of Dust's resources that he could contact the *Balthasar* so easily.

Snowtyger's friend was excited, though how the listener knew this was a mystery even to himself. The mechanical voice was uninflected though the words did come a little more quickly than usual.

"Got something, Gaed Alfred. It happened when I went in to check on that woman's dossier prior to hiring. There was a medical exam, genetic screening –"

"Yes?"

"I couldn't find anything else so I started an in depth on those."

The chief waited patiently. He couldn't see anything to get excited about.

"That's when the world exploded. I hit a block, level six – it had been set to ambush anyone who poked in."

"Were you – did you suffer any damage?" The chief was not quite sure how to phrase his question.

"Some. I'm in repair mode now. But –" This time, for the same unexplained reason, Snowtyger thought he heard determination in the calm, mechanical voice.

"I'm going back as soon as I've recovered. There are ways to get past the block now that I know it's there."

"We don't ask you to risk your life, Dust."

Would there have been a chuckle? Once, maybe. "What's left of it, you mean? I know that, Gaed Alfred."

"Then –?"

"You wouldn't have called me in if this weren't important."

The chief frowned. "Okay it's important," he admitted. "But before you do anything dangerous –"

"I can guess what's coming next."

"Always."

"Damn it, man! Even if I did more than half believe all that stuff, how could anyone baptize a machine? That's what you want, isn't it?"

"I'll ask Father Moto. He's better at theology than I am."

"You do that –" Then, more seriously, "There's something in that file, Gaed Alfred. Something that came before the psych test. Nobody does that kind of block if they haven't got something to hide."

"But –"

"Give me some time and I'll get back with you. And if –"

Snowtyger waited.

"Just so it's on the record," the voice resumed more slowly. "At least I'm *thinking* about that other thing. Okay?"

"Right. You go on thinking about it."

"Yeah."

"I'll be praying for you."

"Thanks, I guess."

As he handed the comm back to the aide, Snowtyger met his fellow Lost Rythan's clear gaze. "You got that?"

With a grin, Heth Xavier gave him the Rythan equivalent of thumbs up.

His people had their priorities.

IT WAS WELL AFTER MIDNIGHT when the travelers reached Harrow. The nebula still rode the sky, putting out the light of the stars, sprawling slightly off center as it trailed tentacles of ghostly lavender lace. There were no lights to be seen in the town as Sergay led the caravan to the camping place on the north lane.

"This is one of the towns where we don't camp in the market square," he explained to Brother Brendan. "It's too big of a place. And anyway I suppose you'd like to keep a low profile."

The travelers were forming their wagons up into a circle as though the leader's unease had infected them all. In the violet tinted half-light, some of the men began quietly leading the horses to a nearby stream while others set up their lean-to tents. No one lit a fire.

"People will still know you're here, I suppose," the Star Brother said.

"Oh, they'll trickle in during the morning. But there's no reason to get everyone talking. Don't want *her* snooping around, do we?"

The Star Brother had shared with Sergay what they had learned from the priest at Welyn, though the boss heard much the same in the course of his day's trading. "But surely your own affairs are beneath her notice," Brother Brendan said now. "She'll have business with the colony leaders."

"Let's hope you're right. But if I was her, I'd want to see *everything*."

They slept the rest of the night undisturbed by any visitor more formidable than a goat, which one of the Lost Rythans chased away from their gear. The lesser suns were in the sky when the camp began to rouse, and the light of the next sunrise was broadening to the east.

Brother Brendan crawled to the opening of the lean-to. The nearby stream had become no more than a line of mist, its fringe of trees invisible. To the south, Harrow was a spectral vision, swathed in the same mist, out of which came the hoarse barking of a dog and the sounds of doors slamming and someone splitting kindling. Once a horse whinnied, to be answered by one or two of their own.

The Lost Rythans were already up, though only Bloodbear was in sight. He had gathered some brush and was busy starting a fire. Several other small fires burned already.

"Where is Ard Matthew?" The Star Brother asked him.

"He's gone with Sergay's daughter to buy milk."

"Oh. Is that safe?"

"She said it was. They are people she knows. Not in the town – outside it."

It was Friday and the smells of breakfast were doubly tormenting. The travelers were frying the local equivalent of ham.

But we can't expect them to adapt themselves to our ways, the Star Brother told himself firmly, trying to muster up some charity. After all, they are still pagans. Uncomfortably he wondered whether God expected him to do something about *that* particular problem and guessed that He probably did.

He was still wrestling with his conscience when a woman brought him a cup of tea. After thanking her, he set it down and crawled back into the lean-to to say his morning prayers. Naturally the tea was cold when he finished, but Ard Matthew and Rhosya had returned, bringing a pail of milk and an armful of bread. It was fresher than anything he had tasted for the past few days and he accepted a chunk gratefully, his mood slowly brightening as he ate.

Meanwhile the pair moved off with their burden, delivering the fresh food to the rest of the camp. The Lost Rythan carried the bucket one-handed while the girl bore the bread. It was some time before Ard Matthew returned alone. He apologized for the delay.

"There's news," he said setting another can of hot tea near the fire to keep warm. "They say the corporate representative is ill. People think she's been poisoned."

"Poisoned!" Brother Brendan exclaimed with his mouth full. "But that will only make things worse for the colony! Pesc already has them entirely at its mercy!"

"Who do people suspect?" Gris Wolfgang asked.

"The farmer where we got the milk – Bran is his name – says that depends on who does the talking. Some say one of the masters, since they've been lording it over the rest all these years and must now give way – and others say it's the druids."

"Ah yes," Brother Brendan murmured. But just who *were* these druids? he wondered. The word meant literally "tree man" and Rhosya had more than hinted that they worshipped the wildwood. Still, the wildwood wasn't a real forest, as surely the colonists knew – and besides it was death to enter.

His speculations were broken off as Sergay came toward them, tea in hand, the sunrise at his back. He looked like a figure out of a myth himself, his wiry form drawn in black, a long shadow stretching before him. The sight reminded Brother Brendan of tales he had heard long ago by the firesides of Gaelway Colony – nights when the children fell asleep to the words of ballads older than the colony worlds, the dreams and nightmares of a land they would never see, sung by drunken men who sorrowed for their lost home on Earth. In those tales men and women had come not only out of trees but from the ground itself, arms filled with gold –

"So," the traveler boss said, spoiling the illusion as he paused to take a noisy gulp of his tea. "Our visitor is sick in bed. Poisoned." He cast sharp eyes on the company. "What happens if she dies?"

Brother Brendan looked down. "I don't want to think about that."

Sergay nodded. "But you must – and my thoughts are probably the same as yours."

"These people from the corporation," Gris Wolfgang said slowly, "they will try to determine who is guilty, won't they? They won't just punish everyone?"

"Why not?" the Star Brother said brusquely. "This isn't Earth – or Lost Rythar. This corporation *owns* the colony. Who is going to stop them from doing anything they like?"

Gris Wolfgang gave him a very Lost Rythan look. "We will have to try," he said.

Brother Brendan nodded. The other man was right; they would *all* have to try. He turned to Sergay. "Do *you* think it was one of the masters? Or several of them working together?"

"Why them? They're vassals of the corporation." The chief scratched at his beard. "They'll still come out on top the way things are, so why make trouble for themselves?"

"Do you think it any more likely –" Brother Brendan looked hard at the boss. "Ard Matthew mentioned druids."

"People talk."

The Star Brother waited patiently, but, "Are you afraid to speak?" Gris Wolfgang asked Sergay.

At this, the traveler shrugged. "They never bothered us any," he said at last. "And it might be we've run into a few now and then. At least those who were on their way to becoming druids, I mean. The others – no." He paused, thinking. "But everything's changing now, isn't it? It's like the end of the world."

"The end of the world you've known. The beginning of something else."

The other man gave him a naked look. "And will there be a place for us in the world that's coming?"

Brother Brendan shook his head. "Not *in* it," he admitted. "So far, I don't think Pesc even knows you exist. Maybe things will stay that way."

"Yes – maybe."

"Now tell me about the druids," the other man went on. "I can see you've got more than the corporation to worry about. Who are they and why are you afraid of them?"

Sergay set down his empty mug carefully and lowered himself to a seat on the ground. "They say – mostly in the north and near the river – that there are people who have found a way to survive in the wildwood. They don't die or get sick when they live with the trees and somehow the wildwood feeds them."

The others waited, watching his face.

"They – *change*," the boss said impatiently, spreading his hands. "They aren't like us anymore. When the change is complete, they would have to disguise themselves to come among human men – if they even do, which I doubt."

"But do you believe those stories?" Gris Wolfgang asked. "That people can survive in the wildwood?"

The other man gave a mirthless laugh. "When you've been here long enough, you'll learn that travelers believe a lot of things others would rather not. That's how we survive."

Brother Brendan raised one eyebrow.

"At Tregarth and the eastern villages, it is no more than an idle tale, if that," Sergay admitted. "Master Tregarth doesn't believe in the druids. But if you asked the Brothers of St. Hubert what *they* believed, you would get a different answer."

It was true Brother Alwyn had hinted at some abomination concerning the wildwood. He had been willing to die in order to avoid it.

"Supposing they exist, would they want to poison the corporate representative?" Brother Brendan asked.

The other man shrugged. "Seems foolish, doesn't it? But I've heard that Pesc plans to kill off the trees."

"That sounds about right," Brother Brendan admitted. "Though I don't see how they can – not all of them anyway."

Sergay shrugged.

"So we really don't know for sure whether these druids would go after the corporate representative," Ard Matthew said. "If they have to disguise themselves in order to mingle with others, that seems unlikely."

"In the end," Brother Brendan pointed out, "what really matters is going to be what the corporation *believes* happened."

There was no answer to this. Or rather, they all knew the answer.

Customers began to trickle in during the morning, though the travelers had done nothing so far to advertise their presence. With Sergay's approval, his guests went off to explore the town. Harrow was large enough that a few strangers would not be noticed, especially if Rhosya went with them. At Brother Brendan's insistence, however, the Lost Rythans donned native shirts and as for himself, while he retained his cassock, he put on the cloak once more to cover the Star Brothers' insignia.

They walked rapidly across the field, soon coming upon a lane which led in among the houses of the town. Ahead lay the churchyard with the towers of the church itself visible above the monuments. The Lost Rythans wanted to stop there first, a request the Star Brother could hardly refuse. Among all the alien worlds they visited, this was their one firm anchor – God's literal presence on the altar of each of the colony churches.

Rhosya held back, however. "I'll wait out here in the churchyard," she said. "I can gather moss for my ointments, as long as the priest doesn't see me."

Ard Matthew was not pleased, but he hardly knew what to say as they hesitated beside the fence. All he knew for sure was that he wanted her safely – and literally – inside the Church.

She may have understood some of this, for she turned to Brother Brendan. "Your god is not our god," she told him flatly. "He wants no part of us nor we of him." It was as though she answered Ard Matthew in the only way she knew – with brutal frankness.

The Lost Rythan winced, but before he could say anything – and what *could* he say, after all? – Gris Wolfgang spoke up.

"That isn't true! How can you even *think* such a blasphemous thing?"

She did not answer.

"Have you a god of your own then?" the Star Brother asked her.

"That is not – I mean, our beliefs would not interest you." She looked trapped as she turned from one to the other of her companions.

Just then two women passed along the lane, pausing to look sharply at the group who stood arguing beside the churchyard gate. Their gaze passed over the men and fixed on the traveler woman. For the first time, Brother Brendan realized that her dress was not like that of the other colonists, consisting of a woven plaid skirt dyed red and blue, gathered beneath an undyed cropped blouse. The other women wore dresses with tailored jackets and their heads were covered with scarves and bonnets while Rhosya's raven hair swung free.

Taking her arm, he led her in among the tombstones. Once out of sight of the lane, he released her at once.

"I should not be here," she whispered, looking back. "They will think I'm a witch!"

"All the more reason to come with us into the church," Gris Wolfgang told her remorselessly.

"You might wait in the vestibule," the Star Brother suggested. "You would be safe enough there. If anyone asks, you are showing the sights to some visitors from the east."

She nodded unwillingly, keeping her eyes fixed on his face.

Ard Matthew began to walk along the back of the building, seeking a way around the side and the others followed. But before they could go far, they were confronted by a rugged ecclesiastical personage who looked as though he expected a robbery and would, judging by the staff in his hand, deal with the intruders accordingly.

TREELIGHT

MARJA SIENKO'S DAYS PASSED IN delirium mixed with moments of unreliable clarity. During one of these lucid interludes, Wells told her she had had an allergic reaction to something in the air or food of the colony and that she should have let the robosecretary test her blood. But before she could respond, she found herself in the grip of Master Frayle. He leered at her, showing his bad teeth in a smile that was almost a snarl.

"Now I have you!" he said. "You won't get away this time!"

She struggled and cried out, "It's the masters! They've poisoned me! They're trying to sabotage the takeover!"

After that, someone held her hands and she felt the true warmth of human flesh. "Don't be afraid. You're safe here."

Nevertheless, she struggled for a moment until suddenly it was another day. "I've got to get up," she said. "They'll be coming – the bishop and Master Madoc. I've got to warn the bishop about Frayle!"

"You're not strong enough to get up." She felt those hands again, holding hers.

Then a robot voice spoke. "Please do not struggle. It is time for your injection."

"Injection? Of *what*? I've had my full spectrum coverage!"

Robot hands gripped her now, and a friendly, smiling face leaned over hers. "You must cooperate," it said. "Your contract requires your cooperation."

Something burned in her blood and then a human arm was around her shoulders and she smelled the human smell. "Here," a hoarse voice said. "Drink this."

She drank and was somewhere else.

All around her stretched the great purple forest. Nothing moved save wind-tossed branches. But there was no wind! They were reaching for her, *arms*, not branches! "Your contract requires your death," the trees murmured, smiling at her in friendly wise. Something pinned her arms to her sides and she struggled until, with a hoarse cry, she woke.

"Where – what day is it?" she asked groggily and a robot voice told her it was Wednesday. She closed her eyes and slept again only to wake in shuddering fear. The trees, she thought. God save me from the trees! They're here – surrounding the house! And then, rather inconsequently she wondered why God should help her. Hadn't she given up her childhood religion long ago? He'd be more likely to leave her to the mercy of the alien forest!

Once more the robot hand gripped her arm and something burned all over her body. "Are you torturing me?" she asked. "Like you did Wells? Am I wearing a slave band now?"

She tried to touch her wrist with the other hand, wondering if she would feel the metalplast there, but she had not the strength to do it. "Wells?" she called. "Wells? Am I a slave now, too? Check my arm!"

But he was not there and she was alone in the purple wood. Once she thought she saw a deer and once a bird flew between the branches. Both were purple, the deer covered with pustules, its fur falling out, the bird a reptilian thing, screeching dismally as it disappeared into the amethystine gloom.

"I'm lost," she moaned. "I'm lost in this terrible place! Will I never be free again?" She felt tears of self pity flow from her eyes, making sidewise tracks from her face to the pillow.

Once more, human hands took hers. "I'm sorry," a low voice murmured close to her ear. "God, how sorry I am!"

She gripped the hands and they were warm and hard – not the metallic hardness of robot hands, but the calloused firmness of a man's hands. "Why – are you sorry?"

But there was no answer. She felt the hands begin to slip away, reached out to grasp a wrist, and felt her fingers trail along the coldness of the slave band.

For a long time she lay there, wondering whether she would die. If she were dying, would they even tell her? Or would she just slip away out of life not knowing – *anything*? Who were her friends, who her enemies – and what did it all *mean*?

"He's been arrested," she said once. "Hasn't he? He got rid of his son's girlfriend and now he's killing me!"

But no one heard. Later a robot hand reached for her arm again and the pain returned along with the nightmares. Purple. The trees and something formless that hunted her. She fled among the squirming branches, her feet making mushy noises on the fungoid floor of the wood that was no wood.

She felt as though she were already trapped in the maw of an alien beast. If she stood still, she would sink into the slime and the hunter would find her there! It was purple – the essence of purple – and there would be nothing left but fragments of her purple-stained bones.

When she came to herself at last, it was another day. "Friday," Wells told her when she asked him. "Don't try to get up yet. You've been pretty sick."

"Did they catch him?"

"Who?"

"Frayle."

"Master Frayle had nothing to do with your sickness. You had an allergic reaction – something they were going to test you for. You were supposed to be tested every few days."

She closed her eyes. "I thought – he was there – we were drinking tea. What am I allergic to?"

"Who knows? It might have been the food or some plant in the garden. Something in the air."

She opened her eyes. "Is that normal when people travel from colony to colony?"

"I don't know anything about medicine," he told her, but his eyes did not meet hers.

Marja snuggled down beneath the quilt. They were alone in the room and for this she was thankful. "You were there while I was sick," she said almost accusingly. "Weren't you?"

He did not answer.

"The robot – it hurt me. It hurt you, too. I saw."

"You spoke of that when you were ill."

"Why?" She tried to read in his face some answer that would make sense. "It was no dream – I *did* see. Why did it do that to you? Why did you *let* it?"

He turned away. "I was being punished," he said. "I broke a rule."

"What rule?"

"A rule of prudence. I caused you embarrassment when we went to see that priest. I put my personal concerns ahead of those of the corporation."

She frowned, trying to see his face. "Did it – do what it did because I was angry with you? If that is so, then I am very sorry."

"No, you had nothing to do with it." He turned back to her. "It was *my* fault, not yours." He drew a shaky breath. "The robot is *good*," he said desperately. "The corporation is good. They – *it* made you well, didn't it?"

"Are they good as God is good?" she whispered. "Is that what you mean? Is the corporation your god?"

She saw a rictus pass over his features, and his eyes blazed for one moment. Then, "You should not say things like that. Don't you know that I must accuse myself if I speak out of turn? If I lead you to believe things that are not right?"

"Why must you accuse yourself?"

"Because I am programmed to do it. You wouldn't want me to be punished again, would you?"

She shook her head.

"Then be more careful," he said. "Believe that the corporation means you no harm. They sent you here to do good to these people – to bring good things to them."

She looked into his tormented eyes as he slowly regained control of his features. He might have been a robot himself now, if it were not for those eyes.

"You are lying," she said.

"Take it back. Take back your words," he whispered. "Do it now – quickly!"

"I'm sorry! I'm sorry," she said, frightened by *his* fear. "Of course my employer means us well. It was the illness speaking. I have been very ill, haven't I?" she faltered.

He nodded, unable to speak.

Later the robosecretary came in. "You must take your medicine now," it said and reached for her arm. She pulled away, but when the thing injected the drug, there was no pain. After a while, Wells brought her a tray with tea and fresh baked rolls.

"I really am feeling better," she told him.

"You've had a long rest."

"Days!" she took a bite and washed it down with tea. "I'm glad *you* didn't get sick!"

"Guess I'm not allergic to anything," he said. Then, "Master Madoc is here. He has been trying to get in all week. Do you want to see him now?"

She frowned. "What about Master Frayle?"

"He sent someone to inquire about you – several times. He didn't think he should come himself."

"I thought he had poisoned me. I hope no one told him."

"No. But he is Madoc's guest."

"I thought he was a murderer," she said. "But it was only servants' talk, wasn't it?"

Her bodyguard waited silently.

"Alright. Let me put on something more formal," she said, looking around. With the efficiency of a real servant, Wells fetched her a wrapper and helped her fold it into a sort of bed jacket.

She looked up at him, smoothing back her hair. "Alright?" At his nod, she told him to send in Master Madoc.

Wells disappeared and, almost at once, the master came in. While he expressed his regret and his compliments, she was aware of him studying her face as though to estimate the ravages of her sickness. What would Master Madoc have done had she died? Would he have treated her successor with the same oily deference?

But Frayle, a small voice said, perhaps *he* would have felt something like regret. Perhaps you have wronged *him*, at least.

She shook away this thought and turned her attention back to her guest. "It was good of you to come," she said, despising him.

"You do not know, Lady, how your sickness has affected the entire village. Father Caron would have come to you – not that you were in danger of death or at least your bodyguard said you were not – but Father did not think –" He trailed off in confusion.

"He did not think I would want to see him in his capacity as a priest," she said. "And he was right. As to anything else, I was too ill. But I am better now and I do have business with him. Tomorrow I will get up."

"That is fine."

"Has there been any word from the bishop?"

Her visitor looked embarrassed. "Not yet," he said evasively. "Perhaps your message hasn't reached him yet what with these new troubles –"

"What troubles?"

"Oh just rumours, Lady. Some difficulty up the river. The – the druids –"

She stared at him. "Who are the druids?" she asked.

He did not answer her directly. Instead, he took out a handkerchief and wiped his face. "They have grown more bold of late," he muttered. "It is even said that they have agents in the towns. But that is not likely. Serfs will talk, you know."

"But who *are* they?" she demanded impatiently.

"The servants of the wildwood. The men of the trees."

She gave him a blank stare.

"They want to destroy the colony," he told her. "They are the enemies of the corporation and of the Church. At first there were very few and we thought they were mad. Who could believe anyone would do such things as they have done? It made no sense."

"They are a subversive group? Revolutionaries?"

"Exactly so. Enemies of progress. Ingrates. They will certainly oppose you if you try to improve our lives here."

"They won't succeed," she said firmly. "And as for the wildwood, I'm afraid it can't be saved. It is a menace to life – and as long as there is a way to do without it –" She was thinking, rather guiltily, of the questions she had put to the robotsecretary about the wildwood's role in keeping up the oxygen supply. Suddenly she remembered also what Wells had said about his home colony – that the eco-system had broken down. Was that also a corporate venture?

"Yes, yes. Of course the wood must go. But perhaps you will tell your superiors of the present danger?" Once more Madoc wiped his face.

"Certainly I will tell them," she promised, wondering what help Hu could send on short notice. The food she had eaten felt like lead in her stomach and she was very tired. "I think you should come back later," she told her guest. "I will see you tomorrow – early."

He rose at once as Wells reappeared from his post outside the door. Marja lay back wearily, listening as they descended the stairs.

She was so tired. And now here was this new problem for her to deal with – whatever it was. Tomorrow she would have to get up and work!

Sleep claimed her, and she only roused once, to see Wells sitting in a chair beside the bed. She gave him a drowsy smile and drifted off again. If there were nightmares this time, she did not remember them. Anyway, Wells would wake her. He would never let the hunter of the purple forest lay hands on her!

As it happened, Rhosya and the priest did know one another and, after a moment, he lay aside his staff. More than once he had entered a sickroom where she had been, passing her in the doorway as she left. Still, neither of them had ever expected to meet here at the church.

Brother Brendan regarded the colonist with frank curiosity. This one, too, was supposed to be trustworthy, and there was something in his face so reminiscent of Father Bryn of Welyn that he wondered if the two were kin. Perhaps his features were not quite so rough hewn, nor his bearing so stern as those of the other priest, but the same inner strength was there to be seen.

"Good morning, Father," Ard Matthew said politely as though nothing untoward had occurred. "We are strangers here and we would like to make a visit to the Blessed Sacrament, if we may."

The priest studied the Lost Rythan. "You came in with the travelers?" It was the same question Father Bryn had asked them.

At this, Brother Brendan told him he was a Star Brother. "We're touring with the travelers," he explained. "It seemed best under the circumstances."

There was a pause while the pastor studied, not the Star Brothers' habit, but the face of the man who wore it. Then, "I am Father Caron," he said. "Come inside – all of you."

Rhosya allowed herself to be led into the sacristy where she hovered near the door. The others crowded the small room, the two Faring Guards towering over the others while Brother Brendan introduced them and himself.

The priest acknowledged these introductions. "I won't waste time asking why you have come and I can't pretend that you will be welcome, either," he said. "We have troubles enough without more offworld interference, however well meant."

Both Lost Rythans stiffened at this, but their innate respect for the clergy kept them silent. "We are not here to interfere," the Star Brother said hastily. "My order sent me mostly as an observer. We have always watched over the Church's welfare on Treelight," he added, watching the other man's reaction.

"You've done us a good turn now and again," Father Caron agreed reluctantly. "At least you get the bishops consecrated whenever we need a new one."

Brother Brendan ventured a small smile. "We had to fight for permission to do even that," he said. "I suppose your bishops are the only citizens of your colony who have ever been offworld."

"They don't talk about it."

"They're not allowed to. We always had to work with Dagon Ltd, you remember, and they set the policies."

"Isolation. Yes."

"And we managed to silence that heresiarch for you," the Star Brother reminded the priest. "The one who tried to set up a theocracy at Bannyclay."

"That was before my time. What did you do to him, anyway?"

Brother Brendan grinned. "It was before my time, too," he admitted. "But he recanted, didn't he?"

"So I've heard. I've also heard the Faring Guard had a hand in it." He gave the Lost Rythans a sharp look.

"I hope you don't think we would ever act against the mandates of your colony," Ard Matthew said seriously. "At least not on purpose."

Gris Wolfbane nodded. "Sometimes," he added, "we are hasty, but we always try to obey the Star Brothers."

They both looked so much like overgrown schoolboys asserting their good intentions that not even Father Caron's attempt at sternness could hold. He burst out laughing. "I see you carry your crosses with you, Brother Brendan," he said. "And now, please come in and see the church." He glanced at Rhosya. "I bear you no ill will, woman. You may remain here in safety."

She gave a confused little nod as first Bloodbear and then Third-Blade handed her their swords and a few other weapons for safekeeping while they went inside. They had gone weaponless to the church at Welyn because that was their only destination, but here in this larger place, it seemed better to go armed. The Star Brother was a bit startled to see just how well armed they *could* go.

And yet, to look at them now, he might have thought they were already saints in heaven. Somewhat rugged saints with earnest, bearded faces and long-fingered hands folded in prayer – at least Gris Wolfgang had his hands folded. His companion still had one arm in a sling.

As he joined them, he prayed for them and for all their homeworld. He tried never to forget that the Faring Guards were exiles, sent away because of feuds and killings in their home colony. Their service to the Star Brothers was their freely accepted punishment, endured in a bizarre mixture of innocence and bloodguiltiness and, for all that, they were as true as any men could be.

Ah well. The people of Gaelway were of a similar sort. Where else did you find a race who valued music above common sense? Who drank themselves silly at every opportunity and bewailed men killed so long ago the very bones of them were dust? As he thought of this, he prayed for his own people, too – and for those ancient warriors of earth, wondering if his prayers might slip down the streams of time and be of benefit to them while they yet lived.

But now he was here on *this* world and it looked like there would be plenty to pray about before things settled down – if they ever did. He prayed for Master Tregarth and the Brothers of St. Hubert and he prayed also for the strange lady sent to Treelight by the corporation to work its will on the inhabitants. And for Sergay's people – and for the souls of the highwaymen they had killed. God have mercy on them all.

Presently he rose and went back into the sacristy. Rhosya was still there, having a timid conversation with the priest. They were discussing the virtues of something called woundwort, but both looked up as the Star Brother came in.

"Thank you," he said simply. "For your hospitality."

The priest grunted. "You came to visit my Master," he said. "Thank Him."

"I did," Brother Brendan agreed. "But I hope we may be at peace, you and I."

"Just don't ask me to spy for the Star Brothers," Father Caron told him. "You may learn what you can and report it to your superiors. But leave us to suffer what we must, without your interference."

"That may be more than we can do," a voice said from the doorway. Gris Wolfgang came in, followed by the other Faring Guard. "You do not know what these corporations are like, Father. Even Brother Brendan has had less experience than we."

"A corporation is not a god," the priest told him. "It is made up of human souls and two of these souls are here now at Harrow. I know what *they* are like, at least."

"Two?" Brother Brendan asked in surprise. "I heard only of this one woman, though I don't even know her name."

"Her name is Marja Sienko. And, yes, there are two. She has with her a slave, a bodyguard named Franz Wells. He is a Christian."

This was a surprise. "Are we likely to see either of them?" the Star Brother asked.

"I don't know. Doctor Sienko has been ill and they haven't been out all this week."

"Yes, we heard that she was ill," Brother Brendan admitted. "Someone said she had been poisoned."

"I'm told it was a natural sickness. She appears to be recovering."

"Then we may catch sight of her."

"Do you plan to announce yourself?" the priest asked him curiously.

The other man shook his head. "The longer my presence remains a secret, the more chance I – or my superiors, rather – might have to –" He trailed off with an apologetic little shrug. "We have no treaty with Pesc," he said. "It wouldn't be too hard for them to remove us."

"So your order *does* intend to interfere. Yet you did not hesitate to reveal yourself to me."

"You are vouched for both by the pastor at Welyn and also by Boss Sergay."

"That old reprobate! Just because I saved him from hanging once –"

The Star Brother looked at him in surprise. "You are the second person who claims that honor," he said ingenuously. "Has he been saved from the same fate twice?"

"Probably more times than that," Father Caron said, with a glance at Rhosya who lowered her eyes and tried not to smile. "Well, your secret is as safe with me as it is with the travelers. But trust no one else while you are here in Harrow! And don't put too much strain on *my* good will either."

There was nothing else to say. Father Caron might not believe it, but his colony was going to need help. Though Brother Brendan couldn't say what form that might take; after all, the nature of their peril was not clear – yet.

Ah well, he thought. These things were in God's hands.

As they reached the market square, they saw that a few booths were set up – mostly foodstuffs. Rhosya stopped to haggle over a round of cheese while one of the vendors pointed out the house where the Pesc woman was lodged. All three offworlders paused to study the façade of a dwelling somewhat finer than most, two storied and decorated with carved and painted shutters.

There was a small garden in front and a walkway leading up to the entrance. The house sported several large windows on its handsome front and even as they looked, a curtain was twitched aside as though someone looked out.

Later that evening, Sergay announced that he was going to visit the Tree-house Inn and would Brother Brendan and his friends like to come along? As it happened, they would, and shortly after the fourth sun disappeared below the horizon, they set out on a roundabout course, skirting the eastern rim of the town until they reached a turnoff. Here the lane became a street of warehouses and tenements where men with watchful eyes faded into the shadows while painted women flaunted themselves in rag-curtained doorways.

The Lost Rythans gave most of their coins to beggar children, forgetting that it was offworld money and likely to cause confusion. They kept their hands on their sword hilts as they passed groups of swaggering youths and looked disapprovingly away from the half-dressed girls.

The nebula was rising as they reached the inn where a small, scar-faced man staggered out, collapsing nearly at their feet. A harp fell from his loosening hands, jangling a protest as it hit the street. Wonderingly, Brother Brendan reached down and picked it up.

CHAPTER 7

MARJA WOKE TO THE SOUND of voices in the corridor. The nebula was shining in the window, brighter than the nightlight burning beside her bed. She felt much stronger than she had and wondered what time it was.

Who was out there? She heard Wells' voice and another. Hadn't she told him not to receive guests when she wasn't there? Not to put himself forward –

Before she could try to rise, her bodyguard slipped in the door, saw that she was awake and hurried over to her side. "The constable has come," he said in a low voice. "He has news for you. Your secretary said I had better wake you. Will you see him?"

She sat up at once. "What is it?" she asked. "Has there been word from the bishop?"

He shook his head. "Better let him tell you," he said, handing her the wrapper.

"What time is it?" Treelight rotated once every twenty-eight standard hours with regard to the largest of its suns and so this arbitrary number was used to mark the standard hours.

"Nearly midnight," Wells told her. "Twenty seven hours."

She nodded. "Send him in and make sure you overhear whatever it is," she directed him.

Constable Wynn was no master. Should he wish to flatter her, it would be with even less finesse than that of Master Madoc. But luckily the thought had not crossed his mind. He deferred to her only as the representative of the reigning corporation and made no effort to recruit her as a personal ally.

"I am glad to see you recovered," he said perfunctorily, "and sorry to disturb you at this hour."

"You would not come without good reason," she said.

He nodded. "We've just had a rider in with news from the north – a village halfway between Harrow and the wildwood. There was a raid and Master Madoc said I should bring you a report. He said you already knew about the druids."

She sat up straighter, curling her hands into fists. "He told me there were rumours of a revolutionary group, yes. Are they coming here?"

The constable shook his head. "That was yesterday, that raid," he said. "We only had official confirmation a couple hours ago. Came down the river to Aber and the townsfolk chased them off. Sunk one of their boats and killed some of them in the water."

"I will need to report this to my superiors," she said. "We can't have civil disorder here. What do these people *want* – do you know? Do they think they can gain independence from the corporation?"

Constable Wynn was not a speculative man. He only shrugged. "The master said you might be able to call down help for us. From them up there, I mean."

"I'll have to talk to the coordinator," she replied. "And I'll need more information before I do."

"You can ask the militia when they get here," he said.

"Yes, I'll do that. Thank you."

When he had gone, she got up. "I'm well enough now," she told the robot when it came in. The thing did not offer any opposition. "Hook me up with Hu," she added while she hunted about for some clothing.

But Pesc 7 was on the opposite side of the planet. The robosecretary told her she would have to wait until morning to talk to the coordinator.

"Alright," she said. "Have you anything at all on file about these rebels? Some reference by a corporate inspector maybe?"

The machine continued to smile at her while it accessed its memory. "Robber bands," it said. "A disaffected religious organization."

Marja pulled on her shoes. "Were any of them called Druids?"

"There is no reference to that. But there still might be a connection with the religious group," the secretary told her. "Druids were ancient worshippers of trees."

She nodded dubiously. "Details?"

"About twenty planet years back an administrator of one of the churches began creating novel doctrines. There was some civil disturbance at the time the Star Brothers came for their regular visit. We do not have details of what happened then, but the disturbances ceased. The order wanted to return yearly for the next decade but permission was denied."

"Was this person saying anything about the wildwood? That it was – oh, holy or something?"

TREELIGHT

The robot continued to smile, its arms at its sides. "No," it said. "The argument concerned the dual nature of Christ."

"I doubt that has anything to do with *trees*," Marja said in irritation and stepped past her secretary out into the corridor. She had to hold onto the railing to descend the stairs. There were lights below – was the constable still here? If not, then someone else was.

She took another step until she was standing where she had been when she saw that robot light coming from the sitting room. As the memory returned, she hesitated. But tonight the house was lit with candles and one or two oil lamps, she told herself. She had left the robot behind her in the upstairs corridor.

After two more steps, someone came quickly toward her, hands outstretched. His handsome face radiated surprise – and relief – as he fixed his blue eyes on hers. It was Master Frayle.

She stopped in embarrassment, remembering the dreadful things she had been dreaming about the man and wondering how she could have cast him in the role of heartless villain. He had no reason to wish her harm. He and the other masters stood to gain more than anyone else from the development of their world, and besides –

But she stifled that particular thought.

Nevertheless, her smile for him was more genuine than the one she had called up for Master Madoc, as she let him guide her into the room and help her to a seat. This time he took a chair, leaving her alone on the bench. She saw Wells turn back from fastening the outer door and, at her nod, he stepped into the dining room.

"I do not think," Frayle said when they were alone, "that I need tell you how concerned I was at your illness. Your bodyguard says that you suffered from something called an allergic reaction. That our world is so strange to you that it made you ill."

"Yes. But I'm recovered now," she said.

"I would not have come tonight," he went on, "knowing how much you need your rest, but I saw the constable leaving and knew you would not only be awake, but possibly concerned at the news he brought."

She was more than concerned. How many other things had the corporation missed, she wondered. How many more holes were there in her briefing – and how dangerous were they?

"He said there had been a raid somewhere by an organization called the Druids," she said quickly. "I believe your militia was involved. They should have more news when they get here tomorrow."

"Ah. But the druids are not a gang as you seem to think." He frowned as though he found the subject distasteful. "They are something quite different."

"I was wondering," she admitted. "I mean, the name sounds more like a cult."

"Like heretics, you mean?" He shook his head. "Not that, either. But they are evil, Lady Sienko. Evil and inimical to the rest of us." He gave her a troubled look. "Their raid was an attack on the very humanity of those people at Aber. Parts of the town had to be burned."

"Burned?"

He nodded emphatically. "Burned. As the druids should be, though this is not allowed. They will only hang."

She looked at him blankly. "What do you mean? I thought they got away."

"There were two prisoners taken. The militia is bringing them here."

"To hang?"

"After they have been questioned, certainly. I'm told there is a bandit in the gaol right now, and Master Madoc will dispatch all three of them together. The crowd likes a spectacle."

Then he caught the look on her face. "I hope this business has not upset you," he said in some surprise. "So soon after you have been ill –"

She swallowed. "Nooo. It's just that we don't – Pesc doesn't allow capital punishment on its colony worlds."

"I'm sorry to hear that," he said, "but surely in a case like this your superiors will understand. The highwayman is a murderer, you see. And these druids are worse. But of course you need not be there when – when justice is done." For just one moment, she thought she saw a look of desperation – of pain almost – cross his face. But then it was gone, if it had ever been there at all.

"I will talk to the constable in the morning," she said, not at all sure of her ground. "I know you have your own customs and that you are –" She had almost used the word "backward" but she caught herself and amended it to "used to executing your criminals. There are many things here that must be changed."

She expected him to say, "Of course", but he didn't. Instead he gave her a look of great gentleness. "I am sorry that so many worries have fallen on your shoulders," he said. "As you say, our customs must be very different from those of other worlds, and there is much for us to learn about culture and refinement and all. But this is not a matter for – that is, we had better proceed with our normal affairs, at least for the time being. We can discuss changes at a later date."

She saw perspiration beading his forehead, but he gave her a kindly smile and stood up. "In the morning," he said, "I will call on you if I may. There should be more news by then, and perhaps you can interview someone from the militia."

"Of course you may call," she said, not sure whether she had not been insulted. Did he imply that such matters were for the men to deal with and that she, as a lady, had best keep out of them?

Something constrained her to add, "And I will also be in touch with *Pesc 7*." But she did not tell him outright that she was going to ask Hu to intervene and stop the hangings. There was no point in borrowing trouble.

He stepped over to her and to her surprise, he took her hand and kissed it. This was something she had never seen done before, except in a vid. But he made it seem so natural that she was not offended. For a primitive, Frayle could be as charming as he was stubborn.

THE PLACE LOOKED LIKE A long disused cellar, though it wasn't, of course. The cobwebs were no more real than the mildew that clung to all the surfaces. Dust almost expected to find a skeleton chained to one of the scabrous walls, but the creator of this scene had apparently not thought of it. At least not yet.

He gave a grim chuckle – a virtual chuckle, that is. Maybe his own virtual bones would be the first.

He had been passing through a series of disorienting corridors – a labyrinth, in fact – and only now did it begin to look as though he had broken into the edge of the restricted storage area. He had found defenses, places of pain and realms of psychedelic madness, and these he had traversed successfully. So far it had been like untangling a knot with no real surprises, only a lot of painstaking tedium.

But now he was coming into a region where anything could happen.

He shook himself, his assumed body responding well as he forced out the last remnants of contamination. He had left a few of the cortex's defenders dead in the hallways, and he had taken wounds which pained him, but did not slow him down. The alarms had been silenced, but that only meant that no outsider – no human being – would be alerted. There were other entities in this place, built-in programs nastier than anything merely human.

The dungeon was quite large and, at first, Dust was at a loss to understand what it was doing here. He expected something to attack him, some creation of the programmer's brain, but nothing did. Instead, it almost looked as though he had come into some sort of loop, a self-perpetuating wasteland where he might wander indefinitely.

He sat down for a moment to think, careless of the filth that adhered to his armor. And then he realized that he was sitting on a chest and that the lid was straining upward. He leaped off at once and stood watching it, gun in hand.

Slowly the thing creaked open, the wood itself crumbling as the detritus of untold centuries – or so it was supposed to seem – slid backward to make a pile on the floor. A hand emerged, looking like a claw in the febrile light.

Dust aimed his gun at that hand, waiting. Sometimes they would talk to you, these guardians. They weren't all mindless robots by any means. Some could be quite sophisticated, some even like himself, the remnants of real human beings. He had met several such in the course of his work.

The lid rose further and something sat up. He braced himself. There was not much chance it would be attractive or even presentable. Already there was a bad smell.

Suddenly the light went out. With an oath, Dust kicked in his infrared vision and leaped back as a long, yellowish form hurled itself in his direction. Claws raked his face and the thing snarled as he brought up his gun and fired. There was some effect but his attacker wasn't *that* sort of construct. Dust quickly metamorphosed the weapon into a sword.

With one swing, he cut off its arm and slashed at a face he was glad he couldn't see very well. The creature howled and kicked his legs from under him, sending Dust sprawling on the filthy floor. Ichor spurted from the creature's wound, making everything slippery as he scrambled up panting, raising his sword for another blow.

"Your head is next," Dust told it.

"Wait!"

He waited. Now would be the time to strike a bargain if they were going to.

"Why did you come here?" it asked.

"Information," Dust replied. "What else?"

"You do not come to sabotage?"

"Not if I get what I'm after."

"What will you pay?"

Dust shook his head. "You know better than that."

"Then I challenge you!"

"Then I take off your head!" With one swing, the thing was done and the construct became a mess on the floor.

At once chests began to open all over the room and creatures by no means homogenous crawled out. Dust backed toward one wall, sword ready as they came for him. He was stronger than these individually, but they were many and he was only one.

Abruptly, something materialized beside him, a woman's form. She was grinning a comradely grin as she raised her own gleaming blade.

And then the creatures were on them.

~

THE INN WAS CROWDED AND most of the customers looked up at once as the newcomers appeared in the doorway, the unconscious harper at their feet. "That is Ewan," Sergay whispered. "They'll be disappointed that he cannot play."

Brother Brendan looked down at the man who seemed to be sleeping peacefully, and then at the harp he held in his hands. It was a lovely thing of a style familiar to him. He ran one finger lightly across the strings.

"Ah, you shouldn't have done that," the traveler said as two or three men rose and came toward them. From another direction, the innkeeper hurried across with mugs of beer. "Now you'll sing for your beer, and no mistake."

The Star Brother nodded. The whole scene brought back memories of another man – a boy, rather, who had gone with his father to the fair. There was fiddle music and, after that, harping as someone sang the old songs of Earth. It was then he had asked to learn to play, he and his brother Seamus.

"Well," he told Sergay, "I suppose I'd better do that." He stepped inside. The others followed, the Lost Rythans pausing to pick up the sodden owner of the harp and deposit him on a nearby table where he curled himself into a ball and went on sleeping.

Without further ado, Brother Brendan lifted the instrument and began to play. It was very like the one he had played before and he paused to tune a string. And, he told his conscience sturdily, it wasn't as though he stepped aside from the path of duty. After all, he was here to serve in whatever capacity God chose for him.

He gave them a song, half in Basic and half in the pidgin Gaelic of his homeworld. He sang of broken hearts and broken heads, which mostly comprised the music of his home colony.

When he had done, they cheered him and a mug of beer was thrust into his hands. Friendly faces crowded about, as even the bemused Lost Rythans were taken to the hearts of the colonists.

A blowsy, red-haired girl seated herself on Sergay's lap, eyeing the offworlders with frank interest. "This is Rhianna," the boss said. "She welcomes us every time we come to Harrow."

"Indeed I do," she said, laughing. "But who are your friends?"

Sergay indicated Brother Brendan, who was still somewhat bemused by their reception. "This one's a member of a religious order," he said wickedly. "On leave, of course."

At this, the young man tried not to blush, as the girl laughed even more heartily. They were dependent on Sergay's good will, but at the moment he found it hard to resist an urge to brain him with the harp. Presently, the two Lost Rythans were introduced, and the girl gave each in turn a winning smile.

As soon as he could, Brother Brendan withdrew from the others and took a seat further away. There, he sipped his beer silently while he studied the assembled company. Their faces reflected the hard experience of years living on the fringes of Treelight's mainstream culture – for it was plain to him that these were the untamed outcasts of the colony. For them, as for the travelers, Pesc offered nothing except annihilation.

The girl had already left her perch on Sergay's lap and was flirting openly with the two Faring Guards, who regarded her with an uncertain mixture of disapproval and curiosity. From another part of the room, a local man was also looking on, his ruddy features beginning to assume an unequivocal expression.

A few other patrons had turned in his direction, as slowly the talk died down. The Star Brother sensed danger and would have risen – but before he could, the colonist stood up, revealing a size and breadth of shoulder that reminded him of Gwern the smith. With remarkable agility, considering his size, the man leaped a table and launched himself directly at Gris Wolfgang.

The Lost Rythan was not taken entirely by surprise, but, even so, the sheer weight of his adversary knocked him to the floor, while a mighty fist connected with his jaw before he could get his hands up to defend himself. Ard Matthew stood irresolute as Sergay motioned him to stand aside.

"Man on man," he said. "This isn't about killing and robbing. Let them fight."

Shaking his head, Gris Wolfgang surged to his feet. The two were of a size – indeed there must be more than a few giants living on Treeworld – and the Faring Guard barely ducked another blow before landing one of his own that left the colonist staggering back, spitting blood.

With a growl, the other man charged and the two closed, each straining for a hold. A bench fell over, along with the men who had been sitting on it. These joined the shouting crowd as some rooted for their own man and some for the stranger. To his amusement, Brother Brendan saw Ard Matthew and Sergay cheering with the rest.

For a moment Gris Wolfgang was overborne, staggering beneath the blows of his opponent. Then the other man – Bran was his name apparently, for that was what his fans were shouting – failed to duck a powerful punch and was knocked to the floor. He scrambled to his feet at once and threw himself on the Lost Rythan.

Gris Wolfgang was ready for him and this time, Bran did not rise. Someone fetched a pitcher of water to throw over the fallen man, while the Lost Rythan bent down solicitously to help him up.

Brother Brendan shook his head at this, but apparently the rules of fair play held. The colonist grinned widely, showing where a few teeth had been knocked out in former fights, and clapped his adversary on the back. "Well done, stranger," he cried, forgetting what they had fought about. "Come and drink with me!"

At this the crowd dispersed as more beer flowed – and more after that. Sometime later, the Star Brother found Sergay sitting next to him while, at another table, Rhianna perched herself on Bran's lap, drinking with the Lost Rythans as though nothing untoward had happened.

And it hadn't, Brother Brendan realized. This whole business was a ritual as old as humankind. Sergay must have known what would happen when he brought his visitors to this place, and he had almost certainly foreseen the outcome. Soon there were calls for more music and, as poor Ewan remained in a stupor, the Star Brother was obliged to provide it.

He played and sang for a while, until they let him lay down the harp. Only then did he get a chance to study the patrons of the inn more closely. He liked them, despite the fact that there were some here who might have been among the robber band back on the Harrow Road. He almost regretted that their kind must soon perish, along with the horses and wagons, the great farms, and the dirt-floored churches.

He looked sidewise at Sergay and saw that the other man knew this, too. There would be no niche for the Treehouse Inn and none for Bran and his giggling lapful. They would be swept away along with the wildwood and anything else that stood in the way of progress and profit.

The nebula was slipping to the other side of the sky when a dusty, thirsty man came in and planted himself conspicuously at the bar. "Beer," he said and when he had drunk, he looked around at the company. "I've just come from the militia," he said loudly. "Brought news from the north."

The others looked up eagerly – those who could still follow what he said. It was plain enough he would not have to pay for his beer.

"The damned druids have attacked a town," the newcomer announced. "Got right in with their slimy treeworms before they were seen."

"Where?" someone called.

"Aber. The people had to burn part of it down."

"They get away?"

"Not all. They're bringing a couple down to hang."

The party broke up soon after this, some thoughtful, some excited, and some too drunk to care. Sergay turned to Brother Brendan who was carefully replacing the harp in the hands of its owner. "So much for tales," he said.

Behind them, Gris Wolfgang was parting cordially from Bran. "If you ever need a friend," the colonist said over and over as he laid one arm about the Lost Rythan's shoulders, "you have only to seek me out. They know me here – Rhianna can always tell you where I am."

"We'll meet again," Gris Wolfgang promised. There was no doubt that *he* had had a good time at the inn, though his Lost Rythan conscience would undoubtedly reproach him for it later. Behind these two, Ard Matthew was taking leave from another pair of boon companions. It had been a much needed break for them all.

As they left, only Brother Brendan noticed another cloaked figure slip out the door, turning in the opposite direction. The Star Brother had seen him earlier, sitting against a wall, neither drinking nor talking to any of the company. What had shown of his face beneath a pulled up hood was dark, almost dirty looking as though he had smeared clay on his cheeks. As he departed, there was something halting in his walk, as though he might be lame.

MARJA OVERSLEPT, PARTLY BECAUSE SHE had been up so late the night before and partly because she was not as fully recovered as she thought. Wells finally came in and woke her to say that a wagonload of boxes had arrived from Madoc Farm. It was the cargo Marja had requested before she became ill and it had been sent down by shuttle three days before from *Pesc 7*.

If the robosecretary had not ordered him to wake her, he would not have done it even then. She had grown thinner during her illness and the veins at her temples were bluish. Even her hair had lost its luster.

"I'll have Tara bring up your breakfast," he told her when he had given her the news about the shipment. "And then would you like me to start sorting the things they sent?"

She shook her head. "I'll see to it, Wells. And tell the – tell Tara I'll be coming down."

When she reached the dining room, she could see the crates piled against one wall. Here would be comfort, she thought. Powered lights and a heater and a well-stocked vid player. There would be things for the masters as well, Madoc and Frayle and the others whose names she could not remember, but who must be drawn into her orbit as soon as possible.

She had not chosen the gifts, which was just as well. After dress goods for the women and liquor for the men, her imagination dried up. Up to now there had been an embargo on anything that might raise the level of technology. Human beings could be endlessly resourceful and the colonists were perfectly capable of dismantling machinery in hopes of studying its principles. It was too much of a risk.

The girl bustled in as she sat down, bringing her what looked like porridge and a plate of sausages along with tea and buns. Marja had made it plain there would be no Lenten fast in her household except when there were guests.

"I must try again to contact the ship," she said as she ate. "Perhaps Coordinator Hu can order them to stop the hangings."

The bodyguard regarded her silently over his teacup.

"There is a policy against capital punishment in corporate colonies," she reminded him sharply.

"Net Central made that law for the corporations," he told her. "It isn't followed."

She frowned. "I know they don't oversee the corporations very closely," she admitted. "But these people seem to have a lot of executions. I'm sure that when I bring it to the coordinator's attention he'll agree that it is too wasteful– of manpower, I mean." She trailed off. Reality was proving a lot more real than anything her training had prepared her for.

Wells did not answer this directly. "You should be able to reach him later this morning," was all he said.

She sat back. "I suppose we could call down the robosecretary to help sort these things," she said. Then, seeing the expressionless look he gave her, she changed her mind. "No, we'll do it ourselves. Let's get started."

Suddenly it felt like Christmas morning – for they had almost always had the means to celebrate this holiday in her childhood home. To be sure, the children had been pleased with very little, but the excitement was what mattered. To get up and know that *this* particular day was like no other!

Wells took a knife from the table and began to pry off the coverings while she groped about in the packing. Yes, here were the bolts of offworld fabric and – for the first time – made up clothing. There were tunics and trousers for the women along with smart-looking jackets and leggings and shoes such as she herself had worn at the university.

"Look!" she exclaimed. "They've got press fasteners and everything. Won't these people be surprised!"

He did not answer as he struggled with a power pack. "Here's your water heater," he said, pulling out a smooth metallic sphere. "Unfortunately you don't have running water so we can't feed into it."

She examined the thing. "It's as though I have to import an entire infra-structure," she said. "But surely we can *pour* in the water, can't we?"

He looked dubious. "I don't think you'll get very much hot water that way," he said. "It's an instant heater – you're just supposed to pipe it through, any amount you want. It keeps flowing, see, and then out this valve here –"

"I don't care!" she said. "I want a hot bath and I'm going to have one!"

Grinning a little, he got up and went to answer the door. It was Father Caron and he did not look pleased as he saw the corporation's largesse strewn throughout the rooms. Marja stood up. "Good morning, Father," she said formally. "Please come in."

He gave her a temperate greeting, nodding to Wells. "I am happy to see you recovered, Dr. Sienko," he said. "Master Frayle told me he had seen you and that you no longer kept to your bed."

She gave him an uncertain look. "Yes," she said. "He came about the – the trouble you've had in the north."

The priest nodded. "I'm afraid this will spoil your good opinion of our colony," he ventured, watching her.

"Not really. I should have realized there would be many things I would have to discover for myself. I mean, Dagon's agents only came every five years and it's beginning to look as though they did not do a very thorough job."

"The Dagon people – usually it was only one man – stayed almost exclu-sively at Madoc Farm," he told her. "I only met one of them and that was because he sent for me to answer some questions about our school. He wanted to make sure the Star Brothers were not involved."

"And were they?"

"No. They are not even allowed to help us in nontechnical ways. We could have done with a great many things which were denied to us unless we could get them from the masters. Education for our children, on any level, was far from being a priority."

He recollected himself. "The Star Brothers sometimes came here," he admitted.

"But they have always been scrupulous about keeping the terms of their agreement. We teach reading, ciphering and catechism. Nothing more was ever allowed."

She set down a lamp, and took a seat. "That will change," she promised. "Education is near the top of the list for Pesc."

The priest sat forward a little, staring at the pile of clothing spilling out of one box. "Well we seem to have gotten along without offworld training so far," he admitted. And then, "What *is* all that?" he could not help asking.

She went over and held up a suit of shimmering blue. When she shook it out, constellations of multicolored stars seemed to bloom and fade, forming clusters that changed position constantly across the fabric.

He reached out a hand and she gave him the trousers and jacket to feel.

"This is what we wear on other worlds," she said. "It is from Earth."

He handed the things back. "No man on Treelight would wear such a thing," he said and Wells turned away, hiding a grin.

"Men don't wear these suits," she explained. "Women do. I haven't opened the men's clothing yet but I hope to see the masters set an example. These things are for their wives and daughters."

At this, Father Caron gave her a shocked look. "Surely not!" he exclaimed. "What do you take them for? Prostitutes?"

At this, Wells had to step into the kitchen.

"But the colors are good – I mean they are better than anything made in the colony. The time of thankless work is over! Your people will have leisure to enjoy life!"

"If they spend their leisure dressing up in those glorified night clothes, they had much better work," the priest said. "Such things are indecent."

She pressed her lips together tightly. Then, "Perhaps the corporation has moved too quickly," she admitted. "I know change takes time. But your attitude certainly does not help. When the bishop comes –"

"You expect the bishop to do great things, don't you?"

"Yes I do! He's been offworld. The Star Brothers took him to Sachsen to be consecrated. He will have seen what you are all missing out on."

"I'm sure he has."

"I want you to begin helping me now!" she said. "The masters have been eager to cooperate, but they do not have the influence you have. Once you priests have been taught how to begin remolding the customs –"

He shook his head slowly. "You cannot buy us as you can the masters," he said coldly.

"Then you'll be replaced!" she burst out angrily. "That is one of the first recommendations I'm going to make. Until we get the schools up and running, you are the only cultural leaders we have and those of you who refuse to cooperate will have to retire."

"Who will replace me?"

She glared at him. "I'm sure not all the clergy are as –" Her voice trailed off as she saw Wells come back into the dining room. He was no longer grinning.

"Stubborn?" Father Caron asked. "Reactionary? Obstructive?"

"Please excuse me," she said. "I've been ill and my patience is not what it should be."

"Nor mine. And I have less excuse. Your corporation is, as you say, precipitate."

A knock on the door announced another caller and Wells went over to admit Master Frayle. The master greeted the priest respectfully and then turned his attention to Marja. Seeing him, she remembered the news of the night before and the probable fate of the captured cult members. Then, seeing him look at her, she remembered a great deal more.

"You find me sorting out the first installment of Pesc's bounty," she said trying to speak lightly. She gestured to the opened boxes. "That thing there," she added, seeing that his attention was suddenly riveted on the water heater, "is going to make it possible for me to bathe without heating water on the kitchen stove."

"May I?" He stepped closer and began examining the sphere, seeking the workings and not finding them. He was plainly baffled as he picked up the power pack.

While she tried to explain to him the principle on which it operated, Wells took a seat next to the priest. Marja could not hear much of what they said to each other but once she heard Father Caron exclaim aloud in irritation. "What is the point?" he cried and then lowered his voice once more. She must have angered him more deeply than she thought.

She determined to ask the bodyguard what they had been discussing, later when her guests were gone. He had been warned already not to deal independently with the colonists and though she would never sentence him to the punishment of the robot, he still needed to be reminded that she was his superior.

Frayle had set down the power pack and was trying not to stare too hard at the rest of the boxes. Marja saw his glance slide over the pile of offworld clothing and decided not to make a point of displaying it. If the priest's reaction was any indication, she had better save such things until the population had had more exposure to offworld fashions.

She turned instead to Father Caron. "So you know that the masters plan to hang the prisoners from that raid," she said, wanting to see his reaction.

"Dangerous vanity," he snorted. "They should have been killed where they were captured!"

Marja stood up in a welter of packing material. "Is that what your church teaches?" she demanded.

"I've always thought it was. What do they do with soul-killers on *your* homeworld?"

"*Soul-killers*? What do you mean?"

Frayle was giving him a warning look and at this the priest hesitated. "These matters do not concern your corporation," he said at last. "Or at least I hope they don't."

She turned to Frayle. "What does he mean by soul-killers?" she demanded.

The master shook his head. "Can you wait," he asked, "until we have a full report on the incident? Otherwise the information you receive may turn out to be false. You don't want to act on a rumor, do you?"

He spoke with such calm reasonableness that she hesitated. "They *are* a cult, aren't they?" she said at last. "What you call heretics. Is that why you want to kill them?" She was thinking about all the religious intolerance of the past and how such an attitude was only to be expected in this primitive colony. There was so much to set right in this place!

"I still don't think I would call them heretics," Frayle said hesitantly. "But perhaps you are right after all."

He had no time to finish as another guest was ushered into the room. This time it was Master Madoc and he did not look happy to see Frayle already in possession, as it were, of the room and of its contents.

Marja greeted him cordially however, and he bowed to her, his features visibly rearranging themselves into something less piqued. His eyes kept slipping sidewise to the pile of boxes against the wall and the things scattered on the floor.

"You come at a good time," she told him with a smile. "I was just unpacking the shipment I had them send down to your farm. I appreciate your arranging to have it brought here while I was ill."

"Naturally I want to do anything I can to aid you in your mission," he said. "And I do hope you are stronger this morning."

She nodded. "Have you news of the militia?" she asked, cutting off another fawning speech.

"I'm afraid they haven't arrived yet," he admitted. "But I expect them within the hour. Of course you will be informed at once."

"You will question them at the gaol?" Frayle asked him sharply, his pale face changing a little as he spoke.

The other man gave him a look of surprise. "Yes. And naturally I expect you to be present."

Again that rictus passed over his features. He turned away for a moment. "I will be there," he said in a low voice.

The priest gave him a speculative look but said nothing.

Madoc, meanwhile was rubbing his hands together as he gazed around at the objects already unpacked. His eye was caught by the bright pile of fabrics and he walked over to examine one of the garments. "These are the fashions of the starworlds?" he asked.

Marja nodded. "I'm afraid they may be too advanced for your people," she admitted. "But there are also some uncut lengths of cloth for your wife to make up."

Madoc held up one of the tunics to his own rotund form as though wondering how it would look. She didn't have the heart to tell him he was holding up part of a woman's suit. Instead, she gestured Wells over to help her unpack more of the shipment.

The bodyguard exhumed a quantity of power packs along with more lamps and a cooker. Another box provided yet another cooker and by this, she knew that the ban on offworld technology was no longer in effect. "Show Master Madoc how to operate these things," she said to Wells. "He may take some of them back with him in the wagon."

The master was enchanted. "But this is almost miraculous," he cried. "A new day – certainly a new day has dawned!"

Frayle nodded, his eyes still on the unopened containers. "I wonder," he said half to himself, "if the corporation has seen fit to send us any weapons?"

Marja looked at him sharply and he gave her a deprecating smile. "We do have our troubles here," he reminded her. "Though we will try not to let them intrude on your programme. But obviously –"

No one mentioned the raid or the prisoners now on their way to Harrow gaol. Father Caron gave Frayle a hard look, however.

It was past noon when everything had been unpacked and Madoc's wagon loaded with gifts for himself and the other masters of the area. Certain items were set aside for Frayle, and he thanked her profusely, though he would not, he told her be returning to his own farm for several days more. He tried not show his disappointment at the lack of firearms among the other things.

Madoc had gone, his presence being required at the gaol, and the priest was once more talking to Wells, when Frayle drew Marja aside. "As I said," he began, "I will be returning home in a few days. Would it be presumptuous to ask if you might be willing to accompany me for a visit to Frayle Farm? With the help of these gifts of yours, we can make you as comfortable – more comfortable than you have been so far. And," he added, "we will pass through Bannyclay en route. It is the seat of the bishop."

The invitation surprised her a little, though perhaps it shouldn't have. "But I must consult with the coordinator," she told him. "It was not planned that I should travel about until more personnel had been landed."

"Of course," he agreed. "I wouldn't want you to do anything against corporation policy. Perhaps I may see you later today? I have duties at the gaol along with Master Madoc, but I could call on you afterward."

She nodded.

At this, the master stood up and took his leave. Marja saw him out. He had come on horseback, accompanied by a servant and she watched the two ride off across the square.

As she turned from the door, she met Father Caron who was also departing. The priest, too, was regarding Frayle and his man as they disappeared into a lane.

"He has invited you to Frayle Farm," Father Caron said without preamble. "Hasn't he?"

She wanted to ask him what business it was of his, but she held her tongue. Let him judge her as he might, the narrow-minded old hypocrite! He wouldn't hold his position for long!

The priest gave her a look that said he had not only read her thoughts but found them amusing. "And you will pass through Bannyclay," he added. "How convenient."

"It seems the bishop can't come to Harrow," she said, trying to sound casual. "So I might as well do him the courtesy of going to see *him*. Unless you think he will refuse to see me?"

"Oh no," Father Caron said, that inward mockery showing in his eyes. "He'll see you alright. Didn't Master Frayle tell you the bishop was his brother?"

CHAPTER 8

THE ADVENT OF THE MILITIA became a triumph, a victory parade that straggled from the north road all the way to the gaol. Of course they weren't all members of the militia, for the small band had acquired a tail of followers collected from most of the farms and freeholds north of Harrow.

From his position near the Treehouse Inn, Brother Brendan had a good view of the grim-faced men walking their tired horses. They had been in the saddle for most of the night in order to show the townsfolk proof not only of their own prowess, but of a menace the masters could no longer ignore.

Their prisoners trudged along as they had all night, arms bound behind them, bare faces pale and marked with strange, silvery lines. Their long hair straggled, bleached looking, but fouled with dirt and blood. They stared straight ahead like sleepwalkers, staggering a bit with weariness.

Brother Brendan tried to move closer as they passed by, for there was something familiar in the pattern of those marks. He was sure the Brothers of St. Hubert had borne such designs in shades of purple – but *they* were dying.

Were *these*? Or was this the fate worse than death the brothers spoke of? The fate they were willing to die to avoid? Had these men been made into something less than human?

The procession passed and all that remained were the boys running behind, shouting and waving sticks in a scene of mock battle. He turned away. Beside him, Ard Matthew had also observed what he had and apparently understood as he had understood.

"God help them," the Faring Guard murmured and the Star Brother echoed his words. It was a prayer rather than an exclamation.

What had happened to these men?

Gris Wolfgang, standing a little behind the other two had either not seen or not understood. But when Brother Brendan told him about the markings on the druids, he grew thoughtful. "Could they possibly have chosen this for themselves?" he asked in a low voice.

"I don't know," the Star Brother told him. "But they are going to hang for it, whether they chose it or not. And people are saying that they have been trying to infect others."

None of the travelers had come to see the parade. When Brother Brendan's party had awakened that morning, rather later than they usually did, it was to find everyone busy setting up pavilions. "Be a fair out here tomorrow," Sergay said. "Got permission from that Master Madoc. There's such a crowd in town and more coming for the execution next week that he seemed to think they needed something to do."

"So you've been elected to keep them out of trouble," Brother Brendan had replied. He could not help being disgusted by the savagery of these people – or rather their callousness. And yet, what if the druids had, in some way, lost their humanity? What if they really *were* trying to infect others?

But if that were the case, they could not be held responsible for their actions. Could they?

"It seems an odd thing," Gris Wolfgang said suddenly, as they made their way back to the camp, "to celebrate the administering of justice in this way."

The Star Brother shrugged. "If it *is* justice," he said. "Though I doubt anyone else is thinking about that aspect of things."

"But that makes it worse," the Faring Guard persisted. "If the men are guilty, then their execution should take place in seemly wise. Their fellow citizens should encourage them to repent of their crimes."

"Come and have some tea," Brother Brendan said, steering his companions to one of the cookfires. Rhosya was there stirring a pot. She looked up as they approached.

"Sergay said you would be hungry. You were out with him last night, I know. Carousing until near morning –"

"He seems no worse for the adventure," the Star Brother said shortly. He did not dispute her choice of the word. If she would have it so –

"My father never is. He is our leader and there are many things he must do for our welfare."

"For your *welfare*?"

"Indeed, he learned much that was useful while he was at the inn."

This was news to the other three. But the older man had not sat with them for all of the time they were there. Perhaps he had been listening in on conversations in other parts of the room.

"The fair is an example," she said. "Because he learned that the militia was coming with prisoners to hang, he went straight to Master Madoc early this morning to ask permission for all this." She waved one hand at the activity in the field.

"Permission they were glad to grant," Brother Brendan said. "Yes, I see. Your father seems to draw news from the air," he added, with a glance at Rhosya. "Certainly he's better at finding things out than we are."

He tried to eat but instead, he kept thinking about the strange silvery lines on the prisoner's faces and the way they had faced straight ahead as they limped along, oblivious, it would seem to the jeers of the crowd and the prodding of the mounted men. Was that bravado – or indifference? Or something else entirely?

His thoughts were interrupted as more and more people began arriving. A number of local merchants had joined in erecting their own booths, and several wagons were parked behind them. Brother Brendan and the others wandered over to look at what they were setting out.

Suddenly Rhosya came panting up, one hand to her side. "Someone from the militia has just been here talking to my father. I am summoned to the gaol to treat one of the prisoners. The highwayman – he was wounded when they captured him, and now they are afraid he will die."

The Star Brother stared at her in surprise.

"Will you come? Master Tregarth told my father that you were to see everything there is to see."

"Yes. Of course." He glanced at the Lost Rythans.

"We will walk about," Ard Matthew told him quietly. "There is much to see – and *hear*."

"Just stay out of trouble," Brother Brendan said as he hurried off with the girl. She paused to snatch up her bag of medicines before she led him back the way he had come. Presently they came to the lane the militia had taken and followed this to the gaol. When they arrived, they saw that a few men had remained as extra guards, but the rest were already dispersing to the local pubs and inns.

The constable recognized Rhosya at once. "Two of the masters are with the captain," he told her quickly, "and they've got the main office. But if you'll come this way." He made no objection when Brother Brendan followed her, assuming, no doubt, that he was one of her many kinsmen. He led them into a musty cell, lighted by one small, barred window high in the western wall.

"Here's Rhyn," he said. "Been here three days but now that slash he's got in his leg seems to be festering. It's made him feverish."

She hurried over to kneel beside a tall young man stretched out on a filthy blanket. His eyes were closed and his flushed face seemed to radiate heat.

"Fetch me some hot water," she said. "and bandages, if you've got any."

The constable, who seemed used to obeying her orders, left at once, locking the door behind him. Immediately the prisoner opened his eyes.

"Just lie still," Rhosya told him as he started to sit up. "I've got to clean this wound."

He blinked at her. "Clean it?" he repeated. "Why?"

"Get gangrene if I don't," she said, peeling off the blood-encrusted wrapping. He cried out as she got to the last part. "I'll wait for the water," she said, letting go. "Soak it off."

She turned to her bag and began sorting out some herbs. "I brought a bottle of beer," she told him. "I'll give it to you if you swallow this potion first. It's for pain and fever."

At this, the Star Brother stepped forward. "I have a med kit at my belt," he said, letting fall the cloak that covered him. "It's got antibiotics."

She looked at him. "This is a medicine?" she asked.

"Kills germs – infection. Makes it go away."

"Be nice to stop hurting," the young man said. "But I won't be needing the leg much longer." He gave the others a rakish grin.

"I'm sorry," Brother Brendan said. "Is there no hope of a reprieve?"

"None at all. They been after me for a while and now I'm fair caught."

Rhosya gave him her herbal drink and he choked it down. Afterwards, she handed him the beer but he was too ill to finish it. "Hope that stuff works soon," he whispered. "Didn't hurt this much when I first got cut."

"Your name is Rhyn?" the Star Brother asked as he bent over and administered a spray injection of antibiotic.

"It was last time someone cursed me."

"Rhyn what?"

"Oh, that's all. Would be, wouldn't it? Don't know who fathered me."

"God would know."

"God?" The man turned slightly, seeming to notice for the first time the habit peeping out from the cloak. "You a priest?"

"Star Brother." There didn't seem any harm in telling him. This Rhyn wasn't likely to either know or care what that meant.

"You shrive a man?"

"Only if no priest is available. I'm only a brother."

"Ah well. They'll have a priest there –"

There presumably meant the gallows. Brother Brendan was rather at a loss what to say next. Obviously the bandit didn't need comforting, and it seemed he meant to die as a Christian. His was a type the Star Brother had not met before.

A few minutes later, they heard the key in the door and the constable came in, carrying a steaming bucket and some rags not much cleaner than those Rhosya had been trying to remove from Rhyn's wounded leg.

Her medicine must have started to work, for he barely moaned as she cleaned the suppurating wound and swabbed it out with something that smelled like vinegar. It was a good choice, Brother Brendan thought. Painful but effective.

"He looks better already," the constable told her.

"Is it certain," she asked without looking up, "that he must die?"

"Oh to be sure. That's Rhyn Red-hand, one of the worst highwaymen in the district. Got friends, though. That's one of the reasons we've been given extra guards." He did not mention the other reason, but both his companions knew.

"And now, I'm afraid, you'll have to wait in one of the cells until a certain person has had at look at the other prisoners," he said apologetically. "Can't have him interrupted and can't have any of them find you here."

He left them in an empty cell. At least he didn't lock the door, the Star Brother noted. He looked questioningly at the straw piled on the floor, but Rhosya shook her head. "Lice," she warned him. "Better to stand up."

Presently they heard footsteps in the corridor, one set booted. Then another door creaked ajar and a cultivated voice told the constable to leave him.

"But Master Frayle, I can't hardly leave you alone with one of *them*."

"The thing is chained to the wall. Now get the hell out of here until I call you!"

They heard the constable retreat.

Presently there were low voices. First that of the master and then that of whatever was chained to the wall.

"I seek word of my son. Evan Frayle. Has he been among you?"

"You ask the servant of the wildwood for news of the living?" The voice was strangely uninflected, but not as though the speaker felt no emotion. There *were* passions latent but not human ones.

"He was living when I saw him last."

"But he may not be now," the strange voice replied. "How do you know you do not see him before you?" The taunt was doubly horrible, spoken as it was in that low, passionless voice.

"I would know."

"I cannot help you. And if he were one of us, neither could he. Until you have been taken in your turn, you may consider him dead to you."

"Taken, hell! And as for Evan, if you gave him your damned drugs –" Frayle stopped. How could he threaten a man who showed such indifference to the fact that he was to hang? What more was there?

"He may have asked for them." There was nothing malicious in the voice and yet the listeners began to feel a great antipathy to the speaker. It was as though a devil were speaking. This Frayle, whoever he was, must be a man of iron nerve, Brother Brendan thought.

"I shall look forward to seeing you hang," the master said, his voice as cold as that of the druid. "And if he has become another such as you, I would watch *him* hang without a tremor."

"Some come to us unwillingly. Had you forgotten that?" Now the words if not the tone were unmistakably taunting.

"Not you, I gather," the other said dryly.

"No, not I. I came by my own free choice from the covens of the north. We sought our master there and found another, even greater!"

"So you were a warlock before you sold yourself to the wildwood?"

The answer was a sound so horrible that Rhosya covered her ears and even the Star Brother turned pale. It might have been laughter, if any could laugh in hell.

The door slammed and they heard the visitor calling angrily for the constable, who came running. "Yes, Master Frayle," he puffed. "Just let me lock that door. Never can tell about these creatures –"

"Let me out of here, you fool." The two pairs of footsteps receded and then there was silence.

"We weren't meant to hear that," Rhosya whispered. "That was Master Frayle, one of the most powerful of the masters hereabouts."

"No, of course we weren't." The Star Brother's mind was in a whirl. So that was a druid. His superiors had never prepared him for something like this! The conviction that Treelight held secrets far deeper than any off-worlder could have guessed, was staggering. Truly, dark things squirmed beneath the colony's seemingly placid exterior.

As soon as the constable came for them, he and the girl hurried out into the sunshine. He wanted to breathe clean air, to feel the warmth of Treelight's suns on his face. He wanted to lose himself in work, fighting the corporation until he forgot that horrible, diabolical laughter.

But he knew he would never forget.

❧

THE MONSTERS FELL BEFORE THEM with an ease that said they had not been designed to face any skilled opposition. For a time, the floor was awash in whatever passed for their blood until the illusion began to come apart. Amid a haze of dissolving images, Dust found himself on a hillside, the girl beside him. Their swords were still smeared, their wounds throbbing – or at least *his* were.

"Where are we?" he asked. He wanted to ask who she was, but he didn't dare. If she were a renegade, then she would tell him. If she were really an ally, she would tell him *that*, too.

She grinned in his face, her own a very good approximation of human features. Her eyes were lavender and her hair, where it peeped out beneath her helmet, was a shade or two darker. "We're on the hill," she said. "At the foot of the mountains. Does it matter?"

He stepped back, not sheathing his sword. "It matters," he said and waited.

"Alright!" she said, laughing. "See, my sword is turning into flowers."

He watched the transformation. As her helmet dissolved – and her hair *was* of a deep amethyst – she made the flowers into a wreath and put it on.

Slowly he let his sword metamorphose back into a gun and reholstered it.

"You're after the treasure," she said.

"I'm after a file," he told her. "I hope you won't get in the way."

"No. Not at all. Has it got a number?"

He waited.

With a shrug, she turned away. "The secure zone is at the top of the mountain," she said. "You'll need help finding it."

He closed his eyes and sniffed. The dungeon smells were gone, but neither was there any scent of flowers. Nor did cool breezes blow down to him from the heights. In fact, the air smelled rather stale.

"Thank you," he said, opening his eyes once more. "I think we'll take the shorter route." He grabbed her arm, propelling her toward a stout, wooden door in the hillside, a door he called into being as they approached.

"Wait!" she cried. "Don't you want to wash? I mean you're all bloody and there's that nasty stuff on your hands."

He shook his head and was clean. Unfortunately, his wounds remained – by which he knew he had taken some real damage in the encounter. "Wait a moment, will you?" he said, stopping.

She had already opened the door and stood within the hill. A gentle glow seemed to emanate from her face and she smiled at him, waiting.

He reached one hand to tap his ear. Someone was trying to reach him – only how could they when he was traveling this way? Might it be a trap?

A voice came faintly but he could not make out words.

"Are you coming?" the girl called.

"In a minute." He tried to tune in and thought he recognized the voice. "Gaed Alfred, is that you?"

"Not quite. I am –" It faded out again.

He moved toward the door. A chill breeze blew out from the depths of the hill and in the pale sunlight, he saw a passage leading upward into shadow. "You sound like Gaed Alfred," he said. "But I don't think we'll have reception – I'm going further in."

"Look – at her face."

Startled, he glanced over at the girl. She had grown more beautiful since he had last looked at her. Her eyes shone and she was beckoning to him. Her armor was melting away to reveal a form of breathtaking allure –

And then he recognized the configuration of those eyes and did the things he must do in order to survive. With one hand he shoved her inside and with the other, he slammed the door. Even as the sound of that closing reverberated in the air, he was running down the hillside, coming to earth just as the mountains blew apart. He was thrown some distance to land against a tree which immediately bent over to enfold him in its barky embrace.

"Okay," he told it. "I'm alright." The tree let him go.

"Gaed Alfred?" he cried in the sudden silence. "I don't know how you did it, but I know that's you!"

"No," the voice came faintly, fading as it spoke. "I am not Gaed Alfred Snowtyger. I am the shadow – of his – prayer –"

For a long time after that, Dust remained hunched at the base of the tree, afraid to look up. When he felt strong enough, he rose and brushed himself off. A path lay where the mountains had been and he began to follow it, still not daring to look back.

What he sought lay not too far ahead.

MARJA GLARED AFTER THE DEPARTING priest, angry that he had had the last word, furious that she could not make him see the necessity of helping her with her assignment. When she turned around, Wells was standing near the pile of packing, his hands at his sides.

"What were you two talking about?" she demanded. "Weren't you punished once already for endangering our mission by your carelessness?"

He started picking up the mess, gathering scraps into an emptied box.

This too reminded her of Christmas morning. "We did not speak of your mission," he said coldly.

"Then what? You were trying to persuade him to something, weren't you? I heard him refuse."

"Yes, he refused." The box was full and now he hunted around until he found another.

"Wells," she said dangerously, "I won't have this. Speak to me or – or you will speak to the coordinator!"

She could not see his face but already she regretted her threat. She was being hateful!

"You infringe on the small preserve of my freedom," he said at last. "But since you only do so out of fear and ignorance, I will answer you." He kept himself turned away, still holding the box in his hands. The slave band gleamed in the light of one of the offworld lamps. "I asked him to hear my confession."

She drew in her breath. "Oh! I never thought –"

"He refused."

"Because you are a foreigner?"

"Because I am a slave." Finally, he turned and the look he gave her was patient, even kindly. "I have been conditioned to absolute loyalty to the interests of Pesc Corp. I must obey them in both letter and spirit if I possibly can. I have no choice."

"And he thinks you cannot be morally free?"

"Oh, that we could probably work out. I know very well which part of me is free to sin."

She waited, her feelings in such confusion that she did not know which emotion dominated. Impatience, shame, pity – or even terror. She understood him, and the reason she understood was because she had once had faith like his – and because –

But she would not follow that thought further.

"You don't have to tell me any more, Wells," she said contritely. "I did not realize."

"But there is more, and I want you to know it," he said, his voice level. "Even though I am constrained to do things I – things that fill me with loathing – they are already done. Or else they are yet to be. But here in the middle of the doing –"

She whitened. "What do you mean?" she whispered.

"Don't ask me that. Remember *that* questions me too, and to make my confession to *it* brings no absolution except –" He held up the wrist with the slave band.

She shuddered remembering that night, Wells making no excuse for himself and the robot hand closing on his arm. "Oh God," she said. "Oh God!"

"If you are silent, it may be that I, too, will be permitted to keep silence."

"But we are doing good –"

"Yes. Tell me that you believe that!"

She turned away. "I must contact Hu and make my report," she said. "I – I won't let anything you have said influence me." Without daring to look at him, she turned and ran up the stairs.

By the time she reached the office, she had regained control of herself. She had other matters to concern her. This business with Wells – might he not be exaggerating some scruple? She knew Father Caron did not approve of what Pesc planned. Had he influenced her bodyguard?

But she had more immediate concerns. The fact that these colonists planned to hang three men was no matter of scruple or private opinion. Such things were not done in civilized places! She opened the door and stepped inside.

Nothing had been done to make of this room a workplace. What need had she for desk or paper or communicator? The robosecretary was everything. No guests would ever be meeting her here for tea and business. Her "office" was partly filled with the stored detritus of living. A table had been set up on rickety legs and a chair beside it. The robosecretary stood immobile before a window so encrusted with dirt that no one could see out of it. Cobwebs hung from the ceiling and there were mouse droppings on the floor.

She had half a mind to order the machine to clean the place up. To scold it as though it were a negligent servant. But she found that when she actually confronted its smiling face, she had not the courage to assert herself or even to affirm her humanity. The thing was Pesc incarnate!

"Put me in touch with the ship," she told it and her voice trembled as she gave the order. She kept her eyes on its hands.

A moment later, the coordinator's words came to her in the uninflected voice of the machine.

"Hu speaking. What progress have you made?"

She told him about her illness, though surely he must already know, and about distributing the gifts he had sent. "One of the masters asked about armaments," she went on. "They have had a few problems with a dissident group of some sort. There was a raid on one of the northern villages."

"Tell him we will consider his request. It might be a good idea to give out some basic weapons, at least to those who show their loyalty to us."

"They've planned an execution," she went on breathlessly. "If we don't stop them, they will hang two of the dissidents. And another man. I think he is a criminal."

"There can be no intervention at this stage. You must support them in those activities that don't interfere with their re-education."

"But hanging! Surely Pesc has a policy against capital punishment!"

"We will later, yes. But for now you must not antagonize their leaders by challenging their authority."

"But we need every person in the colony! This is an immense job and, properly trained, there will be work for each and every one of them!"

"Dissidents and criminals are surely expendable."

She would have said more, but he cut her off. "This situation in the north – and other things – have led to a change in your orders. You will not need to remain at Harrow as your predecessors have done. It would be best if you were to travel around the colony."

This came as a surprise, the more so as she had just been invited to visit Frayle Farm. "I was thinking of that," she admitted and told him about the invitation and visiting the bishop on the way.

"That will be fine. You are also to visit the fringe – the edge of the native vegetation. Can you arrange that?"

"I don't know. Perhaps Master Frayle can take me."

"That would be excellent. Do what you must to persuade him. From what your secretary reports, he sounds like a useful man. And you *are* physically attractive."

She was startled at the order and its implications. Surely she had not heard aright.

"You will attend the executions in your official capacity," Hu went on. "See that you do nothing to offend *any* of the colonists. That is all."

The robot was silent, its mouth quirked into its friendliest smile. She had begun to hate the thing as though it were in truth the human being it sought to emulate. Now she knew for certain that nothing she said or did was secret. Wells must be telling it everything and it, in turn, was telling Hu.

It still seemed odd, she thought dazedly as she turned to escape its glittering eyes, to be hating a machine. It was only the tool of someone else, programmed to do another's will. And why didn't she hate Wells, who betrayed her nearly every second?

Only when she had shut the door behind her, leaving the robot inside, did she begin to breathe freely again. She was repelled by the orders Coordinator Hu had given and disgusted at the mechanical voice coming from that falsely pleasant mouth. It was as though both spoke together, man and machine, telling her that she was not a professional hired for her expertise but only a tool – less, really. She was no more than a lure to draw a man into the service of the corporation!

She caught sight of Wells standing at the bottom of the stairs. Taken off guard, the strain he was under showed plainly on his face. Suddenly Marja was so tired of the whole business that she wanted to run back to her room and lock herself in. It was all coming apart – her mission and her career. Everything!

"Master Frayle is here," her bodyguard said when he saw her.

At this, she hurried down past Wells, almost shoving him aside. The master met her in the sitting room, his face as pale as she had ever seen it, his expression probably mirroring her own. He, too, had seen his world torn wide.

Without realizing how it happened, she was in his arms.

AS THE STAR BROTHER AND the two Lost Rythans made their way out of the camp on Sunday morning, they had to keep dodging Sergay's people, who were busy with last minute preparations. The smell of frying dough and sausages was also a little distracting.

"The fair will be in full swing when we get back," Brother Brendan observed as he stepped over a trailing rope.

His two companions were uneasy. A fair on the Sabbath would have been highly suspect in their home colony, unless it was sponsored by the Church to raise money for some good cause. Luckily, however, they deferred to the Star Brother's judgment.

"Where else can we get a good look at the citizens," he had said. "You don't think those people we met at the inn were typical of the colony, do you?"

There was no answer to this.

The church was well filled – and this was not the only Mass, though it was the only church building in the village. The local custom of providing seats for no one except the masters and their families meant that the three must find places to stand near the back. This they did with a good will, having attended Mass on a number of colonies over the years. Comfort and custom were external things.

There was no chance to see the faces of those at the front. Any attempt to identify the masters – and the representative of Pesc if she had come – would have to wait. Father Caron was a good priest and his sermon on the virtues of fortitude and perseverance in the face of temptation might almost have been aimed against the corporation. It was a high mass and there was a choir.

After they had made their thanksgiving kneeling on the floor among the lesser folk, the Star Brother and the two Faring Guards went out into the churchyard. The better dressed among the crowd would be the masters and their families, of course. Brother Brendan tried to determine which might be the one whose strange interview with the druid he had heard at the gaol. Not the fat, talkative one, he decided; the voice was not the same.

There were several others, bearded men and their half-grown sons. He saw another man join the fat one, good looking, not young but not old either, with a neatly trimmed beard and a fine, athletic carriage. None of the women looked like a corporate representative, though Pesc's agent would probably have chosen to dress like the natives. Still, these all seemed to belong. They had not the look of women who had sacrificed their femininity to serve a powerful and ruthless employer. In fact, most of them seemed rather dowdy.

Outside this select group, the congregation was a very mixed crowd. Militiamen rubbed elbows with what looked like bandits, shopkeepers and their families drifted among freehold farmers and others who, judging by their patched clothing, were probably serfs. Children were everywhere underfoot.

"There's Bran," Gris Wolfgang said suddenly, pointing.

The Star Brother smiled a little. "You chose a worthy friend," he said. "Or rather he chose you."

The other man came slowly toward them, Rhianna on one arm and another girl on the other. This one proved to be Rhianna's sister, Branwen. Obviously a disreputable lifestyle was no impediment to the vigorous faith of the colonists.

"Going to see the fair?" Bran called as he came up.

"Wouldn't miss it," Brother Brendan replied. "After all, we're staying with the travelers at the moment."

"Ah. Thought you might be when you came in with Sergay. Strangers in these parts, aren't you?" Obviously his acquaintance with Gris Wolfgang two nights ago had never progressed beyond a great deal of beery goodwill.

They acknowledged that they were.

"Let's get something to eat." They followed him out through the churchyard, dodging a game of tag, and soon came in sight of the fair. Already there was a crowd. Two women were selling sausages and buns and the group moved automatically in that direction. The Star Brother still had some local money and with this he fed them all. Thank God the fast didn't hold on Sundays!

"Masters over there," Rhianna said suddenly. "The fat one's Master Madoc. Got the biggest farm in the area. Lots of these people are his."

They watched Madoc as he shepherded a group of women and girls among the booths. These all looked enough alike to be his wife and daughters. A few more well-dressed people joined the group but Madoc's distinguished friend was not among them.

"I'd like to get closer," the Star Brother said to Ard Matthew. He had told the Lost Rythans about his visit to the gaol and the very odd conversation he and Rhosya had overhead. "I might be able to identify him if I hear him talking."

He and the Faring Guard separated themselves from the others and wandered over to a rather gaudy tent where Rhosya was selling her tonics. Quite a number of people stopped to ask her advice about their ailments – apparently her coming was awaited and her services much in demand. The sturdy middle-aged woman who appeared to be Madoc's wife was detailing her stomach troubles when they came up.

Madoc and a few other masters waited for her in the entrance, speculating on the corporation's plans in voices loud enough to give Brother Brendan a good sampling. Madoc was telling them of the wonderful new powered lights and the cooker he had been given. It would not be long, he assured the others, before these things would be available to everyone.

"I've heard they'll bring in horseless plows and reapers," one said.

"We'll have to turn away our serfs at that rate."

"Don't worry," Madoc assured them, "there's going to be employment for everyone. This colony will prosper at last and we'll all live like the folk beyond the stars. We'll dress like them and we'll rebuild our towns to look like theirs."

"Horseless wagons," someone said and snickered. "Maybe a house that heats itself."

Madoc flushed a little and would have said something, but at this point the ladies came out and the whole group was swept away toward a small pavilion where Sergay presided over what looked like a roulette wheel. He was in fine form, seating the women at a table, calling for wine from an impromptu bar across what had become the midway, and twirling his moustaches with an elegance that neither Star Brother nor Lost Rythan had so far seen.

"Did you identify your man?" Ard Matthew asked as they watched the proceedings.

"No, I did not. But maybe not all the masters are here yet."

"Nor the corporation's woman." The Faring Guard had apparently come to the same conclusion as the Star Brother.

The gathering was reinforced steadily as more and more of the militia recovered from their exertions of the night before and began to drift in. They were not going back to their post until after the hangings, and now they took full advantage of this opportunity to enjoy themselves. Indeed, some of them were quite drunk already, while a hardy few who had begun drinking the night before hadn't slept at all.

Another group was also becoming more numerous. These did not appear to be townsmen, as they were dressed for the most part in well worn clothing and armed with swords and knives. Their ponytails and long moustaches set them apart from the farm laborers whose hacked off hair seldom reached their shoulders. That and something in the way the newcomers alternately swaggered and slunk about, combined with a measuring look in their eyes, told the watchers that these were men who owed service to none.

The Star Brother pointed them out to his companions.

"The militia are watching them," Ard Matthew observed.

They were indeed – those capable of watching anything at all. The newcomers were also drinking heavily and seemed to have little fear of the law. A few had picked up girlfriends and begun to crowd around the gaming tables. In other places fights broke out, each one surrounded by a cheering mob as people placed bets on the winner.

At last Brother Brendan's patience was rewarded. He looked up suddenly to see a very attractive young woman dressed as the colonists dressed – only her clothes were of finer stuff – and obviously trying to behave graciously to all she met. She was accompanied by the man they had seen in the churchyard, Madoc's friend, and the two were followed by another man, a watchful fellow who had bodyguard written all over his lean and shaven face.

"That will be our quarry," he breathed and Ard Matthew nodded.

"She seems young to have the fate of the colony in her hands."

"I doubt she does. But she makes a good enough catspaw for those who do."

They watched the trio pause to watch while two of Sergay's men gave a wrestling demonstration. Presently, they moved on.

Rhosya had stopped selling for the time being and was telling fortunes. She had set up a table in the shade and already a line of customers waited, many of them male. The desperadoes seemed especially eager to have their fortunes told.

TREELIGHT

"This is not right," Ard Matthew said, giving her a reproachful look. "Either she is taking advantage of these people or else she consorts with spirits she ought not to know."

"I don't think anyone is taken in," the Star Brother said mildly. "I think it's a game with them."

Indeed, the girl was saying witty things as she examined each calloused palm so that both her present client and his waiting friends were kept laughing constantly. "The lifeline is long enough for a rogue like this," she said, drawing one finger lightly across the hand of one of the moustached fellows. "I don't say you'll die of old age –"

"Tell me about the women," he said, laughing with the rest.

"Oh," Rhosya widened her eyes. "Look at these crinkles here." She tapped the places where his fingers joined the palm. "Each one of them is a conquest. Though they are not," she added innocently, "very long."

Behind him someone laughed and a saucy girl stepped forward. "That's easily remedied," she said, reaching for a dagger at her belt. "We'll just take off those fingers."

"Oh," Rhosya told her, laughing, "But see your own line here – why it's still growing! He's a growing boy!"

At this the man took back his hand and laid it over the girl's – the one on the dagger hilt – and laughed into her face. "Better quit while I'm ahead," he said, reaching out a coin to Rhosya with his free hand.

"They're coming this way," Ard Matthew whispered suddenly and his companion turned to see the corporation's representative and her entourage moving toward the table. The crowd of ruffians melted back, all eyes on the three. They must know who she was and they also seemed to recognise the master escorting her, for he earned more than one murderous look – all of which he ignored. Brother Brendan saw one or two other men, who appeared to be the master's guards flanking him as they eyed the crowd suspiciously.

Rhosya looked up at the woman from the stars. "Will you have your fortune told, Lady?" she asked, no longer laughing.

The visitor glanced at her escort and, as he nodded encouragement, sat down, laying her hand out on the table. The traveler girl did not touch it, but bent over peering curiously at the palm.

"You have traveled far," she said, "and there is much here that is beyond the ken of one like me. But I see love –" Here Rhosya cast a shrewd glance at the master. "And great purpose. Your happiness lies in the good you do." For the first time Brother Brendan saw that Sergay's daughter was nervous. Her forehead glistened with sweat.

But the offworld woman only smiled a little. "You don't need my hand to know that I am here to benefit the colony," she said. "But I thank you for the compliment." She said nothing about the first observation – that there was love in her future. Nor did she look at the man beside her.

Her companion had a face both ruthless and proud and, had he not known that this could only be a local landholder, the Star Brother would have taken him for an agent of some offworld power. There was that about him – ambition, perhaps – that marked him as one who saw much further than his fellow colonists and aspired to things they could not even imagine.

"Who is that?" he heard Ard Matthew ask a lean, red-haired desperado.

The other man spat. "That is Master Frayle. Those bastards just condemned a friend of mine to hang."

The Star Brother turned quickly and studied the master's face. Indeed, he looked like the sort who wouldn't scruple to hang a man.

"Your friend," Ard Matthew said shrewdly, "has other friends as well?"

This earned him a suspicious glare. "If it's anything to you, stranger, he has – and Colin Fostered-of-Hwyl is one of them!" At this, their informant moved away and was soon lost in the crowd.

"I think there will be trouble when they try to execute those men," Brother Brendan observed.

The rest of the afternoon – and the evening that followed – was rather an anticlimax. The people threw themselves heartily into their enjoyment, fights became more numerous and finally the militia had to be called to order and marched away. The other strangers had already departed, though the Star Brother did not think they had gone far.

Tomorrow was the day of the hanging.

CHAPTER 9

THE TURNOFF HAD BEEN DISGUISED with brambles, but Dust chopped through them. A shadow was following him now, not interfering, not threatening – just there. He couldn't see it, but he felt it behind him. He was pretty sure it was Gaed Alfred's prayer but he was still afraid to turn around and look.

It followed him through the trail he cut and when he came out in front of the bunker, it was still there. There was a lock on the door and Dust knew the combination. He had learned it some time back, setting off alarms and suffering some damage in the learning. Now he reached for it gingerly, wondering if it had been booby trapped since then.

Behind him, the shadow moved. Something touched him on the back and he felt a cold, clean wind clearing his mind. He inhaled the scent of freshness and remembered some nice places he had been, though he had been too busy to appreciate them at the time. He did so now, feeling a sort of gratitude to whoever had made those places.

"I might die here," he said aloud. "I might not make it back with the files."
The shadow said nothing.

"He told me – Gaed Alfred said he was praying for me. I remembered."
Still there was no answer.

"That might be all it is," he argued. "Just the power of suggestion. I mean, he *said* he would –"

The sun shone and the small breeze fanned his face. The grass was very green and there were trees shading the bunker with their young leaves. An angel stood beneath a willow, watching him.

Dust didn't know how he knew it was an angel. The word just came into his mind when he looked up. "Hello," he said. "Did Gaed Alfred send you, too?"

The angel shook its head.

"Am I going to get killed when I open this door?"

"That's not important," the angel said. "You know it isn't."

"Yeah? Well what about this job I'm supposed to be doing for the Faring Guard? People are counting on me."

"They're not counting on *you*. They're counting on God."

Dust looked down. Suddenly he felt pretty small. Who did he think he was, anyway? Only dust.

"There, that's better," the angel said. "Now go ahead and try."

"And if I do?"

"There you go, thinking about yourself again."

Dust reached for the lock and began feeding in the first coded sequence. As he completed the string of data, a darkness came over his mind and he saw himself for what he was – a thug. He had never been anything else but a crook for sale to the highest bidder. Even the Lost Rythans paid him for his services.

"Don't stop now," the angel said.

With a sigh, he began feeding in the next part of the code. Something clicked in the lock and the trees vanished. For some reason there had got to be a lot of people around him and he recognized some of them.

"You killed me," one man said as another crowded forward. "That time you helped sabotage the Olmstead Base on Networld 13, did you think how many people would die?"

Dust did not look up.

Suddenly he was seized from behind and forced to look. There in front of him was the cross – the one the Faring Guards went on about. There was even someone on it but Dust couldn't see Him very well.

"Every time you struck another, every time you violated My image within you, you struck Me. *You* did this!"

But he could not look at it for long. Everything wavered around him except the lock. Even the angel had disappeared. Dust reached out once more and put in the last sequence of the combination. The contents of the bunker spilled out, filling his memory storage, dragging him down with the weight of them. Some of it he understood – enough.

"Oh crap!" he said, realizing what he had. "I've got to get this back to the exit port. Gaed Alfred's got a real mess on his hands – and that girl, whoever she is –"

But he couldn't get up. The file was heavy and he was not strong enough to carry it. All he wanted was to lie down, to hide himself in the dirt until he turned into real dust, like he was meant to do after the accident, when he should have been dead.

Slowly the lights began to dim until he was left alone in the dark.

⌇

MARJA KNEW IT WAS NO forest. That was only its disguise. It was the planet, waiting until the time was right to devour everything that was not itself. And that time was coming. Already the house rocked beneath her as the ground slowly opened.

"I have to get away," she thought frantically. "Must warn everyone. Pesc will save them – Pesc is *good*."

Then she saw the robots standing in the doorway, waiting to take her down to the waiting maw. They gleamed purple in the light of the nebula, smiling kindly as they stretched out their pain-giving arms. She looked about her wildly and saw that the roof was gone. Outside, the nebula had become a living thing, its gleaming pseudopodia reaching hungrily for the town.

Struggling, she woke herself and lay trembling in the early light. The larger suns had not yet risen, but thank God the nebula had set. She felt as though unspeakable things lay all about her, reaching into her body, crawling in her brain. Someone must help her before it was too late – only it *was* too late and there was no help.

And Pesc was *not* good!

She shook off the half-remembered nightmare and sat up. No wonder she hadn't slept well; today she must witness a hanging. *Three* hangings.

What would her mother have said, she wondered. The Sienko clan had shaken its collective head over her scholarship to Sachsen University, warning her that no good would come of flouting the laws of nature. She should remain among the farms and find a husband with whom to live as the women lived here – a drab life of work and children and piety.

Now she was to attend an execution instead, holding her head up as she watched, showing these primitives that she was no fainting female. Waving aloft the torch of civilization.

While Marja was away at the university, her mother had died. After that, she dared not go back to face the reproaches of her neighbors and relatives. By now she, too, must have been classed among the dead. A lost soul.

She was half dressed when Tara knocked diffidently on the door. "Mr. Wells sent me," she said. "I am to help you dress for the – the doings. You'll be sitting with the masters and all."

"What does one wear," she asked, "to a hanging? Animal skins? Leather and chains? Maybe nothing but paint and feathers?"

The girl stared at her, open-mouthed. "It's for the masters, you see," she explained haltingly. "Something nice and – and dignified."

Wearily Marja took off her clothes and selected a dark dress with a tight jacket. I am in mourning, she told herself. I am in mourning for those who are to die – and also for myself. I am a slave now.

When she reached the dining room, breakfast was laid out as usual. She accepted a cup of tea and looked around for Wells. When she didn't see him, she went back into the sitting room where she found him kneeling beside the bench. She must have walked right past him when she came in.

"Have you eaten?" she asked. He shook his head.

"Well get up and join me. Though, I suppose neither of us is very hungry."

Obediently he rose, crossed himself, and followed her to the table. He seated her and took a chair for himself. "How are you feeling?" he asked.

"About as you would expect." She stirred her tea absently. Then, "Wells," she said, "I owe you an apology. I often do."

"You owe me nothing."

"Well, take it anyway," she told him. "The truth is, I don't have the least idea how to treat you and I don't think I want any injustice on my conscience right now."

He looked down at the table top. "Nor I," he murmured. "But we can't always be choosers, you know."

"Do you know where we are supposed to go?" she asked. "Where we are to sit and all?"

"Master Madoc is coming to fetch you. You will sit with the masters, of course."

"And their women?"

He shook his head. "Their women won't be there. You represent Pesc, and in their eyes you are not a woman. Today you are the embodiment of the corporation."

She looked over at him. "Well, that's blunt."

There were dark shadows beneath his eyes and the line of his jaw looked like skin stretched over bone. "I wish you didn't have to come," he murmured, glancing around as though the robosecretary might overhear. "I want you to know that."

She reached across the table and patted his hand. "Thank you. I won't tell anyone of your disobedient thoughts."

He shook himself free. "Don't think too well of me," he said. And then, "Oh God –"

After one surprised look, she got up and walked over to the window. There were people in the square already, the same crowds who had been amusing themselves at the fair the day before. Maybe she would see that gypsy woman, the one who flattered her so delicately. And the very tall man who frowned as he watched the fortune teller from afar. He did not look like the other colonists with his golden skin and keen grey eyes. There was something dangerous about him. Maybe, like Wells, *he* was someone's bodyguard.

And then, suddenly – she could not help herself – she thought of Frayle. All this time, she realized, she had been trying not to. He was a primitive, a colonist, a man who kept serfs and sentenced people to hang. He said he was a widower, but probably there had been other women in his life – there might even be one now.

And yet nothing seemed to matter except that he had been there when she needed him and, amazingly, that he had needed her, too. She had not asked what sorrow had driven him to her. It was as though, for that time at least, they were not agents of their respective powers, but only two lonely people flung together by forces neither could control.

She watched him arrive and he was not alone, for he rode beside Master Madoc in Madoc's carriage. She saw him looking up at the house front, his gaze suddenly riveted on her face in the window. He did not smile as their eyes met.

Why, she asked herself, must she feel as though she had done something foolish? Something *unprofessional*? Hadn't she been ordered to gain his affections – or at least his trust? She tried not to let this thought go further – tried not to think of Hu's command. That she must ask him to take her to the fringe.

Wells opened the door for Madoc, who had come to escort her to the wagon, jealous as always of his prerogative as the corporation's hereditary contact. When they reached the vehicle, it became even more obvious that relations were strained between the two masters. After gesturing curtly for Wells to sit next to the driver, Madoc placed Marja between himself and Frayle. She was careful not to look at either of them as she perched stiffly on the seat.

They took a different route this time, leaving the square by a street opposite the one that led to the church. After a moment she recognized the road she had travelled when they had first come in from Madoc's farm. A turning led them to the gallows – mercifully empty – and a sort of grandstand that had been erected for the more prominent spectators. A crowd was gathering, turning to watch as the carriage drew up near the platform.

With an adroitness that made her smile – but it was a strained smile – Frayle leaped to the ground and took her arm, helping her to alight while Madoc was still getting his breath back after his own ponderous descent.

"I am sorry," Master Frayle said in a low voice, "that you must witness something like this. You are much affected, and I would think less of you if it were otherwise."

She squeezed his arm in reply.

"The obligations your rank places on you are not to be denied, however," he went on more firmly, "and I know you will face this with courage."

Before she could reply, he had guided her up onto the platform where she was to sit beside him in the front row of seats. They were joined almost immediately by Madoc and Wells. Despite the master's protest, the latter had insisted that he must sit near his client.

"He's right," Frayle said, turning to the incensed Madoc. "There may be trouble today, and this man has been detailed to guard the lady."

The other master glowered for a moment but jerked one hand toward a seat directly behind the others. It was not long before the rest of the places were filled by various masters and town dignitaries.

Out by the gallows, which stood upon its own eminence, Marja caught sight of Father Caron. The masters of Harrow left nothing out apparently.

The sight of the man in his black cassock and hat gave her an uneasy feeling, as though it made of the whole business less of a farce and more of a reality. Three living men would cease to live after this morning's work, she told herself and could not quite believe her words.

She tried again, telling her unbelieving self that their bodies would dangle from the ropes for only God knew how long, and people would pass by and look at them as they slowly withered away –

She put her hand over her mouth, wondering if she would be sick. Dark patches danced before her eyes, and when she closed them she had an attack of vertigo. Madoc hadn't noticed, but Frayle leaned over at once. "Put your head down," he whispered. "You will feel better presently. Don't, whatever happens, let the common folk see your weakness, for we have a duty here, you and I, and we must get through it."

It made her feel better to hear him say, "you and I."

She complied and the black spots disappeared.

Wells spoke softly from behind her. "I've got something you can take," he offered, "if you need it."

She was grateful, but she shook her head. "These people have nothing to 'take' as you put it," she told him. "And until they do, I'd better get through this business without help."

He withdrew in silence.

On her other side, Madoc was preparing to rise and address the crowd. It was his prerogative, apparently, as the major landowner in the district or the mayor of the town or whatever he was. Laboriously, he made his way to a podium where the constable and one or two other worthies awaited him.

When the crowd had been brought to order by dint of much shouting on the constable's part, Madoc began a rehearsed speech. "We are here," he said, "to see justice done. The notorious highwayman Rhyn has been duly tried and sentenced –"

At this, several women began screaming insults at him so loudly that they drowned out whatever else he had planned to say. Nor did it help that the guards chose this particular moment to arrive, half dragging their prisoner who, it seemed, could not walk on his own. Some of the rougher element began cheering, and Rhyn managed to wave to them with his manacled hands before someone struck them down.

Behind, a detachment of militia was marching in the druids. Marja was at first puzzled when she saw them, for it looked as though they had painted their faces with some sort of designs – or else they had dyed their skin instead, leaving some parts undyed. But as they got closer she wasn't so sure.

They were roped together, one after the other and prodded along with pikes, as though no one wanted to touch them. As they reached the empty space in front of the bleachers, she became more and more certain that this was the true color of their skin, preternaturally pale and marked in patterns of rayed silver. Their hair, too looked bleached and she could see the same discolorations on their hands. Their heads were slightly lowered, hiding their eyes. They were limping.

"What is this?" she whispered to Frayle. "What is wrong with them?"

"They have eaten of the fruits of the wildwood," he said curtly, "and it has taken away their souls."

A drug, then. A cult that took drugs and this is what those drugs did to them.

They continued to stare straight ahead, mouths curved slightly in something that might have been amusement, except that it wasn't. With a deep chill, she realized that those faces expressed no human emotions at all.

All three captives were herded together near the gallows. Marja could see the highwayman shrink away from his fellow prisoners while the priest walked briskly toward him. Father Caron ignored the druids as he helped Rhyn to one side and began to hear his confession. When he had given the man absolution, he stepped away, still not looking at the other two.

Despite her enlightened views, Marja was shocked. Didn't *they* rate spiritual consolation? Or perhaps they hadn't asked for it? The druids' rebellion would undoubtedly include not only the colony government but the church as well.

Madoc, who had given up trying to address the crowd, nodded to the constable. This worthy had already had the nooses prepared and they hung waiting all in a row. He motioned the militiamen to bring the three forward as he stepped down to meet them.

Beside Marja, Frayle stiffened slightly and she felt his hand tighten where it rested on her arm. She looked up in surprise, but his face had not changed. Only a drop or two of sweat trickling down his forehead gave him away.

Frayle, she thought, was not as hardened as he tried to appear.

THE LOST RYTHANS HAD LOOKED on with approval as the priest offered spiritual aid to the highwayman but when he ignored the other two prisoners, Ard Matthew, like Marja Sienko, found this disturbing. He gave the Star Brother a troubled look.

"Do you think they've got some disease?" he asked. "But even then, it would not be right to refuse them spiritual aid."

"I don't know. Whatever it is, they look as though they're not really aware of what's going on." He hesitated, remembering the dialogue he had overheard at the gaol. What would such people have to say to a priest, even if he were willing to hear them?

"If they are mad, they should not be killed." There was something comforting in the plain reasoning of the Lost Rythan.

"I know that," his companion replied. "But they have been sentenced to death, and there's nothing anyone can do about it."

However, Brother Brendan too, was disturbed. While there had been some sympathy for the highwayman and a certain amount of odium for Madoc, no one in the crowd seemed to show the slightest pity for the druids. They might as well have been mad dogs.

Turning the image over in his mind, he decided that it must be the true one. To the colonists, that is exactly what they were, mad dogs who worked to spread their madness. No one seemed to think of them as human beings except, perhaps, Master Frayle.

Suddenly he spied a face he knew. Not far away, the bandit they had spoken to at the fair stood twirling one side of his moustache thoughtfully. He was watching the party at the gallows.

Something in his attitude made the Star Brother uneasy. He did not look like he had come to witness the death of a friend. Indeed, he looked much more like a tiger stalking its prey. And he *was* armed. A lot of people in the crowd were.

As he watched, several people got between Brother Brendan and the man – Colin, wasn't it? They must have been part of the militia who seemed to be everywhere – but then these in turn were crowded along by a group of farm boys out to see the hanging. He lost sight of Colin after this.

There were not many women about either, he noted. The few he could see looked like barmaids. A group of them had been screaming insults at the masters not long before and now as they clustered together, their flushed and angry faces promised more of the same.

The Star Brother was still trying to get a glimpse of Pesc's representative. At last he spotted her between Master Madoc and the one who had been pointed out to him as Master Frayle. The offworld woman looked as though she would rather be almost anywhere else and he certainly didn't blame her. He guessed she was here either at the insistence of the masters or at the command of her superiors – or both.

Her recent illness showed in the thinness and transparency of her skin. What would happen, he wondered, if she had to be recalled? At best it could only delay things. But then why had they sent such a young woman – and alone at that? There had to be a reason – he was missing something!

Brother Brendan had tried, as he tried almost every night now, to reach the St. Baltasar. The orbiting chip caught his signal, but whether his transmissions made it into the net, he had no way of knowing. The mothership could be anywhere by now, for Treelight was by no means its only responsibility.

He longed to discuss all that he had learned with Father Moto. So many surprises were turning up, so many mysteries. To say that there was something odd about the Pesc representative hardly began to describe the problem, for there was something wrong with the entire situation. It was not only that Pesc had sent this woman – she couldn't be more than twenty-five – to do a pre-development survey all by herself. She had no staff except that one bodyguard, probably a gunman trained in nothing beyond his immediate job.

Suddenly, without warning, the crowd was shoved back by a surging group of ruffians like the ones Brother Brendan had seen the day before. Quickly they surrounded the grandstand and were already swarming up the sides before the militia realized what was happening.

Everything erupted into shouting chaos. Up on the grandstand, Master Frayle fought them off, swinging a sword with the skill of long practise. Master Madoc had half jumped, half fallen to the ground and was stumbling toward the constable and his men while the other masters were all trying to defend themselves against their attackers.

The offworld woman was flung down between the benches by her bodyguard, who stood over her gun in hand.

Apparently he had no scruples about using it. One of the bandits threw up his arms and toppled down among the crowd. Below, Ard Matthew had drawn his own weapon, but he seemed undecided where to shoot.

"Put that away," the Star Brother ordered. "We're not here to attract attention to ourselves." He turned just in time to see Gris Wolfgang's friend Bran elbowing his way through the crowd, sword in hand.

"Stop him! The fool! Don't tell me he's a member of Rhyn's gang!" Brother Brendan did not wait for the Faring Guards but laid hold of the man himself.

"No," the colonist panted, ceasing to struggle when he saw who it was. "I'm not. But Rhyn's a good fellow and he doesn't deserve to hang!"

"He's a murderer."

For a moment the youth hesitated, and in that moment the militia moved in with pikes and spears and far too many men for the gang to resist. The insurgents broke and ran, pursued through the crowd, which quickly swallowed them.

"Put your sword away," Gris Wolfgang growled and when Bran hesitated, he grabbed it and shoved it back in the scabbard.

"We've got to get him away from here," Brother Brendan said, taking Bran by one arm. "Come on."

They worked their way toward the outer edge of the crowd, only pausing when a cry went up from the direction of the scaffold. The constable had been hit with an arrow, and his men were fighting off another group of outlaws who were trying to wrest his prisoner from him. Apparently the initial attack had been no more than a diversion.

Brother Brendan and the Lost Rythans could not see what was going on, especially after a squad of the militia joined the fray. The ropes, each with its empty noose, swung wildly, and the clash of arms could be heard from where they stood.

After a short struggle, the bandits were beaten back and the constable was helped away from the scaffold. It was only then, with Rhyn still safely in their hands, that the militia realized the druids had disappeared.

On the grandstand, all was still confusion. Two of the masters had been wounded, one of them seriously, and the Pesc woman looked dazed by the sudden violence. She stood between her bodyguard and Master Frayle, who still gripped a bloodied sword in one hand. Of Madoc there was no sign.

Surprisingly, the only gang members left behind were dead. The wounded must have been either carried off or hidden by sympathizers in the crowd. But at the moment, no one was looking for them. Instead, the commander of the militia had ordered a search for the druids.

That effort was hopeless from the start, for the crowd was too dense. After a hurried consultation with the masters – Madoc had come crawling out from beneath the stand – the constable's men decided to go on with the hanging.

The unwounded dignitaries were quickly reassembled. The one remaining prisoner was hustled to the platform and a noose put around his neck. He appeared to be either unconscious or dead. Nevertheless, the commander of the militia gave the order, and suddenly the body swung free, twisting slightly, though not with any sign of life.

"They killed him already," Bran growled and then had to turn away to hide his tears. "Damn it all! He must have got killed in the fighting!"

"Then he did not suffer," Gris Wolfgang told him. "But do not curse. Pray rather that he has atoned for his sins. Or at least," he added, as honesty compelled him, "that he will make it to Purgatory."

"Yeah. You're right. I guess he needs more prayers than curses." The colonist wiped his nose on one sleeve after which he made the Sign of the Cross. "We grew up together, Rhyn and me. He was a great guy."

"He was very brave," Brother Brendan conceded. "I met him at the gaol when Sergay's daughter was called in to treat his leg."

"Damn right he was brave. Went off to join The Band and before you knew it he was their leader. Rotten way to die."

"He wasn't complaining when I saw him."

Gently, Gris Wolfgang began steering the other man away from the scene. "You need a drink," he said.

"*You* can't understand how it is for someone like Rhyn," the colonist said, turning on the Lost Rythan. "Wherever you come from, I bet you been straight all your life – never had to run from the law. Rhyn told me, once it starts there's no end."

"You're wrong," the Faring Guard replied, not letting up his steady pressure on the other man as he hustled him toward the town. "Wrong about me and wrong about there never being an end to evil. If you're not afraid to own up to what you've done, there can still be peace with God and your fellow man. Your friend paid – and we can only hope he paid willingly."

The two went off together while the Star Brother followed, Ard Matthew at his side. "Of course, Gris Wolfgang is right," the Lost Rythan said in a low voice.

"Yes." Brother Brendan smiled at him, envying the simplicity of the Lost Rythan philosophy. But then, things *were* simple if you thought about it.

"It's the other ones who worry me. What was *their* crime?" Ard Matthew asked, destroying Brother Brendan's comforting theory in one blow.

"The druids? I don't know yet." The Star Brother sighed. "I don't think they'll be found. Do you?"

Ard Matthew frowned thoughtfully. "No," he said at last. "There's something uncanny about them, isn't there?"

"Maybe. Or maybe they're just different. At the moment, I'm afraid the worst thing about them is that they are *here*. Somewhere in Harrow."

"Yes," his companion agreed. "I wonder what they will do now that they are free."

THE DAY WAS OVERCAST, WHICH meant that the early suns gave no light at all. By the time the major ones began to lighten the sky, it was raining. Marja sat hunched over the table, listening to the sound of it hitting the windows. She had set one of the heat units going, and the dining room was now the warmest room in the house.

Across from her, Wells was spooning up porridge, not looking at her as he paused to bite into a slice of bread and butter. One side of his face was darkened with bruises and there was a bandage on one arm. Marja had her own share of contusions, and it hurt when she turned her torso sidewise.

Tara had tended to both of them the night before, while Master Frayle stood by. He had suffered no more than a scratch or two, probably because he was so skilled with his chosen weapon. He had killed at least one of the gang and only Marja's protest had kept him from dispatching another one, who had consequently lost no time in making his escape, wounded though he was.

The druids were still at large.

She had thought the sight of a man being hanged would be too much for her, that she would faint or have hysterics or some other disgraceful thing. As it was, the actual execution was an anticlimax. And Frayle had assured her that the highwayman was already dead when they hanged him.

But before that, Marja had seen Wells shoot a man and she had seen Frayle kill another with his sword. These deaths, because they happened so suddenly, had even less effect on her than the long anticipated execution. Perhaps she was becoming calloused after all, as Wells had intended she should back in Bloomhadn Park.

He finished his food and reached for a mug of tea.

"Well," Marja said lightly, "we got through *that*. Though it wasn't what we expected, was it?" The lightness left her voice as she finished speaking.

He did not quite answer this. "You are determined to accept Master Frayle's invitation, aren't you?" he said.

"I have to," she told him in surprise. "I'm ordered to visit the fringe and he seems the most likely person to take me."

"He lives near the wildwood?"

She shook her head. "I don't think so. But he's closer to it than we are here. I'll have to ask him how far it is."

"Does he know he's going to take you there?"

"Not yet. But I don't think I'll have any trouble persuading him."

Her bodyguard stirred his tea with a care it hardly deserved. "You've been told to *persuade* him, haven't you?"

She blushed. Wells had been there when she forgot herself that time, or rather, when Frayle forgot *himself*. No doubt her bodyguard was a non-person as far as the master was concerned, and Frayle probably hadn't even noticed his presence.

"How did you know," she asked suddenly, "that I – what my orders were?"

Wells gave a start. "I know Pesc," he said evasively.

Marja filed this away. So. Was her bodyguard in the confidence of his superiors? Did he have his own orders?

"To answer your question," she said, "we *are* going to visit Frayle Farm. We will also stop on the way to meet the bishop." She spoke firmly, straightening herself in her chair. The effect was spoiled by a slight gasp as her battered ribs protested the movement.

"Master Madoc won't like it," Wells said.

"No, he won't. But I'm not bound to Master Madoc. He might have been the contact person for Dagon Ltd, but they are gone now and I don't think we need him any longer."

"He has influence in the colony."

"So has Master Frayle!"

Wells didn't say anything.

"Anyway, I've agreed to go," she said, "and coordinator Hu has given his permission. He thinks this is my best chance to fulfill my mission here."

Wells set his cup down and rose from the table. "Yes," he said, "I suppose so."

She tried to manufacture a superior smile. "Don't try to outguess the coordinator," she said. "New things have come to light. They've got to be investigated before we can go on. These druids, for instance."

Wells started to speak again and then shut his mouth.

"I don't suppose you approve of Master Frayle," she added. "You're still watching over me like a mother hen. But then you've probably never seen a chicken, have you?"

Wells did not smile though his lips twitched. "You cannot expect me to reply to an accusation like that," he said. "Though I have, in fact, seen chickens before."

She leaned forward. "You are a very good bodyguard," she said more seriously. "I owe my life to you twice over. But you are not trained in social engineering and you have not been sent here to do my job."

He nodded, not taking his eyes from her face.

"You don't want me to leave the safety of Harrow and you don't want me to go anywhere near the wildwood. And I *know* you don't want me to become friends with Master Frayle. Isn't that right?"

"Don't try to guess my wishes," he said bitterly. "I want whatever best serves the interests of my own masters. I am programmed to follow their orders, remember?"

"That is no answer," she said.

"No," he agreed, "I only wish it were."

Marja went into the sitting room and sat down listlessly. She wanted to look at a map, but she would have to summon the robosecretary to display one and she had come to detest its bland face so heartily that she did not.

It was a relief when Master Madoc arrived, accompanied by Master Frayle. The two had been arguing and the argument continued as they came in.

"—safer away from here. With these druids at large, we can't risk anything happening to Dr. Sienko." That was Frayle.

"So you say. But you have lost no time in alienating her from –"

Whatever Frayle would have answered was cut off as the two came into the room shaking water from a pair of umbrellas, which they handed to Wells. They had obviously not meant for her to overhear them, and both looked rather confused at seeing her there.

Marja took each hand in turn, first Madoc's flabby fist and then Frayle's calloused palm. "Good morning, gentlemen," she said. "I am glad you are not suffering from any after effects of yesterday's riot."

Madoc, who had, in fact, twisted an ankle in his hasty escape from the grandstand, thanked her for her concern and limped over to one of the chairs. Frayle waited for her to take her seat on the bench and then placed himself beside her. If he did this with any intention of putting the other master out, he was not visibly successful.

Madoc gave Marja a benevolent smile and, ignoring Frayle entirely, began to speak about the gang's attempt to free their leader. "The Band, they're called," he said, pluming himself slightly in her notice. "They think of themselves as reformers – redistributors of the colony's wealth."

Marja smiled. "Like Robin Hood," she said, but neither of her companions had ever heard the tale of ancient Earth's most famous outlaw and she had to explain.

"Ah," Madoc said. "The stuff of legends. But The Band are quite real, as you have seen. And this Gwyn had a lieutenant who has undoubtedly taken over leadership by now."

"Having failed in their object," Frayle cut in impatiently, "they will be long gone from Harrow."

"I hear," Madoc said to Marja, "that you plan to travel."

"I am going to the bishop," she said, "since he will not come to me." She glanced at Frayle. "Father Caron told me he is your brother," she added, watching his face.

Frayle gave her a rueful smile. "That is true," he admitted. "I am sure he will be happy to meet you."

"But not to come here."

"His duties – he is the only bishop we have, you know."

She nodded. "Then he is a man of some authority, I should think."

Madoc gave Frayle a meaning look. "He is that," the other master agreed.

"And with your influence on my side," Marja said to Frayle, "when I explain to him what we plan –"

At this, Master Madoc had to stifle a snort of laughter. "Oh certainly," he said. "I wish I could be there when you meet."

Marja gave him a hard look but did not ask what he meant. Perhaps it was only spite.

Master Madoc rose. "I'm afraid I have some things to do in the town," he said, "unless –" he turned to Marja "—unless you should require my services?" Once more, he did not look at Frayle.

She shook her head. "After I come back," she said, "I will want to see you. The first priority when I have made my report on the wildwood will be the schools and training centers. They'll be sending down roboteachers and staff as soon as we have places for them to teach."

Frayle looked at her in surprise. "Won't the Church go on running the schools?" he asked.

"They won't be able to. These clergy of yours are not very well educated themselves, are they?"

She had gone too far. "There is," Madoc told her frigidly, "a seminary in Bannyclay."

"Of course," she said hastily, "I meant no offense. I'm sure your seminary is quite adequate. But there are so many things – your people will need technical training in order to run the factories, you know."

She tried not to look condescending. "You must see that the schools will have to be secularized. That is one of things I'll be talking over with the bishop. And maybe," she added as a new idea struck her, "he would be willing to add a few courses to the seminary itself to sort of prepare the clergy for the modern world. It would help things tremendously."

Neither master looked especially pleased with this, so she let it drop. Wells saw Madoc to the door, while Frayle remained where he was.

"I thought," he said when the other had gone, "I should tell you something of our route tomorrow and what to expect." He gave her an apologetic look. "I'm afraid you have seen the height of our civilization, until we reach Bannyclay, at least."

She twisted her hands in her lap. "Frayle Farm," she said. "It is near Bannyclay?"

"No it is not. If we leave in the morning, we should reach the Dagon River by early afternoon. We will cross by the Darkwater Bridge and Bannyclay is on the other side. Undoubtedly my – the bishop will want us to stay with him."

"Oh," she said. "Of course."

"You must allow yourself as much time as you please to conduct your business there," he said. "And then it will be another full day's journey to Frayle Farm. Unless," he added hesitantly, "you have other transportation at your command?"

She shook her head. "You know I don't. Later they will be sending down fliers, but only in pieces. We'll need robots to put them together."

"Then we had better travel by carriage," he told her. "Or would you like to go on horseback and let the luggage follow?"

But Marja had never ridden a horse – at least not since her childhood and then it was only a draft horse. When she told him she did not think herself equal to a day in the saddle, he acquiesced at once.

"I believe you will enjoy the journey," he said, trying for more ease. "The country west of the river is very beautiful. There are plenty of hills and – and trees and things."

"And your farm?"

He gave her a small smile. "I can hardly speak objectively of my family seat. You will have to see it yourself."

"I look forward to that." She glanced around and saw that Wells was nowhere in sight. "Tell me about the fringe," she said abruptly in a lower voice. "You are not far from it, are you?"

"Perhaps a half day's ride. There is a foundation of the Order of St. Hubert where the road meets the Fringe Highway. It is called the West Priory to distinguish it from the others. There are four of them altogether – one for each point of the compass."

"That is a religious order, isn't it?" she said. "And St. Hubert is –" This had been in her briefing, though she had been given no details.

"The patron saint of foresters and hunters," he told her. "We masters carve his image above our doors and on our arms. I have not brought my sword today," he added, "or I would show you."

Remembering her last sight of that weapon, covered with gore, she was glad to be spared the privilege.

"I would like to see this place," she said. "Before we – Pesc, I mean – prepares to deal with the wildwood, I should have a look at it."

He frowned. "Nothing would please me more than to aid you in this," he said slowly, "but the order – I am sure you would not be able to stay at the priory, nor is it safe to camp near the fringe. We would need to return to Frayle Farm the same day."

Another instance of the hidebound prejudice of these people, she thought. But she hid her exasperation. "Of course," she agreed with manufactured enthusiasm. "I would not like to offend the Order of St. Hubert. What are they doing there, by the way?"

"They guard us from the trees," he told her.

"Spiritually, you mean?"

"As to that, I have no idea. They patrol the fringe, however, and set up smaller foundations wherever there is danger of an incursion."

She looked at him blankly. "Do you mean they believe it's coming back? The alien flora?"

He hesitated. "I haven't seen for myself," he admitted. "But guarding us is not the only thing they do. In the past they have eradicated whole sections of the wildwood and cleaned the ground so that it could be planted."

"Oh," she said, prolonging the word. "Oh! Then I really *must* visit them! Don't you see? We can help them with that job. They could work for us!"

Frayle saw. For the first time that morning, his smile was almost genuine.

The rain had stopped. Rising, he asked her if she would like to take a walk with him. She hesitated, looking for Wells.

The master seemed to read her thoughts. "Your man can walk with mine," he said. "That is the price we pay for our position, that we are never quite alone. But," he added, laying one hand gently on hers, "servants can be very discreet."

With a smile, she rose. "Let me fetch my jacket," she said.

CHAPTER 10

BECAUSE RHOSYA WAS STILL BOTH angry and tearful, Ard Matthew started the fire for her and brewed the tea. After a time, she recovered enough to set biscuits baking over the coals.

"Those bastards," she kept saying as she slammed about at her cooking. "First they call me in to treat the man and then they hang him!"

"You knew he was under sentence of death," Brother Brendan reminded her gently. "And you did manage to give him some comfort."

She sniffed and put the lid on the spider.

"I didn't know he was a friend of yours," the Star Brother added. "I thought you were seeing him for the first time when we came into the cell."

Rhosya shook her head. "I didn't know him," she admitted, "not to speak to him, anyway. But once I cut an arrow out of his lieutenant. Before I worked on that fellow, I gave him one of my potions and it made him real talkative." This was punctuated by another sniff. "He just about worshipped Rhyn. They all did."

"I see. I think I may have met his lieutenant. Colin something or other, wasn't it?"

"That's him. You couldn't have asked for a more loyal man."

"I suppose not."

"The Band never robs people like us," she went on. "Rhyn only went after them as could afford to lose a bit. And when Pendaran Creek flooded last year, they were up there helping with the dikes – worked right beside the militia and no one said a word."

Ard Matthew handed her a cup of tea. "That still does not justify robbery," he said. "And people were saying he was also a murderer. Where did they recruit their members anyway? Harrow?"

"Oh," she said vaguely. "From the farms mostly. Runaway serfs and sometimes a younger son of one of the masters."

At the introduction of serfs, the moral tangle became too much for the Lost Rythan and he sipped his tea in silence. There was no slavery on Lost Rythar, but the legality of the institution was one of the realities, not only of Treelight Colony but of the interstellar community at large. Only the Church frowned on this, but could do nothing about it.

Rosya was speaking again. "Colin is the one told me about the druids. He said they lured people away – offered them herbs that brought visions, promised power –"

"What happened to those who took them up on the offer?" Brother Brendan asked.

"I don't know. They were never seen again. Not here anyway."

"How vile!" That was Ard Matthew.

"Yes – I guess so. I've never found an herb like that, though we've got some mushrooms that make you see things all funny. But they also make you sick to your stomach." She took the biscuits off the fire and began setting them on a plate.

"Where is Gris Wolfgang?" the Star Brother asked suddenly.

Ard Matthew looked around. "He was here –"

Then they saw the other Faring Guard in earnest conversation with a young townsman whom Brother Brendan recognised as one of the patrons of the Treehouse Inn. He headed over to where the two were talking.

"It's Brann," he said as he came up. "He needs my help."

The Star Brother frowned, looking at the messenger. "What kind of help?" he asked.

"I – I don't know exactly," the stranger said, stammering slightly. "He only said for me to find this friend of his – Gris Wolfgang."

"It might be something to do with the riot at the hanging," Brother Brendan said slowly. "Is he afraid he'll be arrested after all?"

"I don't think so. He's at a house near the inn. Rhianna's with him."

"I wonder if he's in trouble with one of the gangs," Gris Wolfgang suggested.

"Do you think you can you handle this without giving yourself away as an agent of the Starbrothers?" his superior asked him in a low voice. He didn't really like the look of the messenger.

But the Faring Guard nodded eagerly. "It's alright to use a sword, isn't it? I mean, if I need to."

"The flat of it."

With a grateful nod, the other hurried away, following the stranger.

Brother Brendan waited until they reached the lane into the town and then set off after them. At a gesture from him, Ard Matthew, who had been watching if not overhearing, followed. They were careful to keep out of sight once they reached the first of the streets, snatching glimpses of their quarry up ahead.

"This is not the way to the inn," Ard Matthew said, after his companion had told him of the encounter.

"He said *near* the inn," Brother Brendan murmured absently. "There, they've gone between those two buildings."

He and the other man increased their speed, passing one or two pedestrians, who did not look up as they passed. Hurriedly they rounded a cut-stone warehouse and discovered, between it and the next, a narrow gap leading to a small court behind.

They edged their way through, pausing at the outlet. The little square was hemmed in with the backs of other buildings but they could see no accessible opening into any of them. Then the Star Brother spotted a stairway at the left hand corner across from where they stood. "That must be it," he said.

Moving cautiously, they circled the square until they came in sight of another set of steps leading downward. From below came sounds of a struggle. The Star Brother hurried forward as he caught sight of a knot of men fighting in near silence outside the closed door at the bottom. Only the sounds of their scuffling feet drifted upward to the watchers, along with an occasional involuntary grunt. They were trying to overpower the Lost Rythan.

Two of them had been holding his arms, but he struggled out of their grasp even as the Star Brother approached. Another sprawled on the steps, while a fourth was trying to apply something to Gris Wolfgang's upper arm. It looked like a snake. There was no sign of Brann, though the fallen man looked like the messenger sent to fetch their victim.

With a mighty heave, the Lost Rythan cast off both those, his attackers and, whirling about, sent the one with the snake sprawling. Though the man let go, the thing was already clinging fast, twined about Gris Wolfgang's arm.

With an oath, he snatched it free, leaving a bloody wound, and threw it against the side of the staircase. At once, one of the other men snatched it up and slipped it down inside his shirt. Then they all turned to flee.

Despite his scruples, Brother Brendan did not interfere as the Lost Rythans – Ard Matthew had left off his sling that morning – made short work of the party. The man with the snake-thing died of a broken neck, the others of sword wounds.

When the last body had ceased to twitch, they saw that the faces of three of them were smeared with dirt, their hair darkened with more of the same. Reaching down, Ard Matthew twitched away the shirt of the one who had snatched up the serpent, but there was no sign of it now. His exposed skin, where it was not disguised with filth, was of the same bleached hue they had seen already on the druids, webbed with silvery lines.

After this, the Star Brother turned his attention to Gris Wolfgang. "Let me see that bite," he said, drawing a knife. "Quickly."

Gris Wolfgang took the knife from him and would have cut around the wound but Ard Matthew stopped him. "It's not a snake," he said. "It was something from the wildwood. Look at the wound!"

It was true. There were no marks of fangs, only a round hole where the flesh had been torn away along with the thing that made it.

"It won't be venom. Remember the Brothers of St. Hubert? They were infected by the vines."

"Come on," the Star Brother said quickly, shepherding the others up the steps. "We must get back to the camp. Rhosya may know what to do about this."

Grasping his arm, one hand over the wound, Gris Wolfgang followed while Ard Matthew brought up the rear. They left the bodies to be found where they had fallen, though none of them felt right about this. In the end, they turned once to say a quick prayer for them. There was nothing more they could do if they were not to expose themselves as agents of the Star Brothers.

Fortunately, it was not a populous neighborhood. They passed two drunken loiterers and a girl in a hooded cloak, but saw no one else as they made their way back to the caravan. In all that time, Gris Wolfgang had said nothing. His face was very white, however, and when he looked at Brother Brendan, he could not hide the fear in his eyes.

Rhosya hurried to meet them and when they had told her what had happened, her lips thinned. "Bring him to the fire," was all she said. "We can try to burn it out."

No one argued. Even when she took up a knife and began heating the blade, the Faring Guard said nothing.

"Of all the filthy –" His companion was almost in tears. "Is this how they become – what they are?"

Brother Brendan shook his head. "We can't be sure," he said. "The one at the gaol said he had joined willingly. I believe he considered himself a warlock."

"Then it is even worse."

At that, Gris Wolfgang spoke up. "Brann was not there."

"Obviously, he did not send that man."

"But they knew my name and that Brann and I were friends. They knew that I would come."

The Star Brother nodded grimly, for of course the Lost Rythan had spoken the truth. There was something shocked and childlike in the way he said these things, as though he could not quite grasp what had happened. Deliberate betrayal affected them that way –

But, "We will search for him," Brother Brendan promised. "Afterwards."

Rhosya was very thorough. She wasted no time on any of her potions but set to work immediately with a haste that spoke more loudly than words of the peril. The smell of burned flesh was sickening, but in the face of the Lost Rythan's fortitude under this torture, Brother Brendan forced himself to remain at his side, swallowing bile the whole time.

With both hands on the Faring Guard's shoulder, head bent to keep out of Rhosya's way, the Star Brother could hear him whispering the Miserere as the sweat poured down his face. By contrast, on his other side, Ard Matthew's eyes spoke not prayer but vengeance. It was not going to be easy to keep *him* from doing something rash!

At last it was over and Rhosya went to fetch some herbs for a poultice while Brother Brendan went and got an armful of bedding. Together he and Ard Matthew rolled up the blankets and set them behind the injured man's back.

"Brann," Gris Wolfgang whispered between set teeth. "We must make sure – they haven't – got him." By this the others knew that he at least, would not believe that his friend had been the betrayer.

"I'll go to the inn," the Star Brother promised. "If you will stay here with him, Matthew," he added, turning to the other Faring Guard.

Ard Matthew hesitated. It was not quite an order, but after a moment he nodded agreement. When Rhosya came hurrying back, he stepped over to take some of the things from her hands.

"Set some water over the coals to boil," she said. "We will brew him a drink for the pain. And," – she indicated a jar of pungent salve – "this can go on beneath the bandage."

"Are you sure you got it all?" Ard Matthew asked her in a low voice. "That we were in time?"

She glanced at her patient. "No," she said aloud. "You are a brave man, Gris Wolfgang, and it is only right that I tell you the truth. As long as you are not given any of their foul drugs, you will never become such a one as they are, but I cannot be sure you are not infected. We must wait and see."

The Faring Guard nodded. "Then if it is God's will, it may go with me as it did with the Brothers of St. Hubert," he whispered. "This I can bear so long as it is not the other."

"It may be you have taken no permanent hurt at all," Brother Brendan heard Ard Matthew say before he was out of earshot.

He hurried away to the inn, only stopping to tell Sergay, whom he met returning from the farm, what had happened. The boss listened in silence, but there was something deadly in his face when he had heard the story.

"The wood is closing in on us," he said, setting down the load he was carrying. "We are not true children of this world and we never have been."

"Neither are the druids," Brother Brendan said grimly. "Come with me!"

The two set off down the lane.

THE MAN IN THE TOWER had at least agreed to see him, and for this Gaed Alfred was grateful. Likely his gratitude did not show overmuch, for he had a lot on his mind and he was by nature impatient. When the young hood ushered him in, he had, as always, to duck beneath the lintel of the door, feeling all the while the other man's wary gaze on him.

Fraser May looked up from a screen, his dark gaze traveling further upward than he had expected. "Ah," he said, "they didn't exaggerate, did they? You *are* giants."

Gaed Alfred did not answer this. Instead he stuck out his hand. "Faring Guard Chief Snowtyger," he said crisply. "Thank you for seeing me."

May indicated a seat. "Give it a try, anyway," he said. "I don't know if it will fit you or not."

The chief folded himself gingerly into a chair. "You know what I've come about," he said.

"Yes. You want to get in to see Dust. I'm afraid he's not responding."

"That's why I want a hook-up."

May sat forward. "Do you know what you're asking? If he's gone in too deep, there's some reason for it. He's on a job."

"I know that," the Faring Guard said slowly. "He's working for me."

"Ah. I wondered," May admitted. "Dust mostly works for *me* – in fact that's what he was doing when he got blown up. And that's why he's alive – because he's a good man, and I didn't want to lose him."

Anyone but a Lost Rythan would have been alerted by this coming from a man like May. But he only said, "You mean, you're the one who saved his life?"

"I got them to clean up what was left and set the med techs to work on him. And I backed him when he started this new line of work as a hacker."

"That must have cost a lot," Gaed Alfred said thoughtfully.

May flushed. "Okay, Chief," he admitted with a crooked grin, "you caught me. Sometimes I can be a pretty nice guy."

"He was a friend of yours?"

"He still is; we have a deal going. But he never told me he was also working for the Faring Guard. Or should I say, the Star Brothers, since that is what it comes to?"

Gaed Alfred nodded. "Yes," he agreed. "We Faring Guards work for them."

"So you've lost touch with him?"

"We have."

There was a silence of some moments. Then, "I never pegged him for your sort," May said carelessly. "But I guess you're paying him pretty well."

"We generally pay well," the Faring Guard said blandly. "But also – he knew this was a dangerous job and I tried to dissuade him from getting in too deep. But he wanted to do it."

"I'm touched." May regarded the other man blandly. "I really am. I don't think he'd take a risk like that for me."

"He should. If he owes you his life."

At this, the other man gave Gaed Alfred a narrow look. But the other's face showed nothing except honest concern. "So now you think they've caught him?" May asked. "Whoever it is."

The chief ignored this attempt at fishing. "I don't know. There were some safeguards. I mean, we should have been able to tell if it were just a capture." The Lost Rythan hunched forward, lowering his head a bit so that he could look directly at the other man. "I think it's something else. I've got a hunch."

'You've got a hunch?" May could not hide his surprise. "I thought you Lost Rythans were more level-headed than that."

The chief ignored this. "I don't have to tell you that Dust lives a very strange life," he said. "He isn't always hooked up with reality as we know it."

"Well, what do you expect? Everything in there is virtual. That's why we all – you, too, it seems – need to keep in touch with him if we don't him to float off into the void."

The Faring Guard waited. Fraser May was not the sort of man he would normally visit and he hadn't held out much hope for the outcome of this particular interview.

"So," May said, confirming the other's opinion of him, "what's in it for me?"

Gaed Alfred didn't flinch. "If he goes under, you'll lose his services."

"There's that." Now it was May's turn to wait.

They looked at each other across a gulf, not only of experience but of just about everything else. As a Lost Rythan, the chief could not help showing a certain disapproval – for May's activities were well known – even though he still strove to give him the benefit of the doubt. Had it not been for a conscious effort at compassion when he had first felt the need to contact Dust, he might never have found that deeper well of charity hidden within himself. His *liking* for the hacker had come as a surprise to both of them, but he didn't think he was going to like May very much.

At last he spoke. "If you help us, we'll make it worth your while, of course."

The other man watched the expressions chasing each other across the Faring Guard's face.

"Okay," he said at last, "I'll hold you to that. Meanwhile, you got him into whatever it is and you can get him out." He slammed his hand down on a switch and immediately the man who had shown Gaed Alfred in reappeared. "Take Chief Snowtyger to Dust's station and give him our code to get in."

Gaed Alfred rose carefully, trying not to knock anything over. "There is another man waiting outside," he said. "A Star Brother. I might need him, too."

May gave a curt nod.

As they emerged from the tower, the copper-colored sky was filled with the light of a cluster of copper-colored suns – hence the name of the colony – and the two offworlders donned goggles as they mounted the transport provided. Their driver looked back at them from time to time as he set them in flight above the city. His own eyes had been surgically adapted to the glaring light so that they looked like flat, metallic disks.

"Lost Rythan, huh?" he said once. "And that other guy –?"

"I am a Star Brother," Father Moto told him. "A priest."

"You look kind of like an alien. You both do."

The offworlders did not answer this. A copper-colored man with shining, copper-colored eyes might well consider them alien.

"You still have that feeling?" Father Moto asked the chief once as they flew above a vast stretch of aquafarms.

The other shrugged. "I'm not psychic," he said. "Maybe it's just that he – well, he'd better not get himself killed is all."

After that they were silent for the rest of the trip.

SOON AFTER BREAKFAST – AT which meal Frayle joined Marja while his servants and outriders ate with Wells in the kitchen – they took the west road toward the river. To the south of their way stretched Madoc Farm and for some distance they rode beside fenced pastures where herds of cattle grazed. Madoc also raised sheep, Frayle told her, but these were in another part of the farm. After a short time, the last of the grazing land was swallowed up in brush.

"To whom does this belong?" Marja asked her seatmate. They were traveling in Frayle's carriage with the top down. Behind came the wagon with the luggage. Wells and the robosecretary rode there, along with two more servants.

"This?" The master shrugged. "To Pesc now, of course. Everything does."

"I suppose you could look at it that way," she said slowly, "but possession of a colony world is not the same thing as direct ownership of property on that world."

Frayle sucked in his cheeks for a moment. "When our ancestors settled this colony," he said at last, "Dagon Ltd. set the first landholders in place. They were chosen from among the colonists as those best able to manage others." He gave her a wry smile. "Actually, that is only the official version. Our first settlers were not, as you may have been told, the off-scourings of other world's slums. We masters, for example, are descended from interstellar gangsters who were offered amnesty if they would settle here and work for the corporation."

She stared at him in surprise. "Indeed, I was never told that!"

"I didn't think so. The serfs are different, of course. They came from somewhere else."

"Dagon Ltd made them serfs?"

Frayle shook his head. "Our ancestors did that," he said. "At first, it was considered necessary for the colony's survival. Later, it became fixed in our laws, though many of them are now freeholders and tradesmen. I'd guess there are more of those than there are serfs."

"I see. But you still didn't answer my question," she reminded him. "Who owns this land?"

They were gradually descending while the brush gave way to groves of alders and other terran-style trees. Occasionally the foliage opened out to reveal small streams winding amid ferns and cresses, disappearing into the shadowy recesses of the wood.

"Under Pesc – you must not forget that even the greatest of the farms are held in fief only – no one. This is free land."

"But considering the initial expense of clearing this region from the native forest and planting earth type vegetation, wasn't it wasteful of Dagon not to make use of it?"

He turned toward her, smiling. "Things will be different now," he reminded her. "Our former overlords did nothing to develop the colony because it was only a speculation as far as they were concerned. We did not have the resources to make so many farms as that – and there would not have been enough people to work them if we had."

"Of course. I hadn't thought. But you could have done other things besides farm the land, couldn't you?"

"The region is not entirely wasted. People cut wood here – for building and firing. And there are hunters." His imagination seemed to go no further, Marja realized.

But then, he was right; the population was not large even after two centuries. And with the deplorable lack of technology, what else *could* they have done to develop the land?

After a time, the woodland ended and the terrain grew flatter, shelving gradually as they continued to descend. Marja spotted many small creeks and a few marshy spots where the spring sunshine glittered on open water rimmed with the dark emerald of cresses and other water plants.

Near noon they stopped for a picnic dinner. This was an elaborate affair as a fire had to be built and innumerable baskets and packages unloaded. All of the servants were kept busy save for the two outriders, one of whom cantered over to report.

Frayle did not look up from supervising the tea.

"Men on foot, Master. We saw several."

"How close?"

"Out in the woods. They were trying not to be seen. None have come into the open."

"Hunters," he said. "Or maybe outlaws."

The man waited in silence.

"We are not far from the bridge," Frayle decided. "So long as we remain in the open, you can see if they approach. We will have our meal first and then make for the river."

"Yes, Master." The man turned his horse back the way he had come.

Marja glanced over at Wells who hovered, as always, near her person. Had he heard? Probably he had spotted the watchers himself. But he did not seem overly concerned.

But then, she remembered, her bodyguard was better armed than the colonists. He must have an arsenal hidden about his person. She saw him turn away, moving casually along the perimeters of their chosen site, pausing from time to time to talk to one of the servants.

When the meal was finally ready, there was no table to serve it on. However, the wagon yielded collapsible chairs for herself and Frayle while the rest hunkered down in the grass, eating their plainer fare away from the master and his guest. Marja was amused at the elegance of the serving, though the food was hearty. Frayle was good company, she thought. Between courses he poured the wine himself and told her one or two stories about his colony's history, attentive as always to her comfort and amusement.

Days had passed since the night he had taken her in his arms. Neither of them had made any reference to the incident since. Marja was still unsure of herself and slightly embarrassed. After all, they had both been overwrought at the time and perhaps the embrace had not meant as much as her imagination made of it.

She must not forget, however, that winning Frayle's good will was actually part of her job now. The thought depressed her.

Alert to her mood, he gave her a questioning look. "You are not chilled by this wind, are you?" he asked solicitously. A fresh breeze had sprung up while clouds began to gather in the west.

She shook her head. "Is it going to rain?" She studied the chaos of the multiply sunny sky.

"It may. Are you afraid for your robot?"

"On no! It's more waterproof than we are," she said, startled at his simplicity. She was finding it hard to remember than Master Frayle was a product of a pretechnical society. It was also getting harder, she realised as she saw him wince, to keep from reminding him of this.

She came to her feet abruptly. "Do you see those flowers over there?" she asked with manufactured enthusiasm. "They look like lilies! Have we got time to take a look at them?"

Without a word, he rose and took her arm. The ground beneath their feet was not so dry as the roadway and as they left the road, they had to step carefully from tussock to tussock. One of the outriders turned to flank them immediately and she saw that Wells, too, had risen and was watching them.

Frayle took these things for granted, but she felt hampered by all this attentiveness. It was excessive, surely.

Some three or four hundred yards from the road, they stopped. A sea of white and lavender blooms had opened at her feet so that she gazed at the little dell in wonder, no longer assumed. "Shall I gather some for you?" Frayle asked her.

"Oh yes! I mean, I can –"

But he was already kneeling, snapping off the stems until he had a large bunch, which he promptly placed in her arms. Another man might have said something about the sight of a beautiful woman standing among the beauties of nature, but he only looked his admiration. "No," he said in a low voice, "they should never have sent you here. But I'm glad they did."

She looked down. "You make it harder for me to do my job."

"I would make it easier if I could."

"Yes. I didn't mean that. You know I didn't."

"I know." This time there was no doubt about his feelings – or hers. She forgot Wells and the outrider as he pulled her to him. What did they matter? What did anything matter?

At last he let her go. "They will have packed up by now," he said rather regretfully. "And we must reach Bannyclay this evening."

She nodded, the crushed flowers already wilting in her arms. "Yes –" And then, as something suddenly occurred to her. "I – I don't even know your name! All this time, you have been only Master Frayle!"

"My name is Prydan," he said as he took her hand and started back. "Along with a string of patron saints, of course, not to mention an ancestor or two. But Prydan is enough." He paused a moment, smiling into her face. "And I already know yours – Marja."

"Prydan," she murmured. "I like the sound of it."

Still smiling, he helped her into the carriage.

An hour later, they had their first glimpse of the river. The road had become a causeway with marshland on either side. The outriders reported no more sign of lurkers, though the reeds were man high now, forming brakes even denser than the woodland. But as each of these clumps was surrounded by areas of open water and patches of blooming flags, it was unlikely that anyone could creep up on them unseen. Anyway, the plentiful ducks would give warning.

"That bird," she said once, pointing. "I've never seen one like that."

"A heron," Frayle told her. "And now we are coming to the bridge. It is called Darkwater because the river is so deep at the middle. This is the only river in the colony," he added. "It flows out of the Wildwood in the north and then leaves our lands again southwest of here."

"But where is Bannyclay?"

"This road climbs the bank on the other side of the bridge," he said. "The town is at the top."

She leaned over the side of the carriage to watch the water rushing by below. So this river came out of the wildwood, she thought. You could get into a boat and follow it and it would take you back into the wildwood again as though the colony were no more than an island in a sea of deadly purple. She tried to imagine floating out of the lands of men, and the thought made her shiver.

Beside her, Frayle put an arm about her waist. "Don't be afraid," he murmured. "See – there is the other bank, now."

But I'm not afraid of the river itself, she wanted to tell him. I am afraid of the fringe – of the wildwood. That it will eat me alive.

Dreamily she studied his profile with its neatly trimmed beard, wondering what she was going to do when they got to the town. What *they* were going to do.

As soon as the streets and the traffic of Bannyclay had closed in around them, however, she had other things to think about. The carriage turned down the main boulevard until they passed a cathedral – yes, she thought, a real cathedral here in this tiny colony on a mostly uninhabitable planet! – and then on to a very large stone house.

A group of servants ran out to take the horses. Before Marja had even finished looking at the redoubtable facade, she was being helped down from the carriage. She followed a servant into a spacious hall complete with spotless flagged floor, gleaming wooden furniture and a large crucifix on the wall.

"My brother will expect us to stay here," Frayle said after speaking quietly to what must have been a major domo, "but he is not at home right now. Someone will show you to your room." He hesitated, looking rather uncomfortable.

Yes, she thought, this *is* going to be difficult. He must be on his best behaviour of course, and so must I. Suddenly, ridiculously, she wanted to burst into tears. It was all so impossible and yet it *had* happened! She turned away from him, but then, just as a very dignified elderly lady came to show her to her room, Marja whirled about and gave Prydan Frayle her most dazzling smile.

He was so surprised he almost lost control of his own expression. She did not see what happened next, however, as she followed the disapproving servant up the stairs.

BRANN WAS NOT AT THE inn. Nor was it likely that he would be.

"Haven't you *heard*?" the innkeeper demanded angrily. "He has killed Rhianna – left her dying in her room. Got drunk and beat her to death!"

The other two were stunned.

"He has a weakness for drink, then?" the Star Brother asked slowly. "But to do a thing like that!"

"He was no more a drunkard than most of those bully boys," the man said. "God knows, I try not to judge any of them." Suddenly he slammed a jug down on the table. "But *this* – he'll hang for it if they catch him!"

"Did anyone see it happen?" Brother Brendan asked.

"They heard. She screamed loud enough. She only lived a block over and you could hear it in the street."

"Was he seen?"

The man shook his head. "Got clean away. It was her sister went in and found her. She lived long enough to say it was him, though."

Sergay raised one eyebrow. "She *said* he did it?"

"She said, 'Brann, don't!' over and over a couple times and then she couldn't talk any more. Died this morning."

"This is not good," the boss said quickly. "It will stir things up even more."

"It will be hard hearing for Gris Wolfgang," the Star Brother said. "Brann did not seem like that sort of man."

"No," Sergay agreed. "There's something funny about this."

"Not to the acting constable!" the innkeeper snapped. "And if you have any evidence for him, you'd better tell it to him yourselves. He's been in here questioning everybody and you can be sure he'll be looking for any of Brann's friends."

"Thank you," Brother Brendan told him quickly. "I wish we had the means to clear this up, but we haven't."

He thought for a moment. "I suppose the woman will be given Christian burial?" he asked.

"She'll have what her sister can afford, which is a pauper's grave. They're orphans, you know."

The others exchanged glances. Brother Brendan pulled out the pouch containing the rest of the money Tregarth had given him. "Give this to her sister," he said. "And tell her we are sorry to hear of this thing."

The innkeeper accepted the money and laid it beneath the counter. "I have known these girls since they were children," he said. "And if I could have done any more for them than I have, it would not be wanting."

"I know you would have," the Star Brother told him. "As I don't doubt you have helped others when you could." He turned away before the man could answer, Sergay trailing behind him.

"What will you do now?" the boss asked as they made their way back to the campground. "I don't think we should stay here any longer after all the trouble there's been. No matter what happens, suspicion always lands on the travelers in the end."

"You may be right. But first I must contact the Balthasar – if I can." He looked up to see Ard Matthew hurrying toward them.

Quickly Brother Brendan told him what had happened.

The Faring Guard was as taken aback as they expected. But, "He must be far away by now," was all he said.

"Or a prisoner of the druids," Sergay suggested. "Or dead."

Neither of the others said anything.

Once back at the camp, however, they were faced with breaking the news to Gris Wolfgang. By this time the other man had drunk so deep of Rhosya's potion that his eyes were glazed. She had left him half sitting beside the fire where he made no effort to rise as they came up to him.

Brother Brendan had to tell his story once again.

"He is accused of killing this woman?" the Gris Wolfgang repeated unbelievingly. "Brann would not do that."

There was no answer to this.

"He was not there," Gris Wolfgang said slowly after a moment. "When I came to help him – he was not there!" He struggled to put his thoughts in order. "He must be found!"

"Yes," Sergay agreed impatiently. "But you forget we don't know where to look. And if we did know, then we would probably have to tell the constable. The man's wanted for murder."

Brother Brendan left the group and, choosing a spot behind the lean-tos, he took out the caller and set it for the orbiting transmitter. The sun was high overhead and he had eaten nothing since the day before, but all that must wait.

At long last the thread like voice of the operator came on. "Balthasar." They must be transmitting directly through the net, a difficult and chancy operation.

"Brother Brendan here," he said in relief. "Is anyone available?"

"Gone planetside. We're orbiting Networld 15, but they left a message for you. Wait a minute."

The recording was brief and to the point:

> *Trouble with one of our operatives – we'll get with you ASAP.*
> *Meanwhile Pesc is not – repeat not – planning to develop Networld*

326. The woman is a dupe, but we don't know yet what they're up to. Keep an eye on her – she may need help. Fr. Moto

"Is there anything you want to tell them?" the operator asked. "Can't hold the beam long, but I'm set to record."

Brother Brendan gave a short account of the morning's adventures. "These druids," he finished, "seem to be trying to infect the colonists. Tell Chief Snowtyger about Gris Wolfgang – that he might be infected himself."

He could think of nothing more to say and signed himself out.

As he came back to the others they met him with the news that the corporate delegate was leaving with Frayle, first to visit the bishop and then on to Frayle Farm.

"Anything else?" he demanded. Was this the danger they were warning him against? It would depend on whether the woman was acting on her own or following orders.

Ard Matthew shook his head, eying his superior with concern. "Did you reach the *Balthasar*?" he asked.

Brother Brendan did not answer this. "What is the nearest village to Frayle Farm?" he asked Sergay.

"Dunsever." The traveler chief gave him a shrewd look. "We'll be trading in the west, I think," he said.

The Star Brother nodded. "Yes," he said. "That would be best."

"We'll pass through Bannyclay on the way. You might see this bishop."

"Yes, we might do that," the other man said thoughtfully. "If it can be managed quietly."

"He's a sharp one, I've heard. Frayle's brother."

The Star Brother jerked his head around. "Did you say he was Master Frayle's *brother*?"

"That's right."

It that were true, then Bishop Frayle was the last man he wanted to see – the last who should learn that the Star Brothers had sent someone down to the colony. On the other hand, it might be good to pause briefly in the town and see what news they could pick up. He mentioned this to Sergay.

"They don't like us to camp there," the boss told him. "They don't encourage travelers at Bannyclay. It's a bigger place than this and there's trade enough from the river and that. We're competition."

"Yes, of course. But maybe we could spend a night or two outside the town. Do you have any friends there?"

The older man nodded. "We've got friends wherever Rhosya's done her work. I expect she'll find us a place."

Satisfied, the Star Brother squatted down beside Gris Wolfgang. He seemed more alert now that the brew was wearing off, though the pain must be coming back. "How are you, Wolfgang?" he asked.

The Lost Rythan turned on him a haunted look. "I won't know that for a while, will I?" he said in a low, roughened voice. "I said it would be alright – whatever God decides. But this won't be clean death in battle, where a man makes his peace with God before the fighting begins. I'll have to resign myself over and over –"

Brother Brendan laid one hand on his shoulder. "It's always that way," he reminded the other man. "Death can come anytime. We live in that resignation as well as we can."

Gris Wolfgang felt of the bandage on his arm, winced and let his hand drop. "Promise me," he said, fixing his eyes on the Star Brother's face, "that if – if it looks like I'll be taken over – that you won't let me –" He stopped, looking miserably ashamed. "I would rather be dead," he whispered. "I know it's a sin to ask that of you or Ard Matthew. But once it was the Rythan Way –"

Brother Brendan frowned at the Lost Rythan. "You have done with such ways," he told him sternly. "Anyway, we don't even know if you're infected or not. If you are, we will take you to the Brothers of St. Hubert. They've had experience with this sort of thing and can make sure nothing like that happens."

"Yes," the other agreed, catching at this. "You will tell them how it happened and – and –" He looked down.

"I will tell them."

Gris Wolfgang sat silent for some moments. Then, "What now?" he asked.

"We're going west. I've had word from Father Moto that the corporation woman is in danger and now I hear that she is leaving Harrow. I wish he had been more specific, but they don't seem to know yet what we should be watching out for. Only that the corporation has something in mind."

The Lost Rythan nodded. Then, flushing slightly, "I suppose you've always thought us brave, we Faring Guards."

"Very. I depend on that now."

"It isn't courage," the other man muttered. "It never was. In the olden days, it was pride. Pride makes a man brave, or so my father told me."

At this, the Star Brother remembered his own father, a man who could sing down the angels, as they said in Gaelway Colony. And yet that same man was bested every time he got hold of a bottle of whiskey.

"Pride is too dangerous for us mortals," he said. "I'm glad you've given it up."

"My father said that too." Gris Wolfgang brooded for a moment. "But when we had done with that, we needed something else. We replaced it with faith. I suppose that is the foundation of our courage now." His eyes were overly bright. "We are nothing in ourselves – no greater than any other men. But because we *believe*, we often seem stronger than they are."

"That's as it should be," Brother Brendan told him. "Though you Lost Rythans do have a great deal of physical strength as well. And," he added thoughtfully, "you do more than believe, Wolfgang. You love God."

"But if all that were turned back on us? If I were *possessed* – don't you see?"

"Then you would still have your faith," the Star Brother told him.

Later, Ard Matthew came and helped his friend into the lean-to. But Gris Wolfgang could not rest. When Brother Brendan came in later, both men were still awake.

"Tomorrow, we start for Bannclay," he reminded them. "You must both try to get some rest."

But though they were silenced, he knew that Gris Wolfgang at least, remained wakeful, for he could hear the other man tossing about.

How long, he wondered, until they would know his fate?

CHAPTER 11

IT SEEMED LIKE A LONG time passed before someone found him in the dark. It was like that time he got locked in the cellar at the orphanage. Only he had been someone else then and when he finally got free, he beat the crap out of the boy who had locked him in. No one *ever* knew he'd been crying because he'd got a black eye and some contusions which was enough to hide all the signs.

Now it didn't matter what anyone thought. He was only dust – the grimy stuff that sifted down on things.

"Who's there?" he muttered when a hand fell on his shoulder. But he already knew it would only be some bit of programming disguised as a person, booby trapped like as not.

"I've come from Gaed Alfred. He's got to have the files."

"Tell him they're too heavy. Tell him I can't do it."

But the hand would not let go. At first he thought it was the damned angel again, only it wasn't, because the angel was standing where it had been all along, under a tree. He saw this because it wasn't quite so dark anymore.

"You!" he said in disgust. "You think I'm crazy, but I know you're not real! You're just a figment of my imagination!"

The angel raised one eyebrow and Dust was a little taken aback. He hadn't thought of angels having eyebrows. In fact, he hadn't thought much about angels at all except that Gaed Alfred had fed him some history books and a recording of the Bible which he dipped into from time to time.

"In season and out of season," the angel said, only it wasn't the angel speaking. It was the Faring Guard, quoting some saint about why he would not drop the subject of God even when Dust told him he wasn't interested. "There isn't anything else in the end, but in the meantime, there's chess."

"And beer," Dust had said wickedly. "Bet God won't offer you any." What a smartass he'd been!

"You were that," said the angel, who had been listening in on his thoughts. "But that was before the dark."

Dust looked back into himself and the dark was still there. Only Gaed Alfred was keeping it at bay.

"The files," the other voice interrupted them and someone helped him up.

"I can't carry them all, I tell you! And why should I? I can't face Gaed Alfred now that I've seen the dark. I've sold all of me that matters and now there's nothing left but dust."

"Gaed Alfred knows about things like that," the voice said reasonably. "How do you think he got into the Faring Guard?"

Dust tried to turn, but the grip on his shoulders was too strong for him. "Don't you go putting down Gaed Alfred," he growled, struggling. "He's one of the most decent people I know!"

"So pick up your load and carry it for him – and for this lady, whoever she is, that the corporation's going to double cross."

There was something suggestive in the word, "cross." The file was beginning to metamorphose into a cruciform shape. Clumsily, Dust picked it up.

"Good. Now follow me out."

"However did He do it?" Dust muttered, half dragging the awkward thing over what had become stony ground. "In the Bible, I mean."

"About the same way," the angel said. "You're doing this because you care about someone else more than yourself, only *He* cared for everyone at once."

"Like hell I do! No one ever cared for me and why should I care for them?" Dust told it, but he soldiered on, feeling the wood dig into one shoulder – his armor had melted away some time ago – while his bruised feet became slick with blood. When he couldn't go on any more, he stopped to rest. The sky above remained black and starless because the light seemed to follow him, leaving all distances in a gloom as impenetrable as death.

"Look," he said. "Some of it's coming loose." He reached over and peeled off a strip of wood.

"Let me have that."

"Something's coming in," Father Moto said, watching the screen before him. Gaed Alfred's haggard face looked over his shoulder. The chief had been trying for over an hour to talk Dust back from wherever he'd got lost, but there wasn't any way to tell if he was getting through or not. He just kept saying whatever came into his head – blessings and comfort, affirmations of faith and stuff he remembered from his own youth.

"That's a medical report," he said, reading the screen.

"Not exactly what we want but – look here!" the Star Brother exclaimed.

Snowtyger looked. "We've got to get this to our man on Networld 326!"

"Yes," his companion agreed. "It's plain that woman must not go any-where near the wildwood! And look what they've been giving her!"

Father Moto put in a call to the *Balthasar*.

≈

DINNER WITH THE BISHOP WAS Marja's first exposure to colonial elegance – or any other sort of elegance for that matter. When, within her limited experience, had she ever dined in such state? Her meals in the city were almost always dialed, emerging on retractable plates from the tabletop.

No, these people were not savages, despite their disadvantages. They had developed a way of life as refined as anything higher civilization had to offer. And they did it without machinery or the imports of other worlds, or any of a number of other things.

One of the servants, for instance, had a harelip and another had odd lesions on his neck. She saw them as he bent down to offer her vegetables, though she did not know that they betokened scrofula, a disease so long eradicated on the more advanced worlds that its very name was forgotten. But she did know that modern medical advances could have cured both afflictions. And yet these people worked on.

There were several other guests at the table, masters of the district and their wives, all known to Master Frayle. No one made any effort to introduce them to Frayle's guest, however, and Marja wondered at this. Perhaps they already knew who she was.

The bishop sat at the head, in command of himself and of the situation regarding them all with a look of benignity which might have been genuine – Marja thought it was – though it could not hide the powerful intellect beneath. He had greeted her kindly on his return, but there had been no time for anything but the most perfunctory conversation.

He did not much resemble his brother, though the family good looks were in evidence. But while Frayle's face and indeed his entire body expressed an almost feline strength and energy, the bishop was a man of great stillness. He ate with the economy of one whose mind was not on the meal, studied his guests without seeming to, and was undoubtedly forming judgments of his own.

Marja herself would be an unknown factor so far as he was concerned.

Perhaps he might even consider her a danger to the colony's peace. But though she watched him narrowly, she could gain no hint of his thoughts as he sat listening patiently to the master seated beside him.

Once his glance fell on Frayle, who had taken the seat beside Marja. It was a look of long familiarity in which she thought she could detect a distant but resigned disapproval. Frayle himself was careful not to look in his brother's direction at all.

Later, when the company had dispersed, the masters having evening engagements in the town, she and Frayle sat on with the bishop. His surname was not the same as that of his brother. That name was reserved for the master of the estate. Instead, the bishop used the family name of Rhosyn.

"We are a good sized clan," he told her. "We have several kinsmen who are masters of farms. In fact, one of them was with us for dinner. I hope you will excuse my not formally introducing you to my other guests," he added. "I thought you might like to remain incognito, at least for a time. Though you may be sure you were noticed and speculated about."

His brother frowned slightly. "They will know about her soon enough," he said. "We are on the way to Frayle Farm."

"To be sure. And when you are there, you may call in the whole countryside and reveal whatever you wish concerning the corporate buyout – and Miss Sienko's business in the colony."

"Then you know," Marja said hesitantly, ignoring his use of the archaic "miss", "why I have come?"

"You have come to our world because Pesc has bought out Dagon," Bishop Rhosyn told her. "And you have come to *me* out of your great courtesy. You are very welcome here." He made no reference to her summoning him, though it was a summons he had obviously ignored.

"Thank you," she replied feeling as though she had lost her way in the conversation. "Naturally I had hoped to – to meet with you."

"And my brother Prydan has been so kind as to escort you here."

"We will be going on to the fringe. I would like to see it. I mean –" Actually, she did not want to see it at all and she thought he could tell by looking at her that she did not. There was something unnerving beneath his calm, a patient and discerning strength that his brother did not possess.

"The coordinator has asked me to visit the western part of the colony," she finished rather awkwardly.

This was not quite true. She had been specifically told to visit the fringe itself. Suddenly, for the first time, she wondered why. They were going to destroy the alien flora and, in the end, they would find a way to wipe the planet clean. So, what difference did it make whether their representative saw that flora with her own eyes?

If the bishop saw her perplexity, he gave no sign. Presently the housekeeper came in with tea and, Marja having no experience in local custom, he did the pouring himself.

"I have seen the fringe," he said as he added milk to his own cup. "There is a foundation of the Brothers of St. Hubert – the Western Priory it is called. Unfortunately, they are not allowed to accommodate ladies overnight. Perhaps my brother has told you?"

"We will make it a day trip," Frayle said. "If we leave the farm early enough, there should be time for that."

Bishop Rhosyn nodded. "It is an interesting sight," he said to Marja. "You stand on the edge of the human lands – a bit of old Earth, if you will – and you look out on chaos. It is utterly alien. A reminder that we were not bred for this place."

Frayle smiled his thin, slightly ironic smile. "You draw a lesson from this, no doubt."

"Oh, certainly." His brother was not at all put out. "We are made for heaven," he said serenely, "and we have no true home anywhere else. Though I suppose one could also add that, until that goal is attained, we were designed for Earth."

Frayle looked as though he had heard this before.

"You will come to the cathedral for Compline?" the bishop asked.

Marja and Frayle exchanged a look. "I think not," the master told him. "Dr. Sienko is tired from her journey." He did not offer to go himself.

"Then we will confer tomorrow morning," Frayle's brother said to Marja. "Soon after breakfast. I'm sure my brother will have errands in the town."

This time Frayle could not quite hide a look of vexation at being excluded from the interview, but he overcame it quickly. "Of course. I will join you for luncheon."

They had no opportunity for private conversation as they separated for the night. Their rooms were in different parts of the house and the master made no sign that he would seek her out. She was relieved. Knowing that their relationship had been mandated by the coordinator had rather blighted the whole thing.

As she followed the housekeeper, she thought of Wells for the first time. She assumed that he had, along with the robot, been consigned to a lower region and it was with no pleasant sensation that she discovered otherwise.

"Your guardsman has been placed in the room next to yours," the housekeeper said in a tone of slight disapproval. "And that – that manikin has requested that it share your own room."

Marja sucked in her breath. The idea of the robot standing silent guard over her during the night was almost obscene. But there was nothing she could say to the housekeeper. And Wells would be next door.

She was taken by surprise at the relief *that* thought gave her. On some level, Wells had become her defense against fears both tangible and intangible. She was thinking of this as she entered her room – and saw the robosecretary standing beside the bureau.

Before she could lose her nerve, she snatched up her wrapper and threw it over the robot's friendly face. Afterwards she stationed herself at the window to stare out at the town. She was closer to the fringe now. And the river.

She must have been overtired, for she drifted off still sitting in her chair, dreaming of the slowly undulating river that crawled along from out of the wildwood and back to the wildwood, cutting the colony in two. It sang to her, in words of amethyst light, the lament of the doomed forest.

When she woke later in the night, she remembered Wells next door and slipped into her bed, confident that nothing would harm her here. Even the robosecretary was no more than a silent shadow, muffled in cloth.

In the morning, Frayle went to mass, returning with his brother to breakfast. Rather shamefacedly, Marja had uncovered the robot and gone out, meeting Wells in the corridor. "I want some air," she said.

Obligingly, he led her down into the offices below – he had a knack for becoming quickly familiar with each new environment – and out into a vegetable garden wet with dew. The spring cabbages opened like buds and there were many other plants she recognized from her homeworld.

She told him of her plans for the day. "I should be busy with the bishop this morning and then I suppose we'll be leaving tomorrow," she said. "I don't think it is very far from here to Frayle Farm."

He nodded. "I've been talking to the servants," he told her.

She was not surprised.

"They are a little nervous about your robosecretary. The cook wants the bishop to sprinkle holy water on it just in case." She thought she saw a hint of a smile as he told her this.

"You like it here," she said, almost accusingly.

"Master Frayle's brother is a kindly man."

"The bishop? You met him?"

"Briefly. He asked if I would like to go with him to Compline last night, but of course I could not."

She looked down. "You had only to ask permission. I hardly think there is much danger here," she said.

"You are in danger everywhere."

Startled, she tried to read in his face the things he wasn't telling her. But as always, she was baffled by what she saw. One moment he seemed as forthcoming as a child while the next he closed himself away until he became the stranger he was – the bodyguard assigned by the corporation.

Knowing she might not get an answer, "Will things become more danger-ous," she asked in a low voice, "as we go further west?"

She was right in thinking that he would not answer her. Silently he escorted her back inside and left her in the dining room. A few moments later, Frayle and the bishop came in and they sat down to breakfast.

The two brothers seemed to be on good terms this morning. As always – or at least at this season – there was no meat. She resigned herself to por-ridge and rolls, soon dispatched, and it wasn't long until Frayle excused him-self and departed for his business in the town. She was left alone with the bishop.

"Shall we go to my office?" he asked politely. "Or would you rather come into the sunroom?"

When Marja opted for the sunroom, he took her to a small chamber filled with light. The morning was already warm enough to throw wide the double doors, revealing a different garden, this one full of tulips and other flowers she did not recognize.

"It's beautiful," she exclaimed spontaneously. In fact, it reminded her of some of the nicer parts of Bloomhadn.

He beamed at her enthusiasm. "It's always a blessing when we have a good second spring," he said.

She had forgotten the bizarre pattern of Treelight's seasons. And, she real-ized suddenly, she had once more forgotten Wells. She saw him now, standing outside the doorway. "Shall I wait in the garden?" he asked the bishop.

"Indeed not. You are a part of Pesc, too. Come and take a seat."

Marja felt awkward somehow, explaining her errand, tendering the cor-poration's offer to the colony – and to the bishop himself – while Wells was in the room. It all seemed tawdry, almost as though she were taking advan-tage of the colonists.

Bishop Rhosyn heard her out patiently, putting one or two questions of the sort that made her see things in a new and rather uncomfortable light. When she had finished, he sat so long in silence that she almost wondered if he had fallen asleep.

His response, when it came, took her completely by surprise. He turned to Wells. "Franz," he said – and that was a surprise, too, that he had managed to extract the bodyguard's first name when he spoke to him the night before – "would you wish these things for *your* home colony? Employment for all? Industrialisation? Abolishment of the farm system? Corporate mandated education for the youth? An entirely new orientation of society geared toward financial gain?"

Wells, too, was taken aback. "You ask *me*?" he said with a nervous glance at Marja.

"You came from a colony, didn't you?"

Did he know Wells' story? Marja wondered.

But, "Anything would have been better for us," the bodyguard told him honestly. "My homeworld had to be – that is, some of us were evacuated and the rest died."

"I am sorry," the bishop said. "That was insensitive of me. You – I hope you don't mind me speaking of these things? You are not in a position to make a judgment of your corporation's activities, then."

Wells shook his head and held up one wrist – the one with the slave band.

"And you can add nothing to what Dr. Sienko says?"

The bodyguard's face twisted slightly. "I am programmed to seek only what is to the benefit of my owners."

"And what might that be?"

Wells shrugged. "Whatever they say it is, I suppose."

"Now that isn't reasonable. Suppose I wanted to commit a sin. Would that be in *my* best interests?"

The other man did not answer.

"Your freedom is compromised within and without," the bishop observed thoughtfully. "But still you are a man and a Christian." He leaned forward, suddenly resembling his brother in the force of his attention. "How long," he asked, "since you have received Communion?"

"I am not in a state of grace," Wells told him flatly. "Under the circumstances you could hardly expect me to be."

"We must have a talk later on," the bishop said. "We will discuss the true good of the corporation and the extent of your free will. And if you like, you will make your confession then."

Marja contained herself with difficulty. Not only was this conversation highly distasteful to her, but the bishop had all but ignored her proposal. She made as though to rise.

He turned to her at once. "Please do not be offended," he said. "My priorities should, of course, be different from those of a professional like yourself. As to your corporation's plans for us and my aid in putting them into action, I must ask you for a printed copy of what is wanted and what is offered. I know as well as you do that we owe a debt for this world's development and certainly it needs to be paid."

A breeze wafted the scent of flowers to the party and the bishop suggested they go out into the garden. "You want me to require that our pastors alter the focus of their teaching, I gather," he said as he followed her out the door.

"Oh, Pesc won't stand in the way of religion," she protested. "We only ask that such things be kept out of public life. Otherwise it would take far too long to modernize the colony."

"Of course. And naturally the corporation will want to take charge of the schools."

"Well, they're hardly adequate."

"I suppose not."

"So," she said, "you agree? You will give the necessary orders?"

"Oh as to that," he said vaguely, "I will need a little time to study the matter."

Seeing her disappointment, he held up one hand. "When you return from your visit to Frayle Farm, we will speak again. I will have had time to look over your program by then."

It was plain to her that he was stalling. He was not so quick and decisive as his brother, but he was, she suspected, more subtle. In the meantime, he would certainly be trying to get as much information out of Wells as he could.

Considering the robot's threat of punishment, she didn't think that would be very much.

THE FARMLANDS FELL BEHIND. After that there was brush, which presently yielded to trees. Several of Sergay's people slipped away when the woodland began and it wasn't long before one of them returned for help to carry in a deer. Thus, dinner was assured – at least for the pagans of the company.

Brother Brendan was so tired of bread and porridge that he had half a mind to try his luck fishing in one of the little streams they passed. While the Star Brothers were not bound to keep Lent in exactly the same way these colonists did, he dared not risk giving scandal. Anyway, he thought resignedly, Treeworld's customs seemed to match those of Lost Rythar, which meant that the two Faring Guards would also be horrified if he partook of the venison.

He was peering into the brush, trying to gauge the depth of one of the tiny creeks when the wagon jolted to a sudden stop. A man had stepped out onto the road, hailing them peremptorily.

"Damn robbers," Sergay muttered, reaching for his spear. But then he relaxed. "It's Colin," he said as the newcomer stepped over to the wagon and looked up.

The outlaw gave a start when he recognized Brother Brendan. "Do you know who this fellow is?" he demanded of Sergay.

"Better than you do," the chief told him shortly. "Why have you stopped us?"

With another suspicious glare at the Star Brother, the young man turned back to the boss. "There've been druids. Heading for the river. At least three."

"So many! That makes seven in all," Brother Brendan exclaimed without thinking.

At this, the Band leader vaulted to the seat. His blade was out and pointing at the other man's throat before anyone could move. "What do you know about the druids?" he snarled. "You're a stranger in this district – don't deny it! There's something funny about you and that tall one who was with you at the fair!"

"Put that up!" Sergay ordered, knocking the sword away.

Colin looked from one to the other. "You vouch for this one?" he asked doubtfully.

"I do. Now shut up and let him answer your questions."

Unwillingly the other subsided while Brother Brendan recounted their adventure of the day before. When he got to the end, Colin was nodding with satisfaction. "So much for that lot, then. Good."

Then he thought of something else. "You say it was Brann who sent for this Gris Wolfgang?"

"I hardly think so," the Star Brother told him. "We went to the inn and were told he had been forced to flee."

He could see by Colin's face that he had already heard about the murder. "He didn't do it," the other man said quickly. "I know Brann well enough, even though he's not one of us. He's no killer of women."

"Then where has he gone?" Sergay asked. "Not with you, I take it."

"No. But we'd shield him if he asked us to."

"You'd do anything to break the law," the chief snorted.

At this the other returned him a clear-eyed look. "Wouldn't you?" he asked.

"That's as may be. But Brann is gone, and the girl is dead. Those are facts no one can deny."

Brother Brendan intervened at this point. "Gris Wolfgang does not believe that Brann is guilty either," he hastened to assure the outlaw. "None of us do, but maybe you should talk to him yourself." He hesitated for a moment. "You can imagine the state he's in, not knowing how the poisons of the druids work.

If there is anything you can tell him that would set his mind at ease – that would set *all* our minds at ease – you would be doing a great kindness."

"I wish there were." The outlaw's face grew bleak. "It's all come on us so quickly, these creatures slipping into the town and those other two escaping the hangman, that no one knows what to do. The druids have taken others – your friend was not the only one attacked. They come up the river in boats out of the wildwood, and then they go back the same way, usually with their victims, whose only hope of survival is to join them."

"So you think Gris Wolfbane is probably infected?"

"What did you do for it?"

He told about Rhosya's drastic treatment.

"Then I can't say for sure. None of the Band has ever been caught by them, so we can only go by what others tell us. But if they leave the vine on long enough, then there isn't much hope."

"You're out hunting druids?" Sergay interrupted.

"We are. They tried to take a girl from Harrow. Rhianna's sister. She's in pretty bad shape, but she got away before they could put one of those things on her."

Sergay cursed, glanced at the Star Brother, and shrugged apologetically. "I borrow from your religion," he said with a wry look. "I would not offend my own gods so."

Ard Matthew, who had come up to listen, looked coldly at the chief. "You fear devils, at least," he said. And then, "This kidnapping attempt occurred since we left Harrow?"

The outlaw gazed at him, really seeing the Lost Rythan for the first time. "Yes," he said slowly, still staring. And then, "Where is your home, stranger?" he asked, hand once more on sword hilt.

The Star Brother forestalled him. "You have guessed that we are not of your own folk," he said, "by our accents if nothing else. But you can see plainly enough that we are not druids. Isn't that what matters?"

"Don't try to sound stupider than you are," Sergay added. Then he turned to the others. "I have known Colin off and on for a couple years," he told Brother Brendan. "Rhosya can tell you that while he's a romantic young fool, there's no harm in him. He and his fellows set out to steal from the rich and give to the poor –"

"Can he keep his mouth shut?" Ard Matthew asked, studying Colin's face.

"As long as he stays away from Rhosya's potions, he can."

"I have been in the hands of the militia at Welyn," the young man told him. "It was last autumn when they sought the whereabouts of my chief.

They did not find him that time." As he spoke, he was pulling up his shirt. "Because I did not tell them anything." He turned around to show the lash marks that scarred his back. Certain lighter scars showed that this was not the first time he had been whipped, and the Star Brother wondered about that, though he said nothing.

"I told you he was a romantic young idiot," Sergay repeated, rolling his eyes. "He's got no more sense than –"

But Ard Matthew was satisfied. This was the sort of thing a Faring Guard understood. "We come from offworld," he said abruptly. "And we would travel secretly as much as we can. Though it is hard to disguise a Lost Rythan, I know, for we are a bit taller than average."

Suppressing a smile at this, Brother Brendan watched Colin in order to gauge his reaction.

"So that's what you are!" the outlaw was gazing up at the Faring Guard in awe. Even though he had joined the other two on the wagon seat, Ard Matthew still overtopped him.

"Yes. And this," the Lost Rythan indicated Brother Brendan, "is a Star Brother."

"I was at the gaol," Brother Brendan told him, "when Rhosya was sent in to aid your leader."

For once, Colin was silenced.

"You understand him?" Sergay demanded. "You are to keep quiet!"

A nod. Then, "I have heard of the Star Brothers," he muttered. "They are supposed to be our protectors."

"I wish we had that power," Brother Brendan told him. "God knows you will be needing whatever help we can give."

"There are rumours that this woman from Pesc means to turn everything upside down," Colin said, still eyeing Ard Matthew.

"Which *you* shouldn't mind," Sergay interrupted.

The outlaw ignored this dig. "You would leave things as they are – you Star Brothers?"

"Our main interest in your settlement is spiritual," Brother Brendan reassured him. "We assist the Church here when we can, of course. We do our best to protect you from heresy and – and whatever other evils may come from outside."

"This woman is evil?"

"She is a victim," Ard Matthew broke in firmly. "A dupe. Isn't that right, Brother Brendan?"

"It's the corporation," the other clarified for him. "It is there you will find the evil, at least as it affects your colony."

"Then you may count us friends. We will meet again." Their visitor leaped down from the seat to vanish as abruptly as he had come.

Sergay stared at the place where he had disappeared. "I hope you know what you're doing," he growled in disgust. "The Band may mean well, but they're young and they often act without thinking. That's how Rhyn got himself hanged."

"You think he'll talk?"

"Probably not. But they're going after the druids, and we already know what those druids can do."

"Yes." The Star Brother was only beginning to realize that there was danger not only to those the druids considered useful, but also to any who opposed them.

After Sergay had relayed Colin's warning to the others, he started them off once more, his bowmen riding beside the wagons now, to watch the countryside through which they passed. After a time, the woods gave way to marshland. The bridge lay ahead, and the lesser suns were setting when they saw another figure walking toward them on the road. To their surprise, they recognised Brann.

Before Brother Brendan could stop him, Gris Wolfgang had climbed awkwardly from one of the wagons and was running toward his friend. Sergay drew up with them, reining in the horses as they met.

They did not touch. Perhaps it was that the Lost Rythan felt himself unclean – or else that Brann was uncertain of his reception. They stood apart, looking at one another for a long moment.

The colonist appeared as battered as he had after his fight with Gris Wolfgang. His face was purple with bruises and he swayed on his feet. "I need help," he said at last. "They're after me and – and I didn't do it."

"I know you didn't," Gris told him. "Come to the wagon. You look all in."

"Wait," the Star Brother said. "Who is after you?"

"Druids. They killed Rhianna. And now they want *me!*"

"They won't get you," the Lost Rythan said grimly. "Come on."

When their unlooked-for passenger had been installed in the same wagon with the two Faring Guards, the company set off once more. Brother Brendan was looking straight ahead as the bridge rose before them.

"I don't like this," Sergay said. "We'll have the law down on us if we don't watch out."

"I don't like it either." But the Star Brother wasn't thinking about the law. He was wondering why Brann had not shown more anguish at the death of the girl who had seemed to be his lover.

Could he be guilty after all?

∾

TO MARJA'S EYES, WELLS WAS a new man. In a moment of compassion, she had agreed to go to Mass with Frayle that morning, precisely so that her bodyguard could accompany her. And he *did* receive communion, she noted. It seemed such a small thing to her – no more than a half-remembered symbol of her childhood. But Wells had been willing to risk the punishment of Pesc's robot, perhaps even death, for the privilege of having that small white circle placed on his tongue.

She was moved by this and angry that she was moved. But she kept silent about her feelings.

They departed Bannyclay soon after, taking the west road once more as it climbed slowly out of the river valley. Here the woodland resumed, bright with spring foliage. Scattered among the various greens, cherry trees bloomed in drifts of white, while along the verge were hyacinths and crocuses. For some distance, their way ran beside a creek. Its name, her host told her, not surprisingly, was Frayle Creek.

It was a good-sized stream, and looked rather deep in places. She wondered if it would be possible for a boat to come up this way from the river. And why, she asked herself in sudden fear, would I be wondering about that? As though something might be hunting us.

They reached Frayle's land not long before midday. As they passed one humble dwelling after another, some of them grouped together in small hamlets, he pointed out the timber, the meadows, and finally the plowed fields. The main house, when they came to it, was a sprawling mass of stone and wood with a jumble of peaked roofs and here and there a balcony. It looked as though it had grown, rather than having been built over the years since the colony was founded. The rearing of such a profusion of gables and towers, not to mention the solid structure beneath, might well have taken the full century and a half.

Marja began to wonder just how many people lived there. Her companion was eyeing the house with some complacency, as a man would who guards a treasure placed within his keeping – a *trust*. Something in his expression spoke not only of love but of *patria* – a feeling that went beyond mere surface family pride, and might extend to a ruthless determination to foster and defend the things his ancestors had built, not because they were *his*, but because he was *theirs*.

Then he saw her watching him and his expression changed completely.

"You must be very tired, Marja," he said quietly. "I hope you will be comfortable here."

"Yes – Prydan," she replied. "It is beautiful, your home."

He smiled at her as the carriage drew up into a courtyard flanked by outbuildings. Immediately servants rushed forward to usher the master and his guest up a paved walkway and into the house.

Once inside, Marja looked around eagerly, unable to hide her curiosity. Frayle's house, she saw at once, was less elegant than that of the bishop at Bannyclay. The floors, where they were not flagged, were of wide boards, shrunken in places with cracks between. The walls, too, were unfinished and the furniture was overlarge, with a hewn look. Tables and benches, great chests and safes, all seemed as though they had been literally hacked out of the wilderness – a wilderness that had only been planted a decade or so before the planet was colonized. She got the impression the inmates of *this* house had had greater things to occupy them than either comfort or interior decoration.

They were met by a woman whom Frayle introduced as the housekeeper. She too bore a look of the wilderness, her strong face unlined as yet, but no longer young. Her black hair was threaded with grey and she wore it in a coronet of braids. Her figure was slim in her dark dress, but her hands were large and capable.

She did not curtsey quite – the customs of the colony were not so archaic as that – but she bowed her head slightly as the master gave his commands concerning Marja's accommodation.

"Where are my sons?" he asked when he had finished giving orders.

"Brian is inspecting the shearing sheds," she said promptly, "and Balt has taken a crew into the woods."

He nodded. "I shall want to see the steward," he told her. "And the foreman of the shepherds. Have them wait in the office."

When the woman had departed, he turned to Marja. "I'm sure you understand," he said rather apologetically, "that there are things I must see to after so long an absence."

"Yes, of course," Marja said, with a formality born of awkwardness. "I had not realized how very extensive your holdings were. It must be a great responsibility."

He looked gratified at this. But his caress before he dismissed her to a waiting servant girl was still somewhat distracted. As he turned to hurry away, he was stopped by a rather brawny man with lowering eyebrows and an untrimmed beard.

"They're asking, master," he said without preamble, "what to do with the –" He seemed at a loss for a word. "That thing in the wagon."

"He must mean the robosecretary," Marja said hastily. "It had better have a room of its own – some place I can use as an office. Even a store room would do."

"And your bodyguard?" Frayle asked her. "Surely even he can see no danger here."

She gave him an apologetic smile. "Wells trusts no one. It is his conditioning by the corporation. He's a bit like a guard dog."

The master nodded. "Then give him a room next to that of his mistress," he told the maid. "And find a place for the manikin." A moment later, he was gone.

Marja was given a room as stark and imposing as the rest of the décor had led her to expect. The girl had no sooner left her than two men came in carrying her luggage. They were followed immediately by the housekeeper.

Alone with the woman, Marja found her somewhat formidable. The housekeeper went immediately to the windows and drew back the drapes. The bronze light of the setting suns – one of them was still well above the horizon – gave rosy tints to the unfinished walls, transforming the room into a glowing fairytale bower. Here, indeed, lay peril, Marja felt, half succumbing the the spell of the place. Here anything might happen.

Then the other woman turned around, and her calm face brought back the everyday world, the world of Treelight's frontier. "Dinner will be ready in an hour, Lady," she said. "We do not keep the fast so strictly here as they do further east, but if you object to venison, I will tell the cook."

"Indeed not," Marja told her thankfully. "And what am I to call you?"

"My name is Carhyn, Lady. That will do."

"Then – then Carhyn, can you show me where they've put the robosecretary?"

"Yes, Lady. The *thing* has been given a room at the end of the hall." There was no mistaking the housekeeper's suspicion and distaste for the robot.

Maybe she thinks I'm a witch, Marja thought, and the idea amused her for as long as it took to remember the gallows at Harrow. Then she shivered.

After locating the robot, she asked which room was Wells's. Then, dismissing the housekeeper, she went back into her own chamber. There was a bolt on the inside of the door, and for some reason she found this comforting.

At the appointed time, Wells came for her. "This way," he said, guiding her to the top of a different staircase than the one she had first come up.

She gave him a look of amusement. "You have been exploring?"

He did not deny it. "I'm invisible," he explained. "Or nearly so. And I've already got acquainted with the principle servants. They are all serfs, you know."

She stopped. "Serfs – yes. They would be."

"Slaves in a way," he said cheerfully. "They belong to the estate."

No wonder he got along so well with them, she thought. "What did you think of the bishop's answer," she asked him as they descended the stairs.

"He's a very wise man," Wells told her. "I believe you can trust him to come up with a decision which will be in the best interests of everyone concerned." But he did not quite look at her as he said it.

She gave him a suspicious look of her own. "You speak as a Christian," she said, half teasingly.

He shrugged. "I warned you, didn't I?"

Baffled and uneasy, she followed him to a great hall. The last of the suns was setting, and a roaring fire at one end kept off the chill of the spring night. She found Frayle there, flanked by two younger versions of himself. He had been speaking earnestly to them in a low voice, but broke off at once when he saw her.

"Marja," he murmured, taking her hands. "Come and meet my sons."

Brian was the eldest, the one who was to marry Madoc's daughter, and he proved to be a very serious young man whose dark hair and beard were tinted with auburn. His brother's hair was much redder, while both had the keen blue eyes of their father. Balt, the second son, did not seem quite as reserved as the elder, and she guessed that under the right circumstances, he might prove to be good company.

They all took places at a table ridiculously large, as though there had once been a great many more Frayles than there were now. A longer board, further from the fire, held the servants. It was here that Wells took his place between the brawny porter and another man whose bluff features spoke of hours spent outdoors. He seemed already on easy terms with both of them.

She hid a smile. Apparently there were as many sides to Wells' personality as he had weapons concealed about his body. Then she turned her attention back to her own table.

The master was carving a haunch of venison – at least she assumed that was what it was – and only looked up when he passed her a plate. "I apologise for neglecting you earlier," he said. "But there is much to do here. Perhaps tomorrow you would like a tour of the farm?"

This didn't seem the right time to remind him of their excursion to the fringe, so she assented gracefully to his offer. But did Frayle even guess, she wondered, that all this – his meadows and his sheep and the woods that yielded both lumber and venison – that all of it would soon mean as little to him as the clumsy ovens in which his food was cooked?

She offered him wealth and culture, a place for his colony among the stars. Yet sometimes, as now, he seemed to lack the capacity to understand that the universe did not stop at the borders of this tiny colony. And yet this man was one of the most intelligent and progressive of his people! At times like this, the gap between them seemed too great to bridge. But then –

She was brought out of her reverie by the younger son. He was looking at her questioningly.

"Oh," she said. "I'm sorry. I was daydreaming. Did you say something?"

Balt gave her a knowing grin. "Frayle Farm has that effect on people," he said while his father looked on, displeased. "Just wait until you've seen it all."

"I'm afraid one day will not suffice for that," the master said eyeing his son coldly. "But you may find parts of it interesting."

"I'm sure I will," she said with a smile. Did he begin to understand a little, after all? She planned to call in the waiting crews as soon as they returned to Harrow and, when the wildwood began to fall and a whole continent – a whole world! – opened out around the colony's borders, then at last Frayle would truly see the possibilities.

They finished their meal and the evening in relative comfort. There was one awkward moment when Brian, the elder son, asked if anyone wanted to join him in praying the Rosary. No one did and he left the company early.

Another occurred when the housekeeper brought in wine and Balt jumped up to help her. "Will you have a glass Carhyn?" he asked mischievously but the woman did not look up.

"Thank you, young master," she said distantly, "but that would not do." She did not glance over at Frayle, but he was watching her, his expression gloomy.

After she had gone, the conversation seemed rather forced. At last, in response to a meaningful look from his father, Balt excused himself and left the other two alone. Frayle got up to mend the fire.

"I know it must seem rough living here," he said as he added a log, "after what you've been used to."

"Oh no," she lied, trying to keep her voice light, "it's rather *grand*, I think. Like something –"

"Something out of a history book?" he asked her. "From barbarian times?"

She flushed. "Prydan," she said, "I cannot help it that things are so different on the other colonies. Sachsen has been settled for almost two thousand years. Of course, it would not resemble your – Networld 326."

"Of course." He turned around and she saw that he had composed his features with a visible effort. "You cannot imagine," he said, "the hunger a man feels to belong to the rest of the human family. To learn and to see and to do what others have done and seen!"

"Perhaps I can – a little." But even now she could not bring herself to tell him about her childhood in the backward farm country. She was ashamed to have him know that, even on Sachsen itself, there were places like this.

He dropped the poker and came to her. With his arms around her, she began to feel that they had crossed a bridge after all – though it wasn't that of culture. The look on his face was unequivocal. If she let him, he would lead her to some other room in some other part of the house and they would be alone together for the night.

With her hand linked in his, she turned away from the fire – only to confront Wells, who stood in the shadows, guarding her as always. In confusion, she let her hand slide from that of the master.

Beside her, Frayle stiffened. "You won't be needing your *slave* tonight," he said. "I should be protection enough for the lady," he added to Wells.

She wanted to order the bodyguard to leave them, but the words stuck in her throat. He would obey her only if she reminded him that she was acting under orders – that Hu had told her to do this thing.

With that realization, and the certain knowledge that it was impossible for her to say the damning words, everything was spoiled. Her cheeks reddening, she stepped away from Frayle. "Good night," she told him rather abruptly and followed Wells up the stairs.

Damn the corporation! Damn Hu!

But she did not damn Wells. She did not dare.

CHAPTER 12

THE ROAD TO **B**ANNYCLAY WAS nearly deserted as the travelers approached the outskirts of the town. Rhosya, who had come to join her father and the Star Brother in the lead wagon, directed them to a turnoff where she hopped down and left them. "Keep going," she said, "while I tell the farm folk we are here. I cured their son of the river fever last year and I'm sure they'll welcome us."

The wagons moved on until the road ended in a small meadow surrounded by young trees. Droppings and hoof prints were everywhere.

"I wish," Sergay said, looking around at the mess, "that Rhosya had cured the son of a sheep farmer instead."

Brother Brendan, excusing himself, made his own way in among the trees. It was time to check in with his superiors.

His call was answered at once. "The Balthasar is still orbiting Networld 15," the operator said. "But there's a transmission for you."

The Star Brother waited until, suddenly, he heard Father Moto's voice in his ear.

"Brother Brendan: By the time you get this, we may have more information for you. We'll send it to you as soon as we can. Meanwhile, keep that Pesc woman away from the Fringe. They've been drugging her with something, but we don't know why yet, though we are pretty sure it has to do with the native foliage. See what you can find out. Aside from being toxic, what else is special about it? And keep checking in!"

When he had digested this message, he thanked the operator. "You'll hear from me again," he said. "Maybe later tonight."

"I'll try to keep things open, but don't get your hopes up. You've done well to get through twice in a row."

After signing out, Brother Brendan went to find the Faring Guards and pass on Father Moto's information. While they were discussing what it could mean, Sergay's daughter returned with the farm wife and two of her children. These all carried laden baskets and this largesse served to mollify the boss to the extent that he thanked the woman for her hospitality and even praised the cows that were now emerging from the trees.

"What is my son's life worth?" their hostess cried. "He was in the last stage of the fever when you passed through the town. It was said the travelers knew many secrets of life and death, and I was desperate!"

"Rhosya is a good healer," Sergay agreed.

But the woman was not listening. She had suddenly spotted the Lost Rythans – and Brann, who was emerging from one of the wagons. His face, if anything, looked more battered than it had before and he was holding himself oddly as he shuffled over to the others.

"Another patient of mine," Rhosya said hurriedly. "I must tend to him now. But I do thank you for the bread and cheese."

With a last curious look at the strange company, the farm wife shooed her children from the field. The sight of three strangers had seemed to blunt her friendliness a trifle.

Brann, however, refused Rhosya's ministrations after he had limped over and sat down on a log. Leaving him there, Ard Matthew built a fire, while the girl tore bread into hunks for them and cut up the cheeses. It was plain that Ard Matthew was troubled in conscience about harboring a man accused of murder, and he kept glancing at his superior as though he did not know what to do.

Brann's story was that he had been attacked by the druids and fought free before they could lay one of the vines against his flesh. He had been so battered, however, that after he made it to a hiding place, he could not move from there for some time. When he was finally able to go back into the village, it was only to be accused of murder. After that, there was nothing for it but to flee.

"How many druids were there?" Sergay asked when he heard the story.

"I'm not sure. Maybe three."

"And you fought them off?"

The other man nodded, wincing.

"Here," Gris Wolfgang said, handing him a cup of freshly brewed tea. "We have no more beer, I think –" He glanced at Sergay who shook his head.

"If you don't mind," Brother Brendan said presently, "I would like to see a little of the town before it is full dark."

Ard Matthew stood up. "You had better not go alone," he said and the Star Brother nodded.

The two set off along a lane beside the river. The suns were setting and the nebula had not yet risen, but it was still fairly light. Soon they came to a boulevard where carriages and wagons passed one another in the greatest concentration of traffic they had seen so far in the colony.

"Look," the Lost Rythan said, pointing. "The cathedral!"

His companion turned to stare at the great edifice. It was built entirely of stone in a style that proclaimed what it was while still reflecting the artistry of a people cut off from the larger colonies. It must have taken them many years of labor.

"I'll bet they started that the first year the colony began!" Brother Brendan exclaimed.

The two approached cautiously and slipped inside through one of the smaller entrances. Skirting the open space in the nave, they soon located a side altar where a statue of Our Lady stood, beautifully fashioned of wood.

To Brother Brendan, who was very conscious of the great deeps of space that lay between the inhabited worlds, this was like finding signs of civilization in a wilderness. How far was it from here to Lost Rythar, he wondered, where his order had one of its main centers? How far to his childhood home in Gaelway Colony? Or to the Star Brothers' house on Sachsen? The very suns of these places were but pinprick stars half obscured by the nebula's light.

And yet, once more he saw that it did not matter. The Church cut through time and space even more effectively than the starnet. He felt some of the tension go out of him as he prayed. Beside him, Ard Matthew, too, had come home for this brief time.

The great stained glass windows were darkening when the Star Brother forced himself to rise. They had better be getting back to Sergay's camp, he decided. Tomorrow would be soon enough to see the rest of Bannyclay.

The nebula was well risen when they reached the wagons. Rhosya was brewing some new potion as they came up to her. "I offered to make something for Brann," she said, "but he said he'd rather lie down. He and Gris Wolfgang are in the wagon talking."

The Star Brother turned in that direction, pausing to look up at the sky. It was all God's creation, he was thinking, as the nebula climbed slowly above the horizon, trailing its arms and lighting the entire field with its weird purple glow. What did it matter which world had given him birth? All lay under heaven – even these material heavens themselves!

The peace he had gained in prayer lasted exactly until he reached the wagon.

As he approached, he could hear voices, one of them urging, the other protesting. As he drew nearer, there were words.

"—you will die if you do not. I bring you life –"

"Where did you –"

"Life, starman. Otherwise it will kill you!"

Brother Brendan began to run. He flung aside the flap only to behold a strange and dreadful thing. Gris Wolfgang was backed against one wall, his wide eyes fixed on the other man. With one hand, he clutched his wounded arm shaking his head in terrified denial.

But it was the sight of Brann that filled the Star Brother with horror. The young man held out a handful of some white, squirming stuff which he was trying to force the Lost Rythan to take.

With a shout for help, Brother Brendan laid hold of Brann's clothing – for he could not bring himself to touch his flesh – and dragged him out of the wagon. At this, Gris Wolfgang seemed to break free of whatever had held him. "Don't hurt him!" he cried but it was not clear which of the two he addressed. He seemed too dazed to know.

Ard Matthew and Rhosya came running just in time to see Brann struggle to his feet. He looked swiftly from one to the other as though calculating his chances and then, before anyone could stop him, he turned and loped away, moving awkwardly as though his legs no longer worked as they should. None of the others pursued him.

The Star Brother was wiping his hands on his cloak, hardly realizing what he did. After a moment, he bent over and was sick.

Only he had seen, when he tugged loose the other man's shirt, the paleness and the silvery lines. "He was one of them," he whispered when he could speak. "They got him and – those bruises were his disguise!"

At these words he saw something he had never expected to see. Gris Wolfgang suddenly collapsed, shuddering and half sobbing. Ard Matthew held him until the fit had passed, but he did not seem in much better case. It looked as though the two Lost Rythans had been pushed beyond what their minds could process.

"It all happened so quickly!" Gris Wofgang kept saying over and over. "He was fine just a few days ago!"

"He didn't – you didn't take anything from him, did you?" Brother Brendan demanded.

The other shook his head. "But he was – taken! Changed! Defiled beyond redemption!"

"Don't say that. Say rather that he is already dead."

No one slept much that night and when, during the protracted dawning of the suns, Colin of the Band slipped into camp, he was welcomed with a cordiality that surprised him. Sergay told him what had happened.

"They stole a boat last night," the outlaw rejoined. "We were watching at the bridge, but there was no way we could stop them. Now we know why – Brann was probably aboard."

"Gris Wolfgang is in a bad way," Brother Brendan said. "Brann was his friend, you know. And Brann was changed so quickly!"

"Yes," the young man said grimly. "That seems to be how they operate."

"He was alright just a week ago. And now he is one of them. How could this be? The Brothers of St. Hubert could go on for a year or more before they even got sick."

"It is their drugs, I think. The druids know how to hasten the process."

With a grimace of disgust, the Star Brother told him about the handful of squirming things he had seen.

Colin listened curiously. "We always thought they gave them some sort of brew," he said. "Do you suppose they eat the things?"

But no one knew. The realization that one could be transformed into a druid within days had frightened them all. If Brann – or what had been Brann – had succeeded in forcing Gris Wolfgang to take whatever it was he held, then the Faring Guard, too, might have become such another one.

"Shall we stay here another day?" Sergay asked his guests. "The druids are gone. Maybe we should be off to Dunsever."

The Star Brother considered. "I would have liked to meet the bishop," he said. "But if he is a Frayle, then maybe I'd better not."

"The bishop's alright," Colin said suddenly. "Doesn't even use the same name. Bishop Rhosyn isn't a bit like his brother."

"Then I will go." He wanted to ask how Colin could be so sure of this, but of course the young man would have visited Bannyclay before. He turned to Ard Matthew. "I think I had better take Gris Wolfgang with me," he said.

As Colin offered to guide them, the three left at once while Ard Matthew and Rhosya went to the farm to return the empty baskets. Sergay had decided to move on as soon as they got back.

"You know this place well?" Brother Brendan asked Colin.

"Pretty well. I used to work for the bishop," he added with a crooked grin. "I'm one of Frayle's serfs."

"Then you take a risk coming here!"

"No, I don't. The bishop freed me after I was caught the second time. But he did suggest that I move further east after that."

The other man said no more. Colin must know whether it was safe for him to visit the bishop.

They came into the house through the garden and, Colin's guess being the correct one, met the bishop in the sunroom where he sat reading Marja's sheaf of printouts. He looked up without surprise, recognizing the young man at once.

"I've brought you a Star Brother," the outlaw told him. He hurried over to kiss the bishop's ring and the other two did the same.

"I am very glad," Bishop Rhosyn said cheerfully, "that you have not yet been hanged, Colin."

The other grinned at him.

"And a Star Brother," the bishop went on. "I should have expected you. The Pesc representative has already paid a call. Does she know you are here?"

"No, my lord," Brother Brendan assured him hastily. "And we'd rather she didn't."

"Oh, the lady won't learn anything from me," he assured the other man. "In fact, her employers have such sweeping plans for us that it may be necessary for me to go on retreat when she comes back. I don't like to disappoint that poor girl, but she has no notion what would happen if we put all these plans into effect. I begin to wonder if Pesc is really serious."

At this the Star Brother gave a start – which the bishop did not miss, he was sure. He had contacted the operator once more after the night's events, but there was no further message waiting for him. Was it prudent to tell this colonist what he had learned so far?

He thought he had better wait until he knew more. "You say this woman has been to see you?" he asked instead. "Where is she now?"

"With my brother Prydan. They have gone to visit the family estate."

He gestured them to seats. "Perhaps, Colin, since you know your way about, you will fetch us some tea or something." He glanced at the Lost Rythan. "Beer, as well," he added.

"You've been offworld."

"Well, naturally I had to be consecrated on Sachsen. And wherever things like that happen, one meets Lost Rythans." He turned to the Star Brother. "Now tell me – everything." His voice remained bland, his expression benevolent, but somehow there was no disobeying the order.

Brother Brendan complied, forgetting his original hesitation. The tea had been drunk – and the beer – before he finished his tale. God help him if he'd misjudged the man, he thought when he had finished, but somehow he didn't think he had.

"So Pesc is not telling the lady the truth?" the bishop mused aloud.

"Almost certainly not. My superiors think they are using her in some way without either her knowledge or consent. It's something to do with the fringe – the wildwood. But all they've been able to tell me so far is that we absolutely must keep her away from it."

"I see." The bishop set down the papers he had picked up to show them. "Then we don't have to worry about being modernized after all," he said. His attention turned to Gris Wolfgang, who was sipping his beer with nothing like a Lost Rythan's normal gusto. "What is the matter, my son?" he asked.

Quickly the Star Brother told him about the druid attacks. "They were here at Bannyclay, too," he finished. "They escaped down the river."

"And you," the bishop said, fixing the Lost Rythan with his deceptively mild gaze, "fear that you have been infected?"

"We don't know yet," Brother Brendan said when Gris Wolfgang did not answer. "The wound has been thoroughly burned out, but it was certainly more than a sting."

"Ah. And until you can be sure the treatment was effective, you will have no peace." He was still looking at the Faring Guard.

Gris Wolfgang looked down.

"You have met the Brothers of St. Hubert?"

"We met Marshal Gwilym," the Lost Rythan said in a low voice.

"He is a brave man. Soon he will have his reward and another will take his place. It is the cross they have all chosen."

The Lost Rythan flushed slightly at this. "Yes, your lordship," he whispered.

"You did not choose, however," the bishop said, "and, after all, it may be you will not be asked to carry that particular cross. But if not, you will have another. Surely God wills these things for our good."

He was silent for a moment, watching the other man thoughtfully. "You are ashamed now. But that, too, is vanity. I don't know what God has in store for you, but I know how you should receive it. I think you know that too."

The other man nodded. "I – I forgot," he muttered. "I was afraid."

"You are a Faring Guard, are you not? One whose life is already forfeit?"

"Yes. I killed two men from ambush during a clan feud."

"And this is your penance – to travel from world to world in the service of the Star Brothers?"

"It is."

"Well, then. I can't give you the courage you need, but I can remind you to ask God for it. He'd hardly deny something like that to a penitent trying to do what is right, would He?"

At this, the Lost Rythan finally managed to raise his eyes. "No, your lordship," he said.

In the end, both men went away comforted, each in his own way. Brother Brendan felt suddenly sure they would succeed in saving the colony, because it was worth saving, and his companion stalked beside him, already, the Star Brother was sure, resolved to make up for his lapse.

As for Colin, the bishop's housekeeper had invited him to lunch and, assured that the others could find their way back to Sergay's camp without him, he accepted.

EVEN WITH PART OF IT gone, the cross was a heavy burden. Dust had finally managed to get back on his feet but he couldn't see any reason why he should pick it up again.

"He can come and get it," he muttered to the angel.

"Who?"

"Gaed Alfred. He took that broken part quick enough."

"That wasn't actually Gaed Alfred, you know," the angel told him. "It was only your impression of him. But he did get that part of the file, thanks to you."

"So if that was only my impression of Gaed Alfred, just what exactly are you?"

But the angel didn't answer that one.

"Look," Dust said. "All this god-stuff, it comes from Gaed Alfred. He's infected me. It isn't real."

"You had a pretty good look at what's real," the angel said. "Who do you think told you what a jerk you are?"

Dust gave it a bleak look. "Not Gaed Alfred," he said. "He'd never say anything like that. I must have told myself."

"But he gave you something to measure by. Just like he's been measured and fallen short. Remember?"

"Oh, yeah. I keep forgetting. Those guys in the Faring Guard all used to be – I mean, they're killers, aren't they?"

"So, what are you going to do?" the angel asked. "You're really a mess, you know. Probably worse than they are."

Dust blinked at it.

"Can't fix things, can you?" the angel said smugly. "Have to ask for help."

"You?"

"You know better. You said I'm just a figment of your imagination."

At this, Dust sat back down. "Hell," he said. "That'll teach me to argue with an angel."

Suddenly the hand was back on his shoulder. "Get up," the voice said. "It's going to get darker in here and you need to get moving."

"You again," Dust said, but he said it wearily. He wasn't mad any more.

"This is your chance. You can do something to make up for those people you've killed and all that other stuff you did. For selling your soul to the highest bidder."

"That won't fix it." Dust said, but he was talking to himself.

"You're sorry," the voice said. "At least you can get up and prove it."

"I don't have the energy to get up. Look at me – naked as the day I was born. Lost in the dark with this crazy angel –"

Suddenly he felt a mighty blow that knocked him sprawling on his face. A stone cut him on one cheek. "Get up!" the voice said and Dust got up. As he did so, another piece of the wood splintered away and the cross got a bit lighter.

"But I can't really," he said, not talking to anyone in particular as he made his way up a stony hillside. There were stars in the sky now, though he didn't recognize any of the constellations. Still, it was an improvement.

"Can't what?" the angel asked as it reached over to help him along.

"I can't bring those people back. I can't buy back my soul. Like you said."

"No you can't," it agreed.

Dust dragged the cross up the hill.

In his chair before the banks of machinery, Father Moto nodded. "Here comes some more data," he said.

But his companion wasn't listening. "I think I've figured out part of the problem," Gaed Alfred muttered. "He was ambushed when he went into the Pesc files. And he seems to have picked up a virus."

"Can you fix it?"

"I don't know," the chief admitted. "It's like he's trapped in there. He may not have enough energy to come to the surface."

"Can't you talk him out?"

"I don't know if he can hear me. But I guess something must be getting through or we wouldn't have the stuff we've picked up so far." There were some strands of hair sweated to his face and he shoved these back. "I hate to think of him lost in there."

The priest turned back to the screen and started reading the file segment. After a time, he reached for his communicator.

❧

BREAKFAST WAS AWKWARD. Marja and Frayle did not look at one another. His anger manifested itself in a politeness that, in someone more cultured, would have meant less than it did in him. Why couldn't she have simply spoken quietly to Wells last night, telling him as much of the truth as she had to?

But she knew why. She was not a slave. Her love was not the property of the corporation. And – and neither was Prydan Frayle's!

At this thought, she did venture a timid glance in his direction. He met her look gravely but not unkindly, turning quickly away. While they were eating, the steward was announced and Frayle excused himself to speak with him.

When the master returned, it was only to tell her that he was called away to a different part of the farm and that Balt would provide the tour, if she had no objection. She nodded, not missing a glance between the two brothers. Frayle had started toward her as though to take her hand in parting, but seeing that look pass between his sons, he quickly left the room.

Marja pushed away her plate. Perhaps she was forgiven after all.

"It will be my pleasure," Balt told her, rising after his father had gone. "I've never given a tour before, but then I don't think my father has either – except to Master Madoc." He gave his brother a mischievous glance.

The elder son stood up likewise. "We will say the grace after meals," he said. He had not suggested this the night before, but in the absence of Master Frayle, he seemed determined to stand in his father's place.

Marja endured the prayer barely remembered from her childhood and then followed Balt out of the room. She was not surprised to see Wells, emerging from wherever he had stationed himself during breakfast, trailing behind them.

"I suspect my father was called away to judge a case," young Frayle said as he led her to a side door. "There was a killing while he was away and Brian doesn't have the authority to hang the culprit."

Marja swallowed. This must be one of the regular duties of the masters, she thought. Hanging people.

They took a light wagon. Wells was allowed to sit in the back while Balt drove and Marja sat next to him.

"We've got roads all over the farm," Balt explained, "but they aren't very good. I think my father wants you to see his sheep and certainly the weaving sheds. He's developed quite an industry here."

"Ah," she said. "So you do understand about factories."

"If you mean producing cloth, then we do. Was that what you had in mind?"

Carefully she explained how power could be harnessed – "From the creek?" he asked. "We've got a mill." – and that it could be used to do the work of men.

"That is why I am here," she finished. "Pesc is going to industrialise your colony. You have been held back far too long, you know."

"And my father will be helping you with all this?" he asked.

"Yes. And your uncle, I hope."

At this the young man turned away, half hiding a smile. "You can never count on Uncle the Bishop," he warned her. "One moment it looks like he and my father are thick as thieves and the next they're practically at each other's throats over some moral question."

Remembering the bishop's interview with Wells, she thought she understood perfectly what the young man was telling her.

They drew up before a long series of buildings where a group of serfs, both male and female, labored at great handlooms. In the yard, women were dying yarn in boiling pots of different colored liquids.

"Are they paid to do this?" Marja asked.

Balt looked at her as though he did not understand.

"I mean do they have a share in the profits?"

"They get food," he said, "and their homes. And cloth as they need it."

"This will have to change." She did not look at Wells who stood as always, somewhat apart, watching everything. "Pesc will hardly allow –"

She saw the bodyguard's face tighten. Was he laughing at her? Without realizing it, had she been attributing to the corporation her own opinions? Catching sight of the slave band on his arm, she feared that she had.

Balt either did not see or did not understand. He helped her back into the wagon, his face showing nothing except his own share of the Frayle charm. "Now, what would you like to see?" he asked. "The stables are rather fine. Do you like horses?"

She said that she did, even though they had not been part of her life for some years. Soon he was showing her the colts and several specially fine mares. She stroked their velvet noses and fed them pieces of carrot, while

Wells looked on. She did not think he had ever been close to a horse until he came to Treelight and she could tell they made him nervous.

"That was my brother's mare," Balt told her suddenly. "The one you're petting now."

"Brian's?"

"No, Evan's. Hasn't my father told you about him?"

She shook her head.

"He ran away. He was our uncle's favorite – the old boy wanted to make a priest of him, but the master wouldn't hear of it. I don't think Evan would have liked it, though. He always seemed like a pagan to me."

"So – when did this happen?"

"Last year about this time. He quarreled with our father over something to do with the sheep. Tried to save one of the shepherds from a beating. At first we thought he had joined a robber band, but now the master is convinced he's done worse."

She stared at him, not understanding.

"He's afraid he's gone to the druids."

At this, Marja shivered. "But – would anyone? I mean –" She thought of the strange, warped-looking men at Harrow as they were led out to the gallows, staring straight ahead as though they had already passed beyond such trifling things as death.

"I don't know." He sounded thoughtful.

"What do you know about the druids?" she asked sharply.

"That they honor the wildwood and have found a way to live in it. That they believe our colony is not natural – a disease on the planet. Something foreign."

"Your brother told you that?"

Balt nodded.

"Ah. But how do they live? I mean –" She doubted that this boy could ever have seen a druid. He would not speak so calmly about his brother joining them if he had.

"I don't know how they do it," he said. "If they do. He might have been only telling me something he had heard."

The subject was dropped until, returning to the house, Balt stopped her in the doorway. "Please keep quiet about Evan, if you don't mind," he said. "He shouldn't guess that you know anything about it."

She nodded and the young man hurried off, pausing once to give her a conspiratorial grin over one shoulder. In the hallway, she and Wells met the housekeeper coming down the stairs. "You are summoned, Lady," she said. "By that thing. It is calling for you. The master said to tell you."

"He's here?"

"Yes, Lady."

She hurried up the stairs, Wells at her heels.

"I should have checked in with the ship earlier," she said. "Before we went out, but I forgot."

That was a lie. She hadn't forgotten; she was afraid. She knew that Hu would ask her when they were leaving for the fringe and whether she had secured Frayle's entire commitment by the only means at her command. How could she tell him that she had not done it precisely because she had been ordered to do it?

Frayle was standing outside the office. He turned as she reached the top of the stairs and there was something furtive in his quick movement away from the door.

"It's been making noises," he explained, his voice not quite steady, "and the servants were afraid. Then it started calling for you and when it got no answer, for your bodyguard. Now it has stopped, but I thought I had better remain here in case it started up again."

She opened the door. There was no way she could tell whether Frayle had been in the room. But if he had, he was a brave man, she thought. And a very inquisitive one. She stepped over to the robot. "Dr. Sienko here," she said crisply.

Wells remained in the doorway, the master behind him. When Hu's words came in the robot's uninflected voice, Frayle blanched, but held his ground.

Hu was very angry, but all the while he demanded an explanation for her absence, the robosecretary continued to smile kindly out at the room.

She told him she had been touring the farm and that she was not alone. Master Frayle was with her.

There was a pause. Then, "Is he going to take you to the fringe?"

"He is. Master Frayle has been very cooperative."

Hu cut her off. "If he's here, let him speak to me."

"But – he's a colonist. Surely –"

Hu was adamant. Marja looked over at the master. "Will you –?" she asked.

She could see, now that he had actually come face to face with the unknown, Frayle was finding the situation daunting. The robot itself must have seemed magical to him, perhaps even diabolical. Remembering the witch hanged at Harrow, she halfway expected him to make the sign of the cross and flee.

He did not, however. Visibly bracing himself, he took one hesitant step into the room. "I am here," he told the thing and his voice was as steady as he could make it.

"Leave us alone together," Hu ordered, to Marja's surprise.

"I don't think –"

"You will obey me," the coordinator said, "or you'll never work again."

She stepped away, glancing helplessly at Wells who gestured her out into the corridor. Afterwards, he stationed himself once more outside the room, shutting the door.

They waited together in silence, hearing nothing except a low murmur of the voices within. She could tell when the robot was speaking because the rhythm was not that of a human voice. And she knew that Frayle was answering.

Eventually, the door opened. The master looked like a man who had seen visions. "It – your master would speak with you," he said to Marja and nearly staggered, reaching out to steady himself with one hand against the wall.

She hurried inside. "I'm here," she said.

"This man has agreed to escort you westward to inspect the native flora. I have explained certain things to him, though he is a primitive, and I have secured his unlimited cooperation."

Marja ignored the implied criticism. "But why?" she asked. "Why is it so important that I go to the fringe? That was not my original assignment! I have to get back soon, to meet with the bishop and the other masters."

"Later," Hu cut her off. "You may return to your base – afterward."

She would have protested further, but he interrupted her. "You have your orders," he said. "The corporation is counting on you – and on Master Frayle."

She held her peace, though she already knew that something had gone very wrong and that she was helpless to set it right. Then came the deeper realisation – and how had she been so blind to a fact as obvious as this? – that a corporation that would torture a slave would hardly scruple to destroy its employee. The conviction that she would never again leave Networld 326 was so strong that she wavered slightly, feeling darkness close in on her. What had she gotten herself into? What in God's name had she done?

Frayle was nowhere in sight. There was only Wells waiting in the corridor, his eyes filled with brooding compassion as he escorted her to her room and left her there.

FOR ONCE, THE COMMUNICATOR ACTUALLY summoned him. Brother Brendan excused himself and walked beside the wagon while he listened. Apparently Father Moto was still in the process of digging out information – he didn't say how or from where and there was no way to ask him, for they two were not connected directly. Brother Brendan's reply would have to go to the orbiting transmitter and then take its chances in the net. That would take a while.

Meanwhile he reviewed what his superior had to say. Keep the woman away from the wildwood; he had said that before. She had been drugged with something that would neutralize the toxins but other things would happen if she were exposed and those things might be irreversible. She was apparently a test subject, but for what, Father Moto still didn't know.

So why choose a young graduate in a field like social engineering? The answer: she had been hired because of the results of the genetic scan. She was a natural subject for whatever it was they were trying to do.

Was there a pharmaceutical use for the wildwood that might recoup what they had spent on the colony? But if so, why the secrecy?

Apparently, Father Moto – and probably Chief Snowtyger – had been wondering the same thing. They smelled a rat. So did Brother Brendan. He still did not know the source of their information, but that there was more – one last piece to the puzzle – seemed plain enough.

He went over the facts. A young woman had been sent to Treelight with a fictitious assignment. Unknown to herself, she was to be used in an experiment that might or might not harm her, but very likely would. That alone, while certainly illegal, would not be enough to cause Pesc much trouble, especially if the girl had no one to enquire about her, should she turn up missing.

He didn't need Father Moto to tell him that she would, in the end, go missing. They had hired her, then, for her genes. So why the secrecy? Obviously there must be something that would cause trouble for the corporation. Now he must find out what that was.

The travelers reached Dunsever in the late afternoon and set up camp on the village green. They were welcomed in this particular village, especially since it was market day. As usual, Sergay and his people would provide Sunday entertainment on the green, though there would be nothing so extravagant as the fair at Harrow. This was a more remote region and the people would be satisfied with less.

Despite their late arrival, the travelers managed to set out some of their wares at the Saturday market. As always, Rhosya did a brisk business selling whatever it was she had concocted the night before. Brother Brendan and the Lost Rythans kept out of sight until most of the daylight was gone, only venturing among the late shoppers.

"There's a tavern," Gris Wolfgang murmured, coming up behind the Star Brother. "I heard some people talking about going there this evening." Though the uncertainty still remained, he was doing much better than he had before his talk with the bishop. Because the promise of beer was always a comfort to a Lost Rythan, Brother Brendan agreed immediately to accompany him.

"Perhaps Sergay will come along, too," he said, fighting back a sudden stab of recollection. Their last introduction to one of the local inns had proven disastrous, but he would not dampen his friend's enthusiasm if he could avoid it.

The nebula was halfway up the sky when the Star Brother's party, along with Sergay, set out for the Staghorn Tavern. It wasn't far from the green and already a fair number of patrons had collected. Most of these were villagers, but a few who had come in from outlying farms stayed on after selling their produce. Some of these were serfs.

The four took a table where they could watch the rest of the room. The beer was quite good, though rather dark. Brother Brendan, for one, was glad that hops had been included in the offworld crops introduced by the original corporation, for not every colony made good beer. It must have been quite a task for Dagon Ltd to lay the foundation of this self-contained microcosm, he thought. They had omitted tobacco and proper tea, though what they had was acceptable, but the absence of smoke in the room seemed odd after some of the places he'd been. The Lost Rythans, however, were innocent of that particular vice and did not miss it.

It wasn't long before several voices rose in an argument nearer the fire. The subject seemed to be poaching, and a few of the local masters, including Frayle, came in for a share of, admittedly restrained, criticism.

An old man spoke up. "I remember that youngest Frayle boy. Stood up for my grandson when he was took by mistake. Got him off, too."

"Young Master Evan? He always was a one for running in the woods."

"Reckon where he is now?" someone else said and this was followed by an uneasy silence.

Then, "Well, Master Frayle's taken big game and no mistake! Got a woman from that new corporation! Took her right to his farm."

There were knowing nods and a few "ayes."

A rather dark young man regarded the rest over his mug. "He may have her, but can he hold on to her? Might be he's got a panther by the tail."

Several laughed. Master Frayle wasn't much loved, apparently.

Then another man spoke up. "I'd back my master against any odds," the grizzled peasant said and spat. "He always gets what he wants, damn him!"

"But what," the old man asked, "does he want this time? Not her, I'd think. Not when he's already got that housekeeper of his. Been like a wife to him these ten years, they say."

"It must be real peaceful up there about now," the dark man said, laughing. "Wouldn't surprise me if Carhyn puts a knife in her before it's over."

"You don't know what you're talking about," the peasant told him angrily. "That business with Carhyn's been done with these past two years or more."

"You think he's really after that alien woman?" a red-haired farmer demanded. "Sure, they say the corporation's changed – that we have a new owner. But what's she got to do with it, I'd like to know?"

"Whatever my master wants, he'll get it," the peasant persisted, holding up his mug for a refill. "It don't matter what the corporation does to the colony, he'll always come out on top!"

After that, the conversation turned to sheep, while the visitors went back to drinking their beer.

"How much further is it to Frayle Farm?" Brother Brendan asked Sergay.

"Not far. Hour's drive west. It's a big piece of land – almost a small colony by itself."

"Well, now we know for sure the Pesc woman is there," Ard Matthew observed.

"But if Father Moto's right," the Star Brother reminded him, "they won't stay there long. They'll be heading for the fringe."

"If Frayle will take her, that is," Sergay put in. "These masters have no love for the wildwood. She'll have to give him some good reasons."

"Yes, there is that."

The spring night was almost warm, the nebula filling the few small windows and the open doorway with its lilac glow. A scent of blooming flowers wafted in from outside, almost overpowering the more homey smells of men and fires and beer.

It was plain neither of the Lost Rythans wanted to leave the comfort of the place, and Brother Brendan could hardly blame them. But he needed to check in again with Father Moto, if he could, so in an interval when Ard Matthew had gone up to secure another jug, he turned to Sergay. Would the chief keep an eye on the other two? Lost Rythans had a knack for getting into trouble, he explained hurriedly.

Sergay grinned a little. "You ask much, Star Brother."

"There aren't many I would entrust them to."

At this, the chief laughed out loud. "Go, then," he said. "I'll stay awhile."

Brother Brendan hurried out into the night. Dunsever seemed like a fairytale village, with clean, cobbled streets and well built stone houses roofed in slate. There were so many flowers everywhere in window boxes that their scent was almost overwhelming. Here and there a cow lowed from the stables behind the houses, and this arrangement added another, even more pungent, undertone to the cloying perfume.

The village square lay ahead, lit not only by the nebula, but by the campfires of the travelers. In the uncertain light he saw couples walking arm in arm, while children ran about playing one last game of tag before bedtime.

As he neared Rhosya's fire, he paused to look behind him. The street up which he had just come seemed shadowy now, overhung in places where the light did not reach. A man stood there in the shadows, not moving, the folds of a long cloak stirring slightly in the breeze.

The Star Brother shivered. But then a door opened onto the lane, lamplight spilling out, and the man went inside. Even so, his mood of peace and safety was spoiled. Things had not changed. The druids existed. And Gris Wolfgang would not be secure until his wound had healed with no telltale lines of purple spreading out over his skin. He wished he knew how long that would be.

Pushing away these thoughts, he hurried to the fire and greeted Rhosya. At her questioning look, he assured her that all was well. Her father and the Lost Rythans would be returning later. "I must contact my superiors," he added. "If you will excuse me –?"

The girl nodded. She seemed rather forlorn, sitting by herself beside the fire while she stirred yet another potion. The Star Brother felt a little sorry for her. He knew that any entanglement with a Faring Guard would only lead to heartbreak and hoped fervently that she had not conceived too great a fondness for Ard Matthew Third-Blade. He trusted the young man enough to know that he would not knowingly cause her pain, but Ard Matthew was, after all, a good looking young man.

Still, he could not watch over every detail of his companions' lives, he reminded himself. It would be blessing enough if Sergay could keep them from brawling at the tavern.

He settled himself to his task. As always, it took some time to reach the operator. When at last he got through to the man, he was surprised to hear that his call had been rather impatiently awaited.

"Got something for you," the operator said. "A netcall we've managed to patch through via the Balthasar."

A live transmission from whatever world Father Moto was visiting! Such things were chancy at best and generally far beyond the Star Brothers' usual budget. And then his thoughts were broken into by the voice of his superior.

"Brendan! We were just about to signal you again." The younger man had never heard him as agitated as this.

Then, "We've got them! No time to give you the details, but we know what Pesc is up to! There is just one more piece of evidence we need, and now I'm afraid I will have to countermand one of my orders."

"Yes?" Brother Brendan found that his own hands were shaking with excitement.

"That woman – Dr. Sienko. She will need to visit the native forest after all."

"Gris Wolfgang was willing to have cautery without an anaesthetic because one of the vines latched onto him!" Brother Brendan said grimly. "You haven't seen those druids!"

"I know we ask much. But it is Pesc's intention that she go, and they've got reasons of their own. Hellish reasons –"

"Then why should I help them?"

"You won't be helping them. We are going to record their attempt to get her in there, but you'll have to keep them from actually succeeding."

Brother Brendan gave up trying to understand. He listened as the other man went on.

"You mentioned the druids. Pesc did not know, nor did we, that they even existed. From your reports, it sounds like they have an antidote of their own. They don't die as the Brothers of St. Hubert do when they are infected, but neither do they remain as they were. They are changed."

Brother Brendan thought of the druids going to their hanging. "I don't think it is a desirable change," he ventured.

"No. From what you have told us, I would guess that their minds are affected – probably permanently. In their madness, they seem compelled to give absolute loyalty to the native forest, taking it for a god."

"That sounds about right."

"But even though they are no longer sane, we now have reason to believe that they are by no means unhappy. The forest, in short, is the source of a very powerful and very exhilarating drug. A drug that produces slaves who are not only delighted to serve their masters but who might even do so without detection if they didn't suffer those physical anomalies. In short, with a little adjustment, the forest might supply the perfect tool for subversion, both corporate and political."

Brother Brendan whistled. "But how could Pesc have known about this drug?"

"Dagon Ltd started the line of research, thinking to produce a habit-forming narcotic, and abandoned it fifty years ago, because of Net Central's policies. I don't need to tell you something like that would bring them down on any corporation. Pesc has their records now and have gone on from there."

"And Net Central?" the younger man asked. "Won't they interfere?"

"Not without evidence. Your job is to follow the young lady, see that she enters the fringe – I believe she will be forced to do so by her bodyguard, who has no choice but to obey – and then get her out before she's stung by anything. Afterwards you will hold her until we arrive. You will, of course, be recording the entire incident, or rather we will be doing that through you."

"You want me to –"

"Not you alone. You have two of my best operatives with you," Chief Snowtyger cut in. "Make use of them."

Before he could argue any further, the connection broke off.

Feeling rather dazed, he went back out into the nebula light. Rhosya was still sitting beside the fire, but she was no longer alone. With some surprise, he recognized Colin the outlaw. They were drinking tea together and even from a distance, they looked as though they were enjoying each other's company.

CHAPTER 13

THE DATA **FATHER MOTO** PASSED on to his protégé had not been easy to come by. But Gaed Alfred was determined to extract the rest of the file because the Star Brothers needed it and no Faring Guard ever let the Star Brothers down. However, his friend Dust needed him, too, and the thought of the mercenary trapped in some hell of Pesc's devising tore at him even as he set to work.

So why did he keep thinking he was going about things in the wrong way? Backwards, as it were?

He glanced over at Father Moto once or twice. The superior was connected to the *Balthasar*, transmitting all that they had learned so far. This was the second transmission, the one about Marja Sienko's genetic usefulness to the corporation.

"Dust!" Snowtyger called into the speaker. "Dust – I'm here! It's Gaed Alfred! I know you can hear me – sort of."

The truth was that Dust could not hear the chief at all, or at least not in any ordinary way. That Snowtyger was talking, that the other man wished him well – these things he knew in the sense that they were probabilities and, in his present state, the probable took on what amounted to real substance. Witness the blow on his back from which he still smarted. Had Dust a corporeal body and had he and the chief met in the flesh, such a blow might well have been given to galvanise him into action. He knew the Lost Rythan well enough for *that*!

The dreary hillside seemed to stretch on forever. If Dust, in the process of educating himself, had amassed solid learning in any orderly way instead of flitting about like a hummingbird to drink in whatever took his fancy, he would have noted that his surroundings bore a distinct resemblance to the pagan idea of hades, the land of shades. The angel was a Dantesque touch, to be sure, but even the work of that sober and fantastic Christian came to him as no more than a reference or two Snowtyger might have made while drinking beer after a chess game. The chief was no great reader of the classics himself.

As there was no real way to measure time, Dust's journey might have lasted for years. He could barely remember a time when he hadn't been dragging along the splintered cross. The angel's assistance helped, but then he'd been obliged to listen to all sorts of things he would rather not have had to deal with.

"What do you know about prayer anyway?" he finally growled. "That's what you want of me, isn't it? You want me to ask God to forgive me for all sorts of stuff I never thought was wrong."

"Oh, well, as to that," the angel said, "stuff is stuff. It's *you* that's wrong. You're not what you were meant to be."

"So is that my fault?"

"You needn't keep going on about whose fault it is," the angel said primly. "At least *some* of it's yours. Anyway, now you have a chance to set it all right."

He didn't buy that. Despite the turmoil of his early life, Dust had a strong sense of justice. He knew when things were fair and when they were not. He was just about to give the angel a piece of his mind when a light bloomed over the crest of the hill. Something large was lifting into the air, breathing fire as it came rapidly toward him.

"Oh crap! Now look what you've done!"

Whether it was fair or not to blame the angel, Dust thought it was. If the thing had just kept quiet and not gone on so much about sin and all that other business, maybe the dragon would not have noticed them. As it was, there was no way he could avoid a meeting.

Just as he resigned himself to being roasted alive, the dragon landed in front of him, considerately turning its head to one side. "Welcome, Dust," it said. "I've come to apologise for all this. Pesc has your best interests at heart and we'd like you to come aboard with us."

Dust gave it a sidewise look. He trusted the dragon even less than he trusted the angel, though he was sick enough of the latter's sermons.

"You've been caught up in one of our defense shields, but I can get you out. Why don't you put down that file? It's breaking up anyway and we don't want to lose any more of it than we have already. And then, if you like, we can talk."

"I'll just hang on to it, if you don't mind," Dust told the dragon. "You do the talking and I'll listen."

"As you wish. I couldn't help overhearing you and this – whatever it is. It's been trying to undermine your confidence in yourself."

"You mean telling me I'm not such hot stuff as I thought I was? I never did – think much of myself, I mean. Or at least, I don't now."

"Well, you should. You're good at what you do, Dust, and we'd like you to work for us. If you'd just put down that cross – I mean file – I could explain what we have to offer."

Dust sat down on the stones, glad to take some weight off his burning feet, but he hung on to the cross. He wasn't about to abandon it at the word of the first dragon he met. "You're offering me a job?" he asked.

"You bet. And a prosthetic body to go with it. You don't need to live inside that mechanical junkpile Fraser May built for you. He just did that to keep you under his thumb."

"He's my friend. He saved my life."

"Dust," the dragon said slyly, still keeping its head turned away. "How well do you remember that so-called accident?"

"Enough. Getting blown up is not a favorite recollection of mine."

"You lost a bit of memory when it happened."

"Just what are you getting at?" Dust demanded, reaching down with one hand to rub his foot. Those stones hurt!

"Do you remember your name?"

"I got a name. It fits."

"But your real name?"

Dust didn't answer.

"We looked up some files on your so-called friend, May, and I think you'd be surprised to hear what really happened."

"I think you've got no reason to tell me the truth."

"Dust – you're in denial. Some of this is already available to you. You blanked it out."

"Forget all that," Dust told it. "I'm not interested. But did you say you can give me a body?"

"More or less. It won't be cheap, of course, and that may be another reason old Fraser didn't mention the option. But we can do it – and if you show good faith, we will!"

"Don't listen to him," the angel said. "He just wants you to go on being a jerk."

The dragon turned its snout in the angel's direction, scorching one wing and blackening its white robe. "Bug off," it said.

The angel stood its ground, however, though Dust felt a little sorry for it.

"Look," the dragon went on. "You can't get out of here without help. You'll just go on dragging that thing uphill until you wear out and die. Why bother?"

"I don't know," Dust admitted. "But it seems to be getting lighter."

"That's because you're letting data bleed out to the Star Brothers. We don't like that, Dust, and if it goes on, we could make things mighty uncomfortable for you."

"Yeah. I thought it would come to that."

"So put it down. It's not yours."

"Yes it is." That was the angel speaking. "You put it down and you might never get another chance to be someone decent like Gaed Alfred."

At the name of the Faring Guard, Dust seemed to hear a faint voice calling from somewhere he couldn't see. Suddenly the dragon rose from the ground, somersaulting in the air to come down with its front claws on Dust's shoulders. He sprawled on his back, still hanging onto the cross with one arm, staring up into a pair of golden eyes. Luckily he didn't know that dragons were supposed to be able to hypnotise people or he would have been lost right then.

"Give," their owner said. "Now. You want a job, you can have one. You want a body, that too. But you let go of those files or I'll rip you to shreds and roast what's left!"

In his chair beside Father Moto, Gaed Alfred stopped calling. His voice was growing hoarse. "This isn't working," he said.

The Star Brother turned toward him. "Perhaps not," he agreed.

Because they were old friends, they each had the same idea. Two rosaries appeared and two heads came together over the speaker. The older man began the *Credo*.

There was no way Dust could get out from under the dragon. All the time it kept alternately threatening and promising, it's breath smoky and rather nasty smelling. But somehow, he held onto the cross.

Dust could see the sky from over the dragon's one shoulder and the stars seemed to be moving around a bit. There were faces up there, not angelic exactly, but at least human.

Suddenly the dragon ripped his arm off. The pain was unbelievable and, as the blood spurted, he wondered why he didn't die. Surely he was bleeding to death! But all the while, teeth clenched to keep from screaming, he went on gripping the broken wood with his other hand.

"Let go, damn you!" the dragon said.

The angel had crept closer and laid one hand on his torn flesh. "Hold on," it said. "I think this is what God wants you to do."

Somehow, the dragon couldn't seem to get too close to the cross. His other arm was safe. But now it was worrying one leg. The flames, when they touched him, added to his agony until he felt as though he were going to dissolve in pure pain.

A hand reached down from the sky. Dust looked up and thought he saw the outlines of a room. The two faces were there, Snowtyger and someone else. He couldn't make out what they were saying – or else it was in some other language. *Sancta Maria, Mater Dei, ora pro nobis* –

"Gaed Alfred?" he gasped.

The strange words broke off. "Dust! Come on out of there!"

He strained upward but he didn't dare let go of the cross. The dragon tore off his smoking leg and this time he screamed. "Take hold of the files," he cried when he could get his breath. "Don't let these bastards get them!"

As he spoke, the hand scooped the cross out from under him. At once the lights went out and there was only the dim fire of the dragon's breath – and an agony so great he could hardly think.

"Now look what you've done!" the dragon snarled. "Believe me, you'll be sorry. You haven't begun to pay for this!"

Dust didn't answer. He felt it's claws on his other leg and tried to brace himself.

It was then the angel showed its stuff. While the dragon was busy torturing Dust, there came a mighty rushing of wings, the scorched one shredding away as it flew, and the dragon was knocked off balance by something that landed on its head, clawing at its eyes.

Dust tried to roll over but he could not. The dragon outweighed the angel and in a minute it would tear the thing to shreds. But the angel had done this for *him*! For Dust! For dust –

With his free hand, he grabbed his torn off arm and stuck it back on. Then the leg. The pain became bearable – just – and he stood up. "Gaed Alfred!" he shouted.

"Here."

"I'm coming up!" Snatching the angel from the dragon's claws, Dust leaped into the sky where for one moment, he felt great, brawny arms lifting him until he reached the light. He activated the viewer and saw Father Moto and the Faring Guard.

"Welcome back," Gaed Alfred said. "We thought some prayers might do the job."

MARJA WAS SUMMONED DOWN TO dinner an hour or two after Frayle spoke with Hu. She had spent the afternoon sitting by the window of her room, watching the life of the farm. Servants were always running to and fro, and at least twice she saw the dour housekeeper go out to speak with one of the men.

She knew she would have to come down at last from her place of safety – her tower of illusion. She had been betrayed. Pesc had never intended to let her develop the colony. It was all a lie. So why had they brought her here? Why *her*?

What had Hu told Master Frayle? The master had looked frightened when he came out of the room or, if not that exactly, then at least stirred to the depths. He might stand high among his own people, might well aspire to things higher yet, but in the end, he could become nothing but another dupe of the corporation.

Dinner was not a pleasant meal. There was so much tension in the air that Marja, at least, was glad when it was over. The master excused himself immediately, saying that he had business in another part of the farm. He took his sons with him.

She rose when they had gone. "I'm going out," she told Wells on her way to the door. "You needn't follow."

"Are you wearing your shield harness?" he asked her mildly.

Though she did not tell him, she had left off wearing the thing ever since their arrival at Frayle farm. She nodded, however, and brushed past him. She wanted air – and light. She would watch the sunsets, she told herself. She would remember that she was on a planet and not in the ship with Hu. She would pretend that she was free.

Marja walked quickly past the stables and, spotting the entrance to a path among what might have been azaleas not yet in bloom, she turned into it. To her surprise, she found she was almost running in her haste to escape the house and the robot and the sure knowledge that she had made a grave and possibly a fatal error.

But there would be no escaping Pesc. In the end there was nowhere on *this* world they could not find her.

What *had* they said to Frayle? Had they promised him again the things she had hinted at before? Or had they threatened? Remembering the dazed look on his face, she could not be sure. Of one thing she was certain, however: that he no longer needed her as an intermediary. Hu had taken him away from her.

She stopped, aghast at the train of her thoughts. Was Prydan Frayle no more than a pawn, then? As *she* was? Were they to be separated now because the corporation had found another way to accomplish its ends?

And what were those ends? Why must she go to the fringe? Why Marja Sienko in particular? Again and again it came back to that one same question.

But worst and deepest of all was the shame of being used and cast aside. If the corporation had co-opted Frayle for its ends, then by now he must know more of her own role than she did. Plainly, he did not love her or he would have sought her out to discuss what the corporation had offered him. Frayle must have been using her all along, in the same way she had been ordered to use him!

Marja moved on down the path until it split in two. She chose the left fork which, after a short while, began to descend. The first of the larger suns was setting when she came out on the bank of the creek – Frayle Creek it would be. A little beach led down to the water and there, to her surprise, lay a boat. It had been dragged up recently onto the shore; she could tell by the track behind it.

As she looked up from studying the marks in the sand, she knew suddenly that she was not alone. *Something* waited in the brush. Suddenly it moved!

With a rush, two men leaped out at her, pinning her arms to her sides and dragging her to the ground. Here was a repetition of those former attacks – only this time she was not wearing the harness!

As though the thought had summoned him, Wells appeared from among the azaleas, gun drawn but unable to fire for fear of hitting her. Before he could move forward, a third man hit him from behind, and he collapsed on the path.

Quickly the assailant picked up Wells' gun, but he dropped it at once. It was keyed to its owner and shocked anyone else who touched it.

Only then did she look up at the faces of the two who held her. There was the pale skin she had seen on the condemned druids, there the silvery network of lines, almost like tattooing. The lines ran over every inch of skin she could see –face, hands and arms, even on their necks.

The man who had struck Wells came to stand over her. She had ceased her futile struggles, and now she watched him as some small animal might have watched a snake, paralysed with fear as it moved closer. Her loathing only increased as she traced a detestable facial resemblance between the druid and Frayle's other sons.

"What – what do you want with me?" she whispered. Screaming panic was not far off and she knew she must hold onto her thoughts or she would be lost –

"You are the lady from the stars," the druid said. His voice came out oddly – not like that of a robot, for certainly there was expression in his speech – but it was as though the emotions that underlay the words were not those of a human mind.

"I think you must be Evan Frayle," she said.

"I – was." There was also something a little slurred about the way he enunciated the words, just as his movements were not quite those of a normal man. His coordination seemed to be off.

"Make them let go of me. I can't get away from you," she forced herself to say, drawing on the anger that served her for strength. *Pesc* had put her here, she thought. Pesc was responsible!

To her surprise, the other two released her at once. Only then did she realize how loathsome had been their touch on her. They were *diseased*, she thought, and their skin where it had come in contact with hers was rough and scaly. They gave off a smell like spices, stale spices that made her think of mummies.

"You came here to change things?" Evan said slowly, his pale eyes no longer blue as they might once have been, but some odd silvery color. "To destroy the wildwood?"

"I don't know what I came for," she said, feeling her anger begin to fail her. "I thought I knew, but now –"

"They must not destroy the wildwood," Evan said. His expression did not change but there was something in his voice, the more horrible for having no connection she could see to the anger he should have felt.

"I was told it is poison," she said carefully, wondering if they two, she and this creature, might not be allies. "That it is of no use to the colony. But you – you live there?"

He did not answer this. "I think we had better kill you," he said abruptly, still in that same inhuman tone. "It's no good to make you as we are. That would only bring down the anger of your masters. It is better if you drown here in the creek. Then they will not know."

His words, oddly inflected as they were, shocked her out of her paralysis. "You're mad!" she cried, struggling to her feet. "This – this disease of yours has destroyed your mind!"

The young man watched unmoved while she stood, trembling before him. The last sun's light tinted his pallid features with the false flush of health, doubly horrible in that zombie-like face. His eyes gleamed and his overly pale hair blew about his once handsome features as he held himself crookedly erect.

"You cannot know what we know. We have only joy and more than joy," he said softly. "And even now we would give them to you, if it were not for the danger to the wildwood."

"But if others were aware," she said, trying to reach him with some shred of reason. "If the corporation could be told that the wildwood means so much to you –"

Her voice trailed off. She knew knew exactly what the corporation would do, which was nothing. What did the lives of these colonists mean to Pesc? They were all its property now, she and the farm masters and the druids and even the poor woman she had seen hanging on the gallows that first night. Their welfare meant no more to Pesc than her own.

Almost, staring into those alien eyes, she could resign herself to death. At least it would be a blow struck against the corporation! At least she would die for *something*! Whatever use they had meant to make of her would be foiled!

And then she saw Wells move slightly where he lay on the path. He made no sound as he touched something at his belt. After that his hand fell away and he lay as he had been. A line of blood trickled from one side of his scalp.

At a gesture from young Frayle, the other two grasped her arms once more and began hustling her along the beach to where another path wound through the brush.

"Where are you taking me?" she asked in sudden hope. Maybe they had changed their minds and she was to be held – perhaps for ransom? Might they try to bargain with the colony's new owners?

But, "To a deeper pool," Evan told her. "Your body would be found too quickly here by the path. We played there, I think," he added vaguely. "Long ago – Balt and I."

She fought them then, kicking and clawing, feeling their tainted blood on her skin, their vile flesh beneath her nails. Had she not been fighting for her life, she could never have borne it. As it was, she delayed their progress for some minutes.

Suddenly the brush parted to her right and the druid on that side fell, fountaining blood as Frayle's sword slashed into his leg, severing the femoral artery. The other man released his hold, only to be shot down. She saw Wells run up, holding the gun, blood still matting in his hair, as he aimed at Evan Frayle, who was turning to flee.

"No!" the master shouted in anguish. "Don't shoot my son!"

For a second, Wells hesitated and in that second, the druid disappeared.

Marja had slipped to the ground where she huddled between the two bodies, feeling as though she would never get up again. The defiling wetness of their blood on her hands marked her, and she kept her eyes on the trampled foliage where she knelt, lest she have to look up at the others.

He'll never forgive me this, she thought. She had heard in the master's voice that cry of pain he had tried to keep hidden. He might be able to ignore the presence of Wells, who was only a slave, but he would never forget that she had witnessed his despairing love for this thing that had once been his son.

And then she felt a hand on her arm and, looking up, saw that it was her bodyguard. "We had better help each other along," she murmured, reaching up to touch the wound in his head. And then she burst into tears.

Later, back in her room, she submitted to the housekeeper's ministrations. To her surprise, there were cuts on her arms and an abrasion on one side of her face where she had been thrown to the ground.

"How is Wells?" she asked Carhyn suddenly. Her own rescue meant nothing – she was still Pesc's creature. But something new stirred in her. Had she been able to put it into words, she would have said: I am lost. Therefore, I will try to save whatever I can that is not myself.

"He has gone to speak to the simulacrum."

This got through the fog. "The robot? Why?"

"I do not know, Lady." Carhyn's face gave nothing away, but her hands trembled as she gathered up her medicines. She was looking at something behind the other woman.

Marja turned and saw Frayle standing in the doorway.

"May I come in?" he asked formally.

At her nod, he entered and stood beside her chair. "Your – robot –" He pronounced the word carefully. "It called for me by name. I had come back to the house and found you gone, and then it called."

She remembered the bodyguard fingering a stud at his belt. "Yes," she said uncertainly. "Wells must have sent out a distress call."

"It gave me this," he said, holding out a small metalplast disk. "To guide me to him." He still seemed rather in awe of these wonders.

"It isn't magic," she told him, a hint of contempt in her voice.

He flushed slightly. "Of course not." But he put the thing down on the chest anyway. Then, "You spoke with him – with Evan," he said as though he could not help himself.

She told him she had.

"And how – how did he sound?"

She chose her words carefully, aware that the housekeeper was listening. "It changes them," she said at last. "I don't think he could have been anything like he was before."

"I see. Thank you." He turned and left the room.

Carhyn made as though to follow him and then changed her mind. She picked up her basin and rags. "You will need to rest, Lady," she said and there was no more warmth in her voice than there had been in Frayle's.

Marja got up as soon as the housekeeper had gone. She wanted to see Wells and to know that he had not been hurt too badly. If the thought occurred to her that he, among all the people around her ,was the only one she trusted, the only one on whose goodness and humanity she felt she could rely, she would have denied it. But as she approached the office, she felt already a lifting of the darkness in which she had been submerged.

There were voices within. This time she did not scruple to press her ear to the door and made out the voice of the robosecretary.

"– careless," it said. "You have – too much – talked to the natives "

She could not hear what the bodyguard replied.

Then, "Your arm," the voice said clearly and Marja knew what was coming.

She flung open the door. "Wells!" she said peremptorily, ignoring the machine. "I need you. We are both wanted downstairs."

As he turned, she saw that someone had cleaned the cut on his scalp. The flesh was drawn together with synthoskin which meant the robot must have done it. His face was very pale and set.

Marja met her secretary's bland and friendly gaze. "I'm sorry to interrupt," she told it. "But I must have my bodyguard."

Without waiting for a reply, she turned to go. Wells followed.

When they had gained the stairs, he stopped her. "Thank you," he said. "But you're only putting things off."

"No."

"Mar – Dr. Sienko, I *was* careless back at the creek. And earlier, I did at least hint things to the bishop that – that I was obliged to disclose to the corporation."

"No," she repeated. "It doesn't matter what you've done. That thing will never touch you again. I'll see to it."

He didn't argue as he followed her down to the great room. Frayle was sitting alone before the fire, a flagon in his hands. He looked up as they came in, but Marja could not read that look.

Without waiting to be told, Wells melted into the shadows, leaving Marja alone as Frayle rose courteously and indicated a seat. It was obvious he did not want her here, and she had no wish to intrude herself. But she had to go *somewhere* if she were to protect her bodyguard from the robot.

So, they sat together, two people who did not desire each other's company and must, for different reasons, pretend that they did. She accepted a mug of some fiery drink and was grateful that it dulled her pain. She could only hope it did the same for *his*.

BROTHER BRENDAN HURRIED OVER TO the fire. Colin looked up at his approach and gave him a friendly greeting. They had not seen each other since Bannyclay, when he and Gris Wolfgang had left the young man at the bishop's house.

"You were speaking to your chieftain in the sky?" the outlaw asked him.

"Something like that." He accepted a mug of tea from Rhosya. There was milk in it and a hint of what he could have sworn was whiskey. He glanced at Colin, who grinned and showed him a flask. "Got it back at the river," he said.

"You *got* it?"

The outlaw shook his head. "Present from the bishop's housekeeper. She has a still."

Rhosya bent over to stir the pot. The faint and becoming flush in her cheeks might have been the result of Colin's – or rather the bishop's housekeeper's – largesse. Or it might have been the company.

"She and I understand each other," Colin said complacently. "I bring her game sometimes, and she doesn't ask where I caught it. And, of course, I always compliment what's cooking."

He didn't wink, quite. "What news?" he asked. "From up there." He pointed in the direction of the nebula.

Brother Brendan sipped his tea appreciatively. "I've got to get to the fringe," he said. "And I'm afraid there is little time to lose."

"Ah." The outlaw poured more whiskey into his own cup.

The others were returning at last, something for which the Star Brother was thankful. Otherwise he would have had to fetch them. Since Colin had already been admitted to their confidence, he told everyone at once what Father Moto and the Faring Guard chief had said.

"They don't ask much, do they?" Sergay said. "Just snatch the lady and hold her until they get there. And what do we do with that fancy bodyguard of hers? Or Frayle and his men?"

Ard Matthew was staring at Rhosya curiously. She was indeed looking well – or maybe it was the firelight. "It shouldn't be too hard to prepare an ambush," he said, looking away, "And we've got stunners, if you want that bodyguard taken prisoner."

"Are we supposed to capture the whole party?" Gris Wolfgang asked.

"I don't see how we can avoid it," the Star Brother said. "I'm certainly not planning to kill anyone."

"Her man will have offworld weapons," Gris Wolfgang pointed out. "And he might not be so squeamish."

"Then he'll be our first target."

Sergay shook his head. "Frayle's men are *good*. Don't underestimate what a bow can do. Colin knows."

Brother Brendan recalled Rhosya telling him she had cut an arrow from the outlaw when he was still Rhyn's lieutenant.

"That works both ways," the young man said, laughing. "I'm not such a bad shot myself."

"Does that mean what I think it means?" Sergay asked him.

"You bet. Do you think I'd miss a chance to see a spaceship land?"

"Colin – are you alone?"

"Well, not quite," the young man admitted. "Some of the Band have come. On account of the druids. We're camped in the hills just west of here."

"You're still tracking them?" Brother Brendan asked in surprise.

"We are. The party that stole the boat – they didn't take it on the river after all. They went west instead."

"Then there must be more of them than we thought at first," the Star Brother said thoughtfully. "Maybe quite a few more."

Colin frowned. "Every man that's disappeared in the last few months. From each town, from the farms, from among the woods dwellers. You're right – there could be a lot of them by now."

"We had better go on horseback," Brother Brendan decided. "There is no time to lose."

"Shall I come along?" Sergay asked.

"No. We will return the horses to you, of course, but you needn't come."

They set off while the nebula was still high, Colin leading them to a section of the road opposite his own encampment. "Wait here," he said and disappeared among the trees.

They waited for nearly an hour before they were joined by some six or seven members of the Band. The Lost Rythans, who had been given two of Sergay's largest horses, mounted once more. While they were not expert riders, their lessons were paying off.

It was a grueling ride. Some time after midnight the road passed through Frayle farm, but there was little to see, a peasant house or two, some fine timber and, in one of the meadows, a herd of deer. The outlaws looked wistfully at these as they galloped by, scattering the game.

As they drew up in the courtyard of the priory, the smaller suns were already bathing things in that dreary twilight that was neither proper night nor proper day. Two brothers emerged at once from the shadows.

Not knowing whether Colin would be welcome here, the Star Brother dismounted stiffly and threw back his cloak to show them his habit, explaining in the meantime that their errand was urgent.

One of the pair stepped forward. His face bore none of the purple markings as yet and the look he gave them was both alert and far more friendly than they had expected. "I am Brother Davyd," he said, "and this is Brother Havard. We're real brothers – I mean we both came from the same parents."

"From Frayle Farm," the other added. "We were freed by Master Frayle."

Freed for death, the Star Brother was thinking. But perhaps they had volunteered.

"Did you come that way?" the young brother persisted.

There was no reason to deny it. "From Dunsever. We passed through the farm, but we didn't meet anyone."

They were shown where to put up their horses. If Colin was recognized – and he probably was – neither of the brothers said anything.

"We're on watch," Brother Davyd explained. "Everyone else is in the chapel."

"Has the Mass begun?" Ard Matthew asked him.

"Not yet. I'll show you the way."

It said something about the care that had gone into protecting the colony from worldly influences that Colin and the Band members did not hesitate to follow. The Star Brother wondered, blushing a little at his cynicism, if they were equally sincere when they robbed passing merchants.

When the Mass was ended, Brother Brendan and the Lost Rythans were taken to see Marshal Pwyll. The marshal of the west priory proved to be a tall, rangy man, marked but not yet made ill by the poison of the wildwood. His hair was mostly grey and so was his beard, while his eyes were that shade of blue that made one think of ice. These he turned on his visitors with a scrutiny that would have unnerved most men.

The Star Brother, however, had faced such a look before. Father Moto's eyes were brown, but the effect was the same. As for the Lost Rythans, they had long since been forced to look so uncompromisingly into their own depths that the searching gaze of the marshal could do little to disconcert them.

At last he seemed satisfied. "Now you may tell me why you are here."

He kept them standing while Brother Brendan explained his mission. Only when the account was finished, did the marshal gesture to the wall benches and take a seat himself. "We had heard – dimly, for we have little to do with things outside – that Dagon Ltd has sold our world to another."

They talked for a while about the fringe – and the druids. Yes, the brothers knew of them, though they were seldom seen near the priory. "But they are an everpresent temptation to the weak," the marshal said grimly. "Whether they are here or not."

Brother Brendan found it hard to imagine that anyone could be tempted by what they offered. He said so.

The marshal gave him another long look. "We who are infected must endure the nights as well as the days," he said. "Things seem different then. If it were not that we watch and encourage one another, any one of us might fall. By daylight we see that the druids offer but the seeming of life, though it is really death – a time of dreams and half thoughts, built on the ruins of memory and personality until the last decay is followed by eternal damnation. For none can repent in that state. The last choice they make in this life is to become what they are!"

All three shuddered, and Gris Wolfgang could not keep silent. "Sir," he said, "I have been stung – more than stung, I think – by one of the vines." He showed the Marshal Pwyll the partially-healed mark on his upper arm. "I do not know yet if I am infected."

The older man came over to look at it. "You tried to burn it out, I see. That works sometimes, if we get to it soon enough."

"Then I might escape the illness?"

"You might. It has been some days since this was done, I would judge."

Gris Wolfgang told him it had been.

"Then there is hope for you." The marshal frowned for a moment. "You desire to escape this?"

"I did," the Lost Rythan admitted, flushing slightly. "With all my heart. But now I ask only to bear well whatever God may send."

"That is proper." He stepped back. "Go then and have something to eat, all of you. I will see you again when you have accomplished what you came to do."

They went out and found the refectory. This foundation was smaller than the one at the east end of the colony and fewer of the brothers had been marked. They only saw one or two who were seriously affected and even these managed to get around.

As he munched his bread, the Star Brother wondered what it would be like to live as they did while knowing that a palliative lay ready to hand, that a sick brother had only to leave the place and he would be found by the druids. And he could not help wondering if any of them did so.

Suddenly he wasn't hungry anymore. Laying aside the food, he stood up. The Band sat at a different table and he made his way over to them.

"We have plans to make," Brother Brendan said quietly to Colin. "Let's go outside and look around."

IN THE MORNING MARJA DISCOVERED that there was a chapel in Frayle's house. A priest had ridden out from Dunsever the night before and when she came downstairs the servants directed her to a good sized room, an abutment of sorts on the west side of the structure.

"I – I don't think I –" she said and then noticed Wells. His face was drawn with weariness and remembered pain. By this she guessed that he must have been summoned by the robosecretary during the night and, after all, he had gone.

She bit off a curse. Invention had failed her at the last and when they were obliged to separate near midnight, she had fallen back on simple command. She had ordered him to remain in his room, because she needed guarding. Obviously, he had disobeyed her.

"Damn you," she said in a low voice. "I *told* you not to go in there!"

"I could not convince myself that you were in immediate danger," he said. "I tried, but your command was not enough."

"So, you must make confession to a machine as well as to a priest," she said in disgust.

"I'm not sorry about confessing to the bishop, if that's what you mean. But *that*," he admitted, "was grounds enough for trouble."

"Well you've earned your Mass," she said grimly, relenting. "We will go in."

They found the family gathered near the front of the chapel, the servants behind. It was Sunday and almost everyone connected with the household was there. She took a place on the women's side, though she was the only lady present. The rest of the women, including the housekeeper, must stand further back.

For the first time, she wondered what Frayle's wife had been like, the mother of the two young men who knelt beside their father and of the other one, the druid. How long ago had she died? Judging by the ages of the sons, it might have been some while since.

During the service, when she must kneel in her isolation, she found herself wishing for one single companion, even the housekeeper. The stone was cold beneath her knees, but she did not quite dare to sit through the Mass. The world of Sachsen and its uncaring capital lay lightyears away from this place, but here it seemed to her that all places were in reality one.

Suddenly, looking up, she realised that the chapel was beautiful with its carved statuary and homemade altar. Or maybe *beautiful* was not the right word. But if a better word existed, she did not know it. She thought of the family that had lived here for generations, never doubting that God existed, never failing in their service to Him, whatever sins they might commit. She was sure that Prydan Frayle and his sons confessed those sins at the proper times and that they regretted them, even though they probably went out and sinned again. They were Christians, and that is what Christians did.

As she imagined these things, she felt even more alone.

They returned to the hall after Mass and had a quick meal. The carriage was soon ready, the wagon behind it. Without consulting her, Wells led the robosecretary down to the wagon and climbed in beside it. The thing beamed at him as though they two were old friends, the sharers of many happy memories.

Frayle said nothing as he passed by the slave and the automaton. He took Marja's arm and escorted her to the carriage. It was a silent drive.

They stopped once to rest the horses. Beer and sandwiches were served, but it was a far cry from the elaborate meal they had enjoyed on their way to Bannyclay. There were outriders now as then, and some five other manservants riding or driving the vehicles. All of these were armed.

Frayle ate with her, but he was not at ease. What would happen now if she asked him to pick flowers for her? There were some rather lovely ones, narcissi and such, along the verge.

Abruptly the master beckoned to Wells, who got up from his place among the servants and came to stand beside the carriage.

"You – you have orders," he said. "This Hu person said that you had your orders."

"I cannot discuss these things with you, sir," Wells told him.

"You *cannot?*"

Wells held up the wrist with the slave band.

"But surely – I thought you served the corporation mainly because you were obliged to. I mean you must have some discretion."

"You thought I obeyed out of external fear? No sir, it goes deeper than that."

"This bracelet – it actually controls your actions?"

Wells shook his head. "Not the slave band. *I* have been conditioned to loyalty."

The master looked troubled and then as he thought this over, appalled. "This is the way of Pesc?" he asked. "*This*?"

Wells did not answer.

They resumed their journey. Once or twice Frayle looked at Marja, and once or twice it seemed as though he were going to speak, but when it came to the point, he did not.

She would have spoken to him, but something held *her* back as well. It was not embarrassment; the time for that was past. She was frightened now, afraid of what they were going to do to her. Afraid of Pesc – of what *Pesc* was going to use these men to accomplish.

Obviously, they had secured Frayle's cooperation. Hu must have convinced him. She knew how much he wanted to see the worlds outside, to move among civilized men and to handle their inventions. Prydan Frayle wanted to learn all that the offworlders knew and to escape from the narrow life of his colony. Or rather, which was more likely, he wanted to make of Treelight the hub of his own small empire.

Or could Hu have simply terrorized him into obedience? After all, he was such a primitive that he must nerve himself even to speak with the robot. The coordinator would have known what to say to a man like that; his sort generally did.

She felt a sudden desire to batter Hu's bland face until the blood came, to keep pounding on him until she silenced his lying words forever. She wanted this more than she could remember ever wanting anything before in her life. But it was too late.

The woodland ceased and still the road went on, passing through a waste of brush and barren stretches. It was only when they topped a small rise that she began to see a pale mauve haze that marked the edge of the world. As they descended, the view was eclipsed once more by the green foliage of the colony proper. Then they climbed the next hill and she saw it again – closer.

It was her old nightmare. The great purple beast crouched, waiting – and they were going to feed her to it! She knew this in the way she knew that Pesc was evil and that Wells was helpless to save her. In the way she knew that Frayle cared more for his family and his ambitions and his farm than he had ever cared for her.

When she caught sight of movement out in the brush, she sat forward, praying and not realizing that that she prayed. No matter what she had done with her life, surely God would not let her fall into the claws of the hunter! For one mad moment, she even envied Wells who had suffered and was, if not forgiven, at least spared further suffering until he offended again. He served two gods and one of them was holy –

At this her thoughts grew confused. She barely heard as one of the out-riders came galloping up to the carriage. "Druids," he told Frayle. "Out there."

The master nodded. "They can do nothing," he said dully. "I suppose they are just watching us."

But Marja stood up. "Evan!" she called. "Help me! Evan, if you're out there, *help* me!" It was madness and she knew it. But if she must perish, it would be better to die at the hands of one who was not morally responsible. Indeed, *anything* would be better than to be betrayed by these two men, Wells whom she had trusted and Prydan Frayle whom she had loved.

Frayle pulled her down. "Stop that," he hissed. "Stop or I'll –" He looked back at the wagon where Wells kept watch.

"You're going to feed me to it!" she cried hysterically. "You're going to feed me to the monster at the edge of the world! You're going to *sacrifice* me!"

Her mind became a roaring purple chaos as she struggled in his grip.

Finally, he got through to her. "Marja – Marja! You *must* listen!" He had his hands on her shoulders and was actually shaking her. "Marja, believe me – I would save you if I could!"

"If you *dared*, you mean!" she shouted. "You wanted to live among the stars! *You!*" She put all the contempt she could into her words. "You small, venal man! What is there for *you* out there? The civilized worlds are not for *your* sort!"

He did not answer.

Presently the road forked. In one direction, she saw low buildings but no people. The fringe towered over the tiny settlement. Perhaps the trees had already eaten the inhabitants.

Their branch of the way went on, coming closer and closer to the wild-wood until she could see the individual trunks – only they were far too smooth to be trunks – and the pale lilac vines hanging down. Nothing grew here; an empty length of discolored soil reached to the abrupt verge of the alien forest.

The carriage stopped. "Bring her to me," the robot said pleasantly. "She must have one more dose before she goes."

Frayle took her arm. He looked sick. "I'm sorry, Marja," he said. "I never thought –"

"You never thought? You pretended to make love to me, and all the time you were only trying to get what you could from the corporation!"

At this, he grasped her harder and pulled her from the carriage. "You accuse *me*?" he said angrily. "Isn't that what *you* were doing? Hu told me you had been ordered to make love to *me* in order to win my loyalty to the corporation!"

"*I* –?" She stared at him in shock. It was all so absurd! So unfair! And now he was going to kill her over a misunderstanding!

Wells helped him drag her to the wagon and she saw the robot arm extended. There was the needle like a stinger and then as her own arm was held, she felt the familiar burning pain course through her. "Wait," the robot said, and they waited until some of it passed.

After that Frayle hauled her toward the forest, the dead soil hard beneath her feet. She felt him trembling but whether it was with anger or with fear, she did not know. The ground rose up here and there in strange little ridges and there were hollows, some of them quite large, which they must avoid. Behind the two, Wells stalked silently, still guarding her as he had done all along.

An unfamiliar smell blew toward them from the wildwood, a breath both alien and exciting as though strange spices grew here. Marja had smelled it on the druids and recognized it – only *that* had been the smell of its corruption. This was the freshness of its growth.

Once more she tried to break free. Frayle was a very strong man and Wells was there to see that she did not escape. "No!" she screamed frantically. "Wells! In the name of God, help me!" In the end, she fought so hard that Frayle had to let her go.

Inspired, she turned suddenly on her bodyguard. "Is this for the good of the corporation?" she shouted. "Will this secure its *real* good?"

Wells stopped. She could see the struggle in his face as he took what she offered and tried to make of it a weapon against his conditioning. "No –" he said hesitantly.

And then the ground seemed to erupt with armed men. Frayle's servants came running but she saw one of them go down, an arrow protruding from one leg. A very tall man – a Lost Rythan it must be, only how could a Lost Rythan be here? – aimed a gun and another fell.

"Get down!" Wells snatched at her just as two druids came racing out of the forest. Before Marja could do anything, they had grabbed her and were dragging her in beneath the trees. She saw purple fronds above great amethyst trunks, pale, squirming vines and overall inhaled that spicy scent.

"You – called," one of the druids said in the slurred way they spoke. "Now you join us – after all."

Somehow her bodyguard broke free of the fighting and tackled the man. Behind him, Frayle came leaping, sword in hand, bleeding where an arrow had grazed his side. With one slash he freed her from the other druid. All around them tree-things swayed, vines crawled, and something made sounds never heard in the lands of men. A branch, flexible as no true branch could ever be, reached for Frayle. Like a tentacle, it clutched, teeth like a saw blade running along one side.

Suddenly the two men were fighting the lashing fronds, bleeding where they struck, while Marja tried vainly to beat back the foliage with her hands. At last the three reached the dead earth beyond the range of the forest.

Almost at once, Wells was seized by one of the Lost Rythans and Frayle taken by two young men who looked like outlaws. Marja half fell into the arms of a man in a cassock with a star and a cross blazoned on one shoulder. She was breathing so hard she could not speak.

"Did they get you?" he asked her as another Lost Rythan ran over and began examining her arms and face. "Did one of them sting you?"

She shook her head. "I – I don't think so. I'm alright."

And then in a sudden silence she turned and saw that the men holding Frayle were slowly backing away. The master stood alone, a writhing vine clinging to one wrist like a slave band binding him to the wildwood.

CHAPTER 14

BROTHER BRENDAN RAN OVER TO help the master, but even before he reached him, Frayle had torn the thing from his arm and thrown it onto the ground, stamping on it until it was no more than a faint bluish pulp. Only then did he hold up his hand, where everyone could see plainly the mark of its sting.

"Cut it off!" he shouted in an access of revulsion and terror. "Cut off my hand!"

Ard Matthew ran forward, drawing his sword.

But the Star Brother stopped him. "Wait," he said. "Look at his face!"

At this, the Lost Rythan froze in horror, for there on Frayle's temple was another, larger wound where one of the things had bitten him. In the fighting, he had not even felt it.

He did, however, see the dismay reflected in the faces of the other two as he slowly raised his clean hand to the spot. His eyes widened and a low groan escaped him. Abruptly he covered his face with his hands.

There was no comfort the others could give. Ard Matthew took his arm and led him gently back to the wagon where he lowered the master to the ground, remaining with him while the others saw to the injured. "Let me look at that wound in your side," he said once and Frayle stared at him blankly. "I've got a pressure bandage I can put on."

"Why bother?"

"You must live as long as God wills," Ard Matthew told him sternly.

At this, Frayle submitted to treatment. Afterwards he sat as before, staring straight ahead. Once or twice one hand crept up toward the mark on his face until, with a shudder, he let it drop.

The outlaws released Wells once he had been persuaded to throw down his gun, along with several more weapons of a similar sort. After one attempt, no one tried to pick any of them up. The bodyguard seemed more dazed than anything else as he took a tentative step away from his captors, peering about to see where Marja had gone.

When no one tried to stop him, he walked slowly over to where she stood with the other Lost Rythan. This man gave Wells a suspicious look and would have barred his way.

"It's alright," Marja told him. "He saved me –" And then she realized what she had said. Wells had disobeyed orders! He had defied the corporation, running into the wildwood himself to pull her free!

"How did you get around your conditioning?" she demanded.

His face was drawn and greyish as he stared at her, his mouth working. "I – I don't know," he said and staggered as though he would fall. The off-worlder reached over to steady him. "I told myself that Pesc must be protected. It was like a child – *my* child. I had to make sure it would not hurt itself."

She thought she recognized the bishop's reasoning – and her own inspired words as well. That he must seek out the *true* good of the corporation, that is what the bishop had said. And somehow, Wells had reasoned – had *convinced* himself – that whatever Pesc intended was not in its best interests.

Whatever they intended? "Wells," she said, "*why* was I to be given to the wildwood? Did you know?"

He looked down, his gaunt face flushing oddly, red spots deepening on each cheek. "I knew," he said.

"Then tell me!" She took his hand. "Do you mean to say you knew all along that they were lying to me, that everything I had been told to do here was no more than a cover up for something else? *Tell* me!"

He winced at her grip. "I cannot," he mumbled. "Saving you was only possible because I made myself believe that Pesc would be in danger if I didn't. But I can't do anything more. As it is –" His glance slid over to the robot.

"You!" Marja screamed suddenly, knowing she was being foolish because it was only a machine. But she didn't care! "You won't have him! You – *monster*!" She was reliving part of her old nightmare, a memory out of delirium.

But, "No," the Lost Rythan agreed, half understanding. "That thing is our prisoner now. It won't touch either of you."

Wells turned to him desperately. "You must bind me," he said. "Do you understand? *I* am the one who cannot be trusted!"

At this, Brother Brendan came up and beckoned to Colin. "He's right," he said. "I know how some of these corporate slaves are conditioned. You had better have your men tie his hands. If he's a trained bodyguard, he'll have more weapons about him than those on the ground. Do it now while he still has some control over himself."

The Lost Rythan began a protest, but the Star Brother cut him off.

"I know how you feel, Gris Wolfgang. It isn't fair. But we're doing him a favor, as well as protecting ourselves."

Marja watched in horror as two of the Band tied her bodyguard's hands together behind him and then, forcing him to seat himself on the ground, did the same to his ankles. When they were satisfied, they left and went over to help with Frayle's fallen servants, one wounded, the others merely stunned.

"Now," the Star Brother said gently, kneeling beside Wells, "just how much can you tell us?"

"Very little. I'm sorry."

"If I tell *you*, can you assent to my words?"

"I – I think so."

Mentally, he reviewed the information Father Moto had passed on.

"Then, to begin with," he said aloud, "Dr. Sienko was chosen for this job because of a genetic mutation which made her a perfect subject for an experimental substance, a drug which would make her immune to the toxins of the native flora but very susceptible to its other influences."

"I don't know about that part," Wells said. "The last – yes." He seemed to have some trouble getting out the last word.

"Just nod your head after this. And if it is too hard, we will wait."

A nod.

"So," the Star Brother went on, "the drug was given. It had to be administered in several spaced doses to avoid a reaction –"

"My so called allergy attack!" Marja cried. "I wouldn't let the robot do a physical scan and then I got sick. It was going to inoculate me then!"

"That sounds likely."

Suddenly she remembered something else. "You *did* know, Wells," she exclaimed. "When I was ill, I thought I heard your voice. You were saying how sorry you were!"

Wells did not answer.

She looked over at the Star Brother. "So I was immune to the native forest? It wouldn't have hurt me?"

"I didn't say that," Brother Brendan told her. "I only said it would make you immune to the *toxins*. In other ways, it would have hurt you very much. It would probably have enslaved you, in fact." He frowned in distaste. "You would have been stung if it weren't for your bodyguard – and Master

Frayle." He almost told her then what had happened to Frayle, but he wasn't sure she could take it.

"That sting," he went on, "would have given your system a jolt of pure bliss. Or rather *impure* bliss. And the effect would have continued to some extent, for the rest of your life. I believe that then the plan would have been to remove you to the mothership for further testing in order to develop a vaccine that could be used on ordinary people – those who don't have your unusual genetic makeup, I mean.

"And," he added, "You would cooperate most willingly because you would have been bound to the corporation even more firmly than your bodyguard."

"You mean it's a narcotic? But –"

"It is something far worse. The druids had discovered part of the secret, but it undermines their health, blasts their minds and makes them addicts who must serve the trees or die. This was not quite what Pesc intended, though if they had known of the druids' existence, they would almost certainly have used *them* to inoculate you."

She looked down at Wells. "How much of this did *you* know?" she asked. "That I was their experimental subject? That they planned not to aid the colony but only to exploit the resources of this planet?"

"I knew – all that." The bodyguard did not look at any of them. "I – I was aware that these things were wrong but I could not make it all come together. The bishop showed me how to reason myself into some sort of action. But it was so *hard*!"

"You love Pesc, don't you?" Brother Brendan said gently.

"I must."

"Then be glad we are going to save them from destroying themselves. At least we are going to try." He laid one hand on the other man's shoulder. "Net Central couldn't ignore something like this," he said. "Your corporation would have been broken in the end – annihilated."

"Then if you can prevent this, I will help you."

"Should we release you?"

For a long moment, Wells considered, his gaze traveling to the wagon where the robot sat, its smiling face turned toward him. "No," he said. "Not yet."

At that point Brother Brendan was called away by Ard Matthew. "You need to talk to Colin," he said.

The Star Brother followed him back to the wagon where the outlaw stood over Frayle. The two were glaring at each other. At least for the moment, the master seemed like his old self.

Colin had a look on his face the others had not seen before. "I wonder," he was saying, "if I shouldn't do to you as you did to me the first time I ran away from you – *Master*. How many nights have you spent chained to a wall? How many times have you gone hungry? How many whip marks are there on *your* back?"

"I'm not afraid of you."

"All the more reason to teach you that what goes around comes around."

"You were a serf – and now you are an outlaw. It was only to be expected that you would fall into something worse."

The young man laughed. "Why that makes us equals!" he cried. "Aren't you masters descended from common criminals?"

Frayle glared at him in silence.

Brother Brendan stepped between the two. "This man is not a prisoner," he said, "and your behavior would be out of place even if he were."

"Isn't he a prisoner?" Colin was hardly recognisable as the cheerful leader of the Band. "He was going to do for the Pesc lady, wasn't he?"

"Colin!" Ard Matthew said, coming up to join the Star Brother. "You shame yourself!"

"You," the outlaw sneered, "are a master too, aren't you? Somewhere on some greater world than ours, maybe, but you stand up for each other, you overlords."

"I was a highholder of Lost Rythar," Ard Matthew admitted. "But now I am a Faring Guard. We are not even masters of ourselves."

"What do you mean?"

"We were all once outlaws just as you are, but we have turned ourselves to the service of God."

The young man shook his head in disgust. Slowly he backed away from the group. He did not say anything more as he rejoined his fellows, but presently the Band swept by, galloping back along the road toward Dunsever.

Meanwhile, Frayle looked up at the others gathered around him. His eyes met Marja's – she was staring in horror at the mark on his face. He smiled slightly. "At least you are safe, Marja" he said. "I am glad of it."

She turned toward the Star Brother. "Why didn't you tell me? Is there no hope for him?"

No one answered. Suddenly a voice began calling from above them in the wagon, intoning monotonously over and over: "Wells. Master Frayle. This is Hu. Has your assignment been accomplished? Wells? Master Frayle?"

"Don't anyone answer," the Star Brother said. "Not now. Wait until the other shuttle comes down."

At this, Marja turned to him. "What other shuttle? Do you mean the Star Brothers are coming?"

"Yes," he said, "Our ship is back in the net now. I'm very sorry but, in a way, we made use of you too. Our recording of this day's events is the final piece of evidence against Pesc." He glanced at Wells who had begun to struggle in his bonds. "The recording has already been transmitted to the *St. Balthasar*."

"You lied to me!" Wells shouted. "You made me betray Pesc!"

"No, we have not," the Star Brother told him firmly. "What becomes of Pesc is still in their own hands."

But Wells would not listen. In his own eyes, he had been tricked into breaking the imperatives instilled into him since his earliest days. Now they had to stun him to keep him from hurting himself.

IT WAS LATE AFTERNOON, AND Frayle's wounded serving man had been taken to the priory, along with three others temporarily disabled by the stunners. Frayle ought to have gone as well, Brother Brendan thought, but he wasn't sure whether the master's testimony might not be needed when the shuttle arrived. And Frayle seemed willing enough to cooperate, though otherwise he was sunk in a calm despair.

The bodyguard had meanwhile recovered consciousness, if not the use of his limbs, but it seemed best to keep him where he was. At least Wells held no animus against Marja, believing her completely innocent of any intent to harm the corporation. She had been their victim and as such, had his sympathy, but as for the others, his feelings about them were unmistakable. He hated them with a fierceness that was not his own and, consequently, he was relieved not to be able to do anything about it.

His thoughts about himself were far more confusing. He felt sick with the knowledge that he had done wrong but it was hard to see just where he had failed. Hadn't he tried to serve Pesc in the best way possible by keeping it from a crime that would bring down the wrath of Net Central? Yet the crime had been attempted even though it had failed. Would that be enough to fatally damage the corporation? The Star Brothers had the evidence in their hands and he could do nothing to stop them from destroying his masters if they chose.

In his bewilderment he could grasp only a few things. He, at least, had sinned – but against which god? Had he betrayed Pesc by making his confession to the bishop? Or had he acted against his Faith when he allowed Marja to be taken to the wildwood? And when he had rescued her – was that yet another sin against Pest?

As these thoughts tormented him, he kept glancing over at the wagon, where the robosecretary sat smiling at him like some blasphemous Madonna. It would almost have been a relief to suffer the thing's punishment, for that would save him the greater agony of judging himself. How simple his life had been before this!

Slowly the greater suns began their descent toward the fringe, until at last the offworlders caught sight of what they had been waiting for. A streak of light shot toward them out of the east, resolving itself, as it got nearer, into the sleek form of a shuttle. After circling once, the machine set down neatly on the dead ground, breaking up the hummocks in an acrid fountain of dust.

Slowly the side cracked open. A great meaty hand grasped the flange and with a deliberate grace hardly appropriate to one so massive, Gaed Alfred Snowtyger emerged. The Sector Chief stood for a moment looking around, first at the fringe and then at the group waiting beside the wagon.

To those who had never seen him before, there was something unnerving in the sight of the silver-haired giant with his mighty moustaches and trimmed beard, his shaggy eyebrows and shoulder length hair. He wore the clothing of his homeworld, colorful and barbaric, but the weapons at his belt were modern – a heat gun, a stunner, and a spring pistol. Before anyone could do more than rise, he was striding toward the group.

The two Faring Guards waited respectfully, not advancing as their chief turned to Brother Brendan first. "It's done!" he shouted and suddenly grinned broadly. It was as though another sun came out.

At this transformation from terrifying colossus to something more like a great, friendly bear, the others found it impossible not to smile in return. Of the party gathered to meet him, only the two Faring Guards had ever seen their chief angry, and both breathed a sigh of relief that the mission had been a success.

"You have your evidence?" the Star Brother asked. "Is Father Moto satisfied?"

"He is. And now –" The giant glanced around, spotting the robot still seated in the wagon. "This is the contact module?" His very words shrank the demon thing to its true dimensions. It was only a tool. A machine.

"Yes," Brother Brendan said. "The Pesc coordinator has been trying to get through for most of the day."

Gaed Alfred strode over to the wagon. "Connect me with your boss," he said to the robot. For a moment or two nothing happened and then it spoke.

"Wells? Is that you?"

"This is Faring Guard Chief Gaed Alfred Snowtyger. Are you the coordinator?"

There came a pause. Then, "You have made an unauthorized landing on a Pesc owned world," Hu said through the robot voice. "Not only are you subject to sanctions from Net Central, but Pesc will almost certainly cancel the former agreement with the Star Brothers. And that goes for any other worlds we own!"

"They were going to do that anyway, as far as this one is concerned," Snowtyger rumbled. "And we'll see about the others. But once you set things in production here, you were planning to close this place up even tighter than your predecessors had it. Isn't that so?"

"I don't know what you mean!"

"Then you're not very bright. We've just acquired the last piece of evidence against your corporation. When Net Central learns what you've been up to –"

He did not need to finish. The pause this time was much longer.

"I – I am not responsible for the policies of my employers."

"Damn right. Not responsible at all. So you can pass me on to your own superior," the chief said. "Now."

At a gesture, he dismissed the others. "This will take a while," he mouthed to Brother Brendan. "Have you somewhere to go?"

"The priory." Quickly the Star Brother drew him a map.

"Right." Then, "I'm waiting," he growled. "And so is Net Central."

"He – I mean I can't just interrupt the district manager –" The uninflected robot voice made Hu sound less panicked than he was.

"Suit yourself," Snowtyger said. "But when he hears that you missed a chance to save the corporation –"

"Come on," Brother Brendan told the other Lost Rythans. "We'll leave the wagon here and take the carriage back to the priory."

He glanced at Frayle for confirmation. "One of my men can stay," the master said wearily. "Unless your chief knows how to manage horses?"

"Gaed Alfred can do anything," Gris Wolfgang said sturdily but Snowtyger shook his head. The boundless faith of his juniors was an ongoing embarrassment.

Two of Frayle's men stayed behind after lifting the bodyguard into the carriage where Marja joined him. Frayle sat up beside the driver.

Initially Wells had been propped into the seat, but as they jolted along, he slumped in one corner, eyeing his former charge bleakly. He had not spoken since he had been stunned.

Marja drew a deep breath and turned to him. "Are you alright, Wells?" she asked quietly. "Can – can I do anything for you?"

He shrugged. "Do they still threaten Pesc?"

"I think the sector chief is trying to make a deal with them," she told him.

Wells thought this over. "What sort of deal can he make?"

"I don't know." She was suddenly very sorry for her former bodyguard, caught as he was between the two contending forces. He needed a shave and his hair was plastered with dust and sweat, while his eyes looked large and desperate in his drawn face. She even wondered if the internal struggle might kill him.

On an impulse, she laid one hand on his arm. "You *did* save my life, Wells," she said. "More than once. And at the end, you risked everything to get me out of the wildwood. *These* are the things that matter."

He closed his eyes, smiling slightly. "Yes," he murmured. "I will try to remember that."

They were like two children rescued from an evil enchanter, adrift without knowing what their rescuers intended to do with them.

The carriage was met by two young monks whom Brother Brendan introduced as Brothers Dyved and Havard. The pair quickly took charge of the horses. "Master Frayle's servants are waiting for you inside," one of them said. "But –"

He looked a little askance at Marja as she climbed down.

"I think," Frayle told him, "the marshal will make an exception to the rule in this case. I will speak to him." Despite everything, he carried himself with the same pride with which he had ruled his farm. Perhaps Marja was the only one to really see the desperation in his eyes.

"Cut the bodyguard loose," Brother Brendan ordered, seeing that Wells was unable to get himself out of the carriage. "Will you give us your word not to try to flee – or to do anything foolish?" he asked. "Even if you wanted to, there is nothing you could accomplish now. It's all up to Pesc."

Wells leaned against the wall of the barn, rubbing his wrists while Ard Matthew cut the ropes from his ankles. "Yes – I think I can give my word on that. But remember my limitations. If I see a weak spot, I don't know what I'll do."

"You won't," the Star Brother assured him, "see any weak spots. Anyway, nothing goes to Net Central unless Pesc refuses to cooperate."

The bodyguard nodded tiredly. "There would always have been a danger from the authorities," he said. "Even if *you* had not trapped my owners. I see that now."

"Then you should see something else," Brother Brendan told him. "Or have you forgotten that Net Central is not the ultimate judge before which we stand? The directors of Pesc have offended God."

Wells pondered this slowly. "I – I kept telling myself that when Ma – Dr. Sienko was in danger," he said at last. "The bishop had warned me that the corporation must answer to God for what happened. But thinking of that only worked for a time before my conditioning took over again."

He grimaced. "It's strange. Sometimes God's judgment seems so far away – and then it is as if it were on us even now. Freedom," he added, "takes a lot more out of a man than bondage."

The Star Brother laughed. "In *this* world, anyway." Sobering, he went on, "I know it seems hard to you now because you have just been given some ideas that are new to you. But in your soul, you have always been free – isn't that so?"

But the other man did not answer.

They found the marshal waiting for them in a smaller room off the refectory. Marshal Pwyl greeted everyone with equal politeness but Frayle seemed his first object. He had already been told about the master's accident.

Master Frayle held out his hand, pointed to the sting on his face. "Can these be burned out?" he asked without much hope. "Can you do it?"

"On an extremity – perhaps," the marshal said. "But not the one on your forehead. I'm sure you already realize that."

"Then it will go with me as it does with the brothers?"

"Things will go as God wills. But yes, I think you had better be prepared for that."

Marja did not dare to look at Frayle lest she see his fear. He has paid for his crimes, she told herself, whatever they have been. Greed and ambition, perhaps worse things. He knows this and that he will go on paying until he dies of the wildwood's poison. The last thing a man like Frayle must want would be her sympathy.

"We do not have a proper guest house," the marshal was saying, "but we have cleared out a series of store rooms for you. There are plenty of beds if you will sleep as we do – on straw with a rug thrown over it. You are welcome to stay as long as you like."

Brother Brendan thanked him, looking somewhat embarrassed. "The lady –" he murmured. "I mean, I suppose it is against your rule."

"She shall have a room of her own. Under the circumstances I think we should make an exception." He was still speaking when Brother Dyved ushered in the Faring Guard chief. Gaed Alfred Snowtyger looked rather smug as he addressed the marshal. "Greetings in the name of God," he boomed. "And thank you for your hospitality!"

This finished off Marshal Gwilym's reserve. He grinned back at the Lost Rythan. "I see that your dealings with the corporation have gone well," he said.

"Well enough," the chief told him frankly. "We've got them by the short hairs now, as I made plain to that ass I talked to. Somebody from the central committee. He's going to contact Father Moto tonight. Moto's better at this sort of thing than I am."

Brother Brendan was not so sure of that. In his opinion, the exhortation to be wise as a serpent and simple as a dove applied about equally to the Faring Guard chief and the Star Brother. But he did not comment.

"Perhaps you are hungry?" the marshal suggested. "Since it is Sunday, there will be an evening meal."

The party repaired to the refectory where they were given bread and cheese and soup, while the marshal looked on happily, calling for more beer when it was needed. The other brothers had already finished, so they had the long table to themselves.

Marja could not help comparing this repast with the first meal she had eaten at Frayle farm. The master had carved the meat while his sons sat by, only the family and their guests at the main table while the servants sat further away from the fire. There had been something grand and patriarchal about that life, she thought now.

Suddenly she did not want to go back to the job center at Bloomhadn. Her assignment with Pesc had been both a failure and a humiliation. It was still hard to believe she could have been so gullible. And certainly there would be no reference! At the very least she would have to agree to a block to keep her from revealing anything that had happened.

She repressed a wry smile. To whom would a recommendation be given if she got one? Another corporation looking for someone to spearhead the exploitation of an unsuspecting colony? She could hardly hope to be recruited by another criminal organization – or to see them brought to justice.

And then she remembered Wells. What would become of *him*? Would they exact retribution from their slave because he had disobeyed them at the last? Hu would, she knew, but after this fiasco, Hu would probably lose his job. But would his successor be any kinder to a disobedient slave?

Wells was not eating much, and neither was Frayle. They sat side by side, sharing a bench almost as though they took comfort in one another's presence, one ruined from youth by the conditioning of the corporation and the other, the great man, wearing his death in the marks on his hand and forehead. God had at last made them equals, she thought.

Across the table, the two younger Faring Guards ate hungrily, basking in the good cheer of their chief. Marja, who sat beside Brother Brendan, finally laid a slice of cheese on her bread and munched it slowly, trying not to think about her own future.

Once she dared look up at Frayle. To her surprise, he was regarding her somberly. It was neither fear or anger she saw in his gaze, but only shame. Almost at once each of them looked away.

Choking down her bread, she wished heartily that they had never met.

ON MONDAY, EVERYONE ATTENDED THE morning Mass, Marja included. It had not even occurred to her to stay away, partly because the Brothers of St. Hubert were her hosts, but also because Chief Snowtyger took her presence for granted. There was something about him, aside from the fact that he was nearly seven feet tall, that both comforted and overawed her. Perhaps it was the frightening intensity of his goodwill. He was like a fortress, she thought, and though he rather terrified her, he also made her feel very safe.

Later, over their porridge, she learned for the first time that her robosecretary had been brought inside and was housed in a cell of its own. "Not that we need it now," Brother Brendan explained to her. "Chief Snowtyger and I have communicators to reach our own people. We none of us will ever speak to Pesc again."

She looked down. "None of us?"

At this the giant looked her way. "We made a deal," he told her. "Or at least I hope we did. Now we're waiting to hear if the higher ups have agreed to our demands."

"Your – *demands*?"

Snowtyger gave her a happy smile. "I know there's no question about what an outfit like that deserves," he began, as Wells stiffened, clenching his spoon.

"But it would serve no purpose to destroy them," he went on more smoothly. "They would only regroup in some other form and go on with their deviltry."

Brother Brendan was watching the bodyguard, who had stopped eating to stare at the chief.

"Think of it as a plea bargain," the chief said, addressing himself to the room at large, but looking directly at Wells. "Pesc is not going to fall, much as they deserve to. Instead they are going to pay – quite a lot, I should think."

"But that will hurt them!"

Brother Brendan took up the argument. "It will hurt them for their own good," he explained. "Gaed Alfred Snowtyger – and the Star Brothers – have saved them from themselves this time. If they had gone on with their plans, their activities would eventually have brought on their downfall in any case."

"After a lot more people were hurt," Ard Matthew added. "Millions – maybe billions."

Slowly Wells nodded, the color coming back into his cheeks. "I know you are right," he said. "But it is hard to hear these things discussed as though – as though Pesc were nothing more than –" He could not go on.

"You are divided within yourself," the Star Brother said. "But your reason remains free, doesn't it?"

"Yes, and that only makes things worse."

"Like being possessed," the marshal, who was sitting with them, said. "You do things you would not do if you were free."

"I think it's a little more than that," Brother Brendan said. "His conditioning goes pretty deep."

"It's a hellish thing!" Snowtyger growled suddenly. He reached over and touched the slave band. "This, at least, is in our power. But the other things they have done to you –"

"What do you mean?" Wells asked him. "What is in your power?"

"Wait and see. We'll hear from them soon and then will be time enough."

But it was a longer wait than the chief had anticipated. When Father Moto finally contacted him, the morning was far spent. Most of the party had gone out – though Frayle remained in the chapel – and it took a while to gather them all back together to hear the terms of the agreement.

The Lost Rythans were the hardest to corral, as they had departed with some of the brothers on patrol. Undoubtedly the druids were watching the priory and the brothers were grateful to have the two armed offworlders in their party.

Brother Brendan and the chief had been looking over the cattle – a novelty to Lost Rythans – while Marja, watched as always by Wells, had been pacing about the garden. Frayle's men – all save the wounded one – had gone to tend the horses.

At last, the noon meal forgotten as well as the noon prayers in the chapel – by the visitors at least – Chief Snowtyger got his call. He set the receiver to record so he could play everything back to the others, as soon as they were assembled. The suns were high when they finally gathered around him, listening to Father Moto's voice as it had come from the starship *St. Balthasar*.

There was good news and there was bad. Pesc had agreed to most of the chief's demands. For the first time, Marja and the others learned what these were. The colony was to be resold; indeed, it was already in the process of changing hands.

The buyer was Lost Rythar colony.

"But how could they – I mean where would a poor colony get that kind of money?" she demanded in amazement.

"Oh," Snowtyger told her carelessly, "they didn't ask very much. And we have backers."

The word *blackmail* came to mind, but she did not dare to utter it in front of a man so massive that he had to duck to get through most of the doorways. Still, she told herself, that was the only explanation that fit.

The bad news was that the corporation had insisted that its own personnel remain permanently on Treelight. At first Marja did not grasp what this meant. When she did, it came as far less of a shock that it should have. In some way, she had always known she would never leave the planet, and this was no more than a confirmation of her earlier conviction.

"I'm sorry," the chief told her, when she heard the condition. "But I was afraid they'd insist on something like this. You bear evidence in your blood, see. They'd rather you were killed, but we told them that wasn't an option."

Marja felt a chill run up her spine. Yes, she thought, Pesc *is* like that. Silently she thanked God for the "initiation" Wells had insisted on back in Bloomhadn Park. She had long since passed to the other side of *that* interface, the side where corporations might casually ask for the death of an employee and Faring Guards might, with equal imperturbability, refuse.

"Your bodyguard must also remain, but he is to be freed."

At this, Wells could not keep silent. A low sound escaped him and he buried his face in his hands.

"They will deactivate the slave band – may already have done it."

"Oh God," he cried. "They have cut me off from them!"

Gaed Alfred looked at him in surprise.

"You asked for that," Wells said in a muffled voice. "Didn't you?"

The chief nodded. "Can't leave any loose ends, can we?" he said. He reached over and took Wells' wrist in one hand, putting a sensor to the slave band. "It's dead," he added. "I guess the thing's built into your nervous system, though, isn't it?"

Wells was staring at the band, his expression such a mixture of wonder and horror that Marja feared for his sanity.

"It would have killed you to cut it out before. Now," the chief said, "we'll see what sort of surgery you can have without leaving the planet."

"Someone could shuttle down," Brother Brendan suggested.

"Sure. This is our world now. We'll have to get in some medics for these people." He looked at Wells. "It is their will for you," he said. "They sold you to us and we have made you free. You must accept that freedom in obedience to your first masters – and to us of course."

The bodyguard nodded, still trying to take this in. He kept staring at the band, as though he were afraid it might, after all, kill him. "I understand," he said, shaking his head. "But this will take time to – to sink in. I've worn that band for over thirty years."

Marja moved over to stand beside him. "We have both been freed," she told him. "And yes, it will take time – even for me."

They looked up as Marshal Gwilym came out of the priory. Quickly Chief Snowtyger told him what Father Moto had said.

"And there was one thing more," he added. "We asked for help in dealing with the native flora. They're giving us a vectored genetic alteration – going to spray it on for us themselves. Within a year or two the wildwood will begin to lose its toxicity and very slowly start to yield to the offworld plantings."

"They could have done this all along?" Frayle and the marshal exclaimed at once.

"Yes. They were going to leave things as they were while they harvested their drugs, of course," the chief said. "There was no reason to kill off any more of it if the colony was not to be expanded."

"They told me they were going to wipe it out," Marja said.

"If such a spray was available," Frayle said, still not quite understanding, "why didn't we have it before? Why was it necessary for the Brothers of St. Hubert to fight off the fringe at such cost?"

"It wasn't available," Snowtyger said. "Dagon Ltd. did their best for you when the colony was founded. This is something Pesc developed later on their own as a sort of byway of their main research."

"What else did they develop," Brother Brendan asked him. "What other benefits did they set aside as unprofitable?"

The chief shrugged. "Father Moto won't miss anything. But that's the only one I've heard of so far."

"So, Lost Rythar owns the colony," Frayle murmured. "What will this mean? How will you recoup your investment?"

The chief laughed. "I tried to tell you, our investment wasn't that large," he said. "We're only a name on the deed. The Star Brothers are your protectors now and we are their allies, their – their –"

"You are our patrons," Ard Matthew said to Brother Brendan. "Our guides." He turned to Master Frayle. "We owe the Star Brothers more than we or you could ever repay, for they are the ones who first raised our colony from the darkness of paganism."

"Then the Star Brothers are our real masters?" Frayle said uncertainly.

"I doubt," Chief Snowtyger told him, "you will see much change in your lives here. Not unless you make it yourselves. For your own safety, this will probably be a restricted world for some time to come. Your colony will continue to grow, however, and you or your descendents will be the ones to decide what happens when it is strong enough to open up to the rest of the galaxy."

Most of them had heard about as much as they could take in, and no one had anything to say as they dispersed. The chief had asked the priory chaplain to hear his confession – perhaps the word *blackmail* had occurred to him, too – and Frayle went off with the marshal for a private conference.

Marja sat with Wells on an outside bench, staring at the violet shadow that was the fringe. She saw him looking at the band and wondered what would happen when it was gone. Would he change? After all, she reminded herself, his conditioning had not come from that piece of metal.

"You'd never seen one of these before," he said, seeing the direction of her gaze. "I remember you told me."

She shook her head, no longer embarrassed.

"You said you didn't know how to behave – how to treat a slave."

"Don't remind me of that."

"It's got three modes," he told her. "One to summon, one to punish and one to deactivate. Now I've experienced them all."

"Now you'll soon have it off," she said gently. "Now you are free."

He traced one finger over the metalplast. "I'll never be free," he said. "I think you know that."

"But they can't hurt you anymore. You won't see any of them again."

He shrugged. "I will always serve two masters," he said. "Two gods. Or perhaps one God and one devil."

"You *do* hate Pesc, don't you?" she asked. "It must be like hating a part of yourself."

"I do not hate Pesc."

She frowned, fearing to say more.

"If I hated them," he went on slowly, "then I would remain a slave to that hatred. I have never hated them." He looked up at her. "I don't know if you can understand that. I have only hated the things they did."

"The things they did to you!"

"Those things are done. As a result of them, I must always desire the good of the corporation and all of its personnel. Is that such a bad thing?"

"I don't know," she admitted, "when you put it like that."

"I must put it like that, for it is the truth." He smiled at her. "Master Frayle's brother made me understand. Or rather, he reminded me of things I should have already known. And I did. That has always been my freedom, you see, that I did not give way to hatred."

The larger suns were westering and the smaller had already set when she spotted Frayle and the marshal walking in the paddock. They were deep in conversation. The two Faring Guards came slowly around the corner of the barn, heading in her direction and there was Brother Brendan coming over to join them.

There was something inexorable in the steady pace of the Lost Rythans as they came nearer, something almost portentous. They were like the gods of some stellar Valhalla – the new masters of Treeworld.

Whatever they said about deferring to the Star Brothers, the fact remained that they owned the colony. Chief Snowtyger might say that his people would not interfere in the day to day life of the colony, but was that the truth? By all accounts Lost Rythans had not entirely shaken off their former savagery, and their representatives, the Faring Guard, were recruited from those throwbacks whose deeds had earned them exile.

She stared at their straight-nosed faces, the reddish light making their hair and beards almost ruddy, wondering.

Abruptly, one of them held out his arm to the Star Brother. There, running from a half healed burn above the elbow, a thin line of blue had appeared, snaking downward. Already it had begun to form a faint pattern of branches like some vegetable tattoo – the emblem of the wildwood.

CHAPTER 15

IN THE MORNING, **F**RAYLE HIMSELF insisted on driving Gaed Alfred and Brother Brendan back to the shuttle's landing site. Whether he did this in a spirit of reparation or simply because, he could not resist a chance to see the space craft, who could say? All his personal hopes had been dashed – the plans he had laid for dealing with the offworlders on their own ground, the swathe he would cut among his own people. Everything was to be blotted out in lines of purple.

The chief let him examine the shuttle inside and out, which he did very thoroughly. "I'm not authorized to take you up," Snowtyger rumbled apologetically. "Or I would do so gladly."

"No, I understand."

"Later they might let us bend the rules a little," he added with gruff kindliness, "but it's too early now. No one who had anything to do with – you know. Technically you're evidence."

For the first time, the master managed a thin smile. "It is ironic, isn't it? I would have sold my soul to gain the stars."

Later, he and the Star Brother watched Snowtyger take the shuttle aloft before they drove back to the priory to wait for his return. Once Frayle glanced over at Brother Brendan.

"This surgeon he is bringing," he said. "He is very learned in the ways of your science?"

"I should hope so."

"Then I am happy for Dr. Sienko's man. He is a decent fellow and I wish him well."

"Yes," the Star Brother agreed. "I think he is."

"She is fond of him?"

But Brother Brendan could not answer this. He had only recently met Pesc's delegate, but he suspected that her preference for the company of someone she knew was easily explained by the situation in which she found herself. She was alone on an alien world, as much an exile as any Faring Guard but without the exalted sense of purpose that sustained them. This world, primitive though it was, would be her home from now on.

For a time, they jogged on in silence, the horses somewhat spooked by the shuttle takeoff and glad to leave the area.

When Chief Snowtyger returned that afternoon, he brought along a pair of one-man floaters. With these, he and Heth August Sunbear, the surgeon, traveled much more quickly over the roadway and into the priory compound.

Franz Wells took his place behind Snowtyger and, at her own request, Marja was permitted to climb up behind the surgeon. She was nervous about submitting her former bodyguard to the care of another of these ham-fisted giants and, when they reached the shuttle, her doubts must have shown on her face.

Wells was taken inside the shuttle at once. He gave Marja a quick smile and reached out once to ruffle her hair. But neither of them could think of anything to say.

Gaed Alfred, seeing her distress, also tried to offer rude comfort, assuring her that Heth August had always been a good man to have around after a battle. This did not have the calming effect he intended, however, and she would not be at ease until he allowed her into the shuttle where she waited in one of the acceleration seats while the doctor operated in the storage compartment. After a time, the chief left her alone. She heard one of the floaters start up.

She had been waiting for at least an hour, looking about at the décor, far plainer than that of the corporation shuttle and with a crucifix above the control panel, when she heard horses outside. A few minutes later, she was joined by the Star Brother. "Gaed Alfred told me he'd left you here," he said. "He's talking to Gris Wolfgang."

"The man who –" She gulped. "I was so sorry to see that he is poisoned after all. And the sting was – was cauterized, wasn't it?"

Brother Brendan nodded. "Wasted suffering, it would seem. Only no suffering is truly wasted, I suppose, if we bear it well. Anyway, it was more than a sting since they had held the thing on for some time before he could break free."

"And now he must die." She wasn't thinking about the Lost Rythan, however. It was the fate of Prydan Frayle that was uppermost in her thoughts.

"Dr. Sienko," the Star Brother said hesitantly, "I am sorry that my superiors could not arrange anything better for you and Franz Wells. He is resigned at least, and I hope you will be too. Please be assured that we will do everything we can to help you settle in here."

She looked at him blankly. "Oh – yes." Things were happening so fast that the reality of her exile had still not sunk in. Nor had she come to grips with the fact that the Star Brothers were really the ones in charge of the colony.

"Our visits will become more frequent and our people will stay here longer when they come," he was saying. "We will make a foundation, probably at Bannyclay, with schools and all that. Life will improve."

"I had thought *we* were going to do so much for them," she said vaguely. "Pesc promised, oh, modern comforts and prosperity and education. Freedom from superstition."

"You can't *give* all that to people," he said gently. "They need to make choices of their own – to grow into modern life only if that is what they want."

They sat on in silence, the Star Brother withdrawn into himself. Perhaps he was praying, she thought. He had seemed, when she first saw him, a man of rapid gestures, small and wiry, his quick blue-eyed gaze fairly jumping from one thing to another. Now at last he was still, though it may only have been the transient stillness of a hummingbird.

After another half hour, the hatch finally opened and Heth August joined them. "Finished," he said cheerfully. "He wants to show you – but it's all bandaged, so there's not much to see. But here –" He held out the band, somewhat mangled and trailing connections on the inside. "He said to show this to you, Dr. Sienko, so that you may be sure it is dead."

She could not bring herself to touch the thing. To her eyes it looked as evil as the vines of the alien forest. "To think that human beings put this on him," she murmured. "That anyone would do this to another!"

Beside her, Brother Brendan reached out one tentative hand and laid a finger on the metal. "Yes," he said. "And yet it is so."

Though she had ridden behind him on the floater, Marja had not had a good look at the surgeon. To her surprise, he was not much older than Ard Matthew and Gris Wolfgang, his auburn hair ponytailed and his beard trimmed as theirs were. He had an honest, friendly face with the direct, grey-eyed gaze and long, Grecian looking nose of his race. "Would you like to come in now?" he asked her pleasantly, stepping aside to duck – for he was, after all, a Lost Rythan – through the hatchway.

She rose and followed him. Wells was half sitting in a portable med couch, one wrist swathed in bandages and lying across his lap. He smiled at her. "Now this," he said, glancing down at the arm, "is something I never thought I'd live to see."

She smiled back. "So you don't mind staying here on Networld 326?"

"Not at all." Then, "But this must be hard on you, Dr. Sienko, and I am sorry for your sake that things have turned out this way. But –"

"But when we consider the alternative," she finished for him, "it's not so bad."

"No," he agreed, "it's not so bad."

Later, while she left him there to recuperate, however, she was not so sure. Brother Brendan had come on horseback and, after some argument, persuaded her to mount while he led the animal along the road back to the priory. Once there, they found Master Frayle and the Faring Guard chief leaning together on the fence, watching the horses. "– wants to stay with the brothers here," the chief was saying.

"I'm sure he will be very welcome," the master told him. "Gris Wolfgang is a good man and his courage will be an example to the rest of us."

Gaed Alfred gave him a shrewd look. "I hope that works both ways," he said with his usual directness.

Frayle did not notice Marja as the horse passed behind the two. "I hope so too," he said slowly. "I am one of the patrons of the priory, you know, and I had always thought to end my days here."

The chief did not say anything.

The master flushed slightly. "Many of us do," he said. "We give the dregs of our lives to God. Or so it seems to me now." He paused, looking down at his hand. "I am not so old that this may not turn out to be a blessing."

"This thing – this disease or whatever it is," Gaed Alfred said. "I know some of the brothers have it as well as the marshal. I'm told they can live for years sometimes before they become too ill to get about."

"That is so."

Marja did not know exactly what it was she heard in his voice then. It might have been despair or it might have been some other thing. A dogged endurance that went to her heart.

Later, as the group gathered once more in the refectory, the chief announced that he was taking the shuttle aloft the next morning as soon as he had brought Marja's bodyguard back to the priory. "You," he said to Brother Brendan, "are to remain in the colony for the time being as your order's representative. And your assistants, of course."

Gris Wolfgang looked up at his chief. "You will consider my request?" he asked.

"I'm considering it now. For the time being, you have my permission to remain with the Brothers of St. Hubert, so long as Brother Brendan can spare you. As for the future, I must wait until God's will becomes more clear to me than it is now."

The young Faring Guard nodded without speaking.

"That will be fine," the Star Brother interjected quickly. "I know Marshal Pwyll has invited you to stay, Gris Wolfgang. As for the rest of us, we have been asked to accompany Master Frayle back to Frayle Farm for a few days, until Father Moto finishes his dealings with Pesc."

He turned to Marja. "I hope you will come with us, Dr. Sienko. And Mr. Wells, of course."

To go back as Frayle's guest was the last thing Marja wanted, but she owed it to Wells to see that he was made comfortable. Besides, where else *could* she go now that she was exiled here? Perhaps the Star Brothers would find some sort of job for her, but that must be later, when they had settled in.

Not long afterwards, Master Frayle's personal invitation to her was delivered with a careful politeness that she found more embarrassing than reassuring. Still, for the sake of his kindness toward Franz Wells who had been brought back and had, at the master's insistence, been given a bed in his own room instead of being placed with the servants, she assented more warmly than she had intended.

She bore the master no ill will. Despite his former intentions, he had rescued her and now she owed him a debt she could never repay. It was for her sake he had been stung and, because he had tried to rescue her, he would probably die.

Of course, he *had* once intended to seduce her. That would have been his way to bind her to him as he might have bound a woman of his own barbaric culture. All through, he had acted out of cold-blooded ambition, pretending to a fondness he had never felt for her. And now that all his strivings were at an end, he might well turn to God, she told herself bitterly. Wasn't that what a villain would do in a romance?

But she was not being fair. For she knew now that Frayle did not have it in him to carry his wickedness to its conclusion. He might be mercenary enough to take what he could get from the corporation, but when it came to actually harming her, he had in the end, been obliged to rescue her instead.

So why did she keep feeling that they must come to some explanation? He had complained earlier that *she* had acted in bad faith. And it was true that she *had* been commanded to give herself to him in order to secure his cooperation. But that was not the *real* reason she had – oh, it was all so complicated and unnecessary!

Frayle had been so eager to make a deal with Pesc once he talked to Hu directly, that he could scarce have thought of Marja as a person at all. From that moment, she might have been no more than one of his serfs.

She gave him a covert look. Brother Brendan and the Lost Rythans had gone to the chapel, and Frayle was giving his men some last-minute instructions about the morrow's journey. Seeing that she was practically alone with him, she got up to leave the room. But the master's servants were before her, filling the doorway so that she had to wait.

She was agonisingly aware of Frayle behind her, until suddenly it became unthinkable to leave without saying *some* word to thank him for what he had done. She turned around and there he was, closer than she had realized. For a long moment, they stared at one another.

"I – I must tell you how grateful I am," she began but he cut her off.

"I was responsible for your danger in the first place," he said. "And now I hope I have made amends to you – and to God. At any rate, I shall try."

"You didn't realize," she faltered. "How could you know what the corporation would ask of you?"

"Do you think I didn't know that Pesc was evil? What do you take me for? You can't really think I've never soiled my hands before! Must I be a no more than a child beside you star folk, merely because our world is not as advanced as yours?"

"No," she said miserably. "That isn't what I meant."

But he only shrugged, trembling with anger as he waited for her to go.

Later she too was angry, but it was hard to find an object for her wrath. He had treated her unfairly, implied things she had never thought, never intended.

But she had. Hadn't she been the lady bountiful, distributing her gifts to the masters of Harrow, accepting their homage, guarded by her slave and her robot, escorted by the good-looking colonial? Hadn't she made use of him as much as she could?

Hadn't she?

In the end, even if things had gone as she planned, the only gift she would have brought them was the destruction of all that made their lives worthwhile. Frayle was not a child – indeed, he was a clever man. But he could have had no conception of what would have happened if Pesc had dealt in even the semblance of good faith.

Only now did she see what she had almost done to the colony. If there *were* a God, she thought, her debt to Him must be far greater than Frayle's!

Somehow, she got through that night. In the morning, she was careful to avoid the master, chagrined but submissive when at his orders, she and Wells were placed once more in the carriage while their host went on horseback.

Despite these feelings, she attended to her former bodyguard, making sure he was comfortable. Otherwise, she spent the rest of the time looking out at the passing scenery. This was the landscape of her new and permanent home, she told herself, and she had better get used to it.

Wells spent part of the time dozing because of the drugs he had been given. So it was a shock when he finally addressed her. "This *is* a hard thing for you," he said abruptly. "Staying here. Harder than you let on."

"Oh, I'm sure I'll be given a job of some sort," she told him, turning around. "The Lost Rythans won't let me starve."

"No," he agreed. "Neither of us will starve."

"What will *you* do?" she asked him.

"I – I haven't decided yet." He looked down at the bandage on his wrist. "I know I serve the corporation best by staying here. Now I must convince myself that I might act independently without violating my loyalty."

"Perhaps it will get easier as time goes by."

"I expect it will," he agreed. "But you – you had much more to lose than I."

She tried to manufacture a reassuring smile. "Just now the hardest thing is being the guest of Master Frayle," she admitted. "He doesn't want me there any more than I want to be there!"

Wells considered this. "I don't suppose he wants your pity," he conceded.

"He doesn't want to be reminded all the things Pesc promised him," she snapped, losing patience. "And now –"

"Now he is going to die. Just like that Lost Rythan. He is afraid."

"Not Frayle!"

"Do not mistake courage for indifference," Wells told her. "He may never have thought deeply before, but something like this brings more to the surface than even *he* knew was there."

Marja sat back and closed her eyes while two tears trickled down her cheeks. But whether she wept for her exile or her folly, or for the wretched Frayle, she did not know.

TO DO HIM CREDIT, MARJA'S host had the delicacy not to house her at the manor. Instead, she was given a guest cabin nearby and a maid to wait on her. She would have objected to the latter but, having no skill in housekeeping, this was impossible. Marja didn't even know how to build a fire, and most of Pesc's gadgets had been left behind in Harrow. At least she had the luggage she had originally brought with her to Frayle Farm.

The housekeeper came to the cabin soon after breakfast. "I am sent," she said coldly, "to make sure you are comfortable. We did not have much notice that the party was returning last night." Her eyes were reddened but her face was so forbidding that Marja pretended not to notice.

"Yes – everything is fine." This woman had obviously heard the news of her master's affliction, Marja told herself. And she wasn't taking it well.

"You are expected at the main house whenever it is convenient," Carhyn went on in the same voice. "Your bodyguard has asked about you." There was no mention of the master.

When the housekeeper had gone, Marja put on a light jacket and stepped out into the grounds. Aside from a vegetable garden nearer the main house, and a rather bedraggled row of daffodils, the word "grounds" was something of a euphemism. She walked on cropped turf stepping around a chicken or two until she came to a side door that she remembered from her last visit.

Wells was standing outside it, obviously waiting for her.

"I'm glad to see you," she called with false heartiness. "It's awkward being a guest here. I don't want to just barge in on everyone."

"You would only meet your fellow guests if you did. Master Frayle has shut himself up with the steward and his oldest son. He has a lot of arrangements to make."

"But surely he hasn't shown signs of the disease yet, has he?" she asked rather breathlessly. "It is too early."

Wells shook his head. "But with wounds like that, they say it won't be long."

She looked away, fearing that her face would show too much. "Where are the others?" she asked.

"I think Brother Brendan has gone riding with the younger son," he said, keeping his eyes on the ground. "Touring the place."

She stiffened, remembering her own tour and all that happened afterwards, her terrible encounter with the druids and Frayle's meeting with his son, Evan.

"Perhaps you would like to walk around a bit," the bodyguard suggested hesitantly. "Until they come back, I mean."

She fell into step beside him. "How's your arm?" she asked, seeing that he had it in a sling.

He glanced down at the bandage. "It hurts a little," he admitted, "but would you believe I'm glad of that? It makes everything more real. Still you must think it strange for me to affirm life by the suffering it brings."

She did not think it strange at all, but did not say so. Instead, "It is like being reborn, I suppose."

"Not quite. More like taking off battle armor or crawling out from under a wrecked aircar." He grinned a little uncertainly and then grew serious again as they passed into an orchard.

"There is something I'd like to say," he began abruptly, "but I find it very hard to do so when I must call you Dr. Sienko."

She looked at him in surprise. "Then don't," she said. "Call me Marja. I never thought to tell you that before and I am sorry."

He nodded, staring down at the turf before him. "Marja," he went on, rather awkwardly, "we are both out of a job, you and I. Now Master Frayle has offered me a position as a man at arms and I'm considering his offer. He thinks that he and his sons will benefit by having someone with my experience here."

"Then, by all means, you should accept."

They came to a halt beneath what looked like an apple tree soon to bloom. She, at least recognized it, though Wells probably couldn't tell an apple from an azalea. She felt sorry for him, that he had been cheated out of half his life.

"Marja," he said again rather abruptly, "it's got to be a habit, looking after you. And now this job – I could have a house with it and – and garden space if I knew anything about gardening, which I don't, of course. But would you consider sharing it with me?"

She stared at him in surprise. "Wells – I mean, Franz," she exclaimed, "you're not proposing marriage, are you?" Surely he could mean nothing else.

He nodded.

"But I've treated you dreadfully. And there is your religion. You know I've given up all that sort of thing." But here she doubted she was telling the truth.

Wells saw this, but did not take her up on it. Instead, "If God can wait, so can I."

Suddenly she understood him. What he was offering her was protection, for he was a kindly man at heart and the thought of her cast adrift among strangers on a strange world had touched his pity. He did not love her, at least not in *that* way, but he was willing to take on the responsibility of caring for her. He was, without romance, a romantic.

She swallowed, abashed at his goodness. "I – I don't think I can accept," she faltered. "For one thing I am not worthy of you and –"

Here she was obliged to cut off his protest.

"Please," she said, "hear me out. We would both come to regret it if I agreed to marry you. Oh, I don't mean that we might not be happy together, but it would be at the expense of other things more important to both of us. Isn't that true?"

He did not answer.

"You have a long struggle ahead of you," she went on, "before you are truly free, if you ever are. We both know that. This first release is like – like springtime. But still there is your conditioning and – and the fine weather won't last."

"I would not let that stand in our way," he told her sturdily.

"I know. You would make sacrifice after sacrifice and the truth is, I'm just not worth it!"

"Can't you let me be the judge of that?" he asked.

But, "No," she said. "Here I must guide you, as you have so often done for me. Whatever you choose to do with your life, those decisions must come later. It may be that you will want to marry, but if you do, it will be to someone else, someone who will not be always reminding you of all the things you need to forget."

"I don't – foresee that," he said. "Not to someone else, I mean."

She took his hand. "I can't see the future," she told him. "Neither yours nor mine. But I know that this would be the easy way out and we would regret it."

He did not argue further.

"Still friends?" she asked and he nodded.

"Friends," he repeated, after a moment. "Even that is a new thing, isn't it?"

Much lightened, he because he had done his duty and she because she really had come to love him – but not in *that* way – they turned toward the house only to meet one of the Faring Guards heading in their direction. "I am to tell you, we've heard from the ship," he said. "Pesc is sending down a shuttle to begin spraying the wildwood."

"So soon?" Marja breathed, looking skyward nervously.

"Oh yes. Gaed Alfred put the fear of God into them." Whatever the chief might think of his own actions, his underlings never had any doubt that whatever he did was right.

But something was bothering Marja. "Mr. – ah, what do I call you?"

"My clan name is Third-Blade, but usually I am called Ard Matthew."

"Then, Ard Matthew," she said. "What will become of the druids if the wildwood changes into something else?"

"That will be a slow process. Years, I should think."

"But it will be starting to change now, won't it? How can they live? I mean, what is the secret of their survival, when others must die of the poisoning?"

The Lost Rythan looked away. "Something in the forest itself – some fruit, perhaps. We don't really know."

"And as the genetic structure changes?"

"They will die. There is no hope for them – there never was. The druids' condition cannot be reversed."

"But that's horrible!"

"It is a pity for those they have forced to join them," he agreed. "But the rest chose freely. This is the result of that choice."

He gave her a level look. "I am told they were, or thought of themselves as, wizards before. That they gave their service to the devil." He flushed a little. "Such things do occur, I know, but –" He looked away, his mouth twisting with distaste. "It is something beyond my understanding. In my own colony, it would have been unthinkable."

Marja shuddered a little. "I suppose they *have* brought this on themselves," she said at last. But all the while she was thinking that these Lost Rythans were hard people and how glad she was that they had the Star Brothers to guide them.

Nothing more was said as she and Wells accompanied him to the house. The Lost Rythan might have been sorry that he had spoken so freely, but it was plain he had very little sympathy for the druids.

As soon as they came in, they were told that the bishop had arrived. Frayle and his brother were even now closeted together in the office, but she met Balt in the great room.

The master's son seemed at loose ends, as well he might be, seeing his father not only stricken with the same malady that had taken his brother from him but unlike his brother, determined to die of it rather than go the way Evan had. However, he greeted her as she came in and tried for his old bantering tone.

"Dr. Sienko," he said. "This is a pleasure."

Marja took the young man's hand. How very much he looked like his father! "I am so sorry," she told him and was unable to go on.

Balt shrugged. "He's not dead yet. To tell the truth, I won't believe it until –"

She knew what he would have said. She had seen the blue lattice marks on the Lost Rythan's arm. How closely they must all be watching Master Frayle!

"At least no one else will be infected," she murmured. "Not now that they are spraying the forest."

She stopped, appalled at what she was saying. Evan Frayle was a druid! He, along with the others, were doomed to die as a result of that spraying!

Balt shook his head, his own thoughts following hers. "It *is* a bit late for our family, don't you think?" he said with a grim and twisted smile.

"I – I'm sorry. I should have remembered sooner."

"You actually met my brother, didn't you?"

She nodded unhappily.

"I didn't have a chance to ask you. How was he? Was there anything – anything left?"

He was trying to kill me, she wanted to say. It was a short acquaintance. "I – I don't think you would have known him," she told Balt. "They *change* so and – it is better to remember him as you knew him before."

"So, you would say that the Evan we knew was dead?"

"Yes, I would say that."

Balt nodded to himself. "Evan was closer to me than Brian ever could be, and I missed him a lot after he ran away. I would not like to think he was trapped in some way – still himself, I mean."

"Why did he do that?" she asked. "Run away, I mean."

"Our father. He never understood Evan, though I suppose he loved him. But in the end things were impossible. And there was that girl – maybe you've heard – and she was sent away. Then about the serfs. Evan was always their protector. He wanted to remake the whole colony."

"So, he became a druid?"

"I don't know. Maybe they forced him – or lied to him. They could have told him they wanted the same things he did, you know."

"Maybe they *did* want those things – once," she said, as a new idea occurred to her. "How old was Evan when he left?"

"He was seventeen. Two years younger than I was."

Before he could say anything more, he was called away. There seemed to be a lot of people in the room, all of them strangers to her. Then at last she looked up into a face she knew.

"You!" she exclaimed, recognizing the outlaw who had helped to fight off the druids. "What are you doing here?"

The last time she had seen him, he had been threatening Frayle.

"Came in with the bishop," he mumbled. "He said I might – no, that's not true. He ordered me to come."

"But you're not a serf anymore," she said. "I don't see why you had to follow his orders if you didn't want to."

"No," he agreed. "I'm not a serf anymore." Then, "What I said to Frayle," he told her suddenly. "It's hardly proper for a son to speak like that to his own father. That's what the bishop told me."

"His – *father*?" She was thinking as she said it – was there no end to the unpleasant surprises surrounding the life of Prydan Frayle?

The outlaw shrugged, watching her face. "I think I always knew," he said ruefully. "But I wouldn't let myself think about it too much. Can you see any resemblance?"

Now that she looked closely, she could.

"So, the bishop told me the truth when I went back to see him. After we stopped Frayle and the others from taking you into the wildwood, I mean. He said that Master Frayle didn't know, because my mother was only a serf and she was afraid to say anything. Anyway, they found her a husband. But our Carhyn knew of the affair. She told Bishop Rhosyn about it later after – well I won't go into that. Anyway, he was just Father Rhosyn then and the two brothers were closer than they are now. She's a jealous woman and maybe she hoped the family would do away with me when they knew who I was."

So here was another view of Frayle, not too surprising, she was forced to admit, but sordid enough. "Still, you're alive and well," Marja said crisply. "I suppose you were passed off as the child of your mother's husband?"

"Yes. But there had always been talk. My mother – well, she and Hwyl never did get on and he certainly never pretended I was *his* son."

"But Carhyn actually expected your father to – to –" She could not go on.

"If she did, she made a mistake ,because Father Rhosyn never told him. Besides, even though I didn't like him much, I don't think Frayle would have done a thing like that. Anyway, Carhyn could hardly tell him herself –" He blushed a little as he saw the look on Marja's face. "So," he said quickly, "I'm expected to see him and apologise for my behavior at the fringe. They're talking it over now, I expect – Master Frayle's getting an earful, you can be sure."

But Marja had stopped listening. Once more her mood had changed, to black depression this time. Must she spend the rest of her life in this sink of depravity that was Treelight Colony? To think she had once considered these people innocent!

TWO DAYS LATER, ANOTHER BOMBSHELL burst among them. But this time the news was good – more than good. Pesc had been keeping its bargain, and Frayle Farm, being so near the fringe, they caught sight of the company craft from time to time as they flew in to spray the wildwood. And while this was going on, another of Gaed Alfred's demands came to light: Pesc had been working on an antidote for the poison.

"This may take a while and we can't be sure how well they'll succeed," Brother Brendan told the astonished household. He hesitated to dispense hope when that hope might be disappointed, but he had been ordered to tell the others and he was obeying that order.

Frayle, who had been on his way to his office, froze in the doorway. "And the druids?' he whispered. "Is there any hope for *them*?"

"I don't think so. I'm sorry."

The other man remained where he was, nodding slightly. "Of course," he said. "That would be asking too much."

"Gaed Alfred doesn't know how close they are to success," the Star Brother continued, "but he wouldn't have mentioned it if he didn't believe it was likely. And they are working hard. Everything connected with Treelight Colony must be set in order before we destroy our files."

Colin, who at Frayle's invitation had remained behind after the bishop's departure, looked up quickly and a little apprehensively. Marja, having witnessed at least part of the reconciliation of Frayle with this bastard son of his, could easily guess what was going through the young man's head. If Frayle were not condemned to death after all, if he might go on as he had, ruling his farm and his family, would he still want to acknowledge Colin as his son?

And then, quite suddenly, the full meaning of the news hit her, so that she had to sit down on the first available seat. A hand fell on her shoulder and she looked up to see Ard Matthew regarding her with more perception than she would have expected from a Lost Rythan. "Now," he said softly, "you *must* pray for him if not for yourself." She knew at once whom he meant.

Across the room, Frayle was watching her, but she could not decipher his look. Then, catching sight of Colin, the master turned at once to the young man. "Go and tell your *brothers* what has occurred," he said, emphasizing the word, "brothers."

Slowly Colin straightened himself. "Yes sir," he said. He looked a bit nervous at the thought of bringing this news to the eldest son.

At this, his father gave him a thin smile. "Brian is a realist as well as a dutiful son," he said. "I believe he'll be more glad than otherwise – on both counts."

Marja winced. How *did* that pompous young man take the news that he had an illegitimate brother? Was Frayle only saying what he hoped was true? And then she caught the master looking at her again and blushed, hoping her thoughts had not been too visible in her face.

Meanwhile Brother Brendan turned to the master. "We'll know as soon as they have something," he said. "For your sake, I hope we won't be kept long in suspense."

Suddenly the room seemed too small. Marja made her way outside into the spring garden. Badly kept as it was, she preferred it to the house. She had been much on her own for the past couple days waiting, as they all were, for some sort of closure. Once or twice she had met Colin and Balt hurrying about the master's business and once she had seen Frayle himself, accompanied by Wells, going somewhere in the wagon.

It seemed odd no longer to have her bodyguard dogging her footsteps. She had roamed freely about the estate, though she did not venture back on the azalea path.

After a minute or two she turned to see Franz Wells just coming from the house. "How is the job?" she asked, smiling at him.

"Fine. But I doubt I'll stay."

"But Franz – what will you do if you don't accept his offer? I mean, it sounded ideal."

"I've been offered something better," he said. "Brother Brendan told me."

She waited, not knowing what to think.

"The marshal at the western priory would like me to come there," Wells said slowly. "Even if they develop an antidote for those who are ill, there is still a lot of work to be done. And now, as the wildwood loses its potency, they will go back to clearing new land the way they did before, probably with a lot more success."

"This is what you want to do with your life?"

He nodded. "You were wiser than I, Marja," he admitted. "I'd make a pretty poor husband."

"But you don't just – I mean that's no reason to join the brothers, is it?"

"Who said anything about joining? That might come later, but for now they just need someone to help with the work and to help Gris Wolfgang guard against the druids."

He looked – not quite at peace, she decided, but certainly more so than she had ever seen him before. No one knew yet whether he could surmount the damage done to him in the course of his training and he might end up fighting his conditioning for the rest of his life. Maybe the priory would be a good place to wage that fight.

"Then I'm happy for you," she told him before she turned away, "I'm going for a walk," she added abruptly. "But I promise not to wander far."

"And you'd like to be alone. Right. But if you're not back within an hour or so I'll come looking."

With a smile, she turned away, passing quickly through the vegetable garden.

Unfortunately, her solitude was short lived. Somewhere between the young lettuces and the early asparagus, she saw the back of a woman cutting vegetables. Marja would have taken another way, but it was too late. The figure turned – and it was the housekeeper.

For a long time, the two women stared at each other, until Marja was forced to remember what Colin had said. *Carhyn is a jealous woman.*

With those cold eyes fixed on her, she could have no doubt of the truth of things hinted at. This, too, was one of Frayle's paramours.

"Yes," Carhyn told her, reading the knowledge in her face. "I was his mistress, lady from the stars, while you were never anything but a means to an end. He sees far, does Master Frayle, farther than you might think. He'll survive this and he'll find a way around these Lost Rythans, too."

When she smiled, her teeth were no better than those of most of the colonists. "But you," she said spitefully, "after whoring for those friends of yours in the corporation, they've abandoned you here. What will become of *you* now, star lady?"

"I don't know that yet," Marja told her honestly. "But I hope I never end up like you."

For a moment, she thought the housekeeper was going to attack her, but then the other woman only laughed and went back to gathering vegetables. Fighting down sickness, Marja turned toward the guesthouse, her plans for a walk forgotten. No, she told herself once more, these people were no better, no more simple and good, than those of Bloomhadn Park.

Once inside the cabin, she could not relax. The maid brought her a meal she was unable to eat and tea she would probably not drink. Marja thanked her and dismissed her for the evening.

So Carhyn was Frayle's woman, she was thinking. She remembered how Balt had offered the housekeeper wine and made a joke of it that first evening at the farm. And the way the woman had looked at her then –

The nebula rose in the eastern sky, turning the room into a purple sea. She sat on in her chair, watching the changing light as it pulsed and glowed against the walls opposite the window. Outside, something bayed in the distance and a horse whickered.

Despite the alien skies, the sounds and smells of this place were those of her childhood. A sudden yearning came over her for the years before she had known that she was actually living in poverty and ignorance, before she had thrown everything away in search of a better life at the center of galactic civilization.

It was but a step from remembering her childhood innocence to remembering her lost religion. If a man like Wells could face his future with such faith and courage, how could she do less? And that Faring Guard at the priory – what was *he* doing now? Not moaning about his troubles, she was sure.

Slowly, as the night passed, she tried to break down the wall she had built between herself and the God of her childhood. It was pathetically easy to do. She felt like a three-year old who had taken a wrong turning and, after a short pursuit, been reclaimed by her parents. And yet ...

"I'm not sentimental," she said aloud. "You know that. At least I don't think so."

But now as she tried to make plans for a new life here in this savage place, she realized that she was not – had never been – alone. Her new life would be a life of renunciation, she feared, but it would not be *her* life alone. She was God's creature, His wayward daughter. She would live on with as much grace as she could, she supposed, and one day she would fit into the culture of those around her.

But before she could make any further plans, she fell asleep. When she woke to the sound of someone knocking, the nebula was shining in the opposite window.

Groggily she got up and staggered to the door. Had she been more wide awake, she would have remembered the druids and paused before lifting the latch. But before she quite realized what she was doing, the door was open and Marja was face to face with Prydan Frayle.

"You!" she exclaimed, stepping backwards. "What are you doing here?" It was not a very gracious thing to say and she regretted it at once.

"I was delivering a calf," he told her. "They sent for me." He held up his soiled hands apologetically. "There were complications, and I – well, that is one of the things my father had me trained for."

Marja stifled a sudden impulse to laugh hysterically at the idea of Master Frayle serving as a veterinarian. Instead, she backed away from the door.

"I hope I did not wake you," he added. "I know I should have waited until morning. But one of the servants told me that Carhyn had been seen speaking to you and I – didn't want to wait."

"She told me she was your mistress." Even as she spoke, Marja didn't think this was the right thing to say. But then, what was?

"Oh." He was silent for a moment or two. "But that was all years ago – not long after my wife died. And then somehow she stayed on. The boys needed her."

Marja sat down abruptly on the bench. "You can have your pick of women, can't you?" she said. "Among your *serfs*!" Once more she had been spiteful. Could she do no better than *this*?

He stayed where he was, his lean form backlit by the nebula's light. "I never pretended to be a saint," he told her. It was not a very original thing to say and this time she almost had to stifle a laugh.

"Why have you come here at this hour?" she demanded. "Did you think that because I am exiled, I would be fair game?" This time it was anger that spilled over, anger beyond her control.

But Frayle only shook his head. "I came to ask you a question," he said. "It's something I need to know. It has been preying on my mind."

She could not see his face very well but something in the way he stood there told her that he was far from easy. "Ask it," she said more moderately. "And then you had better go. Your other guests won't think much of your coming here in the middle of the night."

"No." Then, "Your superior – the one who spoke through the manikin – told me that he had ordered you to make love to me. That it was a part of your job to win my confidence."

She looked down at his shadow on the floor. "That is true."

"And did you obey him? Were you only serving Pesc when – "

"I would never obey an order like that!" she cried, her voice breaking. "I was hired as a professional, to make a survey of the colony and to recommend the best way to develop it. I had no idea they were using me – or *you*!"

He took a tentative step into the room.

"It was you," she went on, rising to her feet, "who made a fool of *me*! You wanted what Pesc could give you and you thought that making me *yours* according to the custom of your benighted colony would be the best way to get it. And all the time everyone here knew about your other liaisons –"

"I admit that my intentions toward you were not honorable."

"You pretended to care!"

He hesitated. "I thought you were the one pretending," he said. "And I was angry. I have not been used to being taken advantage of."

"Nor have I!"

"Yes – yes, I can see that. So I thought you would like to know that there was never any pretense on my part. That you needn't feel humiliated. So long as I was under sentence of certain death, I could not tell you lest you think I was asking your pity. Even now I hope you will not misunderstand."

She raised one hand as though to stop his words. "I do not pity you," she said distinctly. "Not at all. Wells told me you were a brave man and he was right." The nebula light turned her flesh the color of amethyst, glowing in the darkness.

"You have seen so many things that I will never see," he went on, almost as though he were talking to himself. "You might well have looked down on me and on my people. Though it made me angry, I understand this now."

"I did," she admitted. "Once. But all that is over. The Star Brother doesn't look down on you, does he? Nor do the Lost Rythans. And they have seen far more of the galaxy than *I* have."

"Then," he said slowly, "we have been true to one another despite everything."

It was an odd thing to say. But, "I suppose we have," she agreed.

"Marja, I still do not know whether I have a future. Perhaps this medicine will come in time but there is no certainty of that."

He paused for a moment and then plunged ahead. "Worse, I dare not make promises I might not keep. I could still go to the priory, except that I would make a very bad monk, you know, and they told me so. Tactfully, of course."

She stared at him in exasperation while he waited, silently regarding her. "Are you so weak as that?" she exclaimed at last.

"I should not have spoken," he said abruptly, drawing back. "I can imagine what you must think of me."

"Don't go yet," Marja said, watching him. "First you must apologise for doubting *me*!"

He started, but did not go.

"That woman called me a whore!" she burst out suddenly. "And I would have been exactly that if I had obeyed my orders!"

She heard him groan. Then, "I do apologise, Marja," he said. "As I am no better than I thought *you* were, it was only to be expected that I would fail to understand your feelings."

"Your apology is not enough!" she cried, beside herself. "I *demand* that you behave with honor! That you be the man I hoped you were! That you truly *are*!" She found she was crying and her anger at this weakness only made her cry harder. Perhaps it was the best thing she could have done.

He made an uncertain movement toward her. "Then – I suppose I had better try to meet those demands," he said. "I mean, not try. I *will*." He waited while she gained control of herself.

"Will you pray for me?" he asked her then, as though it were a perfectly natural thing to ask. "I mean, I rather think you had better," he added, almost setting off the laughter that even now struggled with her tears.

She nodded, unable to speak.

"Thank you."

Suddenly the absurdity of the whole situation was too much for her. She knew she mustn't laugh! She mustn't! "Tomorrow," she finally managed to croak. "When the suns are shining and other people are awake, if this is not all a dream –"

"Yes," he took her up. "Tomorrow, I will come to you, if I may, and we will begin again. That is – if you will permit me."

She reached out and touched his gore-smeared hand. "Yes," she said, "we certainly need to start over."

A moment later, he was gone. Only the light of the nebula filled the doorway, clear and free of shadows.

AFTERWARD

LOOK," FRASER MAY SAID – and they could tell he was uneasy – "Just tell me what business you have with me. I heard about what you did to Pesc, but I've never had any tie with them. In fact, I'm glad you made them eat dirt."

"That does you credit," Father Moto said dryly.

May, who hadn't seen a priest since his mother died, eyed the Star Brother with renewed suspicion. "Has this got something to do with Dust cutting himself off all these months? I mean, if he's decided to work for you full time, that's his decision. I'm not mad."

"You tried to reach him, then," Father Moto said.

May gave him a quick, sharp look, but did not deny it.

"You tried to break in, even though he had changed all his codes. But then of course you were once his caretaker."

"I always looked out for him," the other man said. "I knew him long before he ever got hooked up with your lot."

"Well, he was the one who asked us to invite you here," Gaed Alfred said from his seat across the room. "You saved his life when he had the accident, after all. How could you think he'd forget a thing like that?"

Their visitor did not respond to this.

"Mr. May," the Star Brother resumed, "have you ever given any thought to your own future?"

"You mean here on Copper? Sure. My outfit's pretty secure with the colony council, so don't get any ideas. I'm not like Pesc to go waving a red flag at Net Central." Now, he was definitely on guard, looking quickly from the Star Brother to the Faring Guard. "If you think you've got something on me, just come out and say so!"

"You misunderstand me," Father Moto told him. "I was referring to your *real* future."

May's eyes narrowed. "If you're going to preach at me, you're wasting your time – and mine!" He rose to go, signaling to the pair of guards who followed him everywhere.

"Our time is our own to waste," Gaed Alfred growled. "As to yours, this isn't your party." He stood up.

At this, weapons appeared, especially considering that the chief had one hand in his pocket. Under three pairs of hostile eyes, he slowly drew his hand out, a rosary dangling from his fingers. "My time," he said. "And God's."

"You damn fool! You're lucky my boys didn't burn a hole through your middle!"

"Oh, as to that, I'm wearing a shield. Aren't you?"

Suddenly May laughed. "Okay," he said. "So what *is* the point of all this?"

"Your friend wants to see you," Father Moto told him. "He asked us to arrange a meeting."

"You mean Dust? Have you moved him here?"

"He's moved himself."

At this, an inner door slid open and a tall man emerged. At least he looked like a man, though the body was impossibly thin, the face no more than a mask. "Hello, Fraser," a voice came from somewhere in his chest.

For once, May was struck speechless. Then, "Dust! Is that really you?"

"Pretty much," the other said. "I'm still growing a face."

May reholstered his gun but he didn't take his hand away from it. "I can't believe it," he said tentatively. "I mean, this is wonderful. Did the Star Brothers get you fixed up?"

"Not quite," Dust told him. "Actually I had to go to Earth – Union of Africa. Pesc paid for everything."

At this, the other reached out and touched the metalplast. "I'm happy for you, man!" he said. "This is like a miracle!"

"I suppose it is," Dust agreed, stepping back a little. "Though I know *you* always did the best you could for me."

May drew himself up, his gaze wandering around the room as he tried to assume the right expression. "I didn't even know this sort of thing was possible," he said. "Sure, we did the best we could for you, Dust. If you had seen the mess you were –"

"Well, I couldn't have seen *that*," the other man said slowly. "And afterwards I tried to forget the accident. That was easy really, because some of the stuff was already erased for me. It was only recently I decided I'd have to face up to my memories if I wanted to make any kind of recovery, and that was when I discovered I couldn't find them all. So I hacked the files – *your* files, that is. Do I need to go on?"

May shook his head. "No, I guess you don't," he admitted, his hand once more hovering over the weapon he wore.

"I never was your partner," Dust told him, "or your friend. *You* were the accident. And afterwards, you had me bottled up because I'm good at what I do and you could still make use of me. And besides, you were afraid I might know some stuff – which I do, as a matter of fact."

"Okay, you've got me. I'll pay. Only don't try to take me to court. There's too much on your own plate for that!"

"I had a business," Dust went on. "I was doing good. I could have paid for this body anytime. But you took my memory and you took my outfit."

"I said I'd pay! Can you blame me for latching onto what was practically thrown in my lap? You were doing a job for my rival and you assassinated one of my best agents! What did you expect me to do?"

"I'm sorry about that killing. But you erased my name and some of my life. You posed as my friend."

"Hell, Dust! People like us can't *afford* friends!"

The metalplast figure did not move though it never took its unblinking eyes from May's sweating face. "That's what *I* thought," he said, "when I found out what really happened."

"Well –" Fraser May was at a loss. "Look," he said again. "I can't undo the grenade. So let's talk about damages."

"I'm not going to turn you in and I don't want anything from you. We're quits."

The other man's glance darted from one to the other – the Star Brother, the Faring Guard and the metal man. "Quits?" he said guardedly.

"Of course. Only if something were to happen to me now, those other things I found out would go to Net Central automatically. And the Star Brothers might get mad, too. You don't want to be on the wrong side of the Star Brothers."

Once more May looked around. He was beginning to agree with Dust on that last statement. "Sure, man," he said. "Anything you say. I always thought we could come to some sort of –"

"If you're done, I'll show him out," Gaed Alfred interrupted.

"Fine," Dust told him.

But this was too much. "You damned hypocrite!" May snarled at Gaed Alfred, losing his temper entirely. "We'll see what goes to Net Central!" He raised his gun.

It was the almost last thing he did.

The Faring Guard moved more quickly than even Father Moto had known he could, swinging one fist which, had it connected, would have killed the other man instantly. But at the last second he held himself back and merely knocked him to the floor.

Dust turned to his guards, but no one moved as their boss climbed slowly to his feet, shaking his head in a dazed sort of way. He did not look up at the others.

"I'll show you to the door now," Gaed Alfred said.

"HOPE YOU HAVE FORGIVEN HIM," Father Moto ventured, speaking to Dust. "As you have need of forgiveness yourself."

"Do you think my forgiving him will do any good?" Dust asked bitterly.

"Forgiveness is never wasted," the priest told him. "You did, after all, ask for this meeting – this confrontation. Surely you didn't mean to gloat."

Gaed Alfred came back from his errand. It had been an ugly business and the chief was still a bit shaken at how close he had come to killing May. He risked a glance at the Star Brother and received a nod in return. They understood each other, these two. But now their attention was for their companion.

"So," the chief said at last, "it's just as well you accepted that invitation to visit Lost Rythar while you finish growing into your new skin. You won't want to stay on Copper, I guess. And now that you're baptized, my colony will give you a visa without any trouble."

The sacrament to which he referred had been administered, at Dust's request, during his recent surgery. When the remainder of his cerebral cortex was being transferred to his new body, Father Moto had baptized him with extremely sterile water while the surgeons looked on. He had been obliged to wear a mask and gloves but did not think, in view of the extraordinary circumstances, that this would be any impediment.

"I look forward to seeing your colony," Dust said. "But to tell the truth, I'm almost sorry I learned the truth about Fraser. Do you think that's dumb? I mean, even if he was lying, he gave me a feeling of – well, like I had roots, you know?"

He turned his formless face to the Faring Guard. "Not that I don't appreciate all you've done, Gaed Alfred, and all those chess games. But I thought Fraser was someone from way back."

"You could let your 'way back' start now," Father Moto suggested. "Built some new roots."

"I'm sorry I can't come to see you on Lost Rythar," the chief said, "but you know I've been exiled for life. Still, Father Moto should be able to make a visit or two." He did not add that his own exile stemmed from just such a blow as he had almost given Fraser. For all his penitence, some things did not change very much.

"Then I'll have to visit *you*, Gaed Alfred. Don't think I won't!" The gleaming figure moved toward the corridor door. "Now, if you don't mind, I'd like to be alone for a little while," he added. "Call me when you're ready to leave."

"Well, that's that," Chief Snowtyger said when Dust had gone out. "Back to work, I guess."

"Back to the *Balthasar*," his companion agreed. "As soon as I gather up some things." He laid one hand on the other man's shoulder. "We are what we are, Gaed Alfred. You are a fighting man –"

The chief nodded. "I suppose we'd better pray for May and his gang," he said. "But you know, after what he did to Dust, it's hard. He's a pretty poor excuse for a man, isn't he?"

"Do you want me to answer that?" Father Moto asked, fixing him with a stern look.

The Faring Guard flushed. "Hey," he said suddenly, changing the subject, "shouldn't Dust be using his real name – or at least his baptismal one?"

"I'm afraid he forgot his real name. And when he found it, it was still unfamiliar, probably because he'd been using an alias long before the accident. So he's Dust. *Alfred* Dust, though, as you say."

The other man nodded. "It's an honor to be his godfather," he said. "Even though I'm hardly worthy of it, I suppose." It still rankled that they wouldn't let him in past the microbe shielding for the baptism, but Father Moto, who had had a good look at just how little there was left of Dust's real flesh, did not think the chief would have been edified. Wonderful indeed were the ways of God, he thought, but sometimes it could be disturbing to witness the details.

Slowly the pair – one stooping slightly beneath the low ceiling of their rented quarters, the other holding his head high as he always did – began gathering up their disks and papers. "Sometimes," the priest remarked to Snowtyger, "I feel like a very inadequate *deus ex machina*, sending all those operatives out to different colonies and then watching over them –"

"We get watched over, too," the chief reminded him.

"Of course. And God does a much better job of it."

Snowtyger thought about fetching a beer from the cooler and then changed his mind. Instead, he sat down for a moment in a chair that was too small, stretching out his legs and closing his eyes. There would be plenty of work waiting for them back on the mothership, he thought.

"Yes," he murmured, "thank God –"

Father Moto raised one eyebrow. "For –?"

"For God."

"Ah. Of course." The Star Brother took another chair. He supposed a brief rest wouldn't hurt them. "*Gratias agimus tibi propter magnam gloriam tuam,*" he murmured and smiled at his friend. "We give Thee thanks for Thy great glory."

It was enough for them both.

ABOUT THE AUTHOR

I HAVE BEEN WRITING SOMETHING or other for most of my literate life: children's books, essays, short stories and, as you can see, science fiction novels. I am fulfilling a childhood ambition as well as doing what I like best – and what I think I *should* be doing.

In the science fiction field, you may find my novels, *Godcountry*, *Gelen*, *Sunrise on the Icewolf*, and now *Treelight*, all on Amazon in both print and Kindle editions. These are all in the Star Brothers/Lost Rythar universe, so if you have enjoyed one of them, you will probably enjoy them all. The Star Brothers go where most people don't, seeking out lost colonies and protecting them, when they can, from exploitation. The Lost Rythans – well, Lost Rythar was one of those lost colonies and they are grateful to the Order. So much so, in fact, that they almost literally fall over themselves providing assistance to the Star Brothers who are in turn obliged to keep their "helpers" out of trouble. All of this adds an element of fun to the writing.

Please let me know how you liked the book and what you would like to see next. You can reach me at **lostrythar@gmail.com**.

PLEASE LEAVE A REVIEW ON AMAZON to help other readers who might like this book. Just a sentence or two saying what you liked about it will be a big help.